Please return/renew this item by the last date shown
on this label, or on your self-service receipt.

To renew this item, visit **www.librarieswest.org.uk**
or contact your library

Your borrower number and PIN are required.

Also available by Ellie Dean

ELLIE DEAN

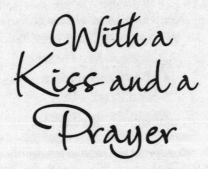

With a
Kiss and a
Prayer

arrow books

1 3 5 7 9 10 8 6 4 2

Arrow Books
20 Vauxhall Bridge Road
London SW1V 2SA

Arrow Books is part of the Penguin Random House group
of companies whose addresses can be found at
global.penguinrandomhouse.com.

Penguin
Random House
UK

First published by Arrow Books in 2018

www.penguin.co.uk

A CIP catalogue record for this book is available
from the British Library.

ISBN 9781784758110

Typeset in 11.5/14.5 pt Palatino
by Integra Software Services Pvt. Ltd, Pondicherry

Printed and bound in Great Britain by Clays Ltd, St Ives Plc

Acknowledgements

People often think that being an author is a solitary pursuit, and to begin with it is just that, but once my story leaves my office a whole team of wonderful people help to make it even better.

I would like to thank Viola Hayden for being such an understanding and joyous collaborating editor during her time at Arrow. It was a huge pleasure to work with you and although I shall miss our chats, I wish you the very best in your new job.

The team at Arrow is always supportive, imaginative and very helpful, and although I can't list everyone here, I'd like to thank Susan Sandon, Becky McCarthy, Emily Griffin, and my new editor – and fellow Aussie – Cassandra Di Bello for their continued and much valued support and advice. You've helped me realise my dream!

No acknowledgement is complete without mentioning my agent, Teresa Chris, who's been my travelling companion on this life-changing journey ever since she got my very first book published back in 1995. She has been unfailing in her energy and enthusiasm to see my career flourish, and thank you is not enough – for without her, I wouldn't be where I am today.

A Map of Cliffehaven

1 Café
2 Beach View Boarding House
3 Doris's House
4 Vet
5 Doctor's Surgery
6 Cliffehaven General
7 Lilac Tearooms
8 The Anchor
9 Ruby and Ethel's House
10 Station
11 Pier
12 Home and Colonial Stores
13 Plummer Roddis
14 Town Hall
15 Fire Station
16 Uniform Factory
17 Bombed School
18 Bombed Odeon Cinema
19 Bombed Church

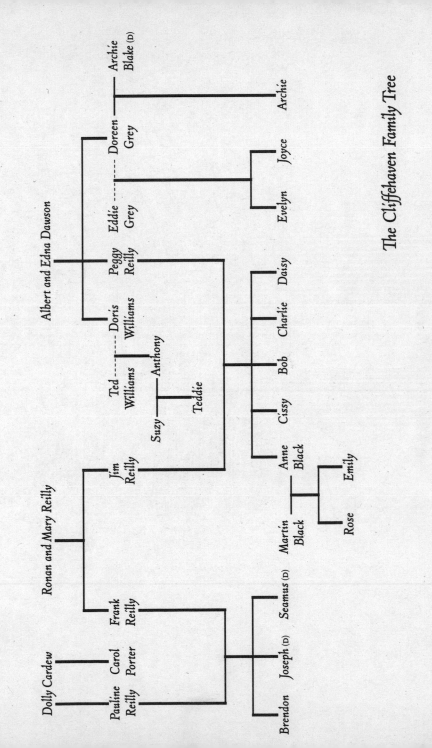

The Cliffehaven Family Tree

I dedicate this book to the brave men who fought in India and Burma, and the stoic women who kept the home-fires burning as they waited for them to come home.

1

Cliffehaven, May 1944

It was Saturday morning and all was quiet at Beach View, except for sounds of activity in the scullery. Peggy Reilly was attacking the last of the mound of washing that had accumulated over the past week. Her evacuees, or her chicks, as she liked to think of them, had seen to their own and the elderly Cordelia's laundry the day before, but having changed the beds and gone through her father-in-law, Ron's, tip of a room in search of discarded underwear, dirty towels and shirts, there had been as much as ever to get through, and half the morning was already gone.

She filled the stone sink with hot water from the copper boiler, added a spoonful of soda crystals, and, having waited for them to dissolve, began to rinse out the sheets before feeding them through the wringer and into the basket. Each dip of her hands into the hot water and every turn of the wringer's handle reinforced her yearning for a proper twin-tub washing machine. Her older sister Doris had been lucky (and rich) enough to buy one before the war.

Peggy knew for a fact that once it was loaded it made short work of a week's washing, and then all one had to do was transfer it into the second tub where it was rinsed and spun, ready to be hung out on the line. Yet, as she and Doris had fallen out yet again, there was no chance of using it, even occasionally.

Peggy switched off the copper boiler, dumped the last sheet into the basket, hauled it onto her hip and carried it into the back garden. She'd thought that by earning her own money at Solly's uniform factory she could have put down a deposit and paid it off weekly; but it turned out that things like washing machines, electric kettles, fridges and irons were as rare as hens' teeth, and so here she was, once more forced to carry on the weekly ritual which ate into her precious weekend off.

The two washing lines were strung across the width of the garden from poles attached to the neighbouring fences. Long, forked wooden props stood at intervals underneath the line, keeping the laundry from dragging across Ron's vegetable beds, which had replaced the lawn beyond the paved area beneath the kitchen window. There was a good stiff breeze which snapped and flapped the washing already pegged out, and the sun was bright when it appeared intermittently between the scudding clouds, so at least everything would be dry and ready for ironing before teatime.

Peggy's gaze drifted over Ron's sprouting vege-table plot and the ugly corrugated iron Anderson shelter, noting that Queenie the cat had found a sunny spot by the flint wall, and was curled in a tight knot, fast asleep. The few chickens that had so far escaped the cooking pot were scratching about in their run. The cockerel, which they'd nicknamed Adolf because of the way he strutted about, was sitting on the roof of the coop surveying his harem with a proprietorial glint in his eye. He was a ruddy nuisance with his crowing at all hours, but as the hens laid a good number of eggs and he was often drowned out by the sound of the planes going overhead, Peggy could almost forgive him.

She let her mind wander as she wrestled with the sheets, vaguely aware of the familiar background noise of the wireless coming from the many open windows of the neighbouring houses as well as her own. Every shop, pub, factory, office and home kept the wireless on now, but Peggy didn't take much notice of it unless it was time for the news, and then the whole of Cliffehaven stopped what they were doing and gathered round in the hope that the growing rumours of an Allied invasion into France had become reality.

It was now almost the end of May, and the number of air raids over France and Germany had increased dramatically. As the news of Allied victories in Italy and the Far East came through, the time seemed right to push their advantage and get rid of Hitler and his thugs once and for all. Yet those in charge appeared to have other ideas, and the

3

waiting was getting to Peggy, just as it was for everyone, for there was still no clue as to when the invasion might happen. But it would – it had to if this war was ever to end.

She looked up as several squadrons of bombers and fighter planes roared overhead. They'd recently been taking off and landing at nearby Cliffe aerodrome day and night, the bombing campaign over the northern shores of France and into Germany increasing in strength and regularity. Her heart swelled with pride as the heavy-bellied roar of the huge British bombers rattled the window panes and sent a tremor through the walls of the old Victorian terraced houses and in the ground beneath her feet. 'God speed and bring you home safely,' she murmured.

Picking up the empty basket to carry indoors, she took a quavering breath as she thought of her darling Jim who was fighting the Japs in Burma; her nephew, Brendon, who'd be returning to duty with the Royal Naval Reserve tomorrow; and her son-in-law, Martin, who'd been shot down and was now a POW in Stalag III along with many of his fellow RAF officers. They were so brave, every last one of them, and all she could do was pray that this war would soon be over and they could return to their loved ones and enjoy the blessed peace which they'd all been denied for too long.

Her thoughts automatically went to Matthew Champion, Rita's lovely young pilot who'd lost his life some months ago in that awful raid over Berlin which had seen so many die or taken prisoner. Rita was putting on a brave face, throwing herself into her work as a mechanic at the fire station and spending every spare moment raising money for the local Spitfire fund – but the sadness and awful loss could still be seen in her wan face and haunted dark eyes, and Peggy's heart ached with the knowledge that there was very little she could do to ease the girl's suffering, except to mother and console her.

With a tremulous sigh, Peggy stowed the basket away in the scullery, then went up the concrete steps into her deserted kitchen. Ron had done his usual vanishing act with his dog Harvey straight after breakfast; Rita, Ivy and Fran were at work; and Cordelia had gone with Sarah and Peggy's little Daisy into town to see if there was anything worth queuing for in the shops – a faint hope, but one that sprang eternal regardless of the stark reality of empty shelves.

She bustled about, clearing the last of the dishes from the drainer and tidying away Daisy's toys. It was a relief to be able to get on without being hindered by her two-year-old daughter, who'd lately become rather demanding when she thought she wasn't the centre of attention – an unfortunate result of her being so well entertained by Nanny Pringle and her assistants at the factory nursery.

Peggy regarded the shabby kitchen fondly, her gaze drifting over the faded oilcloth on the large table, the mismatched chairs and battered old dresser which was covered in all sorts of clutter and no doubt gathering dust and cobwebs. The wireless was burbling away to itself, but a glance at the clock told Peggy it would be an hour before the twelve o'clock news came on – unless of course there was a special bulletin.

She went to the larder in the corner of the kitchen and took out the bowl of pigeon breasts Ron had prepared the night before. He'd been out on the hills at dusk and lain in wait with his shotgun for the pigeons to return to their regular roosts, and had bagged a dozen or more as they'd flown in low on the buffeting wind coming off the sea. There wasn't a lot of meat on a pigeon and the shotgun pellets had made a bit of a mess of them, but getting meat of any sort was a minor miracle these days, and as Ron had assured her he'd retrieved all the pellets, they would make a fitting farewell meal for Brendon on his last night home. Peggy had offered to host the dinner, because Frank and Pauline's cottage over at Tamarisk Bay wouldn't quite stretch to the occasion.

Brendon had had four short days of leave having recently returned from Devon, and his mother, Pauline, had been ecstatic, fussing over him and hardly letting him out of her sight. Peggy feared the inevitable histrionics which would follow his departure, and could only hope that Frank could keep Pauline calm and focused on the need to carry on and remain positive. And yet, Peggy reasoned, perhaps she was being harsh, for Pauline and Frank had already lost two sons to this war, which made Brendon extra precious – and if she'd been in a similar situation, she would probably have felt just as on edge and terrified.

With all the rumours of an Allied invasion, none of them had a clue as to where Brendon would be posted – and he wouldn't enlighten them. But Pauline had refused to even contemplate the idea that he might be involved in the fighting again, and was adamant that he'd be sent back to the London docks. Ron, Frank and Peggy didn't have the heart to disagree with her, even though they thought it was highly unlikely with so many servicemen pouring into every nook and cranny of the south coast.

Peggy also doubted he'd go back to Devon. Something must have happened down there, for she and Ron had noticed how Brendon and his father, Frank, had been grim-faced and tight-lipped on their return. And surely any invasion would leave from Dover, as it was the shortest route to France, and the Pas-de-Calais had been repeatedly bombarded by the Allies recently.

She gave an exasperated sigh at her jumbled thoughts and speculations. The trouble with this war was that no one said anything definite about what was happening, and even the newspapers and frequent radio bulletins couldn't be relied upon to tell the whole truth in case it affected morale. It seemed that all anyone could do was make an educated guess at the state of things, and try to read between the lines.

Peggy determinedly put these thoughts aside as she seasoned the pigeon meat and placed it in her large stewing pot. She then set about chopping the garden vegetables she'd picked earlier. Adding the rich stock she'd made from boiling a ham bone Alf the butcher had slipped her from under the counter, she popped on the lid and put the pot in the range's slow oven. There would be eleven of them round the table this evening if she counted Daisy, so she'd planned to cook new potatoes with fresh mint to go with the stew, followed by an apple and rhubarb crumble. The apples had been stored since last autumn in the basement, the rhubarb picked this morning, and she had just enough plain white flour to make a decent crumble.

Peggy added a pinch of salt to the sifted flour and crumbled the tiny knob of margarine and teaspoon of sugar into the mix and then set the bowl aside. She would top the softened fruit with the mixture nearer to teatime so it didn't go to mush, and serve it with the last tin of condensed milk she'd kept hidden right at the back of her larder. Ron was renowned for digging about in there looking for something tasty, and things like condensed milk, sugar and digestive biscuits had a nasty habit of disappearing.

With everything set for supper, she plumped herself down at the table and took off her knotted headscarf, then shook out her dark curls and ran her

fingers through them. With the lack of decent shampoo, they felt lifeless and straggling, and she
wondered if she should use some of her wages to
treat herself to a trip to the hairdresser's in the High
Street – then dismissed the idea immediately. Fran
was very skilled with curlers and scissors, and happy
to do it for nothing. Wasting money on herself was
too indulgent when there were other, more important things to buy. The head on her floor-mop needed
replacing for a start; Daisy was growing out of everything, especially her shoes; and her own underwear
was falling apart and beyond mending, so that if she
was ever involved in an accident and had to be taken
to hospital, she'd die of embarrassment.

Peggy dug into her apron pocket and pulled out
her packet of Park Drive. Lighting a cigarette, she
glanced at the clock. It was now almost midday, but
as she wasn't due to meet Kitty and Charlotte at the
Red Cross distribution centre until two, she had time
to relax, read her letters from Jim again, fix her hair
and catch her breath. She let her gaze linger on the
photographs she'd lined up on the mantelpiece and
was drawn, as always, to the one of Jim. He smiled
roguishly back at her, looking tanned and fit in his
tropical-issue uniform, and at first glance appeared
younger than the man who'd left Cliffehaven all
those many months ago – but on closer inspection
she could see there were deeper lines etched around
those dark blue eyes which now held the shadows
of stark experience and knowledge. Whatever he'd

witnessed or been involved in had lent him an air of strength and gritty determination which had been lacking in the Jim she knew and loved. He was no longer the scallywag with a roving eye, a carefree nature, and a nose for a shady deal, but a man honed by vigorous training and imbued with pride for what he'd become.

Peggy bit her lip, wondering what he'd seen and done, and how he would settle back into his old life again once the war was over. Cliffehaven might prove too tame for him after all the excitement of Burma, and he could find it impossible to pick up the threads of hearth and home again – especially as the cinema had been blown up along with his job as a projectionist.

She knew he loved her; knew he was longing to come home, but he wasn't the only one to have changed since they'd parted, and their separate experiences must surely have widened the gulf between them. And then there was his little Daisy and the grandchildren growing up with only photographs and stories to remind them of who he was. He would be a stranger to them – and maybe even to her – and that thought made her shiver.

Peggy swallowed the lump in her throat and blinked away her ready tears, cross with herself for being so pessimistic. They would find a way to get through, for they were strong and invincible as long as they had each other, and she had to keep faith in that, and never let it waver.

She reached for the scruffy letters that had arrived earlier, and read the few, hastily scrawled words Jim had written. The ink was blurred from his sweaty fingers, and although he wrote that he loved and missed her and treasured all the letters he'd received from everyone, he gave little hint as to where he was in Burma, or what the conditions were like. Even so, it was clear he had little time to write, that the jungle heat was as bad as ever, and he was probably involved in the skirmishes that the newscaster was now talking about on the wireless.

Peggy folded away the letters and turned up the volume on the wireless as the news continued. The Japanese were retreating at last, forced back by the advancing Allied soldiers at Kohima and Imphal, the imminent monsoon threatening their supply chains and closing off their escape routes. A number of Japanese ships had been sunk in the Pacific and the islands of New Guinea were now under Allied attack.

'Good,' breathed Peggy. 'The sooner they admit defeat, the sooner my Jim can come home.'

The broadcast continued with news that the advancing 5th and 8th armies in Italy had broken through a significant line to take Monte Cassino, and six thousand Germans were now prisoners. There was a new offensive on the beaches of Anzio, and Terracina was expected to fall within hours – and then the Allies would advance on Rome.

Peggy closed her eyes as the newscast came to an end. There was at last hope that the tide was turning – that the Allies were achieving victory after victory. But still there was no hint of an invasion and she burnt with frustration that their leaders seemed intent upon hanging about instead of striking while the iron was hot. She got to her feet, grabbed a duster and set about cleaning the dresser with far more vigour than was necessary. If she didn't do something to vent her pent-up emotions, she'd explode.

Ron was not a man who cared much about his appearance, and so was wearing his usual ragged shirt, old corduroy trousers held up at the waist with a length of narrow rope, an ancient sweater and his long waterproof poacher's coat. A greasy cap was pulled over his thick, wayward hair, the peak tipped down almost to his bushy brows, and his feet were shod in a stout pair of boots, the laces of which had been replaced by thick garden twine.

With Harvey loping alongside him, he left the hills and tramped down the steep slope until he reached the High Street. He had two dead rabbits in one of his poacher's coat pockets, and his sleeping ferrets, Flora and Dora, were curled up in another. It had been a good morning of netting rabbit holes and exercising the ferrets; now he and Harvey were ready for a beer and a sit-down.

He'd arranged to meet his son and grandson – Frank and Brendon – in the back room bar at the Crown, to start Brendon's send-off a little early. They could have met at home or in the Anchor, but the Crown was the only place in Cliffehaven they could really talk away from their women and enjoy a pint or three at the same time. Yet he kept a wary eye open as he approached the pub, knowing that if his Rosie caught him anywhere near the landlady, Gloria, there would be fireworks.

The two women had called an uneasy truce because it was wartime, but there was no love lost between the two landladies of Cliffehaven; they were women on their own, and running a pub was difficult at the best of times – and it didn't help that Rosie hadn't really forgiven Gloria for kissing Ron under the mistletoe two Christmases ago. She'd made it very clear that Ron was never to set foot in the Crown again.

Ron could understand Rosie's reasoning and was quite flattered by it, but as he was completely innocent of any wrongdoing with Gloria, he rather resented being told what he could and couldn't do. At the same time, he didn't relish getting caught coming in here.

A quick glance over his shoulder told him the coast was clear and he nipped into the alleyway at the side of the pub and through the back door, with Harvey following closely behind him.

Gloria was serving behind the bar, and she shot him a wink, and indicated with a tilt of her head that he should go straight through to the snug. Ron winked back and headed to the small private lounge bar at the back of the pub, his gaze feasting on the luscious landlady who, despite her come-hither looks, was most definitely out of bounds.

Gloria had none of the soft glamour and sweet appeal of his Rosie, for she was a big, buxom lass built for sin, with a loud voice and rough ways – but there was no doubting she made a pleasing sight behind the bar, her large breasts undulating delightfully beneath that tight blouse as she pulled pints and kept up a flow of bright chatter. She was a Londoner, but had been running the Crown for so many years she'd become part of the fabric of Cliffehaven, and because she wasn't averse to a bit of harmless slap and tickle, was regarded by her male customers as the salt of the earth and a jolly good sport. To other, more prudish minds she was no better than she should be, and to Rosie, she was a danger to anything in trousers – especially her Ron.

Gloria shrugged off her detractors, seemingly undisturbed by their hurtful sniping, and carried on in her own sweet way. Ron admired her, for he knew Gloria better than most, and despite the brassy hair, heavy make-up and provocative clothes, she had an intelligent, quick mind, and a sharp nose for trouble. In fact, she'd been instrumental in helping to capture a rats' nest of fifth columnists who'd held their meetings in her function room the previous year, and Ron suspected that, being perfectly placed to overhear all sorts of things, she passed on a good deal of useful intelligence to MI5.

He pushed through the door to the snug with Harvey barging before him to greet Frank and Brendon who were waiting there. 'To be sure it's good to have you both to meself for a change,' he said after they'd embraced. 'Once the women get involved you can't get a word in edgeways.'

'It's only because they care, Grandad,' said Brendon, making a fuss of a joyous Harvey. 'You can't blame them.'

'Aye, I know that, wee boy,' he replied, reaching for one of the many beer bottles on the table, and emptying it into the dog bowl Gloria had thoughtfully provided for Harvey. 'But it'll be good to have an intelligent conversation for once. I'm surrounded by women, and this is a rare chance to be away from them.'

They sat in the worn leather chairs and Ron cast an appreciative eye over the laden table, noting the bottle of Irish whiskey nestling amongst the beers. 'I have to say, you've been mighty generous, Frank. This little lot must have set you back a few bob.'

'Aye, it did that, but I can't have me boy leaving without a decent send-off, can I? And Gloria gave me a discount on the whiskey.'

'Aye, and so she should,' muttered Ron.

They drank in comfortable, companionable silence as Harvey's collar tag clanged against the metal bowl in his eagerness to lap up the last drop.

Harvey finally slumped onto the floor with a satisfied sigh and went to sleep, and Ron surreptitiously watched his son and grandson as he packed tobacco into his pipe and took his time to get it alight. There was something between Brendon and Frank – some indefinable thing that had been there ever since Frank had come home from Devon. Peggy had noticed it too, and when Brendon had come on leave a few days later, their suspicions had grown that something bad had gone on down in Devon which now preyed on their minds.

'Are either of you going to tell me what happened down there?' he asked gruffly. He saw the swiftly exchanged glance between them and grunted. 'You know it'll go no further with me,' he said. 'Come on. Out with it. I can see it's eating at both of you, and it'll do Brendon no good to be going back on duty without a clear mind.'

'We've been threatened with a court martial if we breathe a word of it, Grandad,' said Brendon solemnly.

Ron gripped the stem of his pipe between his teeth and leant back in the chair, feeling the weight of his ferrets and the dead rabbits dragging on his coat. 'It was that serious, was it?' He regarded them evenly as they remained silent. 'Let me guess. Those in charge were incompetent. A careless order or lack of proper guidance led to men getting hurt – or worse – just as it did at Dieppe and Gallipoli. And now the whole thing has to be hushed up because it might damage morale and show the public just what sort of fools are running this war.'

'You've got that about right,' growled Frank, slamming his tankard down on the table with such force that the remains of his beer splattered his hand. 'The whole thing was an absolute disaster.'

'Dad,' warned Brendon.

'I don't care if they court-martial me,' he retorted loudly. 'I'm not afraid to speak out to me da.'

'Then do it quietly, son,' cautioned Ron. 'There's no wisdom in letting half of Cliffehaven hear you.'

Frank swallowed the last of his beer, opened the bottle of whiskey and poured generous measures into the clean glasses Gloria had set out. '*Sláinte,*' he said, raising his glass and downing it in one.

Ron drank his own whiskey while Frank poured himself some more. His son's hand was shaking so much the bottle rattled against the glass, and Ron experienced a cold dart of uneasiness. 'To be sure, Frank, you don't have to tell me. I can guess enough to know things didn't go well and that somehow you and Brendon were caught up in it.'

'I was only a bystander,' said Frank, 'but I saw enough, and can only thank God my boy wasn't amongst the dead that day.' He shrugged off Brendon's staying hand, raised his head and looked at his father with bloodshot eyes, his gaze never wavering as he described the terrible scenes on Slapton Sands those two consecutive early mornings when raw, young American recruits had been sent to their deaths during a rehearsal for landing in France.

'The final death toll was over seven hundred,' he finished brokenly.

Ron gritted his teeth, holding back his anger at such an unnecessary waste of young lives, and the futility of ever trusting those in charge to get beach landing assaults right. He'd seen enough slaughter during the first shout, and the knowledge that things hadn't really changed made him sick at heart.

Brendon leant forward, his elbows on his knees. 'As tragic as it was, we're fighting a war, and men die.'

'It was just a bloody rehearsal,' Frank hissed furiously. 'And they weren't men – they were boys – they weren't supposed to die.'

'Everyone knows that,' said Brendon firmly, 'and you can be certain that it wasn't taken lightly by Churchill or Eisenhower. General Addington – the American observer – told me that changes have been implemented to make sure something like that doesn't happen when we—' He broke off and bit his lip.

'You're taking part in the invasion?' breathed Ron, his heart thudding at the thought.

Brendon scrubbed his face with his hands. 'I didn't mean ... That's to say ...' He took a shuddering breath. 'Just forget I said anything – and for God's sake don't say a word of it to Mum.'

'It's all right, son,' said Frank, putting his large arm around his shoulder. 'We understand, and it'll go no further than this room, I promise.' His heavily lined, weathered face showed his anguish. 'But the thought of you going back to the fighting is a knife to me heart, wee boy. If anything should happen to you …'

'I'll do my best to stay alive, Da,' Brendon replied softly. 'But it's war, and we all have to take our chances.'

Ron's heart shrivelled at the thought of the danger the boy would be in. He poured another round of drinks and gulped his own down. 'When you told us you were going down there you said you wouldn't be involved in the fighting,' he muttered.

'I know I did – and at the time, that's what I believed. But it turns out that every man, ship and vehicle that took part in those rehearsals will be involved in the real thing, and I for one am glad of it. I'm sick of hanging about in London like a spare part when I should be doing something useful elsewhere.'

'When will it be?' Frank asked raggedly.

'I've said too much already, Da. Please don't ask me anything more.'

'But it'll be soon?' Frank's penetrating gaze was fixed on his son.

Brendon nodded curtly and poured another whiskey before making a visible effort to change the subject. 'So, what's Aunt Peggy cooking us for supper, Grandad?' he asked a little too brightly. 'Something you pilfered from the Cliffe estate, perhaps?'

Ron understood the boy's need to lighten the mood, but his heart was heavy at the thought that this treasured grandson would once again be involved in the fighting that had already taken his two brothers, Seamus and Joseph and could see that Frank was really struggling to absorb the knowledge that his last surviving son would once again be in peril. Ron battled to keep his tone light and his expression bland as he played along with his grandson's charade that everything was all right.

'Those pigeons had nothing to do with Lord Cliffe,' he said stoutly. 'To be sure they were flying free up on the hills and simply got in the way of me shotgun, so they did.'

Brendon chuckled and shook his head in disbelief. 'If you say so, Grandad.'

Ron grinned back. The whole family knew that the Cliffe estate had been his larder for many years, and although the pigeons had been legally shot, their Christmas dinner had certainly been courtesy of Lord Cliffe's well-stocked salmon ponds and pheasant pens.

He sipped the good whiskey and regarded his silent son, who was drinking it down as if it could wash away his fears and drown out the sounds and sights of what he'd witnessed at Slapton. Ron shared Frank's anxieties and would have given anything to be able to lift the burden of Frank's suffering, but what could he say or do that would make a difference to how they were both feeling? This war had to be won – boys like Brendon had to put their lives in danger to gain victory – and all anyone could do was cling together and pray that they all came home in one piece.

'Let's not dwell on things we have no control over,' he said into the heavy silence. 'Our time together is short enough without getting depressed.' He forced a cheerful grin at Brendon. 'Why don't you tell us more about your young Betty?' he encouraged. 'From what your Aunt Carol says in her letters, she sounds like a nice wee lass.'

Brendon made a visible effort to emulate his grandfather's cheerful tone as he filled Ron in on his girl down in Devon. 'Aye, that she is,' he said, pouring yet more whiskey into the empty glasses as he sang the young schoolmistress's praises. 'I hated leaving her down in Devon, but when this is all over we'll be together again, I'm sure of it.' He finished with a sheepish smile. 'I know you've heard all this before, but she really is the one, Grandad.'

Ron smiled. 'What it is to be young and fancy free,' he joked, the whiskey giving him a pleasant buzz. 'To be sure I remember when I was a lad. The girls couldn't get enough of me back then.'

'You're not doing too badly now,' teased Brendon, whose cheeks were getting flushed. 'You've got a fine woman in Rosie Braithwaite.'

Ron chuckled. 'Aye, I do that, and I count myself lucky that she puts up with me.' He felt the ferrets begin to stir and hoisted them out of his pocket to drape them over his shoulders and stroke their soft fur. 'But if she catches me in here, she'll have my guts for garters.'

The ferrets lay slumped over his broad shoulders, hypnotised by Ron's gentle hands and snuffling with pleasure.

'D'you think it's wise bringing them in here?' asked Frank. 'Rosie wouldn't like it, and I doubt Gloria will either.'

'Ach,' he murmured, 'they're fine, so they are. They're tired and it's peaceful enough in here.'

As if on cue, the door slammed back, making them all jump. The ferrets stirred, raising their inquisitive noses and digging their claws into Ron's shoulders as Gloria bustled in with a large plate of sandwiches.

Catching sight of the ferrets she dropped the plate and let out a screech. 'What the *hell* do you think you're doing bringing them in 'ere?' she yelled.

The ferrets took objection to the loud interruption and before Ron could grab them, they'd shot off his shoulders and scampered at lightning speed across the floor towards the open door.

Ron raced after them in an attempt to bar their escape – but Gloria was yelling fit to bust, the ferrets were too quick, and Harvey was barging about, trying to snaffle the sandwiches from the floor.

'Get them things outta my pub,' yelled Gloria, holding up the hem of her skirt as the ferrets darted between her feet and disappeared into the main saloon bar.

Frank and Brendon were quickly in pursuit and Ron dived after Flora, who was about to disappear up the chimney, managing to grab hold of her back leg. A firm tug, a grasp of her sooty scruff, and she was quickly shoved back into the deepest pocket of his coat.

But pandemonium had broken out amongst the crowd of drinkers as Dora shot between their legs, darting back and forth in search of an escape route through the tangle of screaming women and shouting men.

Brendon made a grab for her, but she twisted away, clawed up the sturdy oak bar and leapt for safety onto the mirror-backed shelves on the wall behind it. Glasses smashed and bottles teetered dangerously as she arched her back, dropped a stinking pile of poo, and let out an ear-piercing screech.

To the accompanying cries of horror at the stench, shouts of encouragement from the servicemen and over-excited barking from Harvey, Brendon and Frank closed in on her, wary of her sharp claws and even sharper teeth.

'Look what it's done all over me shelves,' wailed Gloria. 'You're gonna pay for this, Ronan Reilly, you can be sure of that!'

'Gloria, stop yelling, or you'll frighten her even more,' Ron retorted.

Gloria glared at him, her eyes glinting dangerously, but she held her tongue and her customers fell silent, agog as to what might happen next.

Brendon and Frank closed in with Ron. 'Go slow and easy, boys,' he said, grabbing Harvey to make him shut up and sit still. He murmured soft words as he slowly approached Dora, and gently drew Flora back out of his pocket so they could see each other.

Dora sniffed the air suspiciously and Ron held Flora up so they were nose to nose, and while Dora was occupied with greeting her companion, Frank took a firm hold of her scruff and eased her off the shelf.

Ron tucked them both away in the deepest reaches of his coat. Mournfully eyeing the shattered glasses and bottles on the floor and the odorous mess on the shelf, he gave Gloria a hapless smile. 'To be sure, I'm sorry, Gloria. We'll clean up and pay for any damage.'

'Damned right you will,' she stormed. 'Do you know how hard it is to get glasses these days? And that were a full bottle of gin – worth a king's ransom.'

Ron could see Brendon and Frank were doing their best to clean up the mess with a discarded newspaper as Gloria stood there, her expression thunderous. 'Now, Gloria,' he placated softly, his eyes gleaming with mischief. 'You and I both know where that gin came from and that the bottle was half-empty, so don't be getting ideas of making a profit out of me. To be sure, 'tis sorry I am for the mess, but they were doing no harm until you frightened them.'

'You've got a bleedin' nerve, Ronan Reilly,' she rasped, the gleam of humour in her eyes at odds with her furious expression as she folded her arms beneath her magnificently heaving bosom. 'You come in my pub, let that vermin loose, and then blame me. I don't know what sort of place Rosie runs, but this is a respectable 'ouse, and I ain't standing for it. Cough up the money and get out.'

'But I—'

'Wallet,' she snapped, her hand open beneath his nose, her eyes challenging him to argue.

He could hear the muffled giggles running through the watching crowd, and felt their eyes on him as he scrabbled in his trouser pockets, took out what money he had and placed it in a crumpled pile on the bar.

She eyed the grubby ten-bob note and few coppers disdainfully. 'That ain't enough.'

'To be sure, it's all I have on me at the moment. But I've a couple of fine rabbits to make up the rest,' he said hopefully, digging them out of his coat.

Gloria grimaced and flinched as the dead rabbits were dangled beneath her nose. 'You owe me, Ron, and I won't let you forget it.'

Brendon dug into his pocket and pulled out a couple of notes. 'We Reillys pay our debts,' he muttered.

Gloria stuffed the money into her bra. She stood tall and imposing, her arm as straight and stiff as an arrow, pointing towards the door. 'Out. Now,' she ordered.

Ron returned the rabbits to his pocket and decided the only way to appease her was to use a charm offensive. 'Ach, come on, Gloria,' he wheedled. 'Brendon's leaving tomorrow and—'

'I don't care,' she retorted. 'And if you don't leave right this minute, I'll throw you out.'

Ron felt the tension rising amongst the interested audience and drew himself up to his full six feet three inches and tried to dazzle her with his smile. 'Oh, Gloria,' he crooned with a twinkle in his eyes. 'I know you find me irresistible, and to be sure I'm flattered that one so lovely can't keep her hands off me – but should we not go somewhere more private so we can discuss this further?'

Gloria's lips twitched momentarily, and there was a speculative gleam in her eyes until she remembered their audience. 'Don't flatter yerself. I got my standards – unlike some – and if I'd wanted yer body, I'd've 'ad it. But only after a good scrub-down with soap and water.'

Ron met her challenging gaze as a chorus of cheers and ribald remarks followed this statement. Gloria was now playing to her audience, the town gossip Olive Grayson was lapping up every word, and it was time he beat a retreat. He only hoped he had the chance to explain this situation to Rosie before Olive got in first, for she'd take great pleasure in exaggerating, stirring and twisting his actions into something unsavoury. He caught sight of Frank and Brendon, who were now emerging from the private bar laden with the bottles they'd already paid for, and jerked his head towards the back door.

''Tis sorry I am it has come to this,' he muttered, edging towards escape. 'We'll not be darkening your door again, Gloria.'

The three of them silently left the Crown with as much dignity as they could muster in the light of the amount of alcohol they'd already consumed. Emerging from the side alley, they staggered up the hill to the allotments where Ron's old pal Stan had a nice shed and some comfy deckchairs.

Ron knew where Stan hid his key, and within minutes they were sitting in the sunshine out of the wind, and drinking whiskey from Stan's none-too-clean chipped mugs while Harvey went off to see if anyone might be kind enough to feed him a biscuit or three.

'That went well,' said Frank dryly. 'I expect most of Cliffehaven will hear about it before nightfall as Olive Grayson was watching your every move.' He eyed his father quizzically. 'There were certainly some sparks flying between you and Gloria. You haven't been playing away there, have you, Da?'

'As tempting as it is, I wouldn't dare,' Ron replied. 'Rosie would deal with me as thoroughly as the vet did Harvey.' He eyed the whiskey in the mug, saw an ant about to drown itself and flicked it out with a grubby finger. 'God help me, boys. To be sure she'll hear about this and, like that ant, me life will be in peril.'

'You always did live on a knife-edge, Grandad,' said Brendon with a wry smile. 'How Rosie puts up with you, I really don't know.'

'It's because she loves me,' Ron replied with drunken bravado. 'She's a forgiving woman, so she is, and this'll all blow over, you'll see.'

He chuckled and raised his mug in a toast. 'Here's to women. Can't live with 'em, but can't live without 'em. God bless them all.'

2

The British Red Cross distribution centre had been set up on the vast factory estate which sprawled across the northernmost reaches of Cliffehaven where cattle had once grazed. Situated behind high barbed-wire fencing, it was overshadowed by several barrage balloons which glinted like silver whales above the mass of corrugated iron roofs.

Peggy could have left Daisy with Sarah and Cordelia, but as she spent so little time with her now she was working, she'd decided to take her along this afternoon so they could have half an hour's play in the park before she started her two-hour stint as a volunteer for the Red Cross. She steered the pushchair up the steep hill, then showed her identity card to the guard on duty at the gate and headed for the new building at the far end.

She passed the canteen, which was alive with chatter and the ever-present wireless, and then glanced towards the armaments factory where Ivy worked, hoping to catch a glimpse of her. But it seemed everyone was busy, so she carried on past the tool factory, the parachute manufacturer and the large engineering sheds where bits of planes were being made. There was a wonderful sense of industry, with the sounds of thudding, whining tools echoing from those vast sheds, and Peggy felt a certain pride that she too was now an intrinsic part of the workforce striving to do their best to defeat Hitler. Her sewing of uniforms for Solly Goldman might not be as important as making bullets and bombs, but it paid well and gave her the satisfaction of knowing she was doing her bit. Since she'd given up on volunteering for the Women's Voluntary Service because her sister Doris – queen bee at the WVS – had been such a pain in the neck, she was glad to sacrifice two hours every Saturday to do something charitable.

Peggy's defection from the WVS and her new job at the factory had caused yet another breach in her relationship with Doris – who was now refusing to talk to her unless she wanted something, and although this saddened Peggy, she was determined to do things her way and not be cowed because her snooty sister didn't approve of her working alongside her London evacuees in what she considered to be a common factory.

Approaching the large British Red Cross warehouse, Peggy saw Kitty and Charlotte waiting outside, and smiled as they waved to her. They looked lovely, with one so dark, the other fair, each dressed in dungarees and layers of thick sweaters that didn't quite disguise the fact they were both pregnant. Kitty had been Peggy's evacuee back in

1942, following a terrible accident in the plane she was delivering for the ATA which had left her with a partially amputated leg, and a doubtful future. But Kitty was made of stern stuff, and she'd soon learnt to manage the prosthesis, returned to flying and ended up marrying Roger Makepeace, who was Martin's wingman and best friend.

Dark-haired and usually girlishly slender, Charlotte had been close to Kitty since their boarding-school days, and she too had become an 'Attagirl', before marrying Kitty's rogue of a brother, Freddy, and falling pregnant with twins. Both men were now incarcerated in Stalag III along with Martin, and the girls were putting a brave face on things, determined to do their bit until they could all be reunited.

Peggy hugged them both warmly and kissed their radiant cheeks. 'You both look marvellously well,' she said affectionately.

Kitty laughed and tucked her short fair hair behind her ears. 'I'm just glad I'm not having twins,' she said, patting her bump. 'This one's heavy enough on its own.'

Peggy eyed the walking stick Kitty had taken to using now her pregnancy had advanced. 'You're not finding things too much, are you, dear?' she asked with motherly concern. 'Shouldn't you be resting at home instead of coming here?'

'If Roger can put up with being a POW, then I can certainly manage the added weight on my stump.'

She squeezed Peggy's hand. 'You do worry, Aunt Peg, and there's really no need. The doctor's passed us both fit, and a few hours a week helping out here won't kill either of us – in fact we'd be going quite potty if we weren't doing something useful.'

Peggy smiled at Charlotte, who was easing her back after bending to make a fuss of Daisy. 'Are you sure you've got your dates right, dear? You look as if you're about to pop.'

Charlotte giggled. 'Quite sure. There *are* two of them in here,' she said, caressing her enormous stomach, 'and I'm eating for both of them when rationing allows, so it's hardly surprising I'm so huge. Mother wrote and told me she got quite big with me, so it obviously runs in the family.'

Peggy smiled even though she fretted that both girls were doing too much with only three more months to go in their pregnancies – but then she hadn't exactly rested during any of her own while she was running the boarding house, and certainly hadn't when she'd been carrying Daisy.

She followed the girls into the echoing warehouse, where the sound of the music coming from the wireless was fighting a losing battle with all the chattering. It was a terrible shame that Kitty's parents were in Argentina, and Charlotte's were up in the Midlands, but Peggy was delighted to have the chance to mother them, and was very excited at the thought of three little babies to cuddle and croon over.

Peggy had chosen to volunteer for the Red Cross as it had branches all over the world and was almost wholly a voluntary organisation which did the most wonderful work, not only for the sick and wounded, but for the men and women who were in internment camps. She felt proud that in her own small way she was bringing comfort to those who needed it most.

The three women kept their jumpers and coats on, for it was cold in the warehouse, the concrete floor and iron roof keeping the vast stores of tinned food and medical supplies at the right temperature to stop them from going off. Unstrapping Daisy from the pushchair, Peggy took her over to the knot of little ones playing on mats in a corner under the watchful eye of several sprightly grandparents who'd volunteered for the job while the young mothers packed the food parcels. Once Daisy was happily occupied with a doll's house, Peggy joined Kitty and Charlotte at the long table where the POW boxes were being filled.

The Red Cross provided a bewildering array of different parcels to be sent abroad, some with medical supplies, others with food, or recreational things like board games, jigsaw puzzles and books. Prisoners' next of kin could send their own parcels, but these were strictly checked for anything not on the permitted list of goods, and then weighed before they were sent out. Medical supplies were being transported to the internment camps across Europe, but the Japanese had barred the Red Cross personnel access to their camps and had refused to accept any parcels, which was in direct defiance of the Geneva Convention. Whether the Germans allowed their prisoners to have their parcels wasn't known, but it seemed that at least they were being delivered, and the inspectors permitted into the camps.

The three women set to with a will in the food section, each of them praying that their loved ones would benefit from the tins of meat, vegetables and fish, and enjoy the luxury of butter, biscuits, tins of cigarettes and bars of Cadbury's chocolate. It had been explained to them that each parcel must contain a balance of fat, protein and sugar to supplement what was probably a very poor diet in the camps, and that things like jam, dried egg, tea and cocoa would be a boost to the prisoners' morale.

Once each box was filled and firmly tied with string, it was sent down the line to the women who were responsible for addressing them before they were transported by truck to the mailing centres. There were so many POW camps now that each depot was responsible for a particular area, and the one in Cliffehaven covered a vast swathe of Germany, so it was quite possible that Martin, Roger and Freddy might be the recipients of parcels packed right here at home.

Peggy, Kitty and Charlotte had of course sent their own private parcels as next of kin – even though there was very little available in the shops to make them interesting – but so far there had been no acknowledgement from their men to say they'd received them.

'I don't know how the Red Cross manages to get hold of all this stuff,' said Kitty, picking up a tin of cocoa powder from the great stack behind her. 'I haven't seen cocoa or bars of chocolate in the shops for months.'

'The large food companies have been very generous to donate so much.' Peggy glanced across at the grim-faced security guards who were patrolling the warehouse. 'That's why we have them watching our every move,' she muttered. 'As if we'd stoop so low as to steal from our poor boys.'

'It has been known,' Charlotte said. 'A woman got arrested last week, her pockets bulging with chocolate and tins of butter.' She gave a little sigh and eased her back. 'But I can understand why she did it. The temptation is awful when there's so little to be had in the way of luxuries these days – and frankly, I could kill for a bit of chocolate right now.'

Peggy's mouth was also watering at the thought, but she firmly pushed the distant memory of chocolate away and dug in her string bag for the flask and the paper bag she'd filled with the last of the broken biscuits from her tin at home. 'You're just tired and in need of some sugar. Here, help yourself to some of those, and then have some tea from the flask. I added a bit more milk than usual as I thought it would be good for you both.'

Charlotte smiled. 'You think of everything, Peggy. What would we do without you?'

Peggy giggled. 'I'm sure you'd manage.'

'Actually, I don't think we would,' said Kitty affectionately.

'Bless you, darlings, it's lovely of you to say so.'

The tender moment was broken by a cheerful voice. 'Hello, Peg. I thought I'd find you here.'

She looked up to find Gracie Armitage smiling at her. They'd become friends when Peggy had started at Solly's factory, even though Gracie was a good ten years younger than Peggy. Gracie was the senior cutter at the factory and struggling to raise her daughter on her own while her husband flew for the RAF. Her little girl, Chloe, was only months older than Daisy and they were now almost inseparable.

'Hello, love. I didn't realise you did a turn here.'

'I couldn't before, but it's easier now they've arranged childcare.' She glanced across at the children playing on the far side of the warehouse. Daisy and Chloe were huddled together by the doll's house and no doubt plotting mischief as usual.

'Peace, blessed peace,' Gracie sighed, taking the chair next to Peggy. 'She's been a holy terror all morning.'

'Oh dear, I know how that can get you down,' Peggy murmured. 'Daisy's just as awkward at the moment. It seems to be a phase all children their age have to go through.' She glanced at Charlotte and Kitty. 'Just you wait and see what you've let yourselves in for, girls. And it gets worse as they get older – you mark my words.'

Charlotte and Kitty blithely shrugged off her warning, and Peggy smiled. They were happy in their innocence but wouldn't know what hit them once those three babies arrived, all yelling for attention and causing them sleepless nights.

Gracie chuckled. 'There are some who definitely get worse as they grow older. Your father-in-law is a prime example.'

Peggy checked the long list and reached for a tin of butter. 'He's certainly always getting himself into one sort of pickle or another, but as far as I know he's actually been behaving himself lately.' She glanced across at Gracie, who'd gone rather red. 'Why? Have you heard otherwise?'

'Oh dear,' groaned Gracie. 'You obviously haven't heard.'

'Heard what?'

'I'm sorry, Peg, I thought you'd have heard or I wouldn't have mentioned anything. Ron was thrown out of the Crown this lunchtime. I assumed he'd have come running back to Beach View with his tail between his legs – after all, he couldn't very well go and take refuge in the Anchor. Rosie will have his guts for garters!'

Peggy stared at her in confusion. 'Thrown ...? The Crown ...? What the heck was he doing in there when he knows full well he shouldn't be?'

'I don't know,' Gracie said awkwardly. 'I'm sorry, Peg, I shouldn't have said anything.'

Peggy clucked her tongue. 'I think you'd better tell me what you do know.'

Gracie's blush deepened. 'All I heard was that he'd been drinking in there with Frank and Brendon, and somehow his ferrets got loose and ran into the bar. By all accounts they caused complete chaos and Gloria was so incandescent with rage she threatened to throw Ron out single-handedly.'

Peggy giggled. 'I'd have liked to see her try,' she spluttered.

Gracie shot her an uncertain smile. 'So would I, but she's a big woman, and when roused is probably capable of anything. I certainly wouldn't want to tangle with her.'

'It's not like you to pick up on gossip, Gracie,' Peggy murmured, eyeing her thoughtfully. 'Who told you?'

'It's true I don't take much notice of the latest scandal doing the rounds, but that Olive Grayson who works in the factory loading bay collared me as I was walking up here and filled me in.'

'I'm glad you told me,' said Peggy. 'At least now I know what he's been up to, and can deal with him when he gets home.'

'Olive's a terrible gossip, so I wouldn't be at all surprised if half of Cliffehaven knows by now,' Gracie said. 'Poor Ron. I don't fancy his chances when Rosie gets hold of him.'

'It'll serve him right if she gives him an earful,' said Peggy firmly. 'Rosie has enough to put up with, without his shenanigans.' She gave an exasperated sigh. 'Brendon's due to go back on duty tomorrow, so they were no doubt drowning their sorrows, but why in the Crown when they could have done it at home? I wouldn't have minded.'

Gracie shrugged. 'Your guess is as good as mine, Peggy. Who knows what goes on in men's minds?'

'Well, they'll get a piece of mine when they come rolling in tonight, I'll tell you that for nothing,' Peggy said before once again breaking into giggles. 'I do wish I'd seen the ferrets running amok and Gloria threatening Ron like that – it would have brightened my day considerably.'

Rosie Braithwaite had been rushed off her feet over the last two hours and she was ready for a stiff drink, a sit-down and something to eat before she had to prepare for the evening session, which would probably prove just as hectic. With both her middle-aged barmaids off sick, she could have done with Ron's help this lunchtime, but knowing it was his grandson's last day of leave, she'd accepted he had more important things to do, and had knuckled down to running the Anchor's bar single-handedly.

The one bright spark in her day had been Major Radwell, who, despite having lost most of one arm during the battle for Tunis, had collected dirty glasses, brought a crate of brown ale up from the cellar and changed the barrel when the bitter had run out.

Rosie smiled at him as he stood at the bar quietly drinking his gin and tonic, once more noting how handsome he was with those startling grey eyes and dark hair which held only a hint of silver. He was in his late forties, she guessed, and had lovely manners, and as he'd become a regular over the past few weeks and was probably feeling at rather a loose end, she'd made a point of chatting to him during the infrequent lulls between serving, and found him to be most pleasant company.

She glanced up at the clock and was about to ring the bell to call time when Olive Grayson shoved her way up to the bar and asked for another glass of beer. Rosie didn't like Olive, well aware that she was a malicious gossip, and none too wholesome into the bargain. 'Sorry, Olive. I'm calling time,' she said briskly.

'But you haven't yet, and I'm still thirsty,' said Olive, purposefully shoving the glass across the bar.

Rosie didn't feel like getting into an argument, for it would merely prolong things, and her high-heeled shoes were making her feet ache. 'Just a half, then,' she conceded.

'Ron not helping out today?' the woman asked, her pale eyes glinting slyly beneath the grubby knotted headscarf.

'He's busy with his son and grandson, if you must know,' said Rosie, placing the glass on the counter and taking the woman's money. 'You've got five minutes to drink that, Olive, then I'm locking the door.' She tugged down on the bell pull to signal time.

Olive's unpleasant smile revealed teeth that probably hadn't seen a brush for years. 'So you know where they are, then?'

Rosie took a shallow breath and eyed her evenly. 'If you've got something to say, Olive, then get on with it. I haven't got time to play your silly games.'

Olive slurped down some beer and wiped her mouth on her dirty sleeve. 'Well, if you're going to be like that, I won't bother telling you about Ron and Gloria Stevens.'

Rosie felt a dart of alarm but managed to hide it by keeping her expression blank. 'Then I won't bother listening to it, Olive. Finish your drink and take your gossip with you when you leave.'

She turned to put the money in the till and serve Major Radwell, who was at the other end of the bar patiently waiting for a refill. 'Sorry about that, Major. Another gin, is it?'

'Gloria chucked him out of the pub and sent him off with a flea in his ear,' Olive announced gleefully. 'His ferrets ran riot and I reckon they did at least a fiver's worth of damage, which he offered to pay for with a couple of dead rabbits.'

It took all of Rosie's will power to finish pouring the gin without spilling a drop before she took the Major's money and rang it up on the till. She would not be drawn into Olive's spiteful gossip, let alone react to it. She'd learnt over all the years of running a pub that ignoring remarks like that was the best way of dealing with them. The last thing she needed today was to get into a dust-up with the odious Olive.

And yet as she began to clear glasses and wipe down the bar she couldn't help but hear Olive regaling the last few customers with what Ron had been up to at the Crown and how the sparks had been flying between him and Gloria Stevens. Olive's stories were often embellished, and slanted by her bias, but there was always some truth in her tittle-tattle, and as her story was being corroborated by one of her other customers, Rosie had little doubt that Ron had definitely gone into the Crown and had some sort of altercation with that tart Gloria.

She felt cold with fury that he'd gone against her express wishes, but she was damned if she'd let Olive know how deeply her words had cut, and how hurt she was by Ron breaking his promise never to go into that pub again. Turning back to Major Radwell, she murmured, 'Take your time with that. It's good gin and shouldn't be rushed.'

Olive finished her beer and glared at Rosie, then grabbed her ratty coat and stomped out, muttering that it was hardly surprising Ron spent his time with Gloria Stevens when Rosie clearly had her eye on a bigger catch.

Rosie slid the bolts home after she'd gone, kicked off her tight shoes and returned to the bar. Pouring a large gin for herself and topping up the Major's glass, she wished him luck and downed the fiery liquid in one. Catching the amused glint in his eyes, she shot him a grin. 'It's been one of those days,' she explained. 'One in which I could have done without Olive Grayson and her poison.'

Major Radwell smiled. 'I think you handled the situation very well, Mrs Braithwaite, but I suspect she's out there now spreading gossip about us. Perhaps it would be better if I didn't linger.'

Rosie laughed. 'If you're worried about my reputation, it's far too late, Major. The very fact I'm on my own and run a pub is enough to brand me a scarlet woman. But this is *my* pub and I choose who I drink with. You're welcome to stay as long as you want.'

'That's very kind of you, Mrs Braithwaite. I'd be delighted to keep you company as long as Ron doesn't take objection.'

'I think you can leave Ron's sensibilities out of it,' she said crisply. 'He's not my keeper, and it's become perfectly obvious that I'm certainly not his.'

'Oh dear,' he said ruefully. 'I get the feeling he's in rather hot water.'

'Up to his neck,' she replied, and then grinned. 'And please call me Rosie, Major Radwell. There's no need to be so formal after all the weeks you've been coming in.'

'Very well, Rosie, and you must call me Henry.'

They drank in companionable silence and Rosie tried very hard to put aside all thoughts of Ron's presence in the Crown. 'When will you get your final discharge from the hospital, Henry?' she asked.

'They'll be letting me go any day now,' he replied, 'and I have to think about what I'll do after that.' He drained the glass and placed it on the bar. 'My army career is over, and there are precious few jobs for a man of my age with one arm.'

'It's not like you to be defeatist,' Rosie protested. 'You're still a young man and I'm sure there are lots of things you could do.'

He shot her a wry smile. 'Please don't think I'm courting sympathy, Rosie, but I have to be realistic. The army has been my life since I left university, and it will feel strange not to be a part of something which has provided me with comradeship, work, home and order. '

'I can understand that,' she replied. 'But there must be something you can do. You're clearly an intelligent man with a good education. What about your family? Can't they help in any way?'

He twisted the glass between his fingers. 'I come from a long line of soldiers, Rosie, and was married to the service, which meant my wife left me long ago. My father was a brigadier in India before he passed away, and my brother is out there now fighting with the Chindits. My mother has moved in with her sister to a bungalow in the Cotswolds, and being army widows, both of them are now industriously working for the WI and WVS. I'm afraid there's no family business to step into.'

Rosie poured some more gin, even though it was difficult to get hold of these days, but she felt sorry for him and rather helpless to offer any sensible advice. 'I'm sure things will turn out all right,' she murmured. 'You have experience of leading men, of making difficult decisions and handling problems. Have you thought about try-ing some sort of managerial position – or becoming a schoolmaster?'

He grimaced. 'Perish the thought. I'd rather face the German guns than a room full of inquisitive schoolboys.' He sipped the gin and then gave a sigh. 'Those long weeks in the hospital have given me time to really think about what I wanted to do, and I've come to the conclusion that I must look at what's happened to me in a more positive way. See it as an opportunity, not a disaster.'

'Good for you,' she encouraged. 'And what has that inspired you to do?'

His sudden smile made him look younger, wiping away the hospital pallor and smoothing the lines of stress which had been so apparent only moments ago. 'I've always been an avid reader, which was why I got my degree in English Literature at Oxford – and' – he dipped his chin as if embarrassed – 'it's been my long-held dream to write a book.'

'Goodness,' breathed a wide-eyed Rosie.

He glanced up at her with a shy smile. 'I have no idea of whether I'd be any good as a writer, but I do have a story in mind – in fact I have several.'

'Then you must do it,' urged Rosie. 'It sounds a marvellous idea.'

'But what if I prove to be hopeless at it? What do I do then?'

'You try and get a job at a publishing house where you can read to your heart's content,' she replied firmly. 'But don't give up before you've even started, Henry, or you'll always regret not giving it a go.'

Henry chuckled. 'You're a real tonic, Rosie. That's the best advice I've had today.'

'Glad to have been of service,' she replied, grinning back at him. 'Now, I really do have to get on.' She slid from the bar stool and had to look up at him as he got to his feet. 'Will I see you again this evening?'

'That is a definite possibility,' he replied, 'but would you think it impertinent if I asked you to have lunch with me? I should enjoy your company very much.'

Rosie dismissed all thought of Ron's defection to the Crown and smiled. 'I should like that Henry. But aren't we a bit late? Everything will have closed by now.'

'The dining room at the Officers' Club is always open, and it's not far to walk.'

Rosie had heard the food in the exclusive club was top-notch and was quite excited at the thought of finally seeing what the place was like inside. 'That would be lovely. But first I must make sure the dog's all right, so if you wouldn't mind waiting a few minutes?'

'I'm sure any wait will be worth it,' he said, his grey eyes twinkling with merriment.

Unusually flustered, Rosie retrieved her abandoned shoes, hurried out of the bar and ran up the short flight of stairs to her rooms.

Monty possessed the same enthusiasm for life as his sire, Harvey, and although smaller and more delicate in build, his shaggy, brindled coat and intelligent eyes were the image of his father's. He'd been stretched out on the couch and now he leapt off to greet Rosie, his tail wagging furiously as he jumped up and down.

Rosie made a fuss of him and he followed her eagerly into the tiny kitchen. 'Ron's gone a step too far this time,' she muttered to him, 'and when he does decide to show his face he'll get a right earful and be shown the door, so you're not to make a fuss of him, do you hear?'

Monty cocked his head, more interested in the food Rosie was tipping into his bowl, and the moment it was set at his feet, he gobbled it down with alacrity.

Rosie left him to it and hurried into her bedroom to refresh her make-up and change into something smarter than the black skirt and white frilly blouse she always wore behind the bar. The Officers' Club was very posh, and she didn't want to let Henry down by turning up in anything less than her smartest clothes.

She slipped into a navy linen dress and matching heels, added a string of pearls and ear-studs, and then found some clean white cotton gloves. Placing a fetching little navy and white hat at a rakish angle over her platinum curls, she grinned at her reflection in the wardrobe mirror and nodded in satisfaction. It was amazing how a simple invitation to lunch had wiped away her weariness and bad mood, bringing colour and light to her face and eyes.

'Not too bad for your age, Rosie,' she muttered. 'Not too bad at all.'

Not stopping to wonder if it was the thought of being escorted by the handsome major, the chance to show Ron she could be just as independent, or the opportunity to see inside the Officers' Club which had brought about this change, she grabbed her coat and hurried back down the stairs to the bar and the waiting Henry.

Peggy wheeled Daisy's pushchair through the distribution centre barrier and stopped on the pavement
to say goodbye to Gracie. Daisy and Chloe were
reluctant to be parted and there was a bit of argy-
bargy from both of them until Gracie firmly carried
a struggling Chloe away and headed for her rented
rooms close to the recreation ground. Daisy wriggled and kicked at the foot-plate of her pushchair,
yelling after her little friend.

Peggy tried to ignore her as she turned to Kitty
and Charlotte. 'It was lovely to catch up with you,'
she said, raising her voice to combat Daisy's tantrum. 'Why don't you pop in tomorrow afternoon
for a cuppa? Gracie's bringing Chloe, so at least the
children will keep each other amused so we can
have a good chat.'

'We'd love to,' said Kitty. 'I managed to get hold
of the makings of a cake, so I'll bake it this evening
and bring it round.'

Peggy kissed both girls goodbye, and as they set off
for the little cottage in Briar Lane, Daisy fought to
escape the pushchair straps and yelled even louder.
'Stop it,' Peggy said crossly. 'Behave yourself, or you'll

go straight to bed when we get home, and miss out on Brendon's party tonight.'

Daisy eyed her belligerently and then slumped back with her thumb in her mouth, her tantrum spent – or at least postponed in her mother's withering glare.

Peggy wheeled Daisy down the hill, hoping she'd drop off for a bit of a sleep so she'd be in a better mood by the time they got home, for she had enough to do without having to deal with any more nonsense.

She glanced down to the station platform and caught sight of Ethel gossiping with the two WVS ladies who were running the tea stall. Peggy was about to hurry on when Ethel looked up just at that moment, called out and beckoned her down. Not wanting to appear rude, but disinclined to get caught up in Ethel's thirst for scandal, she checked she could spare a few minutes for a quick chat, and reluctantly made her way through the remains of the booking hall and onto the platform.

Ethel's husband, Stan, was the stationmaster, and had been since his father retired from the post at the end of the last war, and although Ethel worked at the munitions factory with her daughter Ruby, she also helped out at the station when time allowed. Stan had had a heart attack during their wedding reception the previous year, and Ethel's stubborn determination to get him well again had seen him lose most of his excess weight – which made him look much healthier, and had earned Peggy's grudging respect.

Peggy had never really taken to Ethel, for she was rough and opinionated and spoke her mind before thinking, which often caused offence. She'd not been very nice about April, Peggy's one-time evacuee, until she'd got to know her properly. Ethel had accepted that the girl was Stan's niece and had mellowed somewhat once April's illegitimate baby had come along. Peggy was delighted that April had found a warm and loving home with Ethel and Stan. To give Ethel her due, she'd proved to be a stalwart supporter of the girl and a terrific surrogate grandmother to little Paula.

Yet there were things about Ethel that niggled Peggy, and although Stan was a lifelong family friend, Peggy still couldn't think of her as the sort of woman she could confide in and fully trust, for Ethel took umbrage at the slightest thing, was light-fingered, and a salacious gossip with a spiteful tongue.

Peggy greeted the WVS women, who she knew from her time working at the Town Hall – relieved that her sister Doris was not amongst them – and then turned to Ethel, who was wearing a knotted headscarf, dungarees and an oversize railway uniform jacket. 'Stan deserted you, has he?' she asked.

Ethel took the ever-present roll-up out of her mouth and grimaced. 'He went up to 'is allotment two hours ago and I ain't seen hide nor hair of him since.' She grinned. 'Reckon 'im and the others are finishing off all that booze they brought back from the Crown.'

Peggy sighed. 'So, you've heard what happened, then?'

'It ain't difficult in this place,' said Ethel with a shrug. 'Cliffehaven might be swelling by the day with so many people pouring in to work in the factories, but it's still a village when it comes to gossip.' She eyed Daisy, who was now asleep. 'Aw, don't she look sweet?'

'You should have seen her five minutes ago,' Peggy replied dryly. She plonked herself down on the bench next to Ethel and lifted her face to the weak sun, glad of its meagre warmth after the chill of the warehouse. 'How's my April and little Paula? We do miss having April around, and she's so busy these days I hardly ever see her.'

Ethel's usually sour face lit up. 'They're both right as rain. April's got a day off from the telephone exchange, so she and my Ruby 'ave taken Paula to the park for a bit of fresh air. It's good the gels are getting on so well, 'cos I think my Ruby's a bit low at the moment,' she confided. 'What with her Mike all that way up north and no chance of seeing 'im until this war's over, she's worried 'e might go off her.'

'I doubt that very much,' said Peggy. 'Mike's far too smitten for that. It's probably all this hanging about waiting for something decisive to happen that's getting her down. Like the rest of us.'

'Yeah, you could be right,' said Ethel, flicking cigarette ash into a nearby flower tub. 'It's certainly getting on *my* nerves.'

Peggy had known Ethel's daughter Ruby since she'd come down from London, battered and bruised by her brutal husband, who'd since been killed in a motorcycle accident. Like April, who'd come to Cliffehaven after being forced to leave the Wrens when she fell pregnant, Ruby had moved into Beach View, and with the help of Cordelia and the other girls, they had both slowly regained their confidence and sparky personalities. When Ethel also left London, she and Ruby had rented the bungalow Cordelia had inherited in Mafeking Terrace, and now Ethel was firmly ensconced in the tiny railway cottage, Ruby shared the bungalow with another factory girl.

Ruby had met the Canadian soldier, Mike, before he'd been involved in the disaster of the Dieppe raid and lost his sight in one eye. It had been love the moment they'd met for both of them, but their path to happiness had been disrupted by his being sent to the Outer Hebrides for the duration of the war.

'At least the army didn't discharge him and send him back to Canada,' said Peggy. 'And from what Ruby's told me, I gather there are very few distractions up there on that remote island.'

'Yeah, I know. But that don't stop 'er moping about like a wet weekend.' Ethel looked at the station clock and got to her feet. 'I gotta get on, Peg. There's a troop train due.'

'I should be getting back to Beach View too. I dread to think what state Ron and the others will be in when they show up, but I suppose I can't blame them. It's not easy for Frank and Ron to see Brendon leaving again, and with all this talk of an invasion, he could be sent anywhere.'

'I don't reckon Pauline will find it that easy either,' Ethel commented. 'She ain't made of strong stuff, but I bet she ain't turned to the drink. I don't know why men think it's necessary to get drunk at the slightest excuse, and if Stan comes 'ome two sheets to the flaming wind he'll get a right earful and no mistake. His diet don't allow for beer.'

As Ethel bustled off to climb into the signal box, Peggy headed for home. She felt rather sorry for Stan, who was clearly under Ethel's thumb, but as he seemed happy enough to let her boss him about, she supposed she shouldn't be concerned. Her thoughts turned to the long, lively letter she'd received from her friend Dolly the previous morning. Dolly had confided in her long ago about the passionate affair she'd had with the American, General Felix Addington, and Peggy had always advised her to tell him about their daughter Carol, who was equally unaware of his existence. But Dolly had kept the secret to herself until fate had stepped in and brought father and daughter together down in Devon.

Forced to reveal the truth to both of them, Dolly had been terrified they'd turn their backs on her – but her letter yesterday was full of happy plans for the future. Felix and Carol loved her enough to forgive her, and once the war was over, both she and Carol were planning to go to America to be with him and to start again.

'How Pauline will react to that, I dread to think,' Peggy muttered to herself, turning into Camden Road and out of the wind.

Pauline had always been prone to histrionics, and would no doubt make a big issue about her mother deserting her to go and live in America – even though they hardly saw one another now. Dolly was a busy woman with many varied interests, and Peggy could quite understand her thinking that as Pauline was in her forties with a husband to look after her, she didn't need her mother on her doorstep.

'Which is all very well,' Peggy murmured to herself, 'but it's me and Frank who have to pick up the pieces when Pauline falls apart.'

She set aside all thoughts of Dolly and her tangled private life as she continued down Camden Road. There was no sign of Rosie at the Anchor, and Peggy wondered fretfully if she had heard about Ron. Rosie had been her friend for years, and Peggy frequently wondered what Ron had done to deserve her. He'd better hope his Irish charm would smooth this latest disagreement and win Rosie over.

Peggy loved her father-in-law, for although he was scruffy and an unreliable pain in the neck, he'd been her rock since Jim had been called up, and she knew that he simply adored Rosie, and would be heartbroken if she ended things between them. What

Peggy couldn't understand was why he persisted in upsetting her. If he took it into his head to go and see her while still silly with drink, then he was asking for trouble. Turning up full of remorse was one thing, but being drunk and maudlin was quite another.

With her thoughts churning, Peggy didn't stop to chat as she headed for home, but merely nodded to acquaintances, and waved to Fred the Fish and Alf the butcher as she passed their shops. She wanted to get home, have a cigarette and catch up on what everyone had been doing before she prepared herself to face whatever this evening might hold.

She stopped on the corner by the burnt-out skeleton of a bombed house and waited for a convoy of army trucks to rumble up the hill from the seafront. She could see Beach View from here – the home in which she'd been born and raised, and to which she'd returned after her marriage to Jim and her parents' retirement.

It was one in a short row of four-storey Victorian terraced houses which stood in a cul-de-sac halfway up the steep hill. There had once been six, but following a gas explosion right at the beginning of the war there were now only four. The rubble of the destroyed houses remained, but nature had taken over and now it was mostly hidden by brambles, ivy, grass and wild flowers.

Similar terraces lined the hill all the way up to the main road, which led past the Cliffe estate and RAF station to the villages and towns which lay to the north and east, and as Peggy stood there, she noted that just about every roof had missing tiles covered haphazardly with tarpaulin. Damaged chimney stacks had been shored up or demolished, and broken window panes had been boarded over since it was clearly pointless to keep replacing the glass when Jerry persisted in shattering it again. Walls were pocked by bullet scars from marauding enemy fighter planes, and not a lick of paint had touched the doors and window frames since war had started in earnest back in 1940.

Peggy glanced back at the housewives going about their shopping and realised that everyone and everything looked shabby and down at heel beneath the grey clouds that now blotted out the sun. It was a depressing sight, and she yearned for things to go back to the way they once were.

She crossed the road and headed down the alleyway which ran between the backs of the houses and petered out into a track which meandered up the steep hill to the east of the town and along the clifftops. Reaching her gate, she saw that someone had taken in her washing, which was a relief, for it looked as if it might rain again at any minute.

Pushing through the back door, she shut it behind her and gently unfastened the straps to lift Daisy out of the pushchair. She was heavy in her arms, draped over her shoulder and still half-asleep. 'Come on, love,' Peggy murmured. 'Let's get upstairs and see who's home.'

The wireless was on, and Queenie was perched on her usual shelf keeping an eye on everyone as Cordelia washed glasses in the sink, Sarah did the ironing and Rita helped Fran set the table and sort out the seating arrangements. Peggy gave a sigh of pleasure. It was lovely to be in her kitchen again after the icy temperature of the warehouse and the cold walk back, for a fire glowed in the range, and the dim light from the low wattage bulb cast enough shadows to hide the faded linoleum, peeling paint and shabby furniture.

'Oh, Sarah, how kind you are,' she sighed. 'But you shouldn't be doing ironing on your day off.'

Sarah smiled back at her as she hung one of Ron's shirts over the back of a chair. 'Neither should you,' she replied, 'and actually, I quite enjoy doing it. It smells so lovely after being out in the fresh air all day.'

Cordelia turned from the sink. 'We were wondering where you'd got to,' she said.

'I stopped off to chat with Ethel.' Peggy sat down with Daisy on her lap to divest her of her coat, mittens and woolly hat. 'She was keen to find out if I'd heard the latest Cliffehaven gossip, which has evidently spread like wildfire. I suppose you've all heard what happened at the Crown this lunchtime too?'

'Aye, we have. To be sure Ron will be in trouble,' said Fran, her green eyes sparkling with mischief beneath the crisp white nurse's cap. 'I feel quite sorry for him having to face Rosie after today.'

'I wouldn't feel sorry for Ron,' Cordelia said briskly. 'He's a scallywag, and Rosie deserves better.'

'You could be right, Cordelia,' said Peggy, 'but they'd be lost without each other, so I hope this all blows over quickly.' She set Daisy on her feet and the little girl ran straight to Cordelia and wrapped her tiny arms around her legs, smiling up at her winningly and asking for a biscuit and juice.

Cordelia dried her hands. 'Ron should realise what a treasure he has in Rosie and stop behaving like an overgrown schoolboy,' she said, hunting out a biscuit from the packet in the air-raid box that always stood by the door. 'And knowing how Rosie feels about Gloria, I think he's gone too far this time.' She handed over the biscuit with a loving smile at Daisy, and then poured a little orange juice into a cup. 'If you ask me,' she said crisply, 'he's a fool.'

Peggy was used to hearing Cordelia being stern about Ron – it had become a sort of game the pair of them enjoyed, so she didn't take much notice. She took off her coat and gloves and put her arm around Rita. 'How are you, love? I didn't expect you to be home yet.'

Rita hugged her back. 'John let me off early as there wasn't much doing, but he had me stripping one of the engines, so the day didn't drag too much.' Her face brightened. 'And I got a letter from Dad. He's trying to get some leave so he can come down, but I know how difficult things are at the moment, so although I'd love to see him, I'll understand if he can't make it.'

'I'm sure he'll do his best,' soothed Peggy, kissing the top of her head. Rita would certainly benefit from a visit by her father, but with things the way they were, Peggy suspected his army duties would keep him away.

Rita went to fetch another chair from the dining room, so Peggy turned to Fran, whose copper curls were glowing in the firelight. 'And what about you, dear? All those lovely letters this morning – have you heard from your family?'

'Mammy was full of gossip about her neighbours and moaning about Da's lumbago, which he uses as an excuse to get out of doing anything useful around the house.' She grinned impishly. 'He's a lot like Ron, really. Full of Irish charm, and a magician at getting out of things he has no wish to be doing.'

'And you, Sarah?' Peggy asked, knowing full well there had been an air letter from Australia in the morning post, as well as an intriguing one bearing a US forces' franking.

'I've had a letter from Mum, and two from Jane,' she replied, exchanging the cool iron for the one heating up on the range. 'Jane says she's kept so busy with the MOD that there's not even the slightest possibility of getting any leave at the moment, but she sends her love to everyone.'

She dipped her chin and began to iron a pillowcase, her fair hair falling over her shoulders and hiding her face. 'Mum's enjoying living in Australia, and little James is growing like a weed – but she says the heat and humidity in Cairns is very draining and she misses not having proper seasons. After all those years of living in Singapore, she longs for cool English autumn days, cold rain and frosty mornings.'

'Well, she's welcome to them,' chuckled Peggy, hearing the first spots of rain clatter against the window. 'I could do with some sun after the lousy winter and spring we've had.'

As Sarah continued ironing Peggy watched her thoughtfully. Sarah was usually so open about things, and this avoidance tweaked Peggy's curiosity, for there was only one person she could think of who might have sent that letter.

While working in the offices of the Women's Timber Corps up at an Cliffe estate, Sarah had become friendly with an American, Captain Delaney Hammond. He'd since been posted abroad, and Sarah had confessed tearfully to Peggy that her feelings for the captain had gone deeper than just friendship. As he was married and she was engaged to Philip – who'd more than likely been taken prisoner when the Japanese overran Singapore – there could be no future in their relationship. Sarah had struggled to come to terms with her feelings, guilty at being disloyal to Philip, but at the same time battling her deep affection for the married captain.

Peggy had noticed letters going back and forth during the first few months following his departure, but as far as she knew, they'd stopped some while ago – so why had they started again, and more to the point, why was Sarah being so secretive about it? Now wasn't the time to quiz the girl, but tomorrow Peggy was determined to find a quiet moment to talk to her alone and find out just what was going on.

Fran looked at the clock on the mantel. 'I'd better get out of this uniform and grab an hour or two of sleep before supper,' she said through a vast yawn. 'It's been a long, busy day, and I'm on earlies again tomorrow and the operating theatre is booked solid. What time are the others coming?'

'Pauline should be here soon, and I've said we'd eat at about seven. Goodness only knows when the men will turn up,' Peggy said, reaching for her wrap-round apron. 'But they'd better be sober enough to eat their dinner. It would be terrible to waste all that pigeon when it's such a treat to have some meat other than rabbit for the pot.'

'Ron won't have an appetite for anything much when he hears what Bertie and I saw this afternoon,' said Cordelia with a glint in her eyes.

Peggy regarded her with surprise. 'I didn't realise you'd been out with Bertie.'

'He popped in just after you'd left and took me for a glass of sherry at the Officers' Club.' Cordelia sat down, folded her arms and looked at Peggy over her half-moon glasses. 'It's quite surprising who you can bump into at that club,' she said with just a hint of glee.

'Not Ron, surely?' gasped Peggy as Fran hovered in the doorway and the other girls stopped what they were doing to listen.

'Of course not,' Cordelia replied dismissively. 'He might have been an officer during the previous war, but they wouldn't let him past the bottom step looking the way he does now.' She made sure she had everyone's attention. 'It was Rosie.'

'Rosie?' breathed Peggy. 'What on earth was she doing in there?'

Cordelia pursed her lips and tried to look disapproving. 'She was having lunch with that handsome one-armed major.'

'Good for her,' said Fran from the doorway.

'Yes, it's time Rosie had some fun,' said Sarah. 'Ron never takes her anywhere, and Major Radwell's a real gentleman.'

'It might make Ron treat her better if he thinks he's got a rival,' muttered Rita.

'I'm sure it was all perfectly innocent,' said Peggy firmly. 'Rosie's not tied to Ron, and she can have lunch with whomever she pleases.'

'Hmm.' Cordelia pursed her lips. 'They looked very cosy, the pair of them, and Bertie and I agreed that the amount of flirting going on was enough to set tongues wagging for a month of Sundays.'

'Oh, lawks,' sighed Peggy. 'I do hope you're wrong, Cordelia.'

'I might be old, but I still have my wits about me,' she replied waspishly, 'and I know when there are shenanigans afoot, believe me.'

Peggy had met the Major during one of her rare evenings at the Anchor, and could perfectly understand

63

why Rosie might have had her head turned. He was the very opposite of Ron, with his lovely neat appearance and gentlemanly manners. 'Rosie has always enjoyed a bit of flirting,' she said, 'and I don't think any of us should take this too seriously.' She looked at Cordelia. 'What was her reaction when she saw you and Bertie Double-Barrelled?'

'She didn't see us at all. Bertie and I were in the club room where there's a large mirror that reflects the diners through the wide archway. They left soon after we arrived, and were far too interested in each other to notice anyone else.'

'Today has been a bit of a mess for Ron and Rosie, hasn't it?' said Sarah, gathering up the freshly ironed laundry. 'I hope they get ahead of the Cliffehaven gossipers and kiss and make up before the evening is out.'

'Well said – and with that in mind I think it's best if we keep this to ourselves tonight,' Peggy decreed. 'None of it is really any of our business, and it's up to Rosie and Ron to sort it out. Besides, this evening is going to be tricky enough with Pauline likely to get over-emotional and the men raddled with drink.'

'I'll go and warn Ivy,' said Rita, reaching for her ancient fleece-lined leather flying jacket. 'Her shift finished ten minutes ago, so she must be almost home by now.'

4

Totally unware of the brewing storm, Ron tried to focus on where he was going as he made his unsteady progress through the narrow lanes that criss-crossed the area between the High Street and Camden Road. 'Let's stop in for another wee dram with Rosie,' he slurred.

'I don't think that would be wise, Grandad,' cautioned Brendon, who was still quite sober compared to the others. 'We've had enough to drink and Aunt Peggy will have supper on the table by now.'

Ron came to a halt and swayed on his feet as he regarded his grandson. 'To be sure Peggy won't mind if we're a bit late. But I've not seen my Rosie all day, and she'll think I don't love her.'

Frank grabbed his father's arm to stop him falling backwards into a hedge. 'She'll not be thanking you for turning up in this state, Da,' he said, struggling to keep his own balance as his father threatened to pull him over. 'Besides, she might not be in the mood to see you if she's heard what happened in the Crown.'

Ron contemplated this solemnly and then nodded. 'Aye, you could be right,' he said and hiccupped.

He peered blearily through the drizzling rain. 'Where's Harvey?'

'He got bored and went home,' said Brendon, 'and it's time we followed him.' He grasped their arms and gradually managed to keep them on a fairly straight course down the pavement.

Brendon was smiling as he steered them along, glad he was sober enough to witness his father and grandfather in such a drunken state. He could remember his eighteenth birthday when these two – accompanied by his Uncle Jim – had taken him into the Anchor for his first legal pint. Two tankards of bitter had got him very drunk and he'd been half-carried back to Beach View where he'd been violently sick in the back garden before passing out on Peggy's scullery floor. He'd woken the following morning with a blinding hangover only to discover he was sharing a bed with his grandfather's old dog Billy, the pup, Harvey, and a half-chewed beef bone. Now it was his turn to get them home in one piece.

They reached Camden Road and before Brendon could stop him, Ron had broken away from his clutches and was staggering across the road to the Anchor. The door was locked, and there was no sign of anyone being home despite the fact it was almost opening time.

Ron rattled the wrought-iron handle and began to bang on the door.

'Grandad, don't,' hissed Brendon, urgently trying to pull him away.

Ron shrugged him off and staggered back from the door to look up to Rosie's upstairs rooms. He swept off his cap, one hand held over his heart as he missed his footing and ended up standing in the gutter. 'Rosie,' he bellowed. 'Rosie, me darlin' – 'tis your Ron come to serenade you.'

'Grandad, shut up,' Brendon hissed as the sound echoed down the deserted street and his father clung to a nearby lamp post in fits of laughter. Brendon tugged Ron's arm, but it was as if he was glued to the ground.

'Rosie, oh Rosie,' sang Ron, off key. 'Lovely sweet Rosie mine.'

'Oh, Lord,' groaned Brendon. He was frantic to shut him up and drag him away, but even so he could feel laughter bubbling up as Ron continued his cater-wauling. 'Grandad, please stop making that awful racket,' he spluttered. 'You'll get us all arrested.'

'I'll not be leaving until I see my lovely Rosie,' Ron replied, stripping off his coat to leave it pud-dled on the pavement as he promptly began to murder 'The Rose of Tralee'.

'For the love of God, will you stop, Da,' groaned Frank as he slid down the lamp post and ended up sprawled on the pavement, helpless with laughter. 'To be sure me sides are aching, so they are.'

'Come on, Grandad,' pleaded Brendon. 'She's not here and we have to get home.'

Ron threw off his hand. 'Of course she's here,' he muttered. 'She's always here.' He tipped back his head. 'You're waiting for me, aren't you, Rosie – my sweet, darlin' girl? Waiting for your Ron.'

The window above was thrown open and Rosie glared down at them.

Ron tripped over his coat, which sent him staggering into the road before he regained the pavement and weaved back and forth as he tried to look up and keep his balance at the same time. 'Rosie, my love. Oh, my sweet Rosie, let me come in so I can kiss you.'

'I might have known it was you,' Rosie snapped. 'Go home, Ron, and sober up.'

'Ach, Rosie, me darlin', slurred Ron, swaying alarmingly, his cap clasped to his heart. ''Tis beautiful you are in the moonlight. Let me come and kiss the very air from you.'

Rosie disappeared from the window, returning almost immediately with what Brendon instantly recognised as a swill bucket. He hurriedly stepped back into the road as, with deliberate aim, Rosie emptied the contents over Ron's head before slamming the window shut and drawing the curtains.

Ron stared down in confusion as the sludge of vegetable peelings and rotting leftovers slowly dripped from his head, down his face and clothes. 'What did she do that for?' he gasped in bewilderment.

'She obviously didn't appreciate your singing, Da,' said Frank, still helpless with laughter as he sat on the pavement and hugged the lamp post. 'You want to be grateful it was only her swill bucket and not her chamber pot.'

Ron eyed them both aghast. 'But she loves me,' he hiccupped.

'I don't think she does right this minute,' said Brendon, firmly taking his arm and dragging him away before reaching down to pick up the discarded coat and haul his father to his feet. 'Come on, Da, you can't stay there all night.'

Brendon was now almost sober, thankful that Rosie's bucket of pig-swill hadn't splashed his uniform, and the police hadn't been called. He had a bit of a job keeping the other two on their feet, but they finally reached the alleyway and headed for the back gate.

'Whew,' breathed Brandon. 'You stink, Grandad,' he said, eyeing the mess still clinging to him. 'I'd better try and clean you up before Aunt Peg sees you.'

'Ach, she'll not be minding,' said Ron, once again struggling from Brendon's grip, grabbing his coat and weaving his way to the back door.

Brendon let him go to his doom, but while his attention had been on Ron, his father had wandered off, crashed into the side of the Anderson shelter and toppled like a felled oak, head first into the compost heap.

'Bloody hell,' Brendon sighed. 'That's all I need.'

Frank was a big man – tall, wide and a dead weight. Brendon struggled to get him out of the mound of rotting vegetation, but it was hopeless. He'd have to get a wheelbarrow.

'What on earth is going on out there?' asked Peggy from the kitchen window.

'Nothing to worry about, Aunt Peg. We'll be up in a minute,' he replied, wheeling the barrow over to his comatose father who was in danger of being suffocated by Ron's compost.

He heard her say something to the others in the kitchen, vaguely wondered where Ron had got to, and battled to get the majority of his father's bulk into the wheelbarrow. Sweating, fed up, and now feeling utterly sober, he steered the unwieldy barrow back to the path and then came to an abrupt halt when he saw the reception committee on the doorstep.

Peggy and Pauline were grim-faced as they stood, arms tightly folded, poised for battle outside the back door. Cordelia and the four girls were equally unamused as they crowded behind them – carefully avoiding stepping on Ron, who seemed to have passed out on the basement floor beside a fretful Harvey.

'I can explain,' Brendon blustered.

'I'm sure you can,' snapped Pauline. 'But we don't want to hear your excuses. How *dare* you and your father disgrace me like this? You've missed your own farewell dinner that your Aunty Peg slaved over all day.'

Brendon slowly approached with the heavily laden wheelbarrow, his father's long limbs dangling over the sides as he snored thunderously. Perhaps it was time to use a bit of Reilly charm? It usually worked.

'Ach, it was just a few drinks on my last night, Mum. Da and Grandad only wanted to give me a good send-off.'

'I'll give you send-off,' growled Peggy. 'Look at the state of those two. Both stinking to high heaven and out for the count.' She eyed Frank, who was covered from head to foot in compost, and then back to Ron, who was equally filthy. 'You're lucky I'm not built like Gloria Stevens,' she fumed, 'or I'd chuck all three of you out and make you sleep in the Anderson shelter.'

'I'm truly sorry, Aunt Peg,' he said, hanging his head. 'None of us meant for any of it to happen, but Grandad's ferrets got loose in the Crown and then Rosie chucked a bucket of swill over him for trying to serenade her.'

'No wonder she chucked that lot over him. He can't sing – and after what he's done today, it was lucky she didn't throw something much heavier than a bit of swill.'

Brendon heard the stifled giggles and looked up hopefully to find that the girls behind his mother and aunt were trying very hard to keep straight faces.

Peggy regarded Frank, making a sterling effort to stay cross. 'It's not the first time he's ended up in the compost, and I doubt it'll be the last. You'd better bring him in and dump them both on Ron's bed.'

'But they're filthy,' protested Brendon.

'It's them that will have to put up with it,' she said, 'but on the other hand, it'll be me that has to wash the bedding. Better to leave them both on the floor.'

Brendon struggled to get the barrow over the back step, and with the help of the girls managed to get his father out of the barrow and onto the hard, cold scullery floor. As Peggy and Pauline went to fetch pillows and blankets, he eyed the two men and couldn't help but chuckle. It had certainly been a send-off to end all send-offs, and the memory of tonight would live with him for a long time.

And then he remembered that his grandad still had his ferrets tucked away in his coat. Gingerly searching the many pockets he found nothing but two dead and rather squashed rabbits. At some point during the crazy day Flora and Dora had escaped. And now they could be anywhere.

Peggy saw the funny side of it all and was glad to see that Pauline did too – eventually. Once Ron and Frank had been made reasonably comfortable on that hard concrete floor, Peggy served Brendon his portion of supper which she'd been keeping warm in the oven.

He regaled them with all that had happened during that eventful day, which made everyone laugh, and although Pauline was threatening to lose her sense of humour at the shame of it all, Peggy was delighted that he'd had such a rousing send-off. She watched him eat ravenously and gave him half of Frank and Ron's share of the stew. They wouldn't wake until morning, and it served them right to have to go without.

Once Brendon had eaten his fill, he spent a short while talking to his mother and aunt about Betty, and his hopes for their future, and then, because he had a very early train to catch the following morning, he pushed back from the table and went to kiss his mother goodnight.

Pauline had become tearful as the evening progressed, and as Brendon kissed her, she clung fiercely to him until he had to gently but firmly disentangle himself. 'I'll see you in the morning, Mum,' he said, before carrying his kitbag up to the single room that had once been Cissy's.

Pauline sobbed into Peggy's shoulder as his footsteps faded on the stairs, her fear for her son mingled with anger at Frank for denying her the chance to spend Brendon's last night at home in Tamarisk Bay. Peggy comforted her, and as Frank was still out for the count in the basement, she didn't like the thought of Pauline crying herself to sleep in the big spare room at the top of the house, so had reluctantly offered to share her bed for the night.

Peggy lay in the profound darkness long after the house had settled, weary to the bone but unable to sleep. It felt a bit strange to have Pauline beside her, who was a restless sleeper, forever turning, shifting, mumbling and stealing the blankets – so very different to Jim, who hardly stirred all night. Peggy closed her eyes, but her whirling thoughts wouldn't let her relax.

It was clear that Pauline had yet to read her post, for she'd made no mention during supper of her sister, Carol, or Dolly's revelation about Felix being the girl's father, and their future plans. No doubt there would be ructions, and coming on top of Brendon's leaving, Pauline would find it very hard to cope with it all.

Brendon would be leaving within hours for God knew where – Flora and Dora were probably enjoying their freedom somewhere in the hills, and although Ron would be devastated to lose them, it was entirely his fault they'd escaped. As for Rosie, she'd obviously heard about him being in the Crown, and his trying to serenade her had clearly been the last straw.

Peggy didn't blame her one bit for tipping all that muck over him, but what was Rosie thinking by going for lunch with the Major when she must have known Ron would hear about it? The pair of them were behaving like naughty children, and deserved a good ticking-off. But then perhaps Rosie really had had enough of him, and had set her sights on someone who would no doubt prove more reliable and thoughtful. If that was the case, poor Ron would be bereft, and Peggy dreaded the fall-out. Her longstanding friendship with Rosie didn't give her the right to interfere, but if things did go pear-shaped, Peggy knew she'd have to try and smooth the rift between them before it all went too far.

As her eyelids fluttered and her limbs became heavy with sleep, Peggy's thoughts turned as always to her Jim. He would have loved to have taken part in today's boisterous fun, and would probably have ended up in the compost heap alongside his brother, as had so often happened in the past. *Darling Jim,* she thought. *I so wish you were here.*

5

Burma

Jim's thoughts were far from Cliffehaven as he marched with Big Bert and Ernie in the long column of men and hundreds of heavily laden mules and horses through the teak tree plantation and away from the latest skirmish. The Japanese patrol had been lurking in ambush and now lay dead some miles behind them. Their own casualties had been light, but it had been a salutary lesson to stay alert for further attacks.

It was noon, and the air shimmered in the breathless heat, the sweat darkening his shirt and making it cling wetly to his torso as the dead leaves crunched beneath the hundreds of boots and the shrill throb of thousands of cicadas rang in his head like a ceaseless chainsaw. Jim was tired and unbearably hot beneath the weight of his backpack, his mouth so dry it hurt to swallow after not having had a drink for over twenty-four hours. It had become a matter of pride as well as endurance for all of them to still have a full water bottle at the end of the day – but it was also a necessary evil, for fresh water was in extremely short supply, and not even the pack animals had been watered.

The man mountain that was Big Bert marched alongside him, his expression grim, his eyes alert as always for an enemy ambush, but disinclined to waste his energy by talking. Ernie looked small beside him in the midday glare, his hand resting lightly over the stock of his carbine, his eyes also swivelling left and right into the shadeless forest, all too aware that the column was vulnerable. His shirt was also black with sweat, his reddened face streaming with it beneath the broad-brimmed hat.

'I bet we get bloody digging duty again,' he grumbled. 'My belly's stuck to my spine I'm so hungry, and my mouth feels like glue.'

'You and me both,' rasped Jim, his own gaze darting through the endless rows of teak trees. 'We can only hope there's water in the next river – but I do wish those cicadas would shut up. They're giving me a headache.'

They marched on in silence with no sign of enemy, animal or bird, and soon the high-pitched throb of the cicadas faded as they reached their night's camp only to find that the river was dry, its stony bed as rough and parched as their throats.

It was still light, the heat as ferocious as ever as they came to a halt and made camp – but there was to be no rest, for Ernie's prediction had proved right, and their battalion of sappers was immediately ordered to dig defence positions and slit trenches.

Jim worked with a will, the promise of food and sleep keeping him going. Sentries were posted, mortars put into position, and the machine guns sited so they were directed at their northern flank, and to fully cover the east and west perimeters of the open jungle – west where the enemy had been reported, and east where the column had left a wide belt of crushed teak leaves that could easily be followed by an enemy patrol.

It was finally time to eat, but there would be no fires tonight to heat water and food, for it was imperative they remain undiscovered. The meagre meal was soon over, the water bottles remaining untouched as Jim, Bert and Ernie joined the other men in stand-to, equipped and prepared for any action as darkness fell with its usual swiftness.

Jim heaved a sigh of relief as the order to stand down came half an hour after darkness had fallen. The sentries remained at their posts and the signal and cipher men would be kept at work sending and receiving messages for at least another two hours, so it was with infinite thankfulness that his day was finally over that Jim shed his backpack and prepared for the night.

Taking off his boots, he stuffed the socks inside, leaving the laces drawn wide for quick and easy access, and placed his hat on top, the chinstrap tucked beneath them so it didn't blow away. He loosened his belt and top fly button, checked his backpack was securely fastened and used it as a pillow. With his fully loaded carbine between his thighs, muzzle down, breach empty, safety on, he closed his eyes and was asleep in an instant.

The next day's march took them to the edge of the forest where miles of fields, reeds, sandbanks and clumps of bamboo greeted them. A burst of gunfire from the east alerted them to the fact that the fighting patrol sent out to Katha was in action, and every man gripped his weapon in case the Japanese had sent other patrols towards their position.

'Bloody hell,' breathed Jim as they eventually reached the rolling sand dunes that bordered the vast Chindwin River which shone like molten silver in the brilliant sunshine. 'We'll be damned lucky to get the mules across that beast.'

'It's that over there you should be worried about,' said Ernie, pointing to the far bank of the swiftly flowing river. 'We're going to have to tackle it with full kit as well as mules and heavy equipment before long.'

Jim stared at the high, jagged cliff of rock, the headland of which was covered in jungle growth that, from this distance, looked impenetrable.

He blew out his cheeks in a long sigh as he took off his hat and wiped away the sweat from his face. 'At least we can have a drink now,' he said, reaching for his water bottle, diluting a salt tablet in it and downing every drop in three great gulps.

As the lines of mules and packhorses were relieved of their heavy loads and taken to the water for a well-deserved drink, the men rested, snatched a hurried meal, filled their bottles and also drank to their heart's content. But their respite was short, for the officers returned from inspecting the sand bar which was the proposed landing site for the gliders that would bring in their urgently needed supplies and take out their wounded. Having found the sand to be flat and hard enough, and the surrounding area clear of the enemy, they began to issue orders.

Jim, Ernie and Big Bert were sent to dig defence trenches while signallers unloaded their sets, driftwood was collected for signal fires, and men were sent out to reconnoitre their surroundings.

Jim kept an eye on the transport officers as he supervised the digging and got stuck in himself. They'd gone to the water's edge to try and work out the best way to get two hundred and forty mules to swim a mile-wide river from a high and unstable sandbank to a narrow beach and soaring eighty-foot cliff.

'I certainly don't envy them that task,' he muttered to Big Bert. 'Mules are awkward bastards at the best of times.'

'You can bet your life it'll be us poor buggers having to get them over there,' growled Big Bert. 'When in doubt, send for the bloody sappers.'

They were all sweating profusely as the humidity soared and the black monsoon clouds began to gather overhead. The atmosphere was heavy with electric menace as lightning flickered back and forth and gunfire continued to the north. The hairs on Jim's arms and neck prickled and he could feel the air crackling around him as he regarded the tinder-dry fields and tall reeds. One lightning strike and the whole lot would go up and spread faster than a steam train – but at least they had the advantage of water at their backs should they be faced with such an inferno.

The trench digging was finally completed at dusk and having bathed in the shallows of the river, eaten that day's K-rations and smoked a cigarette, Jim was feeling very much better, so he dug out his notebook from his backpack and scrawled a hasty few words to Peggy.

There wasn't very much he could tell her, for censorship wouldn't allow any real detail of where he was and what he was doing, which in a way was a blessing. Peggy didn't need to know what he was going through, for it would only make her fret even more. So he didn't tell her that General Wingate had been killed in a plane crash some weeks before, and that the new commander, Lentaigne, had changed their orders. Neither did he mention that the battle of Imphal was raging and Jim's brigade were on their way to operate against the Japs' lines of communication – which meant they would be heading many miles north-west once they'd crossed the river.

So he wrote that he was fit and well, but that the heat was getting worse, which was a sure sign that the monsoon would break soon. Once that happened, they could all breathe again, as it would force the opposition who didn't have the same amount of back-up to retreat.

He told her he was eating properly and thankful for the knitted socks she'd sent as he seemed to be going through them at a rate of knots. He apologised for the brevity of his recent letters, but his army duties didn't allow much time for anything but to march, eat and sleep. He finished with a kiss and a prayer that the war would soon be over and they could be together again.

Reading it through, Jim saw how his sweat had stained the paper, but it was legible enough in the circumstances, so he folded the slip of paper into the army issue envelope, addressed it and handed it to the officer in charge of communications. His letter would be checked by the censor and then flown out with all the others on the next supply plane – which with luck would be tonight.

Jim lit another cigarette and gazed out over the wide, rushing river which was now a pale gleam of silver in the twilight. It bugged him to think that somewhere back in India there could be a huge sack of mail waiting to be delivered to the men in the jungles of Burma, and in it were likely to be letters from home. It was such a joy to hear from everyone and to receive their photographs and small gifts of socks, underwear and copies of the local newspaper – but there again, it was a two-edged sword, for they merely underlined the fact that he'd been away too long, the distance between them almost immeasurable.

His little Daisy and the boys were growing up without him, as were his two granddaughters – Peggy was revelling in her new-found independence at Solly Goldman's factory, and his two daughters, Anne and Cissy, were young women treading their own paths while they waited for their men to be freed from the POW camp in Germany.

Everyone was doing their bit to hasten this war to victory, and even Pauline had rolled up her sleeves to help out at the WVS while Frank and Brendon had got involved in something down in the west of England – and with the news being relayed by radio to the troops in the Far East, it seemed the tide was at last turning in the Allies' favour.

Jim crushed the last of his cigarette under the heel of his boot and then stretched luxuriously to ease the stiffness in his muscled back and legs. Life had changed radically for all of them – except his father, Ron, who remained as strong and purposeful as always – but when Jim thought of the easy, careless life he'd lived before this war, it was as if it had belonged to someone else, a stranger far removed from the hardened fighting man he'd become.

He stared out at the thundering river, the memories of past battles, the sights and sounds of gunfire and the screams of wounded men flashing in his head like a reel of film. He'd seen enough blood, gore and horror in the dying days of the First War, but the trenches had been nothing like this cat-and-mouse game they were involved in now. Jungle warfare meant being on alert twenty-four hours a day, the tension rising at every sound coming from the steaming jungle, knowing that at any minute they could be involved in a fight to the death against men who seemed to have no concept of fear or compassion.

Jim had seen things that would live with him for the rest of his life, but for now they had to be firmly pushed to the deepest recesses of his mind. Survival was all – he'd deal with the aftermath once the war was over.

His dark thoughts were broken by the familiar drone of Air Commando C-47s advancing. It was now fully dark, but against the star-filled sky he could see that each plane was towing a single glider which would be released over the line of signal fires that had now been lit along the perimeters of the sandbar runway. It was to be a swift turn-around in case the Japanese had spotted the C-47s and came in pursuit, so everyone was on alert.

As Jim was part of the unloading party, he kept his men on stand-by as one by one the gliders whooshed overhead. But they were coming in too high and too fast, so overshot the runway and ploughed into the soft sand, narrowly missing the few trees that hadn't been cleared.

Muttered curses went through the ranks, for now it meant that the assault motorboats they were delivering would have to be dragged over half a mile to the designated river crossing place.

Jim and the others ran with difficulty through the shifting sand and hot night to fetch them. It was a long, painfully slow process as men and mules dragged and hauled the heavy boats through the sand, along with outboard motors, ropes, life jackets, petrol and oil drums, back to the crossing. But the news that the fighting patrols in Inywa and Ma-ugon had driven off the Japanese was cheering and boosted their efforts, so their task was completed well within the allotted time frame.

Returning to the gliders and loading one with mail sacks and the wounded, the men manhandled the gliders into position in readiness for their pick-up. It was a practised and highly skilled manoeuvre which had been used throughout the Burma campaign, but one that only a few of the men had seen, so once all three gliders were in position, they avidly lined the sandbanks to watch how it was done.

Each glider carried two long poles, both armed at the ends with a blue light powered by its own battery, with a third shining above the pilot's cockpit. As the pilot gave his orders the poles were stuck in the sand about two hundred feet in front of the glider and fifty feet apart. One end of a double-length nylon tow rope was fastened firmly to the hook in the glider's nose, and then fixed to the first pole, stretched to the second and then tied very firmly to the nose hook.

The first glider pilot waited, all three lights glowing, brakes off and controls set for take-off. Everyone watched with bated breath as the approaching C-47 lowered a long steel boom from beneath its tail which had a self-operating catch.

The C-47 came in low with its engines throttled back, flaps down, propellers at full pitch. The trailing hook grabbed the taut rope between the poles and snatched it up. The C-47 took the strain, its engines screaming, and as its pilot rammed his throttles fully forward and lifted its nose, the glider – jerked from nought to eighty miles an hour in a matter of seconds – was catapulted into the air, and they both swept away into the darkness as the second C-47 came in for the next glider.

As the last plane disappeared into the night, Jim let out the breath he'd been holding. 'Bloody hell,' he gasped in awe. 'Now that's really something to write home about.'

6

Ron opened a bleary eye and wondered where the hell he was. He felt as cold and stiff as a corpse, his mouth tasted foul, and this was definitely not his bedroom. He blinked to clear his muzzy sight and was immediately assaulted by Harvey climbing all over him and eagerly licking his face.

'Gerroff, ye heathen beast,' he grumbled. 'To be sure your breath is worse than mine.'

He gently pushed the over-eager lurcher away and sat up, only to realise that he must have passed out on the scullery floor, and the snoring leviathan beside him was his son Frank – of Brendon there was no sign. He concluded that his grandson had been sober enough to be allowed to spend the night in a proper bed. Someone had brought blankets and pillows, but he and Frank were both fully clothed, still with their boots on – which meant they must have been comatose, and were now in deep trouble with their women.

Ron wrinkled his nose, recognising the smell of his compost heap emanating from Frank, and memory slowly returned in all its awful clarity. He glanced down at his chest, saw the remains of vegetable sludge glued to his sweater and trousers and grunted in disgust. Rosie had certainly made her feelings plain about his behaviour, and although he hadn't thought he'd been that bad at serenading her, he'd clearly been deluded in thinking she'd appreciate it.

He struggled to his feet and stood there unsteadily for a moment to get his bearings and will his reluctant muscles to work again. He was getting too old to be sleeping on a concrete floor, and should have known better than to drink so much, even though the rare luxury of good whiskey had been impossible to resist.

'Never again,' he muttered – a promise he'd made to himself too many times before, and subsequently broken.

With trembling fingers he drew back his sleeve and looked at his watch. It was five in the morning and much too early to go visiting Rosie to apologise about his attempts to serenade her – besides, he had the ferrets to sort out before he could wash and find clean clothes, and then there was the small matter of appeasing Peggy and Pauline, and of course escorting Brendon to the railway station. It was going to be a busy day.

He dipped his hand into the deepest pocket of his coat and realised with horror that his ferrets were no longer there. He searched each pocket in turn with growing alarm, for he was unable to remember whether he'd put them in their cage before passing out. He stumbled over Frank and staggered into his bedroom – only to come to an abrupt halt. The ferret cage was empty.

He searched his room, his panic rising by the second, but there was no sign of them. Returning to the scullery, he noted that the door to the kitchen had been firmly closed; there had been no kerfuffle to stir him in the night, so it was unlikely they'd got into the rooms upstairs. With deepening dread he dug Frank in the ribs.

'Wake up, Frank. Wake up and tell me what I did with Flora and Dora.'

Frank mumbled something unintelligible and pulled the blanket over his head.

Ron ripped it back and gave him a good shake. 'Frank. Wake up. This is important. I've lost me ferrets.'

Unlike his father, Frank really suffered the morning after a long drinking session, and he painfully sat up, holding his head. 'What happened? Why am I on the floor in your scullery?'

'I don't remember,' Ron said impatiently, 'but by the smell of you, you landed in my compost at some point – just like your brother used to.' Ron squatted beside him. 'Frank, I need you to concentrate,' he said urgently. 'Flora and Dora have disappeared. Do you know where they might be?'

Frank shook his head, which made him wince. 'I don't remember anything after you tried to serenade Rosie,' he groaned. 'To be sure, Da, it was the most fearful racket, so it was.'

Ron realised he'd get no sense out of his son, so he went outside into the garden in the faint hope that his precious ferrets had hidden away in the shed, the outside lav, or the Anderson shelter. The cold, damp air cleared the vestiges of his hangover as he and a fretful Harvey searched every nook and cranny. But they were nowhere to be seen, so with Harvey trotting alongside him, he tramped up the alleyway towards the hills, softly calling for them in the hope they'd hear him and come running as they usually did when out hunting.

A damp blanket of fog was rolling in from the sea, making it hard to see anything, and Ron stood at the top of the track, his spirits plummeting as hope faded. They'd been fine beasts and excellent rabbit catchers, and as he'd raised them from small pups, he'd grown very fond of them. The thought he would never see them again made him immeasurably sad, and it was a long while before he had the heart to turn back for home.

'Come on, Harvey,' he said on a sigh. 'Better get back and clean up before Peggy and Pauline wake to give us an earful. I've a nasty feeling this is only the start of what could turn out to be a very bad day.'

He returned to Beach View to find Frank had stripped down to his underpants and was washing himself in the scullery sink. 'I didn't think it'd be wise to wake the household by using the bathroom upstairs,' he explained, drying himself off with several of Peggy's clean tea towels. 'We're probably in enough trouble with Peg and Pauline as it is.'

'Aye, to be sure 'tis our own fault – so we must take whatever they dish out with suitable humility and dignity.' He grimaced as he shed his spattered sweater. 'I've searched everywhere, but Flora and Dora have gone,' he said. 'I can only hope they found their way into the hills so they can run free and wild. But I still can't work out how they escaped from my pocket. I didn't take them out after we left the Crown – I'm positive of it.'

Frank laid a meaty hand on his father's shoulder in sympathy. 'I'm sorry to hear they've decamped, Da, but there's not much we can do about it, and there are rather more important things to worry about today.'

He eyed the pile of his dirty clothes on the floor. 'Would you have anything half-decent I can borrow for the day? I can't be seeing my boy off to war in that lot.'

Ron nodded. 'You're welcome to anything but me best suit and shirt,' he said gruffly, still mourning his lost ferrets. 'I've some humble pie to eat today, and I can't persuade Rosie to forgive me unless I'm dressed for the occasion.'

Frank followed him into the basement bedroom and let out a gasp when he saw the mess it was in. 'How can you live like this, Da? It looks as if a bomb's hit it.'

'It might look untidy to you,' he replied, picking his way over discarded boots and clothing which were tangled up with old newspapers, dog blankets and hunting equipment. 'But I know where everything is.'

He edged past the open drawers which spilled underwear, old trousers and sweaters, and opened the wardrobe door. 'It looks like someone's ironed me some shirts,' he said, rifling through the crammed hangers, 'and there's me second-best trousers.'

Frank eyed the trousers, which looked clean and pressed, and pulled them on. The turn-ups were a bit short and showed rather too much sock, but at least he could do them up at the waist. Slipping on the shirt he found it strained over his chest, so left the top three buttons undone, but the sleeves didn't reach his wrists. He rolled them neatly up to his elbows and then went hunting through the jumble of clothes in the wardrobe. He found a tweed jacket that was clean but had seen better days, and soon discovered it was at least two sizes too small. 'To be sure, I feel daft in this get-up,' he grumbled, tossing the jacket aside and picking out a thick sweater which appeared to have fewer holes in it than the rest.

'You'd look even dafter covered in my muck heap,' said Ron, reaching for his best dark blue suit and fresh white shirt. 'Go upstairs and put the kettle on while I wash and change. Wee Fran's on earlies today and I suspect Peggy will be up and about soon.'

Once Frank had left the bedroom, Ron sank onto the unmade bed and let his shoulders slump as Harvey rested his muzzle on his knee, his hazel eyes limpid with sympathy. Ron had loved those ferrets – and now, through his own carelessness, he had lost them. He eyed the empty cage and gave a deep sigh. He could only pray that Flora and Dora were the only things he lost today.

Deciding he had to carry on regardless, he quickly washed in the scullery sink, cleaned his teeth, and then had a shave before getting dressed. Eyeing his reflection in the fly-spotted mirror above the chest of drawers, he grimaced. His eyes were bloodshot and even after a shave he looked old, wan and tired – hardly the most dashing of suitors. Perhaps he was a fool to think that someone as glamorous as Rosie could love him enough to keep on forgiving him – but he had to remain hopeful and really put an effort into changing his ways so he became the man she deserved.

Rosie had been woken by Monty whining to be let out into the back garden. She blearily eyed the bed-side clock, and was horrified to discover it was barely six in the morning. Stumbling out of bed, she pulled on her warm dressing gown and padded down the stairs in her slippers to let him out of the back door.

There was a thick mist rolling in, bringing a damp chill to the air which made the scrap of lawn glisten in the pearly light of dawn. She shivered as she stood on the doorstep and waited for Monty to cock his leg and rummage through the undergrowth of the walled garden on the scent of something that had dared to come into his territory. It was probably next door's ginger tom, which had a habit of teasing Monty by parading along the high wall just out of his reach, and using the garden as a lavatory.

She watched the fog swirling through the remaining blossom on the nearby trees. The weather didn't look promising, even though it was almost June, and if it went on like this, there would never be an invasion.

'Come on, Monty. It's too early and cold to be messing about,' she said impatiently as he continued to dodge back and forth, nose to the ground.

Monty gave the outside lav one last inspection and then galloped towards her, his long, skinny legs darkened by the wet grass, tongue lolling and ears flapping, eager now for the ritual of a good rub-down and breakfast.

Rosie grabbed a towel from behind the bar and roughly dried him before going back upstairs. She eyed the empty swill bucket in the corner of her kitchen and pursed her lips. Snowy White's unregistered piglet had lost out on a meal, but there had been a certain satisfaction in tipping it over Ron last night, and she hoped he'd learnt never to serenade her again while falling-down drunk – especially after being seen in Gloria Stevens's pub.

Having put some food down for Monty, who began to gobble it as if he was half-starved, Rosie realised she wouldn't be able to go back to sleep, so she made a cup of tea and stood by the window in her sitting room, to stare down at a deserted Camden Road. The shops were shuttered and locked, the windows of the flats above them blank-eyed with blackout curtains as the sea fret thickened and settled over the roofs in a smothering grey blanket.

The scene was desolate and reflected her mood, for after yesterday she'd come to realise that her relationship with Ron had reached a crossroads – and now she had the real dilemma of deciding what to do about it.

She could accept that he'd drunk too much yesterday – after all, there had been precious few occasions when he could be with his boys, and with Brendon leaving, it was understandable the drinking session had made him emotional. But turning up here causing a ruckus and declaring his undying love for her when he'd gone against her express wishes and chosen to drink in that tart Gloria's place …

Rosie gave a deep sigh. She would usually have seen the funny side of it and sent him off with a flea in his ear, fully prepared to forgive him once he'd sobered up and apologised. But not this time – not when Gloria was involved. Things couldn't go on as they were, for as much as she loved him, Ron had taken her forgiveness for granted once too often.

Her outing to the Officers' Club with Henry had been a revelation, for she'd forgotten how good it felt to be treated as a lady. Henry had been an amusing, attentive lunch companion, asking her opinion on the menu and wine and never once overstepping the mark – so unlike Ron, who usually got into a conversation with an old pal and almost forgot she was there until he fancied a bit of slap and tickle when they got home.

The club itself had proven to be everything she'd expected, for the food had been excellent, the dining room elegantly decorated in muted shades of blue and white, the table laid with crisp linen, heavy silverware and beautiful cut glass. It had reminded her forcibly of the small private hotel her parents had owned during her formative years, for the atmosphere was calm and respectable, the clientele smartly dressed and sophisticated

The Anchor was far removed from what she'd been used to, but it had provided her with an escape from the memories of how devastating her husband James's rapid mental decline had been when he'd returned so damaged from his experiences of the war back in 1918 – and although her customers came from all walks of life, she kept a respectable establishment, had made good friends and come to feel at home and settled here.

Rosie cradled the warm cup in her hands and gazed out through the mist. She liked and admired Henry and was glad of this new friendship, which had brought a different dimension to her life. But the gossips were probably already having a field day, for she'd known they'd been spotted by Cordelia and Bertie as well as several other diners who were regulars at her pub. She'd said nothing to Henry, knowing it would unsettle him, deciding instead to let the gossips make what they wanted out of their innocent luncheon, and concentrate on Henry who had a raft of amusing stories to tell about his childhood in India.

Yet she knew Ron would get to hear about it sooner or later and, conveniently forgetting his own misdemeanours, would turn up here full of righteous indignation before he tried to dazzle her with his Irish charm and coax her back into the same old routine.

Rosie gritted her teeth, vowing silently that she'd stand firm and demand a great many changes before she even considered succumbing again – and yet she knew that although Ron would do his best, he'd soon slip back into his old ways. She wasn't at all sure if she had the will to go through all that rigmarole again.

She and Ron had been courting for years, and although he'd proven to be unreliable at times, and hugely irritating and wayward, she'd been drawn to him so strongly she'd been able to overlook his failings and just love him – but she was tiring of the merry-go-round ride that they seemed fated never to escape. Perhaps if they'd been able to get married like other couples, they could have found contentment, and he might not have been so determined to walk his own path and thereby cause trouble between them. But, with her husband confined to an asylum and no legal way of divorcing him, they'd been caught in a sort of limbo, where they couldn't make any plans for the future until he passed away – which wasn't the best start to wedded bliss.

Rosie fully accepted that this state of affairs hadn't been helped by her refusal to let Ron sleep with her no matter how tempted she'd been – and she had been tempted, many a time, for Ron was an extremely fit, charismatic man. But her strict Catholic upbringing meant that the old lectures on hell and damnation still ruled her life, and she found it impossible to break her marriage vows.

Rosie felt utterly depressed by it all. She was in her fifties, with nothing to offer any man but companionship, and she was simply fooling herself into thinking it would be enough for someone as lusty as Ron, who certainly wasn't short of female admirers. Perhaps it would be kinder to end it now instead of letting it drag on? At least then Ron could find someone who'd give him what he wanted.

She felt a sharp pang of jealousy at the thought and firmly smothered it, recognising it as selfish and unfair – but the spectre of Gloria Stevens taking her place in his affections made her feel quite ill.

She turned from the window to get ready for the day, her dark thoughts milling, her tension rising at the thought of Ron turning up later, full of apologies in the expectation of her forgiving him. It would hurt them both if they were to part – but surely it was the only answer?

Having dressed in slacks and sweater, she pulled on her one pair of flat shoes and a raincoat. 'Come on, Monty,' she said briskly, clipping the leash to his collar and reaching for her umbrella. 'Ron will be busy with Brendon leaving and I need fresh air and space to think things through before he turns up.'

Peggy had woken at the sound of footsteps overhead and water running through the pipes in the bathroom. Fran was up in good time to get to the hospital, and on hearing the quiet voices on the stairs, she gathered Brendon was also up and about. She gave a brief thought to Ron and Frank, who no doubt had spent a very uncomfortable night on her cellar floor, and then slipped out of bed. Pulling on Jim's old dressing gown, and leaving Daisy and Pauline still asleep, she hurried upstairs to use the bathroom and get dressed for the day.

Daisy was still sleeping when she came back down, so she went into the kitchen to find Pauline bustling about and fussing over Brendon as she shot venomous glares at Frank and Ron, who were unusually subdued as they drank their tea. Peggy made no comment about their attire but had to smother a fit of giggles. Ron had certainly pulled out all the stops to impress Rosie, but Frank really did look ridiculous in his father's clothes.

'Mum, stop fussing and sit down,' said Brendon, gently pressing Pauline into a chair. 'Drink your tea and eat something. My train isn't due for a while, and it would be lovely to spend the time we have sitting quietly together as if it was just another ordinary day.'

'But it's not, is it? How can anything be ordinary with this war on?' Pauline burst into tears and fled upstairs to lock herself in the bathroom.

Brendon sighed and sat down beside his father. 'I do wish she wouldn't do that,' he said sadly. 'It makes me feel awfully guilty.'

'Ach, you've nothing to feel guilty about, son,' rumbled Frank, who was clearly still battling a hangover. 'She's always been emotional.'

Peggy wondered if she should go and see if Pauline was all right, then decided it was probably best not to, because Pauline liked an audience for her misery, and without one, she'd pull herself together more quickly and come back down.

She kept an ear open for Daisy waking and sipped the welcome tea as Fran finished her breakfast of dried egg and toast, washed her dishes and reached for her nursing cape. 'Try to get a decent lunch, Fran,' said Peggy. 'I know how busy you get, and you need something substantial to keep you going.'

Fran fastened the cape around her shoulders and smiled. 'The canteen provides a good hot meal, so there's nothing for you to worry about, Aunt Peg. And don't fret if I'm late home. Robert's managed to get a couple of hours off, and is coming to meet me at the end of my shift to take me out to tea.'

'It's about time you two got engaged,' said Peggy, kissing the girl's cheek.

'Ach, we'll do that when he gets around to asking me,' replied Fran with an impish grin that lit up her green eyes. 'But I'm thinking he has rather more important things to concentrate on at the moment.'

'There's nothing more important than love,' replied the ever-romantic Peggy with a happy sigh.

Fran laughed. 'I don't think his bosses at the MOD would agree with you.' She turned to Brendon. 'Good luck, and just remember we'll all be here waiting for you to come home, so make sure you do – okay?'

'I'll certainly try my best,' he replied.

Fran patted his shoulder and ran out of the house, slamming the scullery door with a crash that made Frank flinch and woke Daisy.

Peggy was about to go and fetch the child when Cordelia came into the kitchen and eyed the two older men over the rims of her half-moon spectacles.

'You certainly look cleaner and more respectable this morning,' she said with a twinkle in her eyes, 'but if you're suffering hangovers, you fully deserve them. I've never seen anything like it, and hope never to again.'

'Ach, Cordelia, have a heart,' groaned Frank. 'There's many a time Da and I have had to help you home from the Anchor.'

Her expression sharpened. 'Are you insinuating that I cannot hold my drink, Frank Reilly?'

'Aye,' rumbled Ron, filling his pipe. 'Four sherries and you're away with the fairies, so I'd not be the one to throw stones in glass houses if I were you.'

Cordelia raised an eyebrow, but let the remark pass as she was distracted by Brendon serving her toast and tea. 'Thank you, dear,' she said, patting him on his freshly shaven cheek. 'How very handsome you look this morning. It quite makes me wish I was eighteen again,' she added on a sigh. 'I always did admire a man in a uniform.'

Brendon grinned and kissed her soft cheek. 'Would you be flirting with me, Cordelia?' he teased.

'I very much think I might be,' she admitted with a giggle.

'Will you not be encouraging her,' growled Ron. 'To be sure she's a daft auld woman who should know better.'

'Not as daft as some who can't hold their drink and make a spectacle of themselves in the street by howling at the moon,' fired back Cordelia. She turned back to smile sweetly at Brendon. 'I might be old, but I can still appreciate the sight of a handsome young man – especially when I'm forced to face that ugly scallywag across the table every day.'

Peggy left them to it, for Cordelia and Ron could trade insults all day long, and Daisy was yelling for attention.

An hour later Brendon had said his goodbyes to the other girls, making a special fuss over Cordelia, who'd become quite sombre as she told him how proud she was of him. Now Peggy was walking up the silent and deserted High Street, her heart heavy at the thought of having to say goodbye to her lovely nephew. She'd left Daisy at home with Sarah and Cordelia as the weather had worsened, the sea fret thickening to muffle every sound.

Peggy and Ron shared the umbrella and trailed behind Brendon, who looked wonderfully smart in his dark RNR uniform as he walked arm in arm between his parents. Harvey trotted along, keeping as close to Brendon as he could, as if he knew he was leaving.

She glanced across at Ron, who'd discarded his poaching coat for once and was wearing his old army greatcoat over his suit. 'Rosie will be all right once she sees the funny side of things,' she murmured, seeing his troubled expression. 'You just have to convince her that you'll mend your ways.'

'Aye, I know,' he replied. 'And I do try, Peggy, really I do. But things happen, and to be sure I'm in the soup again without even trying. Now I've lost me ferrets, me grandson is off to fight a war and Rosie will be on the warpath.' He gave a deep sigh. 'To be sure, Peggy, 'tis not a day I'm looking forward to at all.'

Peggy didn't want to meddle any more by mentioning the fact that Rosie had been seen with the Major, for Ron was down in the dumps already, so she just squeezed his arm in sympathy.

Stan was at the station looking rather the worse for wear after his drinking session at the allotment and the ear-bashing he'd had from Ethel on his return. He commiserated with Ron and Frank before grasping Brendon's hand. 'I wish you well, son,' he said fervently.

'Thanks, Uncle Stan,' he replied. 'And when I get back we'll really have something to celebrate, so you'd better get prepared for a proper knees-up.'

Pauline looked po-faced at this, and tried to put on a brave expression as the train appeared around the bend in the track. She flung her arms about Brendon, clinging to him as if she never wanted to let him go, until Frank and Ron squashed her between them as they too embraced their beloved boy and Harvey ran round them with whines of concern.

It was a sad and worrying day, made even gloomier by the fog, but Peggy was determined to smile brightly and give Brendon a warm and positive send-off. She waited to say her own goodbyes, and as the train pulled up to the platform, Brendon disentangled himself, fussed Harvey and then drew her into his arms.

'Take care of Mum for me,' he whispered. 'I love you, Aunt Peg. Thanks for everything, and I'm sorry things got out of hand last night.'

Peggy clasped his face. 'You take care of yourself, and when this is over I want to meet your Betty.' She kissed his cheek, and after a swift hug, he gathered up his kitbag and strode down the platform, Harvey loping after him. Leaving was hard, but long drawn-out farewells were even harder, and it was clear that Brendon had a job to do and was eager to get on with it so he could return home again. Peggy sent up a silent prayer that he would indeed come home, safe and sound.

The four of them stood in a miserable huddle as the troop train hissed and puffed clouds of smoke and steam, and Harvey sat howling on the platform once Brendon had climbed on board and closed the door. Only a handful of passengers alighted, and these were mostly factory workers who hurried away, leaving the servicemen on board who would be going on to the ports, airfields and army camps strung along the length of the coast.

Steam rolled down the platform to mingle with the fog as Harvey continued to howl his anguish at Brendon's leaving. The engine driver blew the whistle and Stan waved his flag. Peggy and the others craned their necks for a last glimpse of Brendon and could make out only a faint figure leaning out of a carriage window and waving as the wheels began to turn.

Pauline broke away from Frank and ran down the platform, calling out to Brendon to stay safe. Frank chased after her and gathered her to him, and they stood in a tight embrace as the train gathered speed and, all too soon, was lost from sight.

'God speed, wee boy,' murmured Ron, tucking Peggy's hand into the crook of his arm. 'To be sure I hate saying goodbyes,' he said mournfully. 'When this war's over and they've all come home, I'll not be wanting them ever to leave again. They come and they go, Peg, and all we can do is watch and wait and do our best to ensure they have a home to come back to.'

Looking towards the forlorn Frank and Pauline, who were still huddled together at the end of the platform, Peggy saw Harvey become animated as a figure emerged through the remnants of the smoke and steam that rolled across the station, and then left the cinder track running alongside the lines and jumped up onto the platform.

She blinked and stared as he approached with a smile and a wave, hardly daring to believe her eyes. 'Good grief,' she breathed. 'It's Rita's dad.'

Big, brawny and looking very workmanlike in his army uniform, Jack Smith strode towards her with Harvey at his heels. 'I fell asleep and only just woke up when the train began to pull out,' he explained. 'It was this fellow's howling that woke me,' he added, giving Harvey a hefty pat.

'Oh, Jack, we're so pleased to see you,' cried Peggy, throwing her arms about him. 'Rita will be thrilled.'

Jack's brown eyes twinkled as he vigorously shook Ron's hand. 'I managed to persuade my CO to let me stop off for a couple of hours and catch the later train to meet up with the rest of my regiment. He's a fair sort of chap, and once I explained the situation with Rita, he agreed immediately.'

Peggy had known Jack all her life; had comforted him when Rita's mother had died, and done all she could to help as he struggled alone to raise his young daughter. To see him now caused a confusion of emotions, for although she was delighted that he and Rita could snatch a precious couple of hours together after being apart for so long, she felt a jolt of dread. It was clear that Jack's time working as a mechanic in the army motor repair shops in the Midlands was over, and that, like Brendon, he would soon be involved in the promised invasion.

She kissed his cheek and gave him a gentle nudge. 'Don't waste precious time hanging about here with us,' she said. 'Rita was heading for the fire station as we came to see Brendon off, so you should find her there.'

Jack didn't budge, his expression anxious. 'How's my girl really doing, Peg? Her letters don't tell me much. Is she coping – after Matthew?'

'Oh, Jack,' Peggy sighed. 'She's doing as well as she can. Matthew was such a lovely, sweet boy, and his death came as a terrible shock to all of us. Seeing you will help no end, so get down there and find her.'

He hitched his kitbag over his shoulder and ran down the hill, his heavy boots echoing in the stillness of the damp and dreary morning.

Turning to Ron, Peggy plastered on a smile. 'What a lovely surprise for Rita,' she said shakily, 'and how thoughtful of his commanding officer to give him permission to stop off. It's good to know there is still kindness in this troubled world.'

Ron stood back and smiled down at her as he handed over the umbrella. 'And now let's hope that kindness is shining down on me today. I'm off to see Rosie. Wish me luck.'

She nodded and watched him hurry away with Harvey, as always, at his side. He'd need a heavy dose of luck – but Rosie always forgave him, and he'd no doubt come bouncing back home later, full of the joys of spring.

'I'm taking Pauline home,' said a drawn and sad-eyed Frank. 'Thanks for putting up with me last night.'

'That's all right,' Peggy replied softly. 'It was quite like old times, and certainly gave us all something to laugh about – which has to be good in the circumstances.'

As they left the station and went their separate ways, the stresses and strains of the past years began to tell on Peggy, and she decided to go to the little church that overlooked the sea to the east of the town. It was peaceful there and she needed a few quiet moments to pray for the boys and girls who were risking their lives so their country could be free – and to gather her senses so she could face the coming hours and days with strength of purpose to keep the home fires burning and everyone's spirits high.

Ron straightened his tie which threatened to strangle him, brushed the damp from his greatcoat and smoothed back his hair. Taking a deep breath, he walked purposefully up the alleyway to the side door of the Anchor. Deciding it might be best if he knocked first instead of just waltzing in as usual, he ordered Harvey to shake himself dry, for Rosie wouldn't appreciate him doing it indoors.

He rapped on the heavy oak door and waited. But there were no answering footsteps on the other side. He frowned and shot a questioning look at Harvey, who whined as he put his front paws against the door and began to scrabble with his claws.

Ron's apprehension rose as he knocked again, waited impatiently for half a minute and then reached for the doorknob. Rosie had locked the door. He stood and stared at it as if by sheer will he could force it open. There were several explanations as to why it was locked; Rosie might still be in bed; she could be busy in the bar getting ready for the lunch-time session; or she could be out walking Monty. Or – and this sent a shiver through him – she was in there and refusing to see him.

He left Harvey whining and scrabbling at the back gate and strode out of the alley to peer into the windows, but was frustrated by the closed shutters and blackout curtains. He stepped back into the street and looked up at her windows, saw that she'd opened the curtains up there, and wondered if she was hiding from him. Looking round, he managed to find a couple of bits of loose grit on the pavement and threw them at her sitting-room window.

'Rosie,' he called. 'Rosie, I know you're there. Stop messing about and let me in.'

'You're wasting your time, Ron. She's gone out.'

Ron swung round to face his old friend Sergeant Williams, the local policeman. 'Where is she, Bert? I need to see her.'

Sergeant Albert Williams was the same age as Ron and a fellow survivor of the Somme. He would have retired if it hadn't been for the war commandeering all the younger men, but he enjoyed his job and it kept him out of the house and from under his rather bossy wife's feet. He was a large man with a ruddy face, a kindly disposition unless roused, and a penchant for a drop of whisky should it be offered in return for a blind eye being turned to one of Ron's minor law infringements.

'I heard about your run-in with Gloria yesterday,' he said, rocking back and forth in his size twelve boots.

Ron gulped. If Bert knew about that, then probably Rosie did too – which meant he really was in very deep trouble.

'Are you sure Rosie will want to see you after that awful caterwauling?'

Ron stared at him in astonishment. 'How the hell do you know about that?'

Bert tapped the side of his bulbous nose. 'People think I don't know half of what goes on in this town, but they'd be surprised at how much I hear and see. I turn a blind eye when things aren't serious, as you know, and although you were in danger of disturbing the peace last night, I thought Rosie's punishment was severe enough to let you off a night in the cells.'

'So where's Rosie gone at this time of the morning?' Ron demanded.

'She's walking Monty down on the promenade.' He grabbed Ron's arm as he was about to dash off. 'But she's not alone, Ron.'

Startled, Ron looked back at him. 'Who's she with?'

Bert pursed his lips, clearly working out how best to reply. 'Let's just say she's with the same chap who took her to lunch yesterday at the Officers' Club,' he said reluctantly.

Ron could feel the colour drain from his face, and he staggered a bit before he regained his senses. 'Chap? What chap? Come on, Bert, spit it out.'

Bert's meaty hand rested on Ron's shoulder. 'I'm sorry, old chum. I thought you must have known, seeing as Cordelia and Bertie were in the club at the time.'

'Cordelia said nothing about it. Who is this man taking my girl out to lunch?' snarled Ron. 'I'll soon settle his hash.'

Bert's expression hardened. 'Now, you just hold on there, Ron. There's no profit in going off like a loose cannon before you know all the facts. I'm sure there's nothing in it – and besides, you can hardly go round starting fights with one-armed war heroes.'

'The Major?' gasped Ron. 'My Rosie's been seeing Major Radwell?' Rage infused his face. 'How long has that been going on?'

The other man shrugged. 'I have no idea. They haven't been seen together outside the Anchor before yesterday.' The heavy hand again pressed down on Ron's shoulder. 'Look, I'm sorry, old pal, but you must see that a good-looking woman like Rosie is bound to have her admirers. Perhaps she only went out with him because she wanted to get her own back on you seeing Gloria yesterday.'

'I did *not* go to the Crown to see Gloria,' Ron protested. 'I was there drinking with Frank and the boy.'

'Aye, that might be the case, but gossip has it you and Gloria were sparking like fireworks.' Bert leant closer. 'We both know there's no love lost between Gloria and Rosie, and the very fact you were in there would be enough to cause trouble. Hell hath no fury like a woman scorned, Ron. You should know that by now.'

'That's not Rosie's way,' Ron muttered, although he was beginning to have his doubts. 'If she had something to say she'd come out with it straight – not go off with another man behind me back.'

He could see from Bert's expression that he wasn't convinced. Heaving a sigh, he shook his head. 'I rather liked Major Radwell. Thought he was a decent sort. It goes to show how wrong I was, doesn't it?'

'Don't jump to conclusions, Ron,' the other man cautioned. 'It's never wise and often makes things worse.'

'I suppose I'd best go home then,' Ron mumbled.

'See that you do,' warned Bert. 'I don't want to hear there've been fisticuffs between you and the Major.'

'You and Rosie might not think much of me at the moment, but I'd never stoop that low,' Ron said bitterly.

'I know you wouldn't dream of it usually, Ron. But when matters of the heart are involved, common sense flies out of the window.'

'To be sure, Bert, I'm thinking if I had an ounce of sense I'd not be in this predicament now.' Ron shook his head dolefully and then brightened with hope. 'I don't suppose anyone's reported seeing two ferrets, have they?'

'Sorry, Ron. I'd have told you if they had.' He looked suitably sympathetic. 'It seems you're having a rather bad day, old chum.'

'You can say that again,' muttered Ron.

He dragged a reluctant Harvey out of the alleyway and headed back towards Beach View, aware that his old pal was watching his every move. Yet, as he reached the junction, he couldn't resist looking down towards the seafront – and saw Rosie walking up the steep hill with Monty and the Major.

Slipping into the deep shadows of the bombed-out house on the corner, he stilled Harvey and held tightly to his collar to stop him rushing off to greet his pup.

Rosie was laughing at something the Major was saying as they ambled along arm in arm, seemingly oblivious to the damp drizzle that was dripping from the umbrella he was holding over her.

Ron eyed the Major, hating to admit that he was a good-looking man despite having lost most of one arm, and although he had to be several years younger than Rosie, they made a handsome couple. He grimaced at how at ease they seemed to be as they slowly approached Camden Road and finally turned down towards the Anchor.

Ron pulled up his coat collar and shivered as he watched them go into the side alley. What the hell were they both doing out this early? Had there been more than lunch involved, or was this a chance meeting and the Major was merely escorting her home before he went on his way?

Ron bunched his fists, the jealousy burning in him when he saw a light go on in Rosie's sitting room. He could see her at the window, chattering and smiling over her shoulder before pulling the curtains against the dreary day and effectually shutting Ron out.

He stood there in the damp chill trying to decide what to do as the foghorn mournfully moaned its offshore warning. He could march over there and demand an explanation – or let himself in as usual and feign surprise at catching them together and wait to see what they had to say for themselves. Or he could just storm in there and punch the Major on the nose.

The latter wasn't really an option, even though it might give him a fleeting satisfaction – for Rosie would never speak to him again and he'd feel an utter heel at doing such a thing to a man who'd sacrificed so much for his country. Yet Radwell had a flaming cheek, chatting up his girl and treating her to posh lunches. Hero or not, Ron would see to it that he'd get his comeuppance one way or another.

Ron chewed his lip and came to a decision. 'Come on, Harvey, it's time to get out of this finery and go for a proper walk so I can think. I'll get to the bottom of what's going on – but play it clever and not go in all guns blazing like she'd expect.'

Harvey looked up at him, his head cocked to one side, his eyes puzzled. His beloved human was clearly worried about something, and although he had a fair idea what it was, it seemed he didn't want his help in solving the problem – which he could if only Ron paid proper attention to him.

Harvey looked back at the Anchor and, with a snort of disgust, trotted after Ron in the hope they might be going home for a second breakfast and a good rub-down with a towel.

7

Peggy's spirits had been lifted somewhat by her visit to the church on the hill, but when she arrived back at Beach View it was to discover that Cordelia and Ivy were looking after Daisy, and there was no sign of anyone else.

'It's been all go here this morning,' said Cordelia once she was satisfied that Brendon had left without too much hullabaloo from Pauline. 'Ron came home in a foul mood, which doesn't bode well as far as he and Rosie are concerned – but he refused to tell me anything, just got changed into his usual disreputable old clothes and went out again.'

'Where's Sarah?' asked Peggy, reaching for the teapot. 'She was supposed to stay here and help you with Daisy.'

Cordelia gave a shrug. 'Ivy and I can manage perfectly well,' she said briskly. She finished wiping Daisy's sticky mouth with a damp flannel, and the child rushed off to help Ivy finish the big wooden jigsaw Ron had made her for Christmas.

'That's not the point, Cordelia,' said Peggy. 'She said she'd be here.'

'I know, but she got a telephone call shortly after you'd all left. It seems she'd forgotten she was supposed to be meeting one of her friends for a day out. And with so little time for fun, I could hardly stop her, could I?'

'I suppose not,' muttered Peggy, wondering if Sarah might be avoiding Beach View, for it was unlike the girl to forget anything – least of all a planned day out.

Ivy put the last piece of the jigsaw in place and then pushed back her chair. 'Andy come in earlier to tell me 'e got tickets for the pictures this afternoon. So if you don't mind, Aunt Peg, I'll go up and get changed. We're having a bit of lunch at the British Restaurant first, and if I don't get a wiggle on, I'll be late.'

'Of course not,' said Peggy. 'You go and enjoy yourself, and thanks for staying to help with Daisy.'

'It's no bother,' said Ivy cheerfully before running out of the room and up the stairs.

'At least someone's happy,' said Cordelia. 'But I'm worried about Rita. She and Jack popped in, just before they went back to the station for Jack to catch his train. It was plain to see Rita was thrilled to have a few hours with her dad, but was dreading saying goodbye again. And with everything that's happened recently ...' Cordelia trailed off. 'Anyway, I haven't seen her since.' She gave a worried sigh. 'It's all so very unsettling, this coming and going, and I dread to think what will happen in the next few weeks. All those young men, the fathers, brothers and sons ...'

Peggy put her arms around the elderly woman and held her close. 'Please don't, Cordy,' she murmured, 'I can't bear to see you upset.'

'I'm getting too old for all this uncertainty,' Cordelia replied, dabbing her eyes with her handkerchief. 'Brendon leaving this morning brought it all home again. I've been thinking about my brother's boy Jock out in Singapore, and Martin, Roger and Freddy in that camp, and Jim and Brendon. Now Jack's caught up in it too. When will it all end, Peggy?'

'I don't know,' she replied helplessly.

Peggy looked down at Daisy who was clinging to her legs, her little face puckered with concern for Cordelia. Fixing a smile firmly in place, she put her hand on Daisy's shining black curls and said brightly, 'Chloe will be here soon. How about you find your favourite picture book so you can show her your lovely colouring in?'

Daisy happily trotted off to the toy box in the dining room.

'It's my nephew Jock and Sarah's fiancé Philip who worry me the most,' Cordelia confided. 'I don't know how Sarah and Jane are managing to cope with the lack of any real information coming out of the Far East, and the terrible rumours do nothing to assuage the awful fear that they might be dead.'

Peggy had heard those rumours too, and she shivered at the thought of what might happen to Jim if he was taken prisoner in Burma. She kissed Cordelia's soft cheek. 'We'll get through this together,' she murmured. 'And when it's all over, we'll be stronger and braver and ready to face any struggles that might come with peace.'

The solemn moment was broken by Ivy rushing through the kitchen on the way to meet her Andy, and Daisy toddling in with her colouring book.

Yet, as the day continued, Peggy couldn't quite dispel the feeling that something momentous, a turning point in this dreadful war, was in the offing, and it would affect them all. She could only pray it would be to the Allies' advantage.

Despite the awful weather and Peggy's worry over where Rita and Sarah might have got to, her mood had been lifted after lunch by the arrival of Kitty, Charlotte, Grace and little Chloe. As the children played and squabbled, the women had sat down to catch up on things, discuss plans for the babies' arrival, and the possibility that at least Charlotte's mother might be able to get down when the time came. They swapped knitting patterns and cooed over the matinee jackets and bootees Peggy had kept once Daisy had grown out of them while they ate Kitty's delicious cake over numerous cups of tea.

Peggy had just regaled them with the events of the previous day when Ron returned looking very purposeful. He glared at the laughing women, grunted something unintelligible in response to their teasing, and shot back down to his basement bedroom.

Harvey was soaked through and slumped down by the fire with a deep sigh to quietly steam dry and fill the room with the less than delightful pong of damp dog.

'Poor old boy,' said Peggy, reaching for a scrap of towel to dry him off. 'You've been out all day and must be exhausted.'

Harvey's eyes were beseeching as he rolled on his back for her to rub his tummy, and then went to sit by his empty bowl.

Peggy took the hint and scraped some of the left-overs into it, before putting the kettle back on for another pot of tea.

Harvey made short work of the scraps and then collapsed by the fire again, nose on paws as Queenie curled up against his belly.

Ron returned to the kitchen half an hour later looking very smart in his suit and greatcoat, Jim's dark blue fedora set at a jaunty angle above one shaggy brow. 'I'm off to the pub,' he muttered. 'Come on, Harvey.'

Harvey opened one eye, wriggled his brows, and promptly went back to sleep.

'It looks like you're on your own,' chuckled Peggy. 'Good luck.'

'To be sure I shouldn't have bothered getting up today,' Ron grumbled before heading outside again and slamming the door behind him.

His departure triggered a bustle of fetching belongings and dressing once more for the outdoors. The afternoon had sped past and none of them had realised just how late it was. Peggy followed them down the path, holding tightly to Daisy's hand as she waved them goodbye at the gate.

Peggy stood there until they'd gone out of sight, and then turned back towards the house. There was still no sign of Rita or Sarah, and with the grey day closing in and the foghorn once more moaning out at sea, her concern for little Rita deepened. She was in a fragile state of late having lost her beloved Matthew, and Peggy was apprehensive that seeing Jack might have done more harm than good to Rita's state of mind.

Hurrying back into the kitchen, she glanced again at the clock. 'If Rita isn't back by the time I've got Daisy in bed, I'm going out to look for her,' she said to Cordelia.

'But where would you start?' Cordelia asked fretfully. 'This is a big town now, and if she's gone out on that motorbike, she could be anywhere.'

'Then I'll go to the fire station and get John Hicks to drive me to all her usual haunts first,' said Peggy with determination. 'She could be all alone in a state about her father, or worse still could have had an accident on that motorbike and be lying out there somewhere injured and in need of help.'

Ron strode through the gathering gloom, the mournful sound of the foghorn echoing his mood. The day had been a disaster so far, but he was determined to end it on a high note. He'd come to the conclusion that he'd been in Rosie's bad books too often to placate her with flowers or chocolates, and that if he was to keep her, he'd have to go about things differently. The long walk in the hills had cleared his head and made him see their relationship from her point of view, and he'd been chastened to realise how careless he'd been towards the woman who meant so much to him.

He opened the door to the Anchor fully expecting to see the Major in his usual place at the end of the bar by the till, but there was no sign of him – which was a relief, because he wasn't yet ready to face him and be polite. Pushing through the crush of people, he noted how few servicemen there were, and that the majority of the customers were locals and factory workers – a sure sign that something was afoot with regard to this rumoured invasion.

Ron finally managed to get to the bar, but one glance told him Rosie wasn't there either. He tried not to let his imagination run away with him, and waited patiently until one of the part-time barmaids caught his eye.

Beryl and Flo usually worked in the factory canteen up on the industrial estate, and when Rosie was in a bind, she called on them for help, even though they weren't as efficient as her usual two women.

'Hello, Ron,' said Beryl, her matronly figure swathed in a floral wrap-round apron, her plump face flushed with her exertions. 'Rosie said you might pop in to lend a hand, and goodness knows, me and Flo could use you tonight.'

'Where's Rosie? Upstairs, or changing barrels?'

'She had to go out,' said Beryl, swiftly clearing dirty glasses from the bar as Flo continued to pull pints. 'Didn't say how long she'd be.'

'She were looking ever so smart,' piped up Flo. 'So she were off somewhere important, I bet.'

That nugget of information didn't make him feel the least bit better, but as both women were clearly struggling to cope, he took off his coat and hat and dumped them on the coat rack in the hall before returning to the bar.

His mind was working furiously as he filled glasses and took the money, and when there was a lull, he approached Beryl again. 'Did she say where she was going?'

The woman shook her head. 'She just said it was important, and if she wasn't back before closing to lock up for her.'

Ron frowned and went back to serving until he had a chance to speak to her again. 'Did she go out on her own?' he asked Beryl, who was older than Flo and less inclined to exaggerate.

'I don't know, Ron,' she said impatiently. 'She opened up for me and Flo and then left through the side door. But she took Monty with her, so she can't have gone far.'

Ron felt enormously relieved. If she'd taken Monty then she wasn't off to some posh dinner or the theatre with the Major – but where the heck could she be?

'No sign of the Major this evening,' he remarked nonchalantly.

Beryl shrugged. 'He doesn't come in every night, and with the weather so bad I doubt he could get a lift in from the Memorial tonight.'

Ron considered this and decided it made sense, for the military hospital was situated on the other side of the surrounding hills, but jealousy sparked at the realisation that the Major had managed it earlier this morning, which didn't ease his concern over where Rosie had gone tonight – and if she really was on her own.

He continued serving, his gaze drifting repeatedly to the large clock above the bar as yet another hour passed. The noise level was rising along with the cig-arette and pipe smoke that now hung in a thick pall beneath the heavy beams of the low ceiling. Someone was bashing out a tune on the old piano which encouraged others to try and sing along, but it was a horrible noise, and he wondered if that was how he'd sounded the night before – in which case he couldn't blame Rosie for upending the swill bucket on him.

It was getting hot and stuffy in here, but the black-out rules meant they couldn't throw open windows and doors, and all the noise was beginning to give him a headache. *I must be getting old*, he thought dolefully, *for I usually enjoy a lively night – but it's not the same without Rosie, and that's a fact.*

It was gone eight o'clock when he heard a kerfuffle by the door, looked up to see who was causing it, and saw a white-faced Peggy pushing her way towards him. Dashing from behind the bar, he led her into the relative quiet of the narrow hallway. 'What's happened?'

'It's Rita. We can't find her, and we've looked everywhere in Cliffehaven.'

Ron hid his alarm as he sat her down on the stairs and took her cold hands in his. 'Who's we, and where have you looked?' he asked firmly.

'Andy and Ivy have taken a small van from the fire station, and John Hicks has gone out in the other. Her motorbike isn't at home or the fire station, so they've been to the cinder track, up to the farmhouse ruin, and asked all the people manning the clifftop guns if they've seen her, but no luck. Andy and Ivy have been all over town, back to where she used to live, knocking on her friends' doors and looking in the recreation ground, the allotments and the parks – but there's no sign of her.'

She paused to take a breath through chattering teeth. 'I've been to the hospital, but Fran hasn't seen her, she's not listed as a patient, and she's not in any of the pubs either.'

Ron's mind whirled with all the possibilities. Rita was a lively little thing, mischievous too, but she was also a solitary soul, preferring her own company when things worried or upset her. And a lot had happened to the girl over these past few weeks

– culminating in her father's unexpected visit, which must have further increased her anguish when she'd had to watch him leave again so soon.

He looked up as Flo handed him a glass of brandy which he cupped in Peggy's trembling hands, encouraging her to drink. 'Thanks, Flo. Can you and Beryl manage without me for the rest of the evening? Only there's something I have to do.'

'Yeah, of course. But what about Peggy?'

'I'm taking her home,' he replied.

He grabbed his hat and coat, waited until the glass was empty and then helped Peggy to her feet, almost relieved to have someone else to worry about instead of Rosie. 'I have a feeling I know where she might be,' he said as he steered her through the side door and into Camden Road.

'Then I'm coming with you,' she said.

'No, Peggy, girl. You're going home to thaw out before you die of the cold. And I'll have no arguments about it.'

'But—'

He maintained his grip on her waist and hurried her outside and along the pavement, towards Beach View, his mind working out how to get where he needed to be in the quickest time possible. 'Is Harvey out with the others?'

'No, he's at home sulking because they left without him.'

As they reached home at last Ron hustled Peggy indoors and gave her a nudge up the concrete steps.

'Go and get warm while I organise meself,' he muttered as Harvey flew down the steps to greet them both and almost knocked Peggy off her feet.

Peggy trudged up the steps and Ron swiftly changed into his old clothes and sturdy walking boots while Harvey watched him in puzzlement.

Ron stripped the blankets off his bed and rolled them with the sheet into a tight bundle which he tied together with garden twine, checked that his lamping torch had new batteries, wrapped a thick scarf round his neck and crammed his woolly hat over his ears. Slinging the bundle over his shoulder, he picked up his small haversack which contained a first aid kit and a flask of brandy.

Stomping up the steps into the kitchen he was met by the sight of Cordelia and Peggy sitting wide-eyed and fearful by the fire. 'I'll send Harvey back when I find her,' he assured them, reaching for Rita's colourful scarf which was lying on the kitchen table.

'But what if the others find her first? How will we let you know? How are you so sure you know where she is?'

Ron had no answer to all of these questions, for he was acting purely on instinct, and his knowledge of the young girl he'd known since she was a baby. He left the house with Harvey, and set a fast pace along the alleyway and up into the hills.

It was an unusually cold, damp night, the temperature dropping rapidly, and the very fact that

Rita was still out there somewhere told him she must be in trouble. Rita was a thoughtful, sweet girl, and no matter how troubled she was, she would never knowingly cause Peggy worry like this.

Ron tramped up the steep hill and was soon engulfed in the thick fog that was rolling in from the sea. Visibility was down to a few feet, and the dampness in the air would be washing away any scent. He gently grasped Harvey's jaw, looked him in the eye and held Rita's scarf to his nose. 'Seek, Harvey. Find our little Rita.'

Harvey snuffled at the scarf then ran round in a wide circle, nose to the ground, tail stiff with concentration.

Ron doubted he'd come across it yet, especially if the girl had brought her motorbike up here, so while Harvey was tracking back and forth, he set off towards the ruined barn.

He could see very little and the fog would have been debilitating to anyone who didn't know these hills as well as he did. Sure-footed, his sense of direction honed by many years at sea and in these hills, Ron kept going until he could make out the darker shadows of the ruined barn emerging through the swirling fog. Although Peggy had said it had already been checked, he gave it a cursory inspection anyway, and Harvey got quite excited for a moment, but then he lost the scent again, so Ron turned northward and began to descend towards the forest and farms of the Cliffe estate.

Reaching the high chain-link fencing topped with barbed wire, he came to a halt and once more drew Rita's scarf from his pocket.

Harvey sniffed deeply, searched amongst the gorse and long grass by the fence and then worked his way along the perimeter until he reached the country lane in the valley. The fog was thinner here, the visibility just good enough to make out the fields of wheat, and the ghostly white fleeces of grazing sheep.

Ron followed him, watching his every move. If his instinct had been right, Harvey should pick up her scent very soon.

Harvey stood in the lane, sniffing the air, his ears pricked – and then he shot off towards the airfield.

Ron hurried after him, straining to hear his bark which would signal that he'd found her.

It came within minutes, muffled by the fog and very distant.

Ron strode towards the sound, his boots crunching on the loose gravel of the country lane as he passed the silent fields and approached the far reaches of RAF Cliffe's runways and security fencing. There were no planes tonight, and the fog was now rolling over the hills into the valley, deadening all sound but for the frantic high-pitched and urgent barks of his dog.

Harvey galloped out of the fog, saw Ron, gave a single bark and turned swiftly back at the faint cry for help.

Ron frowned as he broke into a trot. That wasn't Rita's voice.

He found them at the side of the road, half-hidden in the undergrowth of a high hedge, the mangled motorbike on its side in a nearby ditch, Harvey going back and forth between them, whining with concern.

Ron patted his head and praised him quickly before fighting his way through the brambles to the two girls who were huddled together for warmth and comfort.

'I don't know how you found us, but thank God you're here,' said Sarah tearfully through chattering teeth. 'We've seen no traffic for hours and although we've been calling and calling, no one's heard us.'

Ron hid his surprise at seeing her. 'Where are you hurt?' he asked, switching on his torch and taking in their deathly white pallor, their scratched faces and the awkward angle of their limbs.

Rita's brown eyes were huge in her ashen face as she tried to move her leg and gave a sharp gasp. 'It's my knee and Sarah's ankle and arm.'

He untied the bundle and swiftly wrapped them in the blankets, for although Rita was wearing her fleece-lined leather flying jacket and thick trousers, Sarah had only a lightweight overcoat over a cotton dress, and both girls were trembling with shock and the cold. 'How did this happen?' he asked, glancing at the damaged motorbike.

'Yank army truck going too bloody fast round the bend back there, clipped the rear wheel and knocked us flying,' Rita rasped. 'They couldn't have felt the collision, because they just kept on going.'

Ron handed over the brandy flask, noting how Sarah was cradling her arm against her chest. He tore the sheet to make a sling and gently eased her arm into it before turning his attention to her ankle. 'It doesn't look broken,' he muttered, 'but I'll strap it up for now.'

He turned to Rita when he'd finished, and eyed the thick leather trousers. 'What about your knee?'

She grimaced. 'There's not much you can do about it unless I take these trousers off, and it's far too cold for that. I'll be fine, really.' She finished off the brandy. 'We're a couple of cripples and the bike looks written off. What on earth do we do now?'

Ron sat back on his haunches. He calculated the distance he'd have to go to get help from either RAF Cliffe or the American HQ on the Cliffe estate. 'I'll go and get help from the Yanks,' he muttered. 'It'll be quicker than trekking round the airfield to the guard house.'

He tucked the blankets more tightly around them, hoping they would be enough to stave off the cold while he was gone. 'Huddle together to keep warm. I shouldn't be long.'

'Can Harvey stay with us?' pleaded Sarah.

Ron shook his head. 'I'm sending him home to let everyone know I've found you. They've been out searching since six o'clock and must be frantic by now.' He tied Rita's scarf to Harvey's collar. 'Home, Harvey,' he ordered.

Harvey dithered and whined, clearly loath to leave.

'Home. Now,' said Ron, his tone stern.

Harvey went hurtling into the lane and was soon swallowed up by the fog.

Ron handed the torch to the girls and strode away, breaking into a steady trot as he headed through the rapidly thickening fog towards the main gate of the Cliffe estate. The blasted Yanks were always driving too damned fast in those great heavy trucks, and it was a miracle the girls had survived such a collision if the state of Rita's bike was anything to go by. And if he had any kind of back-chat from the guard on the gate, the man would soon learn not to mess with Ronan Reilly – or any of his family.

Peggy had been pacing back and forth; repeatedly going down to the scullery door to peer into the thick blanket of fog, straining to hear any sound that might herald Ron's return. Her worry over Rita was now all-encompassing, and not helped by the fact that Sarah seemed to have gone missing as well.

Andy, Ivy and John Hicks had come back from their fruitless search, and Fran had just arrived from her shift in the hospital theatre, to make tea and comfort poor Cordelia.

'To be sure, Grandma Cordy, they'll come home and wonder what all the fuss was about,' Fran soothed. 'I expect they lost track of time, and with the fog and everything are finding it difficult and slow to get back.'

Peggy wanted to believe her, really she did. And then she heard a sharp bark and the furious scratching of paws against the back door and flew down the steps.

'Harvey, oh, Harvey, good boy,' she cried as he rushed in. She looked up at the gathering in the kitchen doorway. 'Ron's found Rita – look, this is her scarf.'

There was a general sigh of relief before the speculation began as to where and how he'd found her, and how long it would be before they got home. And then Cordelia's soft voice broke through the chatter. 'But where's Sarah? Why isn't she here?'

Peggy rushed to her side and held her close. 'She's probably still with her friend,' she soothed. 'And if they've gone to the pictures they won't be back for another hour, so please try not to worry, Cordy.'

'She should have telephoned to let us know what she was doing,' said Cordelia crossly. 'With this fog closing in, she must have realised we'd be worried.'

Peggy accepted she had a point, and decided that when the girl did come home she'd give her a good talking-to. But the relief of knowing that Rita was safe with Ron was all she could think about at the moment.

She bustled about, feeding Harvey, and then drew back the blackout curtains on the kitchen window. The fog meant there wouldn't be any air raids tonight, so it didn't matter if the light was showing – and if the warden didn't like it, he could shove it under his tin hat.

The shrill ring of the telephone made them all jump, and Ivy shot off to answer it. Returning a minute later with a beaming smile, she said, 'That were Ron. He's up with the Yanks at Cliffe. Rita and Sarah are being seen by their medic – nothing too serious – and then they're coming 'ome in the commanding officer's car.'

'Thank goodness for that,' breathed Peggy, sitting down with a bump on the hard kitchen chair. 'But what on earth is Sarah doing all the way over there and why do they need medical attention?'

Ivy shrugged. 'Ron didn't say. But their injuries can't be too bad, otherwise they wouldn't be coming 'ome, would they?'

'I'm just thankful they're both all right,' said Cordelia on a tremulous breath.

So was Peggy, but she said nothing as she bustled about getting the rabbit stew warmed for when they got home. It was a foul night, and what was needed now was a hot meal and drinks and the sanctuary of home. But Sarah had a lot of explaining to do before the night was out.

Sarah was all too aware that she had a great deal to explain when she got back to Beach View, and as there was no way of avoiding it, she steeled herself against Cordelia's disapproval and Peggy's anger.

She sat next to Rita in the soft leather seats of the enormous staff car as Ron sat in the front, chatting to the driver, who was inching the car along the main road into Cliffehaven. She was at last warm and out of pain from her fixed dislocated shoulder and wrenched ankle, thanks to the hot cocoa laced with brandy and the strong pills the American medic had given her, but the shock of the accident still made her tremble and shiver.

It had all happened so fast. One minute she was riding pillion behind Rita, the next she was flung into the air, landing with an enormous thud onto the verge, the motorbike crashing over her on its way into the ditch. Sarah was very aware of how lucky they'd been, and the thought of what might have happened made her feel quite ill.

She stared out at the luminous grey of the night's fog which enveloped everything around the crawling car, masking landmarks and wiping away all sense of direction. She wasn't in the habit of telling lies, or being secretive, but this solitary lapse had taught her a very sobering lesson, and she vowed silently she'd never do it again.

'You're going to have to tell Aunt Peggy,' murmured Rita, who'd been divested of her leather trousers and was now wearing American army camouflage over the heavy bandaging on her badly twisted knee.

'I know,' sighed Sarah. 'And I'm really not looking forward to it. I love her so, and hate the thought of losing her respect.'

'She'll be all right once she's calmed down,' soothed Rita. 'She's bound to be cross with both of us, but we both know her bark is worse than her bite and it never lasts very long.' She grimaced as she tried to get her leg into a more comfortable position. 'I'm just sorry we've put her through all that worry. She frets enough over us all, and must have been going through torture tonight, running round trying to find us.'

Sarah nodded, her low spirits ebbing further. 'I feel terrible about adding to her fears, and horribly guilty about what I did today.'

Rita took her hand. 'There's nothing for you to feel guilty about. We're all struggling, Sarah,' she said softly. 'And when there's a chance to grab a little happiness, we have to take it. I'd have done the same, believe me.'

Sarah returned the pressure of her fingers in silent empathy as the car slid to a halt outside Beach View.

Peggy and the others must have been looking out for them, for as Ron and the driver got out of the car the door was flung open and a stream of light glittered in the fog. Peggy rushed down the steps with Ivy and Fran, and swamped the two girls with kisses and hugs as Harvey danced around them, and Cordelia watched from the doorway with Andy and John.

The driver scooped Sarah up in strong arms as Ron lifted out Rita, and they were carried up the steps into the hall and through to the kitchen. Everyone was talking at once, asking what had happened and how bad their injuries were, while Peggy bustled about insisting the American driver had something to eat and drink before he made the long, perilous drive back to the camp.

Sarah hobbled straight to her great-aunt and awkwardly embraced her. 'I'm so glad to be home,' she breathed close to the soft cheek. 'And I can't begin to tell you how sorry I am that you've been so worried.'

Cordelia stroked back her fair hair and gazed into her eyes. 'At least you're home safe now. I couldn't bear the thought that you both might have been alone out there on such an awful night.' She frowned. 'What I can't understand is why you were there in the first place. I thought you were meeting a friend?'

'I was – in a manner of speaking,' Sarah confessed. 'But I'll explain everything later when it's quieter.'

Cordelia raised an eyebrow but said nothing more as the American finished the cup of tea, wished them luck and hurried off with one of Peggy's paste sandwiches to keep him going on the long drive back to base.

The talk went on round the table as Ron and Rita tucked into the stew and Harvey sat patiently waiting for a morsel to come his way. Sarah had little appetite, but she forced down as much as she could and left the rest for the clever dog who deserved it far more than she did. She was aware of the questioning look in Peggy's eyes every time they exchanged glances, and knew it wouldn't be long before she had to reveal where she'd been today – and who with.

Once John and Andy had left, the chatter dwindled into silence as the late news came over the wireless – and when it was realised that there was nothing about the promised invasion, the girls prepared for bed. Fran was on earlies the next day, so was Ivy, and as they helped Rita up the stairs, the silence in the kitchen deepened and all eyes turned to Sarah.

She lit a cigarette and to her dismay found that her fingers were trembling so badly she could hardly hold on to it. 'Firstly,' she began hesitantly, 'I want to apologise for my behaviour today. It was thoughtless and unkind after all you've done for me, and I promise never to lie to you again.' She looked from Peggy to Cordelia and then to Ron, trying to read their thoughts in their expressions.

'To be sure, wee girl, you were not the only one to cause worry today,' muttered Ron.

Sarah managed a faint smile. 'Thanks, Ron, but it's no excuse.' She licked her lips and took a deep breath. 'I got a letter yesterday from Delaney Hammond.'

'The American captain from up at Cliffe?' asked Cordelia.

Sarah nodded. 'He's been promoted twice since leaving Cliffe, and is a Lieutenant Colonel now.'

Peggy didn't look impressed. 'I thought you two had stopped writing to each other,' she said flatly.

'Not really,' Sarah confessed. 'We don't write as often as we once did, but we're still in touch, and as I'm up first most days I collect my post, if it has arrived, and read it at work.'

She looked at Peggy, silently imploring her to understand. 'Delaney telephoned this morning to say he was being flown into Cliffe for an important meeting, and would be there for a few hours before he had to fly out again to join his new command. And I had to see him, Peggy.'

Peggy patted her hand. 'I can understand that, my dear,' she said softly. 'But was it really wise to start things up again when there's still no news of Philip?'

'I know it wasn't wise, and yes, I feel horribly guilty about Philip, but with things the way they are, I needed to see him just once more before he got involved in the fighting again.'

'He's no kind of gentleman to leave you to walk home all that way alone in such appalling weather,' said Cordelia crossly. 'No Englishman would have been so ungallant.'

'That was my fault entirely,' Sarah said quickly. 'He couldn't leave the aerodrome because he was officially on duty, and I insisted upon walking home despite his offer of trying to get a car and driver.'

She lowered her head and let her long fair hair fall over her burning cheeks. 'I wanted to spend every last moment with him, you see, and had planned to walk back along the road instead of over the hills as I usually do from the estate. The fog wasn't that bad when his plane took off, so I thought I'd be all right.'

She dared to look up. 'I know he's married, and I know it's shameful to feel like this when I should be thinking only of Philip – but I can't help it.'

'There can be no future in it, Sarah,' said Peggy, lovingly tucking a loose strand of hair behind Sarah's ear. 'So why torture yourself by going to see him?'

'I needed to know if it had all been a bit of a fling – just a mild flirtation between two lonely people far from their loved ones who'd made rather more of it than it warranted – or something deeper.' She took in a ragged breath and blinked back her tears. 'In a way, I wish we hadn't met today, because it's just made everything far more complicated – for both of us.'

'Well, I'm sorry, dear,' said Cordelia crisply. 'But if you will play with fire you'll get burnt. It was unfair of him to keep writing to you – let alone turn up here and disrupt everything. I hope he realises how very difficult he's made things for you.'

Sarah nodded. 'It's difficult for both of us, but we had to grab this last chance of seeing one another. None of us know what the future holds, especially with all this talk of an Allied invasion – and it would have been simply awful if we'd not met, and something happened to him.'

Peggy drew Sarah into a gentle embrace. 'We do understand, really we do. But we're worried about you. I wish you'd confided in me, I wouldn't have been cross.'

Sarah hugged her back and then dried her eyes. 'I know, but I was scared you might think less of me for falling in love with a married man when I'm already engaged.'

'Silly goose,' Peggy chided softly. 'When it comes to matters of the heart we have no defence against our feelings. Of course I don't think less of you.' She smiled into her eyes. 'I'm just glad you and Rita got back safely – but what was she doing all the way out there?'

'She'd been on the hills overlooking the airfield to watch the planes coming in and going out. She told me she felt closer to Matt by just being there, but as the fog rolled in and she realised it would be too dangerous to ride back cross-country, she headed down to the valley to take the road home.'

Sarah grinned. 'She almost ran me over – going too fast as usual – but it was a relief to see her, even though it was a bit hairy riding pillion.'

'You were lucky you weren't both killed,' said Cordelia with a shudder.

'I put in a full complaint with the commanding officer up at Cliffe,' rumbled Ron, 'and he assures me the driver of that transport truck will be severely punished, and that Rita's bike will be restored as soon as possible.'

He slowly got to his feet and came round the table to kiss Sarah on the cheek. 'It's good to have you both home again. Now Harvey and I are off to our beds. It's been a long, exhausting day.'

It wasn't long before Sarah was in her own bed, and as she lay there in the darkness listening to Fran snuffling in her sleep, she snuggled down beneath the blankets, closed her eyes and relived those precious few hours she'd spent with Delaney.

She'd thought she was in love with Philip when he'd asked her to marry him, but what she felt for Delaney was far deeper and stronger – an irresistible force against which she had no defence.

Her smile was soft as she thought of the kisses and caresses they'd shared, but her troubled conscience refused to let her sleep despite her exhaustion. How could something so very wrong feel so utterly and wonderfully right?

8

Burma

The moonlight was glowing on the turbulent water
as two heavily armed platoons of Gurkhas and
Riflemen climbed into the assault boats and motored
out into the middle of the great Chindwin River
towing other boats behind them. Jim and the men
on shore were alert for any sight of the enemy; the
machine gunners' thumbs on the double-tap button, the mortar-men poised with ammo in hand,
the launchers' sights set on the jungle-clad cliff on
the other side.

The tension was broken by the roar of three
Mustangs flashing up from the south at low altitude
to heavily bomb the line of Japanese telegraph poles
on the far side of the river and give support should
the men on the ground come under attack.

Jim and Ernie stood armed and ready next to Big
Bert to watch as great fountains of earth exploded
beneath the fighters, and then gasped in awe as the
pilots turned up-river and came in even lower, dip-
ping a wing almost to ground level to rip out the wires
still attached to the telegraph poles. Jim found he'd

been holding his breath and let it out in a great gasp as the brave and utterly fearless American pilots flew away to circle lazily high above them on guard duty.

But there was no time to stand and stare, for men, equipment, horses and mules had to be moved across the river and the sky was already lightening as a red flare went up on the far bank to signal it was clear of any enemy and the advance guard was dug in on the clifftop.

As the day wore on and the heat rose, the crossing of the Chindwin became a battle of wills between the stubborn mules and the equally stubborn but rapidly tiring men who were sweating, swearing and straining to get the animals to the other side while it was still light. A string of twenty or so beasts would be forcibly led into the water, only for them to panic mid-stream and head back to shore, while others fought their handlers and restraints, kicked out viciously and threatened to sink their huge yellow teeth into anyone who dared get near them as they refused to leave the shore.

Jim and his men were utterly exhausted; soaked with sweat, stripped to the waist and at the very end of their tether as they leant far out over the boat's gunwales to drag the two mutinous and spitting mules by their halters through the water. Jim had lost count of the number of times he'd made this journey, but it seemed these particular beasts had finally got the right idea and were now swimming – albeit reluctantly.

They reached the bank and passed the mules over to their handlers, and then sank on the ground to drink deeply from their water canteens and bolster their flagging energy by eating some of their K-rations before they had to do it all again.

Jim looked around him. The shore was littered with mules, saddles, damaged boats, ropes, radios and stores as men struggled to bring in more of the recalcitrant beasts and tried to bring some order to the chaos. He squinted against the glare of the sun and checked his watch. The day had flown, and within a couple of hours the sun would begin to sink and it would be night again.

'We should have completed the crossing by now,' he muttered to Ernie who'd flopped into the sand beside him. 'But I reckon we've got less than a fifth of those damned mules across the water. At this rate, we'll still be at it by nightfall.'

'In my experience,' said Big Bert, lighting a smoke, 'neither mules nor horses can be made to do a long river crossing in the dark – so we'd better try and get as many as possible over before then. Without them, it'll be us carrying all the equipment.'

Jim grabbed his carbine, wearily got to his feet and roused the other men, his gaze trawling the skies and his surroundings. The operation had been conducted during the glare of the day, and it had hardly been silent. If the enemy was nearby, the entire day's work would have been in full view for at least five miles in both directions, so he had to assume that the Japanese knew they were there and what they were doing.

He glanced across at his commanding officer who was standing sturdily on the sand, his binoculars sweeping both shorelines, his expression grim. He didn't envy the man's task, for even if the Japs didn't have a strong enough force to attack and prevent the crossing, they could certainly inflict casualties – or tail and harass the column before it reached the designated operations target, which was still many miles away.

Jim climbed wearily into the assault boat after the men in his platoon and sat at the stern with his carbine arching a slow sweep along the jungle ridge behind them as men on horseback attempted to bully the mules across the water. Getting the men and horses across before dusk would be easy, but without the mules to carry their heavy weapons, reserves of ammo, demolition sets, medical stores, tools and radios, they'd be useless if they came under attack.

Jim and the other men had made another successful crossing, but getting two or three mules at a time over the river was making a very small dent in the large number that still milled about on the shore, so he wasn't surprised when his commanding officer ordered everyone to be still and listen.

The man was thin to the point of gaunt, his khaki shorts billowing above deeply tanned, sinewy legs, his face weathered by his years of commanding troops in India and Africa. But looks were deceptive, for he'd proven to be as strong and resilient as the mules, and had earned great respect from all of them for his leadership qualities and common sense.

'This isn't a decision I've made lightly,' he said to the half-circle of commissioned and non-commissioned officers standing before him. 'All crossings will stop at fifteen hundred hours. Forty column will head back with the excess mules to join forty-nine and ninety-four column in their mopping-up operations.'

Jim glanced across at the officer in charge of 40 column and knew he'd have a tough march to catch up with the others, for they were already two days ahead.

'Brigade HQ and the rest of thirty column will cross the river and continue on to our rendezvous point. We'll be short on mules, but we do have the horses, so we'll just have to make the best of it and carry what we can.'

Jim and the other men worked on until three, and then in a haze of exhaustion crossed the Chindwin for the last time. Having wrecked and sunk the boats and outboard motors so the Japs couldn't use them, they loaded up the few mules and horses with the heaviest of the stores and equipment while an advance party went to reconnoitre the steep and barely discernible path that wound its way along the face of the cliff to the top.

Jim festooned himself with carbines and extra ammunition and then staggered beneath the weight of his overladen pack. He was at last getting some insight as to why the mules were always so bloody-minded – and could perfectly understand it.

He glanced across the river to see 40 column disappear into the sand dunes with the rest of the mules, and then began the awkward climb up the rough and winding cliff path, which he suspected was home to poisonous snakes and biting insects. The heavy pack threatened to drag him backwards as he negotiated tree roots and used vines as thick as his arm to cling to and steady himself, not daring to look down into the deep ravine where jagged jaws of rock waited to catch the unwary, and the river thundered over vast boulders, sweeping all before it.

He gained the top, and as the others scrambled up beside him to wait for the mules, horses and handlers to arrive, they took in the view – and it did nothing to raise their spirits.

The trees were over a hundred feet high, the dark, dense jungle stretching for miles beneath the setting sun and gathering storm clouds. Rocky, jungle-clad ridges soared above the canopy, which meant there would be plunging valleys, swift rivers and Burmese villages hidden within them, as well as the Japanese, who had been sighted twenty miles to the north, and whose gunfire could already be heard.

Jim steadied his breathing, eased his tight leg muscles and adjusted the straps of his backpack, which he'd padded with his spare shirts to stop them rubbing his sunburnt shoulders. He hadn't slept for thirty-six hours and could have dozed off right there and then, but he tipped the brim of his hat low over his eyes to cut out the glare of the sinking sun and exchanged a knowing glance with Ernie as the Gurkhas drew their machetes and began to hack a way through the jungle. They were in for a very tough few hours.

A flash of lightning and a deep crash of thunder were swiftly followed by a deluge of warm rain which battered down on them, drenching them in an instant and making their loads even heavier. But at the commanding officer's hand signal they fell into line and purposefully began to make their way once more into the familiar realms of the lethal unknown.

9

Rosie returned to the Anchor just before the Town Hall clock struck one in the morning. She unclipped the leash from Monty's collar and wearily kicked off her high-heeled shoes before padding up the short flight of rickety stairs to her rooms, frowning at the darkness, certain that Ron would have been waiting for her. And yet there was no sign that he'd been here at all, which came as a bit of a shock.

Having closed the blackout curtains before she'd left, she switched on the light and hunted for a note – but there was nothing more than the hessian bag of the day's takings on the dresser. She wondered if he was playing some sort of cruel game with her to get his own back. It was unlike him, but if he was, then she really didn't have the time or patience to play along. She took off her coat and scarf, shook the damp from them and left them draped on the back of the armchair before going into the kitchen to make a pot of tea.

Monty hurried after her and began to push his empty bowl towards her with his nose.

'You've already eaten very well this evening,' she chided softly, reaching for his special biscuits. 'But you've been a good boy all day, so I suppose you've earned an extra treat.'

Monty made quick work of the biscuits before noisily lapping at his water, and then sprawling on the couch for a snooze.

Rosie smiled wryly. She envied him, for there was a great deal to do before she could snatch an hour or two's sleep and be prepared for what would surely prove to be yet another exhausting and emotional day.

She made the tea and went into her bedroom, still puzzling over Ron's absence and lack of communication. She'd been so certain that he'd come into the pub tonight, for he'd promised to help out, knowing her usual two barmaids were off sick. If this was his idea of a game then it had backfired, for she'd expected better of him and was singularly unimpressed.

Taking her case from the top of the wardrobe, she began to pack everything she might need for her time away, and as she folded her best suit and silk blouse and hunted out her good patent leather shoes, she felt the weight of sadness settle in her heart for what might have been.

With her suitcase packed and ready at the bottom of the stairs, she finished the cup of tea, slipped on her sturdy shoes and thick coat, and had a last cigarette as she waited for Monty to stop messing about in the garden. He seemed agitated and wary, constantly darting towards the outside lav and then jumping away with little yips and yaps.

She breathed an exasperated sigh, turned on her torch and went out to see what was causing such excitement. 'Has that blasted cat got locked in there again?' she asked.

Monty gave a sharp bark and danced on his toes, his tail going like a metronome.

'Oh, for goodness' sake,' she muttered, yanking open the door, ready to give the cat a boot up the backside to send him on his way. But there was no flying bundle of hissing ginger fur shooting out, just two pairs of gleaming eyes watching her from the deepest shadows behind the toilet bowl.

Rosie's heart thudded at the thought of rats until she dared to shine the torch into the corner and saw Ron's two ferrets looking anxiously back at her. 'Oh, lawks,' she breathed. 'You're all I need tonight.'

She hesitated momentarily as she thought about what to do, and how the heck they'd got into her garden in the first place – then saw they were edging out of their hiding place towards the open door. She swiftly closed it, made sure the latch was firmly in place and then hurried inside, Monty loping along with her.

Digging about in the cupboard under the stairs, she unearthed the old cat basket she'd once used when her long-deceased Sooty had needed to be taken to the vet. Lining it with one of Ron's old sweaters which he'd left on the coat rack in the hall, she put a spoonful of dog food on a saucer before shutting an over-excited Monty in the kitchen.

She returned to the outside lav, then paused for a moment to remember how Ron handled his ferrets. Flora and Dora were nice enough when Ron was holding them, or they were behind the bars of their cage and docile, but the thought that they were probably hungry and frightened made her nervous. She shuddered. She'd seen their claws and teeth and knew what damage they could cause to unprotected flesh.

'You can't dither about out here all night,' she muttered, steeling herself to open the door. 'Neither can you leave them where they are.'

With the basket open and almost filling the doorway, Rosie squatted down and softly called to the frightened animals. 'Come on, Flora, Dora. Come into this lovely basket so I can get you home.'

The ferrets eyed her suspiciously, their whiskers twitching as they sniffed the air and cautiously advanced on the scent of Ron drifting from the sweater, and the temptation of the dog food in the saucer.

'Good girls,' Rosie crooned, ready to grab them by the scruff should they suddenly take it into their heads to make a run for it.

Flora and Dora slowly squirmed into the basket and began to eat ravenously. Rosie fastened the straps as quickly and quietly as she could and then carried them carefully into the bar, surprised at how heavy they were. She picked up the keys Beryl had dropped through the letter box after locking up, and went outside.

It was now past two in the morning and the streets were deserted, the blackout intense, but at least the fog seemed to have lifted, which augured well for the journey she would be making later. She cautiously switched on her torch and slowly made her way past the shuttered shops towards Beach View.

'And where do you think you're going at this time of night?'

Rosie nearly jumped out of her skin as Sergeant Albert Williams loomed out of the deep gloom of a shop doorway. 'Good grief, Bert,' she gasped, clutching at her thudding chest. 'You almost gave me heart failure. Don't you ever go home?'

'Not if I can help it,' he replied, eyeing the cat basket and the torch. 'The wife's a far harder taskmaster than my inspector.' He nodded towards the torch. 'You're breaking the blackout, Rosie. By rights I should fine you.'

'Please don't do that, Bert. I've had a bad enough day as it is, and I need to get these ferrets back to Ron. He must have mislaid them when he came serenading the other night, and is probably frantic by now.'

'Aye. I reckon Ron mislaid a good many things that night – including his dignity,' the policeman replied with a smile. 'Why don't I deliver them to Beach View for you? It's too late for you to be roaming about on your own – you never know who might be lurking about and up to no good.'

'That would be very kind of you, as long as you don't mind.'

Bert took the basket. 'It's a bit early for house calls, so I'll take them back to the station and deliver them once it's light.' He grinned broadly. 'It's been a while since I had my own ferrets, so it'll be a pleasure to keep them company.'

'Thanks, Bert.' Rosie hesitated, wondering if she should ask him to pass on a message, and then decided not to. Albert Williams knew everyone's business, and his wife had a way of getting it out of him so she could spread it all over town – and what she had to tell Ron was very private. 'Goodnight then,' she said.

'Goodnight, Rosie,' he replied, his curiosity about what she was doing out and about at this time of the morning still clear in his expression.

Rosie wasn't about to enlighten him, so she quickly made her way back to the Anchor, locked the door behind her and glanced at the clock. The time had flown and now there was no chance of getting any sleep before she had to leave again.

With a weary sigh she plodded back upstairs, released a howling Monty from the kitchen and sat down to write a short note to her most reliable bar-maid, Brenda, in the hope she'd run the pub during her absence. Slipping the front door key into the envelope, she sealed it and set it aside to deliver later. The letter to Ron was far harder to write, for she knew it would be difficult for him to read, no matter how she penned it – but she owed him an explanation, and wasn't about to simply disappear without a word. To avoid any confrontation, she would give it to Stan to pass on after she'd gone. She could rely on Stan.

It was barely five in the morning when Rosie hurried down Camden Road to slip the note with the key through Brenda's letter box in the certain knowledge that if Brenda was still not well enough to take over the pub, she'd organise someone else reliable to stand in.

She had just returned to the Anchor to pick up her case when the chauffeur-driven car purred to a halt at the kerb. Not waiting to be handed in, she climbed into the back where Henry Radwell was waiting for her, and ordered Monty to sit on the floor. She smiled at Henry, who was looking very smart in a beautifully tailored civilian suit, and far too chipper for this unsociable hour.

'I see you're embracing your first day as a civilian,' she said lightly. 'How does it feel?'

'Rather strange,' he admitted 'But now I have your company, I'm coping remarkably well.' He eyed her affectionately. 'More to the point, Rosie, how are you?'

'I've had better nights,' she replied with a wry smile. 'I'll tell you all about it on the way. But would you ask the driver to stop at the station for a minute? I need to speak to Stan before we leave.'

The driver duly stopped and Rosie hurried to the platform where a troop train was starting to pull away. Her heart sank, for unusually, there was no sign of Stan – just Ethel, fag in her mouth as usual and looking distinctly sour. Rosie felt a pang of concern that Stan must be ill for his wife to be on duty at such an early hour, but she had other, more pressing things to worry about and didn't really want to get into any sort of complicated exchange with Ethel.

Rosie didn't like Ethel and the feeling was mutual, even though they'd had little to do with one another. Rosie suspected Ethel was jealous of her – though goodness only knew why – and she considered Ethel to be coarse and uncouth, and not nearly good enough for darling Stan, who'd been a mainstay of this town for most of his life.

Rosie clutched her letter and wondered if she could trust the woman to deliver it without steaming it open to read the contents. It would be a gamble, but one it seemed she couldn't avoid, for Ethel had spotted her and was eyeing her and the car with curiosity.

And then, to her relief, Rosie saw Peggy's snooty sister Doris emerging from behind the WVS tea and sandwich wagon to close the shutters. Rosie didn't like her either, for she was a complete cow to Ron and Peggy with her hoity-toity ways, but she suspected Doris was more reliable than Ethel, and not half as nosy.

'Would you mind delivering this to Beach View?' she asked pleasantly. 'It's rather urgent, so I'd be very grateful if you could do it today.'

Doris eyed the letter that was being held out to her and then glared coolly down her nose at Rosie. 'This town has a perfectly good postal service. The letter box is over there.'

Rosie bit back a retort and managed to keep her tone reasonable. 'I'm very aware of that, but this needs to be delivered today.'

Doris raised a severely plucked brow. 'Then I suggest you do it yourself. I'm far too busy, and certainly don't have time to go out of my way to Beach View.'

Rosie shoved the letter at her, making Doris automatically clutch it to her chest. 'Please deliver it for me,' she said anxiously. 'I have to go away for a while, and it's really important Ron gets this today.'

Doris held her gaze for a long, cool minute and then pocketed the letter. 'I'll do my best,' she said, 'but I have a great many important tasks ahead of me today, so it might not be until later.'

'That's very kind of you,' breathed Rosie. 'Thank you, thank you.'

She turned and hurried back to the car, unaware that Ethel had joined Doris on the platform and they were watching her departure with great interest – and that within minutes of her departure, Rosie's letter had changed hands again and was now buried deep in Ethel's trouser pocket.

Ron was just emerging from the outside lav after his morning constitutional, and a lengthy peruse of yesterday's newspaper, when he heard heavy footsteps approaching along the alleyway, so went to investigate.

'Hello, Bert, you're out and about early. What can I do you for?'

'I'm returning lost property, Ron.' Bert hefted the cat basket aloft.

Filled with joy, Ron hurried to relieve his friend of the basket and check on his precious ferrets. 'Where did you find them?' he breathed. 'I've looked everywhere.'

'Rosie found them in her back lav, so I said I'd bring them over.'

Ron frowned. 'But why not bring them herself? Surely she's not so cross she can't even face me?'

Bert measured his reply. 'It was a bit late when she found them, and she didn't want to wake up the house,' he said solemnly. 'So I kept 'em overnight. Fine creatures, Ron. Made me wish I could have my own again, but the wife won't hear of it.'

Ron eyed him suspiciously. He'd known Bert since they were in short trousers and could always tell when he was hiding something, for his ears went pink – but he said nothing, for he'd get whatever it was out of him soon enough.

'Ach, Bert, 'tis a wonder they've come to no harm. Will you be coming in for a cuppa so I can thank you properly?'

'I should be going home,' Bert replied reluctantly.

'I insist,' said Ron, giving him a nudge towards the scullery door.

Bert stood firm. 'No, really, old chum. I have to go home. The missus will give me earache as it is, and if I stay out much longer she'll come to find me – and you know what that can lead to.'

Ron certainly did, for despite his size, Bert was terrified of his harridan of a wife who probably weighed less than six stone soaking wet, but possessed a voice akin to a chainsaw and a steely determination to make Bert's life a misery. 'Before you go, Bert, can you tell me when Rosie brought you the ferrets?'

'Late last night,' he replied, his gaze drifting beyond Ron's shoulder as he edged towards the gate. 'Too late for visiting, that's for certain.' He reached behind him for the latch and fumbled it open.

'Rosie went out yesterday lunchtime,' said Ron. 'You seem to know everyone's movements in this town, so where did she go?'

'I don't know,' spluttered Bert, at last able to get through the gate and into the alley. 'Stop badgering me, Ron, and just be thankful she found Flora and Dora and that they've come to no harm.'

'But—'

'No more, Ron.' Bert waved a meaty finger at him. 'You're getting to sound like the wife.' With that he turned on his heel and almost broke into a lumbering run as he made his escape.

Ron stood deep in thought at the gate for a long while, and then took his ferrets indoors. He'd go to see Stan later, and ask him for some of his special roses from his allotment to give Rosie as a peace offering and to thank her for finding his ferrets – and then he'd find out just what she'd been up to. But in the meantime he would tend to Flora and Dora, who must be very unsettled after their long ordeal.

10

The planes had been very noisy all night, and Peggy could only assume that as soon as the fog had lifted, the heavy bombardment of the northern coast of France was on again. Her hopes were high that the invasion had begun as she bathed and dressed herself and Daisy, but when she went downstairs to the kitchen, it was to discover that there'd been no mention of it on the wireless, so she had to conclude it had yet to happen.

She kissed Sarah and Rita good morning and settled Daisy on a cushion so she could reach the table. It was still very early, but the girls had seen to breakfast and were already washing up the dirty dishes Fran and Ivy had left behind in their rush to get to their shifts on time.

'Oh, you are good girls,' she said, having to shout above the racket being made by the RAF. 'But you mustn't think you have to clear up after everyone just because you can't go to work today.' She eyed the heavy strapping on Sarah's ankle and Rita's knee. 'How are you both doing after yesterday?'

Sarah placed tea and toast on the table and cracked open Daisy's boiled egg so the toddler could dip in her toast soldiers. 'My shoulder feels a bit bruised where the doctor manipulated it back in place, but my ankle certainly won't let me walk all the way to Cliffe.'

She shot a glance at Rita, who was, unusually, wearing a skirt and jumper and determinedly tidying up discarded knitting and newspapers, even though she was clearly in pain and had to rely on an old walking stick of Ron's to get about. 'You need to have a word with Rita,' Sarah confided. 'Her knee has ballooned to such an extent she can no longer wear her trousers, and Fran told her she should go in for an X-ray to make sure she hasn't broken something. She even offered to send an ambulance out, but Rita refused.'

'Fran's being over-cautious,' said Rita. 'It's just a nasty wrench, and now Ron's lent me this stick, I can get down to the fire station and help service the engines while there are no raids on.'

'Well, I think you should heed Fran's advice,' said Sarah sternly. 'You could have done some real damage, and walking on it will make it worse.'

'Don't fuss,' Rita muttered. 'If I go to the hospital I'll be kept sitting about for ages waiting to be seen, and I have better things to do with my time.'

Peggy could see how the girl was favouring the other leg and doing her best to hide the pain the injured knee was clearly causing. She glanced at the clock. 'If you feel you can walk to the fire station, you can make it to the hospital,' she said firmly. 'We'll go together on my way to work – and I'll have no arguments about it.'

'Do I have to?' moaned Rita. 'I hate hospitals.'

'None of us like them, dear, but there are times when they're a great blessing,' said Cordelia, coming into the room with the morning's paper. She kissed the top of Daisy's head, carefully avoiding the eggy mess on the child's face. 'Goodness,' she breathed, catching sight of the pot of blackberry jam on the table. 'Where did that come from?'

'Ivy brought it home yesterday. I didn't ask where she got it,' said Peggy, going rather pink as she tucked into her breakfast.

'I suspect it was from Ethel,' said Cordelia with a sniff of disapproval. 'That woman does a roaring trade on the black market and seems able to lay her hands on most things now she has a friend working in the factory canteen.'

'Oh, dear,' sighed Peggy. 'I do hope her shady deals don't cause any trouble for Stan. He's such a dear man, and it would be awful if her carrying on made him ill again.'

Cordelia rolled her eyes as yet another squadron of bombers and fighters thundered overhead. 'It's not jam that will do the damage, but that awful noise,' she said crossly. 'I do wish they'd get on with this invasion. All this disturbance so early in the morning is most unsettling.' She switched off her hearing aid and began to read the newspaper.

Peggy shared an amused glance with the two girls and finished her breakfast, still with one eye on the clock. 'Where's Ron?' she asked, holding on to Daisy so she could clean her face of egg and jam before she trotted away.

'He went out with Harvey really early,' said Rita. 'He's cock-a-hoop, because Bert Williams brought his ferrets back.' She grinned. 'Rosie found them hiding in her outside lav, so he's planning to go and see her later and try to mend things between them.'

'That's good,' said Peggy. 'I hate to see him so down.' She reached for Daisy's coat and hat. 'It's time for us to go, Rita. Do you want that ankle checked as well, Sarah?'

Sarah shook her head. 'It's really not too serious, but I'll come with you both to make sure Rita *does* see a doctor, and then help her home if she needs it.'

Rita blew out her cheeks and dragged on her battered flying jacket. 'It's a lot of fuss about nothing,' she complained, 'but if it makes you happy, I'll see the doctor and then get to the fire station.'

They left Beach View five minutes later, and although Daisy was perfectly capable of walking to the hospital, Peggy decided that it would be expedient to put her in the pushchair. Daisy didn't like this idea at all, and made a terrible fuss all the way down Camden Road, but with both girls hobbling, their progress was very slow.

The hospital was quiet, so Rita was seen quite quickly before being sent off to the X-ray department in a wheelchair – which she liked as little as Daisy had appreciated her pushchair.

Peggy sat in the waiting room trying to amuse Daisy with a colouring book while Sarah's ankle was looked at, and when the girl came back with a bright smile to say that it was only twisted, she sighed with relief.

'You'll soon be out and about again as long as you rest it well,' she soothed. 'I just hope the Yanks responsible for all this get their comeuppance. They had no business to be racing about so carelessly down that country lane – and as for just leaving you both …' She looked at her watch. 'I'm going to be late for work,' she fretted. 'Whatever are they doing with poor little Rita?'

The answer came half an hour later. Rita was returned to them in the wheelchair, her leg bound from ankle to mid-thigh in a plaster cast, her mutinous expression needing little explanation. She glared at Sarah and tightly folded her arms. 'Don't you dare say I told you so,' she warned.

The nurse smiled at Peggy and handed over a pair of crutches. 'Your daughter's got a hairline fracture at the top of her tibia, and there is some damage to the hamstring and muscles surrounding her knee. The cast will have to stay on for six weeks, I'm afraid, but after that she'll be as good as new.'

Peggy didn't correct her mistaken belief that Rita was her daughter, for in a way she was just as much a daughter as her beloved Cissy – who was stationed up at Cliffe aerodrome and much missed. 'Thank you very much, nurse. We'll make sure she doesn't overdo things.'

The nurse grinned as Rita scowled. 'Best of luck with that,' she said, passing over a box of pills and a slip of paper. 'These are to combat the pain, and she has an appointment with the doctor in six weeks' time. Any problems, please don't hesitate to bring her in.'

'I am still here, you know,' grumbled Rita as the nurse bustled off. 'Anyone would think I'd gone deaf and daft as well as crippled.'

'At least you've still got a leg – unlike poor Kitty,' said a practical Sarah. 'And she doesn't moan and carry on, so neither should you.' She took the crutches from Peggy. 'Come on, Rita, it's time to call in at the fire station and then go home.'

Peggy grinned, for Sarah was being unusually bossy, and although Rita was making a great show of being out of sorts, she could see the girl was grateful for her businesslike manner and lack of sugary sympathy.

Peggy waited until Rita had practised with the crutches, and then followed them out of the hospital as far as the gate. 'I know it'll be horribly frustrating,' she said, kissing her cheek. 'But please try and be nice to poor Sarah. She really does have your best interests at heart.'

'I know, and I'm sorry I've been such a brat,' Rita replied with a rueful smile. 'Go to work,

Aunty Peg, and stop worrying about everything. We'll be fine.'

Peggy dithered at the gate with Daisy and watched them make their slow progress along the uneven pavement. She was anxious Rita might trip and topple over, but it seemed she'd got the hang of the crutches and was now moving quite confidently towards the fire station, swinging along in an almost piratical manner, calling out to her colleagues who were watching from the forecourt.

Peggy gave a sigh of relief that both girls would be all right after their ordeal, and hurried down Camden Road to the vast clothing factory which sprawled the length and breadth of an entire block. Solly Goldman was an old and much loved friend, and he'd understand why she was so late and not make a fuss, but it would mean losing an hour's wages, which would make her a bit short at the end of the week when the milk and paper bills had to be paid.

Once Daisy was ensconced happily in the nursery under the watchful eye of Nanny Pringle and her two young assistants, she took a couple of puffs of a cigarette and then hurried into the factory, which was humming with activity, the ever-present wireless providing background entertainment.

The building had once housed a fashion clothing business but had been extended during the war years to cope with the growing demand for uniforms. Solly had always had a keen eye for what was needed and had got in early when he realised the war really was coming and the forces would need to be clothed, so he'd invested in bigger and better machinery, taken on more machinists and was now conducting a roaring trade.

And yet Solly wasn't all about making money, for he was a generous benefactor of many charities and had been instrumental in helping to organise the rescue and safe transport to England and America of Jewish children who otherwise might have been slaughtered or imprisoned by Hitler.

Solly was waiting for her by her machine. He was as wide as he was tall, with dark hair and brown eyes that missed nothing. He wasn't a handsome man, but he was charismatic, and all the machinists were a little in love with him.

He looked at his gold watch. 'Oy, vay, Peggy. You're an hour late, and I was getting worried. Do you have a problem at home that I can help with?'

Peggy quickly explained her lateness as she shrugged off her coat and settled at her machine. 'I'm sorry, Solly, but I'll make up the hour.'

His large, soft hand rested lightly on her shoulder, the diamond winking in his gold ring. 'You don't have to, Peg,' he said quietly. 'I know you work twice as hard as everyone, so you won't miss out on any pay.'

'But that isn't fair on the others,' she protested. 'I can't let you do that.'

He made an expansive gesture with his hands. 'My Rachel would have my guts for garters if I didn't,' he said, with a twinkle in his eyes. 'Now, I must get back to my accounts. We'll speak later perhaps.'

Peggy smiled as she threaded the machine and picked up the first of what would be many pairs of navy bell-bottoms she'd sew that day. Solly might consider himself to be in charge, but it was Rachel, his wife, who quietly oversaw everything that went on and kept Solly under her delicate but very firm thumb.

Ron stood on the top of the hill, the fresh, salty wind blowing in his face from the sea, and watched the bombers and fighters take off and land at Cliffe aerodrome. They'd been busy since before dawn now the fog had lifted.

He lit his pipe and idly watched Harvey darting in and out of the gorse and through the long grass, tail windmilling, nose to the ground in search of who knew what. Ron's mood was lighter today, for Flora and Dora were safely at home, and there was real hope that Rosie had forgiven him – although it was odd that she hadn't brought the ferrets herself, and Bert had been very cagey about it all.

Ron saluted the fresh batch of planes which screamed overhead, and decided not to go to Tamarisk Bay this morning to check on Frank and Pauline. He had enough problems of his own, and the last thing he needed was Pauline moaning and wailing and making his Frank's life a misery.

He turned for home, planning to get changed, see Stan about his roses and then go to the Anchor.

'Come on, ye heathen beast,' he rumbled at Harvey. 'To be sure you've watered every blade of grass, and that tank must be empty by now.'

He tramped across the rolling hills, acknowledging greetings from the soldiers manning the big guns that lined the clifftops who'd become friends over the past few years, and was just about to descend towards the alleyway when he was disconcerted to see Bertie Grantley-Adams striding towards him.

Bertie was looking his usual dapper self – the ultimate country gentleman in plus fours, tweed jacket and hat, and sturdy brogues – but behind that facade and bristling moustache was a man of great bravery and intelligence who'd honed his skills as a saboteur and spy during the first shout, and was now working secretly for MI5. Ron hadn't known him before he'd become a constant companion to Cordelia, but soon realised they had a good deal in common, for although they were retired, they both still had an allegiance with their old paymasters, and were often called upon to do some undercover work.

Peggy and the girls at Beach View had come to like and respect Bertie, even though they fondly mimicked his plummy accent and called him Bertie Double-Barrelled behind his back.

'Hello, old chap,' said Bertie heartily. 'Thought I might find you up here.'

'It's not like you to be out and about at this hour,' said Ron. 'Has something happened I should know about?'

Bertie took a moment to light a small cheroot and watch the planes going out over the Channel. 'I heard from a mutual friend early this morning,' he said in the sudden lull between the flights.

'Oh aye?' Ron tamped down on his impatience, for Bertie never got straight to the point and he'd learnt long ago that it did no good to rush him.

Bertie continued to smoke his cheroot as another squadron of planes took off. 'She would have telephoned you, but with so many people in the house, she couldn't be sure of getting hold of you.' Bertie's eyes gleamed in the early morning sun as he turned to regard Ron. 'She knows you well enough to realise you'd probably be out at this early hour.'

Ron realised then that he was talking about Pauline's mother, Dolly Cardew, who unbeknown to her daughters was working for the SOE and not living out a quiet retirement in Bournemouth. Dolly was in direct contact with several agents who were being flown into enemy territory, and one of them was Danuta, the young Polish girl who'd lived at Beach View at the start of the war. 'Is this about Danuta?' he asked fearfully.

Bertie nodded, his expression glum. 'She was betrayed and taken by the Gestapo the night she was due to return to England,' he said. Seeing the shock in Ron's face, he hurried on, 'But it's not all bad news. The Allies bombed the prison and she managed to escape to a safe house, and will very soon be on her way to England by fishing boat.'

'That's marvellous news,' breathed Ron. 'To be sure I feared for that brave wee girl, and many a time I deeply regretted sending her to Dolly.'

'It was what she wanted,' said Bertie, 'and she's proved to be extremely useful to us as well as resourceful.' He stamped out the butt of his cheroot beneath his brogue. 'But I'm sorry to say she suffered during the Gestapo's interrogation, and it's touch and go as to whether she'll survive the Channel crossing.'

Ron felt the blood drain from his face as his imagination ran wild.

Bertie squeezed his shoulder in consolation. 'She's a born survivor, Ron. If anyone can pull through it, she will. Arrangements have been made to pick her up quite close to Cliffehaven so she can be taken straight to the Memorial Hospital.'

Ron took a deep breath to steady his racing heart. 'When is she expected?'

'Before dawn tomorrow. I'll tip you the wink when I hear she's arrived, but it might be a while before she's well enough for visitors.'

Ron's heart clenched at the thought of that young, vulnerable girl being in the hands of those Gestapo brutes. 'The others have no idea of what she's been doing,' he murmured. 'But if I don't tell

Peggy she's at the Memorial and she finds out, there'll be hell to pay.'

'I'm sure you'll think of some explanation to satisfy her,' said Bertie comfortably. 'Sorry to dump this on you so early in the day, but Dolly was adamant you should be told. I suspect she might put in an appearance as well – the girl has come to mean a lot to her – but of course she'll cover that by visiting Pauline.'

Ron sighed. 'It's a tangled web, all this secrecy, isn't it, Bertie?'

'It certainly is, although the worst-kept secret is this invasion. Everyone is discussing it in quite fine detail – right down to the fact that gliders will be used – although where they get the information is a mystery.'

'There's loose talk amongst the troops, and with the influx of servicemen pouring into the south, it's quite evident that something's afoot. People aren't stupid.' Ron narrowed his eyes against the glare of the sun on the sea. 'I just wish they'd get on with it now the weather's cleared. I don't suppose you know when it will happen?'

Bertie grimaced. 'Sorry, old chap. Those on high are keeping it very close to their chests.'

Ron nodded and shook his hand. 'Thanks, Bertie. Will we see you later?'

'It's a fine day for a round of golf, but I'll pop in later and take Cordelia to afternoon tea at the club.' He strode off towards the golf club which sprawled beyond the northern boundaries of Cliffehaven, a sprightly, neat figure with an energy that belied his advanced years.

Ron headed down the hill to Beach View, his worries about Rosie momentarily forgotten amidst his troubled thoughts on Danuta's plight. The girl had escaped the horrors of the Warsaw ghetto and come to England in search of her fighter pilot brother, who'd tragically been killed shortly before her arrival. Danuta had been pregnant at the time, and when the baby had been stillborn, she'd become determined to play a part in bringing Hitler down. She'd lost everyone she loved, and was filled with such anger and pain that he and Dolly had feared for her ability to stay cool in dangerous situations.

But Danuta had proved to them that she could channel that fury into a steely determination to survive and do as much damage to the enemy as she could, and had played an intrinsic part in rescuing Martin, Freddy and Roger from the horrors of Buchenwald concentration camp. Now she needed to be loved and cherished, and Ron knew there was no one better placed to do that than darling wee Peggy. Yet how to explain why Danuta was back in Cliffehaven at the Memorial, which had been designated as a service personnel hospital?

Deciding he'd think on that for a while, he put it to the back of his mind as he came down into Cliffehaven. He made his way through the labyrinth of narrow streets behind the Crown to the High

Street, and then over the humpback bridge to the station.

'Hello, Stan,' he said cheerfully. 'How are you holding up on this fine day?'

Stan grinned back at him. 'I'm as fit as a fiddle. Ethel took over here this morning so I could have a bit of a lie-in, and it's done me the world of good.' He eyed his friend and winked. 'I hear you're in a spot of bother with your lady love,' he said. 'Was it some of my roses you were after?'

Ron grimaced. 'Aye, I am that. I've a nasty feeling I have lots of humble pie to eat today.'

'It'll take more than roses, Ron, if the gossip about her and the Major is true.'

'That's what's worrying me,' Ron confessed. 'It's not like Rosie to shut me out and avoid me like this, and I'm thinking I'm in deep trouble this time. The Major is something I hadn't bargained for.'

Ron regarded him sympathetically. 'Women are a mystery, Ron, and she's probably only using him to get her own back for Gloria,' he said. 'Help yourself to the roses. You know where everything is. I'd come with you, but with all the troop trains in and out, I can't leave the station.'

Ron thanked him and hurried up to the allotments. Having gathered a large bunch of beautiful, heavily scented pink roses, he tied them with string and carried them back down to the Anchor. It was almost midday, so Rosie should be getting the bar ready for opening time.

The shutters were open so he tapped on the window as he peered into the gloom and saw someone moving towards the door. Whipping off his hat, he cradled the roses and waited nervously as bolts were slid back and the key rattled in the lock.

But it wasn't Rosie standing there with a wide smile, but Brenda, and for a moment he was lost for words.

'Hello, Ron. Are those for me?' teased Brenda, who was still snuffling a bit from her heavy cold.

'To be sure I'll bring you some next time,' he replied quickly to cover his disappointment. 'Is Rosie upstairs?'

Brenda left the door open and led the way into the bar as the Town Hall clock struck twelve. 'She's gone away for a while.' She finished placing clean glasses on the shelf beneath the highly polished bar and took the towels off the beer pumps.

Ron felt a stab of alarm. 'Gone away? Where, and for how long?'

Brenda shrugged. 'I have no idea, Ron, sorry. She posted a note through my door early this morning asking me to run the place until she got back. She didn't say how long she'd be away, or where she was going, but she's taken Monty with her, thank goodness. I have enough to do without looking after a lively dog.'

Ron's thoughts whirled and his pulse raced in panic. Travel restrictions were tighter than ever, and anyone wanting to leave Cliffehaven would have to have a valid, urgent reason, and go through a lot of rigmarole, before permission was granted – unless, like Doris, she had friends in high places. Could Major Radwell have such influence, and if so, had they gone together – and where to?

That idea made him feel quite ill. If she'd gone by train then Stan would have said, for with Ethel on watch, she'd have told him; especially if Rosie had been travelling with Radwell. The coaches no longer ran, and Ron could only surmise that she'd hired a car as she'd done once before when her husband had taken a turn for the worse.

'Do you know how she went?'

Brenda shrugged. 'I have no idea, Ron.' She looked over his shoulder as a group of factory girls came in. 'I'm sorry, but I've got to get on. Will you be coming in to lend a hand in the evenings? Flo and Beryl are on night shift this week, and I'm not really up to coping on my own with this horrid cold still lingering.'

Ron knew when he was beaten, yet he wasn't about to give up on Rosie, that was for sure. 'Aye, I'll be in,' he said, carefully laying the bunch of roses on the counter. 'You'd better put these in water and take them home after you've finished here,' he muttered.

He dug his hands into his coat pocket and plodded down to the promenade. He didn't feel like going home, or talking to anyone; he just wanted time and space to think, for the events of the past few hours had knocked him sideways and he was beleaguered by doubt and the most awful, sickening guilt.

He had only himself to blame for Rosie's lack of faith in him, for he'd hardly been trustworthy of late, acting like a fool, going his own sweet way without a thought for her feelings. It was no wonder she'd decamped without a word. And to add to his guilt and fears about Rosie it was his fault that Danuta had put her life in danger, for without his interference, she would never have become involved with Dolly and her spymasters.

11

Peggy had gone outside to sit in a deckchair along-side Cordelia and enjoy the last of the warm sunshine while she drank her tea after supper. Daisy was in bed at last, Sarah and Fran had gone to the pictures to see *Gone With the Wind* for the third time, and Rita and Ivy were washing the dishes. They were chattering away like sparrows as they discussed their day and tried to assess how Rita's bike would get mended and brought back to her, since there were rumours flying about Cliffehaven that the Yanks had moved out very early that morning.

'I don't know where those girls get their energy,' sighed Peggy to Cordelia, who was trying to unravel her usual mess of knitting.

'The enemy's over the Channel, dear,' she replied with a frown. 'Really, you do worry me at times, Peggy. Are you sure you aren't doing too much?'

Peggy smiled and patted her hand to reassure her that she was fine. She was too tired to repeat what she'd said, and when Cordelia had her hearing aid switched off, conversations got far too compli-cated – especially after the worrying events of the previous day and the long hours she'd put in at the factory.

She watched Cordelia struggling to make sense of what she'd done with her knitting, and gently took it from her to see if she could unravel the tangles. It proved to be beyond her too, so she unwound it all and started again, swiftly completing several rows before handing it back.

'Thank you, dear,' muttered Cordelia. 'I don't know how I get into such a mess. This is only supposed to be a square to add to the blanket I'm making. It's hardly complicated.'

She began to knit, promptly dropped two stitches and gave a deep sigh of frustration as she failed to pick them up properly and dropped two more. 'I'm all fingers and thumbs,' she said crossly, abandoning the square and stuffing it into her knitting bag. 'This blessed arthritis makes everything difficult, and I did so want to finish the blanket before we have another winter.'

'I wouldn't fret on it, Cordy,' soothed Peggy. 'The weather will get warmer now we're almost in June, and you'll find the arthritis will ease.'

Cordelia glared at her. 'Betting on whether or not I'll ever finish it in a blue moon is hardly a very kind way of putting it,' she said. 'I thought better of you, Peggy Reilly.'

Peggy took a deep breath and pointed to Cordelia's hearing aid, willing her to turn it on. But before she could repeat what she'd said, Ron came stumping out of the basement in his second-best attire.

'That expression would sour milk,' said Cordelia, twiddling her hearing aid and making it screech. 'Whatever's the matter with you today?'

'Nothing,' he replied moodily, jamming his pipe in his mouth and lighting a match.

'Well, something's up,' said Peggy. 'You've been going about all day in a terrible grump. Is Rosie still being stand-offish?'

Ron got his pipe going before explaining about Rosie's sudden departure and her lack of any communication with him. 'I'll be working at the Anchor when I'm not on fire-watch or Home Guard duties,' he said, 'so don't expect me back until late.'

Peggy and Cordelia watched him trudge down the path and through the gate, Harvey following closely behind. 'It's odd that Rosie didn't leave some sort of message for him,' said Peggy. 'It's so unlike her to hold a grudge – and Ron's behaviour the other night couldn't really be classed as all that unusual. She knows what he's like with a few beers inside him.'

'Perhaps it was one time too many,' said Cordelia sagely. 'Every woman has her limits as to how much she will stand from her man. I certainly wouldn't put up with it.'

Peggy silently agreed, and could only hope that Rosie hadn't done something stupid to get her own back on Ron. 'You're lucky Bertie's such a gentleman,' she murmured.

'I wouldn't have it any other way,' said Cordelia stoutly. 'But even he is inclined to go off unexpectedly at times, and can be very evasive about what he's been up to.' She gave a little sigh. 'Men are strange creatures, Peggy, and despite being almost eighty, I've never been able to understand what goes on in their heads.'

'Well, there's no doubt Rosie has got Ron properly worried this time. I wonder what's caused her sudden disappearance, and whether it's all to do with Major Radwell. I seem to remember he was due to be released from the hospital this week – and if anyone could get a travel permit, he surely would.'

'I wouldn't jump to conclusions, Peggy. Rosie has a good head on her shoulders, and charming as Radwell is, her heart, rather foolishly, still belongs to Ron.'

'I hope you're right,' Peggy murmured, aching for the pain her beloved father-in-law must be suffering. If only Rosie had left a message of some sort – even if it was to tell him it was over – then at least he'd know where he stood. But it was the uncertainty that was weighing him down.

Their conversation was interrupted by the sound of someone knocking on the front door. 'Who on earth can that be?' Peggy muttered, twisting round.

'I'll go,' shouted Ivy from the kitchen window.

Peggy and Cordelia shared a glance and smiled. 'It must be Andy,' said Peggy, settling back into her deckchair. 'Though he usually comes in the back way. I do hope there's nothing wrong.'

She strained to hear the voices now drifting through the open kitchen window, but couldn't make head or tail of what was being said, which was most frustrating. And yet that didn't sound like Andy's voice, and it certainly wasn't the plummy tones of Fran's Robert. With a frown, she eased herself out of the chair and went into the scullery just as Ivy and Rita appeared in the kitchen doorway.

'It's all right, Aunty Peg,' said Ivy. 'That was someone from Cliffe bringing Rita's bike back.'

'That was quick,' breathed Peggy. 'But I thought the Yanks had left Cliffe?'

Rita gingerly made her way down the concrete steps on her crutches, her face alight with excitement. 'It isn't a Yank,' she said, 'but he says it's as good as new. I told him to bring it round the back so I could have a proper look at it.' She reached the bottom of the steps and grinned. 'And here's me thinking it was abandoned and I'd never see it again.'

'Oh, darling, that is good news,' said Peggy, giving her a hug. 'Now mind that step, and don't trip on the loose paving slab outside.'

Rita rolled her eyes and swung over the threshold with ease before hurrying down the path towards the throaty burble of a well-tuned machine.

Ivy giggled. 'I ain't seen her that lively for weeks, but I reckon it ain't all to do with getting 'er bike back. You should see the bloke what brought it.'

'I hardly think she'd have her head turned so quickly after losing Matt,' said Peggy rather sternly, and then saw the tall, handsome young man climb off the motorbike and smile down at Rita, who was grinning delightedly back at him. 'Oh,' she breathed. 'I see what you mean.'

'His name's Peter Ryan,' said Ivy rather breathlessly. 'He's an Aussie bomber pilot,' she added unnecessarily, since this much was obvious from the insignia on his dark blue uniform and cap. 'And certainly a sight for sore eyes, ain't 'e?'

Peggy and Cordelia took in the long, rangy figure, broad shoulders and handsome face beneath the closely cropped brown hair which shone like a conker in the last of the sun, and silently agreed with Ivy.

'What's he doing with Rita's bike when the Yanks were supposed to be fixing it?' asked Peggy.

Ivy shrugged. 'I dunno, but it sounds like he done a good job.'

Peggy and Cordelia watched with avid interest as Rita and the young man chatted happily while they inspected the motorbike. 'They certainly seem to have taken to one another,' said Cordelia.

'I'm not surprised,' replied Peggy with a chuckle. 'The Australians we've met have always been able to charm the birds out of the trees. Remember how they took over the cooking that Christmas and brought us our first chickens hidden in their overcoat pockets?'

Cordelia giggled. 'Indeed I do. A bunch of scallywags, but very likeable.'

'Look out,' hissed Ivy, patting her hair in place. 'She's bringing him over.'

Peggy stood to greet the young man as Rita made the introductions.

'G'day, Mrs Reilly,' he drawled, his large hand swamping her fingers. 'How ya goin'?'

'I'm going very well,' she replied, looking up at a tanned face and straight into a pair of thickly lashed, startlingly blue, mesmeric eyes. Gathering her senses, she introduced Cordelia, who twittered and blushed as the Australian shook her hand and smiled at her.

'Peter's done a marvellous job on the bike,' enthused Rita. 'It's running better than ever.'

The Australian looked rather bashful. 'Aw, it was no bother, Rita. I've got bikes at home, and I enjoy tinkering with engines.'

'I'll put the kettle on,' said Peggy, hoping she'd find out more about this charismatic young man over a cup of tea.

He twisted his cap in his hand. 'That's real kind of you, missus, but I thought Rita might like a ride before I have to get back to Cliffe.'

Peggy gasped. 'Oh, I don't think—'

'I'd love to,' breathed Rita. 'Come on,' she said, tugging on his arm. 'What are you waiting for?'

Peter Ryan grinned at Peggy's concerned expression. 'No worries, missus; reckon she'll be right. Catch you later.'

Peggy anxiously followed them down the path with Cordelia and Ivy trailing behind her. She stood at the gate and watched Rita abandon her crutches and settle on the seat behind the Australian, her damaged leg stretched out so her foot rested on his thigh.

Peggy's heart was beating faster than usual as the engine roared, Rita put her arms about his waist, and they went hurtling down the alley at what looked like breakneck speed before shooting out onto the main road and roaring up the hill.

'He'll get her killed,' fretted Cordelia tearfully. 'You should have stopped them, Peggy.'

'I wish I had,' she replied on a tremulous breath. 'But you know Rita when she sets her mind on something. Nothing will shift her.'

'Rita knows what she's doing,' soothed Ivy. 'And so does he, 'cos he told us 'e used to do a lot of dirt-track racing back in Darwin.'

'But not with a girl on the back with a broken leg,' snapped Peggy. 'I shall be having a strong word with the pair of them when they get home.'

But Peggy never did read them the riot act, for when the Australian brought Rita home a couple of hours later, the girl had been glowing and unscathed from her risky adventure, which made Peggy realise it had been just what she'd needed to lift her spirits.

However, she did still worry about this new friendship, and as she closed the door on the cheerful young man and returned to the kitchen to make the evening cocoa, she began to gently probe Rita about him.

'What's an Australian doing up at Cliffe aerodrome?' she asked as they sat in the quiet kitchen. 'I thought most of them had been sent to the Middle East or out into the Pacific.'

Rita's laughing eyes regarded her over the rim of her mug. 'He's done more than his share of flying ops, so he's been ordered back to train up new pilots and have a break from combat duties.' She sipped the cocoa. 'He was shot down twice, saw his brother and best mate killed, and although he won't admit it, he's exhausted and on the edge of losing his nerve.'

'He seems quite gung-ho when it comes to tearing about on your bike,' countered Peggy. 'And how come he ended up with it when the Yanks promised to repair it?'

'He's got an American pal based at the Cliffe estate who was going to mend it. But he got new orders and had to leave, so Peter took it on.' Rita put down the empty mug and eyed Peggy calmly. 'He's nice and friendly and a good mechanic. We both love bikes and enjoy dirt-track racing, but that's as far as it goes, Aunty Peg – so don't go getting romantic ideas into your head.'

'It never crossed my mind,' retorted Peggy, going a bit pink. 'I'm just worried that all that charm and easy-going attitude will be hard to resist.'

'He's not Matt and never will be,' said Rita firmly. 'Pete and I have shared interests, and get along well – but that's all it is.'

Peggy gave her a hug and a kiss and sent her off to bed, still not totally convinced that friendships between the sexes could remain platonic, for the initial attraction that had drawn them to one another could so easily be a precursor to something deeper – especially during wartime when the future was so uncertain. Rita was vulnerable; he was a charming, battle-weary hero far from home who shared her passion for motorbikes and was far too likeable. It was a situation Peggy was determined to keep a very close eye on in case Rita got hurt.

Ron woke early the next morning to find a slip of paper had been slotted through the cat-flap. It was from Bertie.

> *Our friend has arrived, but had to be rushed into theatre. I wouldn't tell anyone just yet in case she doesn't pull through, but I'll leave it to you to decide what to do about visiting.*

Ron crushed the note in his fist and sent up a silent prayer to whichever God was listening that Danuta would prove resilient enough to overcome whatever horrors the Gestapo had inflicted upon her. He had no fears that the doctors at the Memorial might not be skilled enough to repair her, for he'd seen the miracles they'd performed on patients not expected to survive – but there was still this sickening guilt and fear that he'd been instrumental in her plight, and if she didn't pull through, he'd have the burden of that guilt haunting him for the rest of his life.

He opened the door to let Harvey out, and then put a match to the note and watched it burn to ash in the scullery sink. Washing it away, he went back to his bedroom to get dressed and see to his ferrets. In a strange way, he felt perversely glad that he had Danuta to worry about as a distraction from his fears about Rosie and Major Radwell. In the grand scheme of this war, his falling-out with Rosie was a very minor event, even though it broke his heart. There was little he could do about it but keep faith in Rosie and take each day as it came until she returned home. He could dedicate himself to being around for Danuta, when he so clearly hadn't been around for Rosie.

Going outside to feed the chickens and gather up the eggs, Ron dodged the vicious cockerel which had taken a great dislike to him, and firmly shut the gate on the pen. 'To be sure, Adolf, you need to mind your manners, or you'll be next for the pot,' he warned.

Upstairs in the kitchen, he found Sarah waiting for the kettle to boil, dressed in her WTC uniform of jodhpurs, green sweater and sturdy shoes. 'Good morning, Ron. Lovely day, isn't it?' she said cheerfully.

'Aye, it is that, especially when the hens have laid so well.' He carefully put the bowl of precious eggs on the wooden draining board. 'Are you sure your ankle will take that long walk, wee girl?' he asked in concern, eyeing the heavy strapping.

'It's much better today, thanks, Ron, so I thought I'd give it a go. If it's too painful, then I'll try and get a lift back this evening, but the work will be piling up and it isn't fair to leave it all to someone else.'

'I'll walk up there with you,' he said, slapping a couple of slices of the gritty mess that passed as bread these days onto the hot plate, and setting a pan of water to boil the eggs beside them. Rationing meant they were allowed one egg a week if they were lucky enough to find any in the shops, and he was eternally grateful to those young Australians who'd brought them the stolen hens on that Christmas Day at the beginning of the war.

'Ivy told me about Rita and the Australian chap who fixed her motorbike,' said Sarah, pouring out the tea. She grinned. 'I think Ivy was rather bowled over by him, but I'm glad Rita's got the bike back in one piece – I know how much she treasures it.'

Ron had heard all about the Australian from Peggy, and rather shared her concerns that Rita might be falling too hard and too fast for the young man they knew so little about, but as Sarah was also on the horns of a romantic dilemma, he kept his thoughts to himself.

'Aye, her father found it abandoned a couple of years before the war, and Rita helped him to restore it. It was a labour of love for both of them, so it was, and very much a part of her close relationship with her father, so of course it's precious.'

He added the eggs to the boiling water and set the timer. 'She was a bright wee girl even at that age,' he said fondly, 'and Jack taught her all he knew about machines, which has stood her in good stead.'

'I wish I had a skill like that, but I'm afraid I wouldn't know a piston from a pillion.'

Ron chuckled. 'We all have our different talents, Sarah. It's what makes life interesting.' He glanced up at the clock and hurried to turn on the wireless so it would warm up in time for the early news.

They were already eating their eggs and toast when the announcer declared that the news that morning seemed positive. The 5th Army had broken through the German battle lines and was now engaged in fierce fighting right on the outskirts of Rome. The city was expected to fall within hours – which would secure the first major victory of the war in Europe.

Meanwhile, there had been fresh Allied landings on islands near New Guinea, and the Russians were preventing the Germans from strengthening their position in the Romanian hills. Nothing much had changed on the home front, but there was a stern warning that anyone caught breaking the travel restrictions would be heavily penalised.

Ron grunted as the news came to an end. 'Still nothing about an invasion. What the divil are they waiting for?'

Sarah cleared away the dirty dishes and pulled on her coat. She glanced out of the window and gave a soft groan. 'The sun's gone, and there are some nasty black clouds rolling in. It looks as if we're about to have more blessed rain.' She reached for her umbrella, hat and scarf. 'If this weather doesn't improve there'll never *be* an invasion.'

Ron silently agreed, for beachhead landings had a tragic history of failure, even when the weather was fair. After the debacle at Slapton, he doubted very much that Churchill and Eisenhower would risk more unnecessary deaths by sending them into the Channel during such rough conditions.

He rammed his old cap over his untidy hair, dragged on his tweed jacket and checked he had his pipe and tobacco. If he was going to persuade the matron at the Memorial to let him see Danuta, then he had to look reasonably respectable. He clicked his fingers at Harvey, who was hoovering up toast crumbs from beneath the table, and the three of them left the house for the challenging walk to the Cliffe estate.

It took longer than usual, for Sarah was still going cautiously on her twisted ankle and the wind had risen in strength, hampering their progress, but they reached the top without incident and Sarah took a deep breath of satisfaction.

'I'll be fine from here on,' she said. 'It's all down-hill, and as I'll be sitting at a desk all day, I'll have plenty of time to rest it for the walk back.'

Ron grinned and patted her shoulder. 'I know how much you like your independence, but if you can get a lift home, then do so. Better not to overdo things too soon – and it could be tipping down by then,' he added, looking up at the scudding black clouds.

He kept an eye on her until she reached the country lane and disappeared out of sight. Then he stood for a moment to watch the planes take off and land beneath the ominous clouds which were now masking the sun. He could smell the rain in the gusting wind, and feel the chill of it through his jacket as huge, white-capped waves rolled in to explode against the base of the chalk cliffs and scatter glittering sprays of spindrift. Gulls shrieked, battling to stay on course, and the poor men manning the big guns along the clifftop were huddled miserably in the lee of the sandbag defences in their greatcoats and tin hats.

'So much for summer,' he grumbled softly before slowly descending the hill and heading for the Memorial Hospital which lay beyond the fields and grazing sheep, hidden by spurs of private woodland which stretched along the far horizon.

He found he was sheltered from the wind as he reached the valley and as he crossed the ancient stone bridge, he paused for a moment to gaze into the clear water of the meandering river that fed the reed beds several miles to the west. He called to Harvey, who was splashing about trying to catch a frog, and then tramped up the rutted track, breathing in the scents of wild onion and garlic.

The hedgerows on either side of him were displaying the jewelled colours of dark blue speedwell, golden marsh marigolds, dog violets intertwined with pale pink dog roses and the froth of white hawthorn blossom. Crows had built their nests in the treetops, pigeons and gulls were pecking in the lush grass of the grazing pastures, and despite the wind and the threat of rain, Ron could hear the beautiful song of a skylark high above him.

He knew there were quicker, easier ways to get to the hospital, but he loved this walk. He rarely met anyone, and the peace and solitude reminded him forcibly of why they were fighting a war, and how very important it was that they won it. He carried on walking as Harvey investigated the ditches beneath the hedgerows and whined in frustration as he saw rabbits feeding beyond that impenetrable barrier of bramble thorns and stinging nettles.

The woods behind Agatha Fullerton's property stretched for five or six miles, and hidden deep within them was a dark, cold pool where Ron went hunting for eels – but that was not his mission for today. A high boundary fence ran between Agatha's land and the large manor house estate that had once belonged to the Finlay-White family, but Ron had made a gap in it long ago, which he'd disguised with tree branches, and it had yet to be discovered. Perhaps, once he knew how things stood with Danuta, he'd come back, for there was nothing tastier than a bowl of jellied eel.

Ron was familiar with the tragic story of the wealthy Finlay-Whites, for he'd known the grandson, who'd joined the same regiment as him at the start of the last war, and like so many others, neither he nor his father had survived the trenches. The dowager had worn black from that day on, rather like Queen Victoria when she'd lost Albert, and having no heirs, she'd willed Holmwood House and the entire estate to the armed forces in memory of her lost loved ones.

Ron passed his secret gap in the fence with barely a glance and reached the top of the track to lean on the five-bar gate and look down at the Finlay-White Memorial Hospital for Injured Servicemen. Apart from the addition of a new west wing, the house didn't look very different from when he'd once worked there as a part-time odd-job man and gardener. The bricks were mellow ochre, the many windows looking out from beneath fancy gabled roofs to sweeping lawns and neat flower beds.

His eyesight was still as good as ever, and he could see people moving about on the terrace and croquet lawn accompanied by nurses and orderlies whose uniforms glowed white in the gathering gloom. He felt a deep pang of sadness for the many young lives that had been lost or irreparably damaged because of the war, and prayed that Danuta had come through the operation.

It was still very early, so Ron lingered for a while to smoke his pipe and reminisce. Kitty had been a patient here, and so had Mike Taylor, young Ruby's Canadian. Both had suffered life-changing injuries, but they'd pulled through and were living life to the full, so he had to keep faith that Danuta would too. He fully admitted to himself that he was reluctant to go down there and find out how she was, and silently berated himself for being a coward before tapping the spent tobacco from his pipe and clambering over the gate.

'Come on, Harvey,' he murmured. 'All this speculation does no one any good.'

He strode down the lawn towards the terrace as the first drops of icy rain splattered over him. By the time he'd reached the double doors, the terrace and croquet lawn were deserted, so he ordered Harvey to wait beneath a nearby bench and pushed his way into the hall. He could hear voices and the squeak of rubber-soled shoes on polished floors, and wrinkled his nose at the reek of disinfectant before he headed for the matron's office.

Ron had always been wary of matrons, for past experience had proved they stood no nonsense and rarely had a sense of humour, but today he was feeling quite confident. The battleaxe who'd once ruled this place with an iron fist and sour temperament had long since been moved to another hospital, and Ron hoped her replacement would prove to be more helpful and understanding.

He took off his cap, smoothed his hair and eyebrows, and rapped lightly on the door.

The door opened and Ron's heart sank. The officious Matron Billings from Cliffehaven General, with whom he'd had several unpleasant run-ins, stood in the open doorway.

Her gimlet gaze pierced him with disfavour. 'What do you want at this hour, Reilly?'

He gripped his cap and returned her stare. 'I've come to enquire about a patient who was brought in very early this morning.'

'Visiting hours are from two until four,' she said briskly as she began to close the door on him.

Ron shoved his boot in the narrowing gap. 'I'm Miss Chmielewski's guardian,' he said firmly, 'and therefore have a right to know if she came through her operation.'

The large bosom rose and fell as the narrowed eyes regarded him. 'I was not aware that Miss Chim ... Miss Chemyl ...' She gave up the struggle. 'There is no mention of you in her notes,' she said coldly.

'I doubt she has any notes,' retorted Ron. 'But you know very well that she used to live with us at Beach View when she worked in the laundry at the Cliffehaven General. You were the matron there at the time.'

'I can't be expected to remember everyone,' she snapped. 'And I'm not at liberty to discuss patients with the likes of you.' She glared at him and attempted to close the door, but Ron's heavy boot was still in the way.

'I'm not leaving until I know if she survived the operation,' he said.

'If you don't, I shall call security and have you thrown out.'

Ron smiled, for he knew that security consisted of two elderly, overweight men who spent most of their time drinking tea in the storeroom and reading the *Racing Post*. He decided to play her at her own game, and removed his foot from the door. 'I'll be back at visiting time, then. What ward's she on?'

'She's in the recovery room at present, but will be transferred to Women's Surgical when the surgeon is satisfied with her progress.' Matron closed the door with rather more force than was necessary.

Ron grinned, for now he knew Danuta had come through the op. All he had to do next was find the recovery room. He hurried down the corridor, his memory of past visits taking him straight to the doctors' changing rooms. Making sure the coast was clear, he slipped in and quickly swapped his jacket and cap for a white coat and a stethoscope which he found conveniently tucked in one of the pockets.

Bundling his cap into his jacket pocket, he strode out into the grounds and quickly deposited the jacket next to a rather bewildered Harvey who was sheltering from the rain beneath a rhododendron bush. 'Stay there and look after that,' muttered Ron. 'I won't be long.'

Returning inside, he finger-combed his hair into some sort of order and strode with purpose towards the operating theatres which were situated in the new west wing. He'd studied how the doctors swept importantly about when he'd briefly been in hospital, so knew that with the right swagger and wearing a white coat, he would pass muster.

He smiled vaguely at patients hobbling past on crutches, and nodded solemnly at the few nurses, who obviously didn't recognise him, but who clearly thought he belonged there. He continued on until he reached the two theatres and then followed the signs to the recovery room. Pausing to look through the round windows cut into the swing doors, he saw four occupied beds, and the back of a nurse who was sitting at a table in the middle of the room.

He took a breath, pushed through the doors and strode to the table. 'I've come to check on Miss—' He met a pair of very familiar, laughing brown eyes.

Nurse Hopkins giggled softly. 'Hello, Ron,' she whispered. 'What on earth are you doing here in that get-up?'

'It's a long story,' he said, tipping her a wink. 'I need to see how Danuta is.'

'If Matron catches you we'll both be in trouble,' she replied, looking over her shoulder towards the door. 'But Danuta's doing very well, considering, and the surgeon is quite hopeful she'll make a full recovery. But it'll be a long haul. She suffered some terrible injuries.'

Ron could see the girl had been moved by Danuta's plight – just as she had when she'd nursed Kitty through her painful recovery. 'Can I see her?'

'Just for a second, then you must go, Ron.' She cast another fearful look towards the door, then led him to the bed in the corner.

Ron's heart twisted as he looked down at the tiny figure that was almost lost in the whiteness of that hospital bed, and the cage which had been placed over her feet to take the weight of the bedclothes. Danuta's little face was bruised and battered, her nostrils plugged with bloody gauze beneath the thick strip of tape. Her fair hair had been hacked in lumps from her head, one arm was in plaster, the fingers of both hands heavily bandaged; and as he gently lifted the sheet at the bottom of the bed, he saw that her feet were also swathed in bandages.

'What did those devils do to her?' he managed hoarsely.

'We were told she'd been caught in an air raid,' Nurse Hopkins whispered back, 'but we could all see she'd been tortured.' She blinked back her tears and replaced the sheet over the cage. 'Her nails had been torn out, her nose and arm broken, and there were burns.' She swallowed hard. 'Burns all over her body. Someone had punched her so hard the surgeon had to remove her spleen – and ...' She swallowed again. 'There were other things, Ron, too awful to mention.'

Tears blurred his sight as he reached down to gently touch Danuta's wrist. 'You're home safe now, wee girl,' he managed gruffly before he turned away. 'Thank you, Nurse Hopkins. I'll be back at visiting time.'

He strode out of the recovery room before he made a fool of himself by bursting into tears. Dragging off the white coat, he rammed the stethoscope back in the pocket and left them on a nearby chair, and then hurried outside into the rain.

Ron could feel the rage building inside him as he gathered up his jacket and broke into a run towards the trees. And once he'd negotiated the five-bar gate, he let it out in a great anguished roar that echoed through the trees and down into the valley.

The rain battered his tear-streaked face as he lifted it to the lowering sky and bellowed his pain and wrath against the men who'd done such a thing – and against the all-seeing, all-loving God who'd turned a blind eye and let it happen. 'Why, God?' he stormed. 'Why Danuta when it should have been me or those Nazi bastards?' he yelled, his clenched fists raised to the heavens.

But there was no answer and Ron's shoulders slumped as he lowered his head and wept.

12

The past week had been fraught with worry and tension, and as Peggy slowly walked back from Sunday mass with Daisy, she hoped that things would calm down; the weather would improve now they were into the fourth day of June, and the invasion would finally get under way. They'd all thought it had started the previous day when massed squadrons of aeroplanes had swarmed across the Channel, and warships had been sighted off the east coast – but it turned out it was simply another bombing raid on the Pas-de-Calais.

And yet, as the new week loomed, very few of Peggy's worries had been resolved, and she suspected things wouldn't improve for a while yet. Ron was moodier than ever, often disappearing early and not returning until after closing time at the Anchor. He'd still not heard a peep from Rosie, and although it obviously bothered him, Peggy had begun to wonder if there was something more serious on his mind. He didn't look at all well and was often distracted, rarely dredging up a smile or rising to Cordelia's gentle teasing. Peggy had tried to winkle out of him what was bothering him but, as usual, he refused to enlighten her, so she could only assume that whatever it was, he was determined to deal with it on his own.

Sarah and Rita were also causing her concern, for Sarah had gone very quiet the previous day after the post had arrived and had brushed off Peggy's gentle questions, saying she was missing her mother, and wished wholeheartedly that they weren't living on opposite sides of the world. But again, Peggy wondered if there was more to it.

As for Rita, she'd been enlivened by the Australian's rather too regular company, and although Peter Ryan was utterly charming, Peggy fretted that he seemed to have a lot of free time considering he was supposed to be tutoring cadet pilots. Was he all that he seemed – or was she just being over-protective of Rita?

She waited while Daisy picked some dandelions and daisies from the grass verge, and watched as fighters and bombers thundered overhead. They'd been noisy since five this morning, and as she looked out to sea, she could make out the dark palls of smoke rising from the distant shores of France. The raids had grown in intensity of late, and Peggy was amazed that there could be anything left to bomb over there.

She took the wilting flowers from Daisy and held her little hand as she continued along the narrow road towards Beach View. She'd heard nothing from Pauline since Dolly's letters, and Peggy was rather relieved that she seemed to have accepted things and not made her usual fuss – or if she had, poor Frank had borne the brunt of it.

She gave a sigh as she reached the cul-de-sac and regarded the pile of rubble that had once been two fine houses. Beach View looked as shabby and unkempt as the others in the row, with bullet scars pockmarking the walls, the lovely stained-glass windows on either side of the door replaced by strips of hardboard. The brass knocker was almost black from lack of polish, and the concrete steps hadn't been whitewashed for years. There had once been fancy wrought-iron lamps set into the sturdy pillars either side of the bottom step, but they'd been shattered during a raid, and Ron had taken a rasp to them and cut them off at the base. Jim wouldn't recognise the place when he came home.

Disheartened, but determined not to let it spoil her day, she continued up the hill and along the alley to her back gate.

Daisy grabbed the dandelions and daisies and ran ahead of her to Cordelia, who was sitting in a deck-chair reading the newspaper with Queenie curled contentedly in her lap. 'Gan-Gan, look what I got,' she yelled, shoving the flowers at her, and making the cat skitter off to the safety of the shed roof.

'They're lovely, darling,' Cordelia replied, taking the poor things from the child's hot little hand. 'But I think they might need a bit of water, don't you?' She struggled out of the chair and found an empty jam jar in Ron's pile of things to be taken to the tip by the back door, then filled it from the outside tap and let Daisy arrange the flowers.

Peggy smiled as she watched them. Daisy adored Cordelia and the feeling was mutual, and it was heart-warming to see them so absorbed in each other. Daisy's unexpected arrival had given new purpose to Cordelia's life after the boys had been evacuated to Somerset, and with the girls regarding her as a grandmother, she felt loved and useful.

'I'll put the kettle on, and open that kitchen window,' she said, giving the elderly lady a kiss on her soft cheek. 'The house could do with airing after all the rain we've had.'

'There's a surprise waiting for you up there,' said Cordelia, with a twinkle in her eyes. 'It's the reason we've kept the window shut.'

Peggy hurried indoors, taking off her hat and coat as she ran up the concrete steps. The heavenly aroma of roasting lamb greeted her as she pushed through the kitchen door, and with a gasp of delight, couldn't resist opening the oven.

Golden potatoes were sizzling nicely alongside roasting carrots and onions, and the fat was crisping on the half leg of lamb. Her mouth watered as she hurriedly checked on the door to the scullery. She now understood fully why everything had been kept tightly shut. Neighbours would smell the cooking meat and questions would be asked – and as she had no idea where the meat had come from, it would make things very difficult, especially if it proved to be stolen or purchased on the black market.

'Doesn't it smell wonderful?' said Rita, swinging into the room on her crutches. 'Pete brought it over and swears he got it legally.' She giggled. 'I suspect he chatted up one of the women in the canteen at Cliffe and swapped it for a couple of cartons of American cigarettes.'

'That was very enterprising of him,' murmured Peggy, who wasn't totally convinced by Rita's story. 'Will he be joining us for lunch?'

'He's on duty all day, unfortunately, but he wanted us all to have a treat by way of thanking you.'

'Thanking me?' said Peggy with a frown. 'What on earth for?'

'For putting up with him and feeding him tea and biscuits.' Rita grinned. 'He knows you don't really approve of him.'

'I …. I …' Peggy stuttered.

Rita gave her a quick hug before filling the kettle. 'Go and sit in the sun while I make the tea. Lunch won't be ready for almost an hour, so me and Ivy can come and sit with you before we dish up.'

'Where are Fran and Sarah?'

'Fran's lying in as she's on nights next week, and Sarah's gone for a walk down on the prom.' Rita's bright brown eyes were suddenly clouded with concern. 'She's really not herself since she met up with Delaney, and I think she's finding it very difficult to come to terms with the fact there can be no future in it. He's hardly likely to dump a wife and two kids for her, is he? And once the war's over and he goes home to America, he'll probably forget all about her.'

Peggy nodded, her expression sad. 'It's all a terrible mess, but there's nothing any of us can do but be there when she needs us.' She put her arm about Rita's narrow waist. 'And I don't disapprove of Peter – I'm just concerned you'll get into a similar tangle.'

Rita rested her head on Peggy's shoulder. 'Please don't worry about me, Aunty Peg. I'm a big girl now, and can take care of myself.'

Peggy kissed her, her thoughts flying to Cissy who'd been inclined to get romantically attached at the drop of a hat until she'd met her American pilot – and then wistfully remembered herself at Rita's age. She'd thought she'd known it all too, but in reality she'd been little more than a child when she'd met and married Jim in haste. She harboured no regrets, for the marriage was a happy one, but she knew how very lucky she was to have found the right man when so many girls of her generation had rushed into things only to find they'd made the most awful mistake.

Sunday lunch was an absolute triumph – a rare feast in these austere days, to be savoured and celebrated. Everyone was in party mood as they tucked in, and Peggy decided that a bottle of Ron's rather lethal parsnip wine was in order. Consequently they were all a little tipsy as they sat back, replete and contented.

Peggy lit a cigarette. 'I can't remember the last time I had a proper Sunday lunch,' she said. 'And I'd forgotten how delicious roast lamb can be.' She smiled at Rita. 'Peter certainly knows the way to a woman's heart.'

Rita went a bit pink as she gathered the dirty plates for Ivy to carry to the sink. 'He'll probably turn up in the week, so you can thank him then.'

'It's a shame Ron missed out,' said Peggy. 'He used to love his Sunday roast.'

'I've put his share on a plate, so all he has to do is warm it up and add hot gravy when he gets back from the Anchor,' said Ivy, busy washing dishes at the sink. 'The fat's been run off and put in a jug, and I've scraped the bone so Queenie and Harvey get their share.'

'I'll boil the bone for stock,' said Peggy dreamily. 'It'll certainly add some flavour to the next rabbit stew.'

'To be sure I've had enough rabbit to last me a lifetime,' muttered Fran. 'When this war's over, I never want to see another one.'

'We're all jolly lucky Ron brings those rabbits home,' said Cordelia, eyeing Fran over her half-moon glasses. 'He's not much use in the scheme of things, but you can't deny that he's a good provider of meat when most people have to go without.'

The tranquillity of Peggy's kitchen was broken by the jangling of the telephone in the hall, and she reluctantly went to answer it. Before she could even say hello, her sister, Doris, was already in full flood.

'Well, I hope you're satisfied,' Doris barked. 'You were the one who encouraged her, and now she's left me high and dry. This is an appalling way to carry on, and I will *not* stand for it, do you hear?'

'I don't know what on earth you're talking about,' Peggy managed as Doris paused to take a breath. 'And I don't appreciate you telephoning me on a Sunday just to bully me.'

'Pauline has handed in her notice at the WVS and left me with no one to cover her shift,' snapped Doris. 'You'll have to come in. I simply can't be expected to cope here on my own.'

Peggy gripped the receiver. 'If you have an issue with Pauline, then I suggest you drive over to Tamarisk Bay and have it out with her. I'm not coming in, Doris, and that's final.'

'I don't see why I should use my precious petrol when you have nothing better to do than lounge about at the weekends,' said Doris crossly. 'It wouldn't hurt you to get some exercise by walking over there.'

Peggy gritted her teeth. Doris had a nerve talking to her like that, but then she never did stop to think before she opened her trap – and that had always led to trouble. She forced some calm into her tone. 'You use your car all the time,' she said. 'One little trip to Tamarisk Bay won't put a dent in that hoard of petrol I know you keep hidden in your garage.'

'I need it to get about to do my charity work,' Doris said tightly.

Peggy let the silence stretch, determined not to be bullied into doing something she really didn't want to do.

'Well, I can see I'll get no help from you,' Doris said eventually. 'But then I'm not surprised. You're no doubt too taken up with Ronan Reilly and those girls to care about me – but then I'm only family, so obviously don't matter.'

'I'm not playing this game, Doris,' Peggy said evenly. 'You might be family, but I've seen and heard precious little of you since I started working at Solly's – unless you want something.'

'You know my feelings about you working at that ghastly factory,' Doris retorted.

'I certainly do. Now, if you've quite finished, I'd like to get on with my Sunday.' Peggy firmly replaced the receiver and took a deep breath before she went back to the kitchen.

Cordelia eyed her quizzically. 'Let me guess; that was the dreaded Doris.'

'How on earth do you know that?'

'Because you've gone all pink, your shoulders are up by your ears and you've bunched your fists,' said Cordelia with a twinkle in her eyes. 'I know she winds you up like a clock, but really, Peggy, you shouldn't let her.'

'That's easier said than done,' she replied, realising Cordelia was right as she uncurled her fists and eased the tension in her shoulders. 'It seems Pauline has deserted the WVS, and it's all my fault,' she sighed.

'I couldn't stand that woman bossing me about a minute longer,' said Pauline, stepping through the scullery door and into the kitchen. She sniffed the air. 'Can I smell roast lamb?'

Everyone shook their heads and tried not to look guilty.

'It's just a lamb bone I've been cooking down,' said Peggy, crossing her fingers beneath the table at the fib. She got up from the table and hugged her sister-in-law. 'It's lovely to see you, Pauline. Come in and have a cup of tea.'

'I could certainly do with a cuppa after that walk. Frank's mending nets and sorting out the engine on his fishing boat, so I thought I'd come over to ask your advice.'

Peggy's spirits wavered as she poured out the tea. 'Is it about what to do now you've stopped volunteering with the WVS?' she asked hopefully.

Pauline took a sip of tea, and watched over the rim of her cup as the girls and Cordelia quietly left the kitchen with Daisy. 'I've already signed on to volunteer for the Red Cross,' she said. 'I was impressed by how organised they were, and how pleasant the people in charge are. I've had it with Doris and her snooty cronies ordering me about like a skivvy.'

'Well done you,' breathed Peggy, now understanding why her sister had been so cross. 'So what advice were you looking for, Pauline? You and Frank are all right, aren't you?'

'We muddle along very nicely now we talk more and discuss what's bothering us. We still mourn our darling boys, but we do it together, and of course Brendon is never far from our thoughts.' Her voice wavered, and the cup rattled in the saucer as she put it down.

Peggy had a horrible feeling she knew where this conversation was leading, but said nothing as Pauline lit a cigarette and made a visible effort to control her emotions.

'I don't know what to do about Mother,' Pauline said finally. 'She's probably too embarrassed to say anything to you, but she wrote and told me about Carol's father.' She paused for effect but then hurried on before Peggy could say anything. 'It turns out he's General Felix Addington, who was overseeing whatever was going on in Devon. She hadn't been expecting to see him ever again, but his turning up like that forced her to confess the truth, to him and to Carol.'

'She wrote to me about it too,' Peggy murmured.

Pauline stared at her. 'Why would she do that?'

'We've been friends a long time, as you very well know, and she wanted me to be aware of what had happened in case you needed support,' said Peggy. 'I can understand that it must have come as an awful shock, especially to Carol, but, happily, things seem to have been resolved.'

Pauline glared. 'Resolved? Not as far as I'm concerned,' she snapped. 'Mother has obviously lived a very rackety and secret life – which is shame enough for me and Carol to have to contend with – and she would have continued in the same vein if it hadn't been for that American inconveniently turning up and forcing her to come clean.'

Pauline took a shallow breath and continued before Peggy could comment. 'She lied to Carol, lied to Felix, and now I'm wondering just how many lies she told me.'

Peggy could see that Pauline was close to losing control. 'Why would you doubt her, Pauline?' she asked calmly. 'You've always known who your father was. Dolly never made a secret of that.'

'How can you be so sure?' Pauline retorted. 'When someone can live a lie like that for over twenty years, then she's capable of anything.' She stubbed out the half-smoked cigarette forcibly in the ashtray. 'Who's to say the man whose name is on that marriage certificate was my father? She's clearly had many lovers over the years, and could easily have had an affair and passed me off as his.'

Peggy saw the light of battle in Pauline's eyes and knew she wouldn't let this go easily. 'You're letting your imagination run away with you, Pauline,' she said earnestly. 'Dolly was barely seventeen when she married your father, and certainly wasn't the sort of girl to have affairs – in fact, she's had very few over the years. She liked men and they liked her, but until she met Felix, she'd kept them all at arm's length.'

'You can't possibly know that,' said Pauline flatly. 'Mother's secretive and a proven liar; she could have been up to anything – especially when she was in London or working as a translator abroad.'

She crossed her arms tightly about her waist. 'In fact, I've begun to wonder if she really is living in Bournemouth, because there's never any answer when I ring her there.'

'Dolly was never a tart,' Peggy said evenly. 'She made mistakes, just as we all do, but that doesn't mean you can condemn her. She married your father because she was young, naïve and thought she loved him, and he let you both down by walking out shortly after you were born.'

Peggy could see Pauline wasn't convinced, so pushed the point. 'When she met Felix it was love at first sight, and she truly thought they had a future together until he confessed he had a small son and a sick wife at home who he couldn't divorce. She was devastated, unable to tell him she was expecting his baby because she'd wanted more from him than an affair. She didn't want him to stay with her out of duty, or become a long-distance father who would probably lose interest in Carol when he was caught up in his life in America.'

'She said all of that in her letter, but I can't believe any of it,' Pauline interrupted, on the verge of angry tears. 'And now I don't know who I am, or where I came from. I can't forgive her for that.'

Peggy felt a stab of exasperated pity for this woman who found it impossible to see things from anyone's point of view other than her own. 'I'm sorry you feel that way,' she said, reaching for her hand. 'I know it's a lot to absorb, but I promise you, Dolly never lied about your father.'

Pauline looked mulish, clearly not willing to believe or forgive.

'Imagine how your sister felt when she discovered the truth,' Peggy continued softly. 'And yet both she and Felix have been able to forgive Dolly. They love her too much to stay angry with her, and now all three have a chance of starting afresh.'

Pauline snatched away her hand. 'And that's another thing,' she rapped out. 'It's all very well them going off to America to play happy families, but what about me?'

Peggy sat back in the chair and regarded Pauline squarely. 'You have a husband and son, a lovely home and a good life here in Cliffehaven. After the war you and Frank will be able to travel to America, and I'm sure Carol and Dolly will return to England frequently to visit you.'

'Frank and I don't have the sort of money it would take to go to America,' Pauline said bitterly. 'And if

Mother turns up here expecting to be welcomed with open arms, I'll refuse to see her.'

Peggy tamped down on her impatience. 'Dolly has always adored both you girls, and it would break her heart if either of you turned your back on her. Don't be angry with her, Pauline. She's only human, and deeply regrets her past mistakes.'

Pauline mopped her eyes with a handkerchief. 'She didn't regret leaving us with our grandparents while she swanned about the world doing goodness knows what,' she muttered. 'And even when Carol and I lost our loved ones, she was in such a hurry to get back to her exciting life that she stayed barely more than a few days.'

'She knew she'd get on your nerves if she stayed longer,' said Peggy. 'You know what she's like – never still, always busy at something. But she stayed until she was sure you could cope, and besides, you did have Frank and me and Ron to get you through those dark days.'

'Carol had no one,' Pauline argued. 'My little sister was mourning her husband and baby and she was left all alone down there in Devon.'

'Carol wanted to be alone after the funeral,' Peggy said firmly, her patience all but spent. 'She told Dolly she needed time and solitude to absorb all that had happened, and virtually ordered Dolly back to Bournemouth – so don't make up your own version of things to suit yourself, Pauline.'

'But how will I cope when my entire family goes off to America?' Pauline wailed, twisting her handkerchief in her fingers. 'It's so unfair of them to abandon me like this.'

'Oh, do pull yourself together, Pauline,' said Peggy, her patience finally snapping. 'You hardly see either of them as it is, and you have Frank and Brendon to look after you. You'll just have to get on with your life and look forward to the grandchildren coming along once Brendon gets married. Carol and Dolly will visit, I'm sure, and before you know it, you'll be so busy with Brendon's little ones, you won't have time to feel sorry for yourself.'

Pauline reddened. 'If that's what you think, then I've obviously made a mistake coming here,' she muttered, pulling on her coat and tying the scarf beneath her chin. 'I thought at least I'd get some sympathy from you.'

Peggy had had enough of this never-ending circle of self-pity and blame, and was relieved that Pauline was planning to leave. 'You asked for my opinion, Pauline, and I'm sorry if it offends you. Why don't you talk this over with Frank? I'm sure he'll be more understanding.'

Pauline grunted. 'He said the same as you, so it looks as if I'm going to have to deal with this on my own – as usual.' She picked up her handbag and left the kitchen, slamming the scullery door behind her.

Peggy slumped back in her chair and blew out her cheeks. 'That went well,' she muttered. 'So much for a quiet Sunday.'

Ron had left Brenda to lock up the Anchor so he could get to the hospital for visiting hours. He'd come every day since that first secret visit, and had timed it well today, for as he approached the five-bar gate, he heard the clock above the old stable block strike two. He clambered over it as Harvey squeezed between the bars, and then hurried down the lawn towards the terrace where the patients were enjoying the brief appearance of the sun.

Harvey had become used to this new routine, so was quite happy to be fussed over and fed snippets of cake and biscuits while he waited for Ron's return. His presence had been noted by Matron Billings, but when she'd ordered him to be evicted, there had been such an outcry from patients and staff that she'd unwillingly let him stay – on the understanding that one misdemeanour would see him banished.

Ron headed for Danuta's room. The corridor was quiet, but he could hear the murmur of voices coming from the wards he passed along the way, and the rattle of the tea trolley as it was wheeled from ward to ward by one of the nurse probationers. Of Matron Billings there was no sign, which was a huge relief, for she never failed to berate him over something when she saw him.

Danuta had been moved to a private room which overlooked the sweep of lawn to the back of the old manor house. She had yet to wake properly, and this had caused Ron some alarm until little Nurse Hopkins explained that she'd been heavily sedated to counteract the pain and help her to heal.

Ron pushed open the door to the quiet, darkened room and froze in delighted surprise as the neat little figure in a silk suit and fetching hat turned in the bedside chair and smiled back at him.

'Dolly,' he breathed, rushing to take her hands and look into her lovely face. ''Tis glad I am to see you. When did you arrive?'

'Very early this morning,' she whispered back, glancing towards the bed and the still little figure beneath the white sheet. 'I had a run-in with that ghastly Billings woman, but soon put her in her place, so she won't bother either of us again.'

'How did you manage that?'

'A letter from Winston Churchill works wonders,' Dolly replied. 'Especially when it's full of praise for the sterling work she's doing here.'

She grinned up at him impishly, reminding him of the young girl he'd first met all those years ago. 'I hear from Nurse Hopkins that you managed to sneak into the recovery room. You are naughty, Ron, but I'm so glad you've never changed.'

Ron tried not to look flattered by this praise. He drew up a second chair and regarded Danuta. 'Did

Nurse Hopkins tell you about her injuries?' he asked softly.

Dolly nodded. 'It's a miracle she's still alive – but I blame myself entirely for what happened to her. I knew she'd been compromised, and should have insisted she return home sooner.' She gave a deep, remorseful sigh. 'But she was determined to rescue those airmen before she left – and thank God she did. Hitler's order to have them executed as spies was delivered within hours of their escape.'

'You're not the only one to feel guilty, Dolly. To be sure she's been preying on my mind ever since she left Beach View.'

Dolly held his gaze for a long moment. 'She's a brave, brave girl,' she said finally. 'And if she hadn't come to us, she'd have found another way to get her revenge on those who murdered her family.'

Danuta stirred restlessly and her eyelids fluttered as she mumbled something.

'What's that?' asked Ron, leaning closer. 'I didn't catch it, Danuta.'

'She's talking French,' said Dolly, gently touching the girl's battered face. 'She's saying she's just a waitress in a bar and knows nothing.' Dolly blinked rapidly and cleared her throat. 'She obviously still believes she's being held by the Gestapo.'

'You're safe now, *acushla*,' murmured Ron, the old Irish endearment coming so easily in this emotional moment. 'Ron and Dolly are here, and no one will ever hurt you again – never – do you understand?'

Danuta turned towards his voice, her eyelids still fluttering as she fought to wake.

'There's no need to fight against sleep, little one,' soothed Dolly. 'Ron and I will watch over you from now on.'

Danuta lay still, her tense shoulders drooping against the pillow, her body sinking into the mattress as if she realised the danger had passed, and she was with people who loved her. And then she opened her eyes and took a swift look around her before settling first on Dolly and then Ron. 'Where is this?' she asked, her voice roughened by lack of use for so long.

'You're in hospital, just outside Cliffehaven,' said Ron, finding it hard to talk through the lump in his throat. 'Welcome home, Danuta. We're so very happy you've come back to us.'

Danuta managed a wan smile. 'I too am happy,' she whispered. She turned her head on the pillow and looked at Dolly. 'Please not cry,' she said, reaching out her heavily bandaged hand to lay it on Dolly's wrist. 'I soon be well to fight again.'

'We'll talk about that when you're fully recovered,' replied Dolly gruffly. 'For now you must rest.'

'Invasion has come? War over now?'

'Not quite yet,' said Dolly, still struggling with her emotions. 'But soon – very soon.'

Danuta relaxed once more into the pillows. 'Is good,' she said on a sigh. And then she frowned. 'Where is Peggy? Why she not here?'

Ron glanced across at Dolly, who nodded back. 'I've yet to tell her about you,' he admitted, 'but the minute she knows she'll be with you like a shot.'

'You not tell Peggy because you think I die?' Danuta had a glint of humour in her sunken dark green eyes.

'To be sure I knew you weren't dying,' lied Ron, 'but it would have upset Peggy to see you as you were.'

Danuta nodded, and then her eyelids began to droop. 'Lovely Peggy,' she murmured sleepily. 'She like mama – I have miss her.'

As Danuta fell into a deep, drugged sleep, Ron unashamedly wiped his eyes with his grubby hand-kerchief. 'If I'm to tell Peggy and get her up here before the end of visiting time, I'd better be going,' he said gruffly.

'There's no rush,' said Dolly, clearly finding it hard to control her own emotions. 'That letter from Churchill means we can visit any time we like.' She shot him a watery smile. 'Dear Hugh arranged it all, even to the point of virtually drafting the letter so every point was worded to make life easy for us.'

Ron had never met Sir Hugh Cuthbertson, who was head of MI6 and Dolly's boss, but he knew him by reputation and the snippets of information Dolly had confided to him over the years. 'Thank him for me when you next see him,' he said, getting to his feet. 'To be sure that's a debt we can never repay.'

Dolly smiled up at him as she took his hand. 'He wouldn't dream of asking you to,' she replied. 'Now, go and tell Peggy. I won't be here when you return, but I'll see you tomorrow.'

'Will you be staying with us?'

She shook her head. 'I'll be with Pauline. She's yet to reply to my letter, and I suspect she's not too happy with me at the moment, so I have to try and smooth things over.'

Ron had only a vague idea of what she was talking about because he hadn't really been listening when Peggy had told him about the to-do with the American general down in Devon. 'To be sure, wee Peggy will be glad of your presence,' he sighed. 'The poor lass has enough on her plate at the moment.'

Dolly nodded her understanding, and Ron left the hospital, his emotions all over the place. He was delighted that Danuta was on the road to recovery, but how to tell Peggy – how to explain the terrible injuries? He should have asked Dolly, he realised, as he grabbed Harvey by the collar and dragged him away from a huge slice of chocolate cake someone had carelessly left on a low table.

Harvey wasn't too pleased about this, but then saw a rabbit loping across the lawn and shot off in pursuit.

'Heathen beast,' Ron muttered fondly. 'I wish my life was that uncomplicated.'

*

Peggy and the others had come in from the garden as the sun disappeared behind thickening clouds and the wind strengthened. It looked as if they were in for yet another cold, wet night, but the turn in the weather hadn't stopped the fighters and bombers, for they'd continued their seemingly endless raids right through the day.

Peggy's mood had lightened as she'd played with Daisy and her dolls. The kitchen was quiet but for the soft background music from the wireless as she waited for the early evening news, and she was feeling very content. But Rita had become bored with sitting about doing nothing, so she and Ivy had gone down to the fire station to see Andy and the others and spend a bit of time in idle chat, taking some rock buns they'd bought from a bring-and-buy fund-raising event.

Sarah had gone upstairs to write letters, and Fran was at the kitchen table darning her black stockings, which she'd need when she went on night duty the following afternoon. Cordelia had fallen asleep over her library book, her spectacles askew on her nose, her hearing aid switched off because of the racket the planes were making.

Harvey came galloping into the quiet haven like a whirlwind and joyfully tried to lick everyone, startling Cordelia awake and knocking over his water bowl, and making the cat arch her back and hiss at him.

'For goodness' sake, Harvey,' said Peggy, getting up to clear the mess from the floor and having to fight him off as he tried to climb all over her. 'Will you calm down and behave?' She eyed him more closely as he sat and panted. 'What's that in your whiskers? What have you been eating now?'

'It's chocolate cake,' said Ron, stomping up from the cellar. 'I wouldn't be at all surprised if he was sick before the day's out. He's been stuffing himself silly.'

'Where on earth did he get hold of chocolate cake?' gasped Peggy.

'At the Memorial.' Ron threw his cap onto the table. 'The patients seem to think he needs feeding up.'

Peggy stared at him in puzzlement. 'What were you doing up there?'

'I was visiting someone,' he said, helping himself to a rock bun and sharing it with Daisy, who'd come to lean against his knee.

'Don't eat that,' said Peggy sharply. 'We've saved you roast dinner, and it'll spoil your appetite.'

Ron's eyebrows shot up. 'Roast dinner? Since when?'

Peggy explained as she heated up the gravy and took the plate out of the warming oven. Placing it in front of him, she grinned. 'There. You weren't expecting that, were you? And don't give any to Harvey, he's got his here,' she added, putting the bowl down for the dog.

Ron beamed back at her and tucked in.

Peggy sat down and watched him eat, delighted that he was enjoying this surprise gift. She waited until he was mopping up the last of the gravy and juice with some bread, and then asked, 'So, who were you visiting up there?'

He finished eating, and with a sigh of great pleasure, pushed his plate away and began to fill his pipe. 'To be sure that was a feast, Peggy. There's nothing better than one of your roasts.'

'Ivy and Rita cooked it,' she replied, almost dismissively, before repeating her question.

'I was visiting our little Danuta,' he said, 'and before you get into a tizzy, you should know that she's on the mend.'

Peggy was shocked into silence, and it was Fran who piped up. 'What's Danuta doing up there, Ron? It's a service personnel hospital, and she's a civilian.'

Ron got his pipe going and puffed clouds of sweet-scented smoke into the kitchen. 'She got injured during a bombing raid, and had to be transferred there so the specialist surgeons could deal with her,' he said smoothly.

'How did you know she was there?' Fran continued. She remembered Danuta very well from her stay at Beach View, and the struggle she'd had getting a job at the Cliffehaven General despite the fact she was a qualified theatre nurse.

'A pal of mine told me,' he replied.

'How badly injured is she?' demanded Cordelia.

'Quite seriously,' he admitted. 'But the doctors at the Memorial are the best, and she'll recover, although it might take a bit of time.'

'How long has she been there?' Peggy was close to tears.

'A few days,' said Ron, not quite meeting her steady gaze. 'She was very poorly when she was first admitted, and I didn't want to worry you in case ...'

'In case she didn't pull through?' Peggy's anger rose swiftly to the surface and she glared at him. 'How *dare* you keep this from me, Ronan Reilly? You know how much I care for that girl, but you kept all this to yourself. Would you have bothered to tell me if she'd died, or were you planning to keep that secret too?'

'Now, Peggy, girl, there's no need to take on so,' he protested. 'Of course I would have told you.'

'But in your own good time – like everything else,' she stormed. 'Honestly, Ron, there are times when I could throttle you.'

She shoved back from the table, glanced at the clock and slumped down again. 'And now it's too late to visit today,' she said in exasperation. 'The poor little love must think I've deserted her, being in Cliffehaven all this time and none of us have visited her. How could you be so cruel not to tell me earlier?'

Ron abandoned his pipe and gently took hold of Peggy's arms, drawing her closer. ''Tis sorry I am I've upset you, wee girl,' he said softly. 'But it was not done purposely. Danuta only woke today, and she's asked for you. So go and get your coat, and I'll ring Fred the Fish and see if he'll give us a lift up there.'

'But it's gone visiting time,' Peggy managed.

'Danuta's a very special girl,' he replied. 'We can visit her any time we want.'

'She must be, if Matron Billings has agreed to that,' said Fran briskly. 'The old witch is the last person to bend the rules.'

'Aye, well, Matron Billings has had direct orders from some of Danuta's very well-placed friends, and even she has to obey them,' said Ron, leaving the table to telephone his old pal Fred.

Fran frowned and looked to Peggy and Cordelia for enlightenment. 'What friends? I thought she was working at St George's Hospital in London?'

Peggy shrugged, unable to reveal her knowledge of Danuta's dangerous missions in enemy territory. 'I neither know nor care,' she replied. 'I'm just thankful that she's alive and well enough to ask for me.' She slipped on her coat and hunted out her best shoes. 'Do you both want to come with us?'

'You go, dear,' said Cordelia, clearly upset by Ron's revelation. 'I'll get Bertie to drive me over when she's feeling up to having more people around her.'

Fran was still looking puzzled as she shook her head, making her copper curls bounce on her shoulders. 'I'll stay and put Daisy to bed. I can get a lift from the General and pop over there tomorrow before I have to be on duty.'

Peggy sat squashed between Fred the Fish and Ron in the rather smelly van, her handbag clasped on her lap, her pulse racing as they rattled up the steep road and turned into the hospital driveway. She hadn't been up here since Kitty had been a patient, but she knew Danuta couldn't have been in a better place to recover.

She was tense, eager to see the girl, but trying hard not to imagine what might have happened to her to bring her here, for the last she'd heard of Danuta, the girl was in Germany, helping to rescue the Allied airmen who had been shot down – so it was unlikely she'd fallen victim to an air raid over here. But whatever the reason she was here, it was now her turn to repay the girl for her bravery, and to reassure and mother her, and provide the peace and love she'd need to recover.

Fred stayed in the van, and promised to wait for as long as they needed.

Peggy and Ron hurried through those familiar corridors, passing men and women on crutches or in wheelchairs, the remembered odours of boiled cabbage and antiseptic unavoidable.

Ron quietly opened the door, and after peeking in, stood aside to let Peggy enter.

Peggy's heart was thudding as she tiptoed into the deeply shadowed room and approached the bed. She gave an involuntary gasp as she saw the bruises and bandages, and had to cover her mouth with her hand. 'Oh, Danuta,' she said softly. 'Oh, my darling, sweet girl, what happened to you?'

Danuta opened her eyes – eyes filled with pain and the horrors she'd seen – and then she let out a sigh and reached up her arms to Peggy. 'Mama Peggy,' she whispered. 'Mama, I come home to you.'

Peggy's tears pricked her eyes as she tenderly held the girl to her heart. 'I'm here, darling. I'm here.'

Ron quietly left the room. They didn't need anyone but each other for now.

13

Burma

There had been skirmishes and ambushes from the moment they'd scaled that riverside cliff. The fighting had been fierce on both sides, and although they'd wiped out several rats' nests of Japanese, some of their number had been killed or wounded.

However, despite this, Jim was getting a real sense of this strange and beautiful country into which he'd been thrust. Blue-hazed mountains soared above lush, jungle-clad valleys where hidden villages of bamboo huts lay by crystal-clear rushing rivers that fed into neat paddy fields. Unfamiliar bird calls were accompanied by the tinkling of tiny bells in ornate little pagodas bedecked in frangipani and smelling of burning incense, while saffron-robed Buddhist monks walked barefoot from village to village, and long-horned cattle cropped contentedly as white egrets hitched a lift on their backs to feast on the ticks and flies they found there.

The people were slender and brown-skinned, the men mostly bare-chested with a wide length of brightly coloured cloth wrapped around their waist to fall to their ankles. The women were elegant in their sarongs – or *longyi* – daintily modest in small white tops as they moved to some slow inner rhythm which made them almost glide along as they carried baskets of produce on their heads in the heat of the day. It all looked so peaceful, but Jim knew the Japs often hid out in those villages, bringing death, destruction, and often slavery to these gentle people who'd been caught up in a war that was not of their making.

The mountain range Jim and the rest of the long column had just negotiated led to a broad valley which ran for approximately forty miles north towards another precipitous mountain. This valley was almost entirely smothered in jungle except for a few scattered Burmese villages and the cultivated areas around them.

Morale was high amongst the men, for the time for games of hide and seek with the enemy was over, and the Chindits had been ordered to engage and drive out the Japanese in a series of ambushes, and make it impossible for them to use the area by destroying their communications, arms dumps and vehicles. It was what they'd trained for and why they'd borne the privations and effort to get here, so each man was ready and eager to get to work, bring the fight to the enemy and rout him once and for all.

The idea was to let the enemy know they were there in force, heavily armed and ready to fight, so they set off at a deliberately fast and noisy pace to intimidate the already disorganised and fleeing Japs.

It would take three days to reach the end of the valley, where they would set up operations at the foot of the towering mountain.

As the long column of men, mules and horses progressed boldly along the single road that had been carved through the valley, Jim could see the villagers working knee-deep in the water of the paddy fields, bent at the waist beneath large conical hats woven from strips of bamboo as they planted the green shoots of rice. At the sound of their approach the villagers stopped and stared at them – first in fear, and then in awe, some of the dainty and very pretty girls shyly waving and smiling before they returned to their work, their babies secure in slings on their backs.

Jim rather fancied the hats, and could probably have purchased one for a few annas, but there was no time to stop, and it would just be one more thing to carry. The brightly patterned *longyis* the women wore were pretty too, and he wondered momentarily what Peggy would look like in one – and then dismissed the idea. The hats and sarongs suited this place and these people – and neither Peggy nor Cliffehaven were ready for such exotic things.

Having reached the end of the valley, their commander set up a temporary HQ, arranged for the first supply drop, and after a brief rest, ordered Jim's column to attack the Japanese posts to the west which had been sighted by air intelligence. The idea was to keep the Japs occupied during the next three days of air drops but to avoid getting pinned down.

Jim, Ernie and Big Bert eagerly followed their senior officer in Indian file into the dense black jungle of a starless black night. Jim could hear the man walking in front of him, and the breathing of the man behind, the creak of mule harness and the clink of metal on metal – but although his night vision was usually very good, he was virtually blind in what felt like an endless void of utter darkness.

They were closing in on the co-ordinates given to them by air-recon, so they walked more slowly, alert and ready for action.

And then all hell broke loose at the head of the column. Explosions ripped through the jungle in great flashes of blinding light to rain dirt and debris down on him as stuttering bursts of gunfire opened up, the bullets zinging in from all directions as the Bren guns roared and shook the earth beneath his feet.

Jim dropped to his belly, firing into the jungle at the unseen enemy, trying to gauge by the flash of his gun where he was hiding, when a terrified mule broke free and almost trampled him in its crazed bid for escape.

Jim lobbed a grenade into the jungle and followed it up with a long burst of rapid fire, aware that the man next to him had slumped against him and was probably dead.

He swiftly reloaded and pumped more bullets towards the few flashes of light that were still coming out of the all-enveloping darkness, and then, as suddenly as it had begun, it was over.

The call for cease-fire went down the line and everyone slowly got to their feet to check on their wounded and mop up any surviving Japs who might still be lurking. Jim counted three dead, including the man who'd fallen beside him, and one of the mule handlers. The one wounded man would have to be strapped on horseback and sent back to the temporary HQ to be ferried out after the supply drops – how long he'd last was anyone's guess, for he'd taken a belly shot, which usually proved fatal.

Jim breathed a sigh of relief when he heard Ernie and Big Bert talking nearby, and then took the dead men's identity tags and handed them to his senior officer before covering the bodies as best he could in palm leaves and jungle debris. There was no time to dig graves, however shallow, but their final resting place would be marked as a co-ordinate on a map for those back at HQ, who would do the debriefing after the operation and inform the next of kin.

The men returned from the Japanese hideout to report no survivors, so after the padre had said a swift prayer over the makeshift graves, everyone gathered up their weapons and ammunition and continued their march, aware of the rattle of gunfire and the thuds of explosions in the distance. It was going to be a long three days, but Jim's blood was up and he was ready for anything.

14

Peggy had spent an hour with Danuta, but for most of that time she'd merely held her hand and watched her sleep. She was glad the girl knew she was there and that no harm would come to her, but on her return home, Peggy had spent a restless night, worrying about her.

It had broken her heart to see Danuta looking so frail and small in that hospital bed, but despite what she must have gone through, there was still a light of determination in her green eyes when she spoke, which gave Peggy hope that she would pull through.

She opened her eyes, stretched and then turned to look at the photograph of Jim she'd placed on the bedside table the day he'd left for India. 'I wish you were here, my love,' she whispered. 'I miss you so, and it's been ages since I heard from you.'

He smiled back at her and she felt such yearning to hold him that it was almost a physical pain which she curled into beneath the bedclothes.

'Mumma? Mumma wake now?'

Peggy swiftly pulled her emotions in order and turned to smile at Daisy, who no longer needed the sides up on her cot and had got into the habit of clambering onto the bed at Adolf's first raucous crow. 'Yes, darling, I'm awake,' she replied, pulling her daughter to her and holding her soft, warm little body close, needing this loving contact to counteract her loneliness for Jim.

Daisy put up with this for less than a minute and then pushed away to slide back off the bed. 'I hungry, Mumma. Want beckfist.'

Peggy's precious moment was over, and she reluctantly got out of bed to glance at the clock and prepare for another long, busy day. The planes were noisy again, even at this hour, and her pulse beat a little bit faster in the hope that the invasion may have begun.

Yet, as she got herself and Daisy washed and dressed, Peggy wondered how on earth she was going to fit everything in today. She couldn't afford to miss part of her shift again, and certainly didn't want to let Solly down after he'd been so kind in giving her the job in the first place – but she was determined to visit Danuta at some point, for the thought of her being alone up at the hospital was just too much to bear after all the girl had been through.

'I wish I still had my car,' she muttered as she pulled a brush through her tangled curls. 'It would make life so much easier.' She had a fleeting hope that maybe Doris might lend her the Austin, and instantly dismissed it. They were barely talking, and after yesterday, she didn't feel like going cap in hand asking for a favour, only to be shown the door with a flea in her ear.

Once she and Daisy were ready, Peggy looked in on Cordelia to see if she wanted help getting down the stairs. She was getting very unsteady on her feet, and Peggy constantly worried that she might take a nasty tumble.

'I can manage perfectly well,' Cordelia said rather huffily. 'Please don't fuss, Peggy. You have enough to do without running about after me.' As if to prove the point, she headed purposefully for the stairs and, with one hand gripping the banisters, the other grasping her walking stick, she negotiated each stair with great care until she reached the hall.

'Well, that's not right,' she said crossly. 'Where's my newspaper, and what happened to the early post?'

'The paper boy must have slept in,' said Peggy. She was still trying to get used to Cordelia not being at her best first thing in the morning when she'd once been so bright and lively. 'Perhaps there's no mail for anyone today,' she added wistfully.

'It's simply not good enough,' Cordelia snapped. 'I can't eat breakfast without my newspaper and crossword.'

'We'll just have to make do with the news on the wireless until it's delivered,' Peggy said placatingly.

'I don't like the wireless news,' grumbled Cordelia. 'It's always so gloomy.'

Peggy bit down on a smile as she followed her into the kitchen to find that Sarah was just finishing her breakfast, and Ron was feeding Harvey and Queenie. The wireless was on, but there were still a few minutes to go before the eight o'clock news bulletin.

Ron frowned at Cordelia, who rather pointedly turned off her hearing aid and glared back at him. 'What's got into her this morning?'

'No paper and no post,' replied Peggy, settling Daisy on her cushion so she could reach the table.

'There was some post,' said Sarah quietly. 'But both letters were for me.' She put her hand on Peggy's shoulder. 'I'm sorry, Peggy. I know how much you wanted to hear from Jim and the others.'

Peggy felt a bit put out that she still hadn't had anything from Jim – or, for that matter, from Anne or the boys, despite the fact she'd written to them nearly every day. 'There's no need to feel sorry, Sarah,' she replied. 'There's always the afternoon delivery. Perhaps I'll get something then.'

She watched the girl pull on her coat, ready for the long tramp over the hills to Cliffe, and was tempted to ask if her letters had come from Delaney – then decided it was none of her business. 'It must be quiet up there now all the Americans have gone,' she said instead.

'It is a bit, and there's talk that the Women's Timber Corps will be moving to another site very soon. The forest at Cliffe has been thinned enough, and what's left must be preserved to encourage new growth.'

Peggy stared up at her in confusion 'But where would they go? And would you have to go with them?'

Sarah shrugged. 'Nothing's decided yet, but the possibility of Scotland has been mentioned.'

'Scotland! You can't possibly go all the way to Scotland,' protested Peggy.

Sarah giggled. 'I have no intention of doing so. This is my home now for the duration, and if they do move on, I'll find work in another office in town.'

'Well, thank goodness for that,' breathed Peggy. 'I couldn't bear the thought of losing you.'

Sarah kissed her cheek. 'The feeling is mutual,' she murmured. 'Now, I'd better be off, or I'll be late. At least the weather seems to have improved a bit.'

Ron turned up the volume on the wireless just as Sarah was about to go down the steps to the basement, and as the announcer's excited voice came into the room, she turned back and sat down at the table, making urgent winding signs to Cordelia to turn on her hearing aid.

'Early this morning it was revealed that the German troops had been ordered to withdraw from the city of Rome, and to defend it against the advancing Allies outside the city's walls. Despite dogged resistance from the Germans, the first American soldiers of the Fifth Army reached the centre of the city late last night,' said the announcer.

The occupants of Peggy's kitchen held hands in awed silence as he continued, his excitement clear in his usually calm and measured tone.

'Rome is the first of the three Axis powers' capitals to be taken and its recapture will be seen as a significant victory for the Allies and for Lieutenant General Mark Clark, the American commanding officer who led the final offensive.

'The people of Rome have poured into the streets to cheer and wave and throw bunches of flowers at the victorious liberators who are even now parading through the city. The Romans also massed in great numbers in St Peter's Square, to call on Pope Pious to give the victors and the citizens of Rome his blessing.

'The Pope has now appeared on the balcony to address the throng and give thanks that the holy city of Rome with its irreplaceable treasures and ancient buildings has been saved from destruction by the agreement on both sides that the battle should be fought outside its walls.

'First reports from the city say it has been left largely undamaged by the occupying German forces. The water supply is still intact and there is even electricity – recent blackouts are reported to have been caused by engineers reluctant to restore power for the occupiers. Most Romans remained in the city during the occupation and many refugees also fled there, consequently food supplies are now extremely short, so the Americans' first task is to set up food and medical stations throughout the city.

'In a broadcast from the United States, President Roosevelt welcomed the fall of Rome with the words, "One up, two to go." But he gave a warning that Germany had not yet suffered enough losses to cause total collapse to the regime – and this seems to be borne out by a defiant statement from Hitler's headquarters in which he said that "the struggle in Italy will be continued with unshakeable determination to break the enemy and forge final victory for Germany and her allies".

'The American military authorities in London have paid tribute to the British General Sir Harold Alexander, who has been in overall command of Allied forces in Italy, describing the campaign as daring, unconventional and brilliant.'

Peggy gathered up a bewildered Daisy and smothered her face in kisses as Cordelia and Sarah hugged. 'I can hardly believe it,' she breathed. 'Oh, Ron, this is only the start of it, I'm sure, and once the invasion goes ahead it will be Paris next – and then Berlin.'

'Aye, it's a great victory, so it is, but don't get too carried away, Peggy, girl. There's a long way to go yet, and by the sound of it Hitler's nowhere near ready to surrender.'

Peggy would not allow his pessimism to spoil her joy, so she clasped his grizzled face between her hands and gave him a resounding kiss. 'Don't be such an old grump,' she teased. 'The Allies are in Rome, the sun is shining and—'

'You're going to be late for work,' he interjected, his blue eyes twinkling.

'Oh, lawks, so I am,' she gasped, grabbing Daisy's coat.

'Before you go rushing off, there are things I need to tell you.'

'What things?' She paused in the act of getting Daisy into her coat and shoes, a prickle of fear threading down her spine.

'I'll be visiting Danuta in the mornings and for a short while each afternoon, and I've arranged for someone to drive you up there at the end of your shift. As Rita and Ivy are taking over the cooking and so on, there's no need for you to be rushing about in a tizzy and worrying about everything.'

Peggy had been so sure it would be something bad he had to tell her that she slumped in relief that Ron at last seemed to have turned over a new leaf and was being more thoughtful and caring than before Rosie's departure. 'But what about Daisy?' she fretted. 'Danuta isn't well enough for me to take her up there.'

'Fred's Lil will mind her, so you're to stop worrying, d'you hear?'

'Oh, dear,' she muttered. 'I hate causing so much bother to everyone.'

'Go to work, Peg,' he said firmly.

Peggy and Sarah left the house together and parted company at the gate. Peggy felt as if she had wings on her heels as she and Daisy walked down Camden Road, and it seemed the happy mood had infected everyone, for there were smiles and waves and even laughter in the endless queues outside the shops. She cheerfully replied to the greetings, and waved to Fred the Fish and Alf the butcher as she passed on her way to the factory.

Peggy left Daisy in the nursery and hurried into the factory to find that the happy atmosphere had lightened the usual dull Monday morning feeling, making the chatter and laughter louder as the wireless blared out.

'It's wonderful news, isn't it?' enthused a radiant Gracie as they hung up their coats. 'Today Rome – tomorrow Paris!'

'That's what I said,' replied Peggy, 'but Ron doesn't seem to think it will be that easy.'

'It'll be easy if we get on with this blessed invasion,' grumbled Gracie. 'Once our troops are in France, Hitler won't stand a chance of keeping Paris.'

'Oh, I do so hope you're right.' Peggy pushed through the cloakroom door and into the main body of the factory to be met by a wall of noise from the machines, the wireless and the loud chatter and laughter of the machinists, cutters, loaders and warehouse staff.

'We'll talk at break time,' shouted Gracie. 'Solly's promised everyone an iced bun as a treat to celebrate the victory.'

Peggy grinned and nodded before quickly heading for her machine. The thought that this war might soon be over battled with the delicious anticipation of an iced bun – the likes of which hadn't been seen at Beach View for years – and she sat down with a will to begin her shift.

Whether it was the happy atmosphere, the rising hope for the future or the enticement of that bun, it seemed that everyone worked with a greater will that morning. The buns duly arrived from Solly's cousin's bakery in time for elevenses, still warm from the oven, the icing sweet and deliciously gooey.

Every woman gazed in awe at the heavily laden baker's trays and almost reverently chose a bun and took as long as they could to savour every crumb as a beaming Solly took over the vast canteen urn and saluted the victory with a mug of tea.

The excitement of the day had dwindled, the sweetness only just still lingering in her mouth as Peggy finally cut the thread on her twenty-fifth pair of bell-bottoms and sank back in her chair to ease her stiff neck and shoulders. She'd worked like a Trojan and the hours had flown, but it would be several more hours before she could really rest and take in the enormous events of the day.

'Do you have time for a cuppa before you go up to the hospital, Peg?' asked Gracie, who'd heard all about Peggy's one-time lodger and her terrible injuries caused by bomb-blast during their lunch break.

'I would have loved a cuppa, but someone's picking me up, so I daren't keep them waiting.' She gave Gracie a quick hug, waved goodbye to the other girls and hurried off to fetch Daisy from the nursery.

Fred's van was waiting outside the gates, and she smiled at Lil as she approached. Lil was a tiny woman, born in the East End, and very protective of her Fred, who was a bit inclined to flirt – quite harmlessly as it happened – with his female customers. She put up with most things, like his gambling and fondness for a pint or three, but woe betide any woman who dared to overstep the mark.

Lil could often be quite fierce but she had a heart of gold, and despite the pair of them being in their sixties, they'd taken in four little brothers who'd been orphaned during a particularly nasty bombing raid. Fred was a big, bluff man who adored her, but he was also terrified of her finding out some of the things he and Ron had got up to over the years – a misguided fear, for Lil knew everything and only chose to use that knowledge when it suited her.

Lil climbed out of the van and hugged Peggy before picking up Daisy and making her laugh as she whirled her around. 'Come on, gel,' she said, climbing back into the van. 'You sit on Aunty Lil's lap for the ride home. And when we gets there you got the boys to play with, and some lovely fish for yer tea.'

Peggy frowned. 'Er, I thought Fred was driving me up to the Memorial?'

Lil laughed and shook her bottle-blonde curls. 'Lawks, love, you don't wanna be going visiting in this smelly old thing.' She jabbed her thumb over her shoulder. 'You got a posh ride and won't end up stinking of fish.'

Peggy looked behind the van and saw a small black Austin purring at the kerb. The low sun was glinting on the windscreen, so she couldn't see the driver until she climbed out.

'Dolly! What on earth are you doing here?'

Dolly grinned. 'I bumped into Ron, and he told me about the girl and your need of a lift each evening. So here I am – your chauffeur at your service.'

Dolly gave her a tremendous hug and Peggy caught a hint of expensive perfume.

'I'm actually down here to see how Pauline is after she got my letter and didn't reply to it,' Dolly said. 'She all but showed me the door,' she added with a delicate grimace, 'but she'll find she can't get rid of me that easily.'

'Good for you,' said Peggy, climbing in beside her, delighted but rather flabbergasted by her friend's unexpected appearance. 'She came to see me and was thoroughly beside herself about it all.'

She regarded Dolly who, as usual, looked younger than her years, was beautifully dressed, and radiant with happiness. 'It's a shame she can't see beyond her nose,' Peggy said, 'because it's so obvious you're blossoming now you and Felix can be together.'

Dolly chuckled. 'I feel about sixteen,' she admitted, 'and with Carol being so very sweet and forgiving about everything, I count myself one of the luckiest women in England – if not the world.'

She switched on the engine and checked her appearance in the rear-view mirror. 'It's ripping news about Rome, isn't it? Such a romantic city,' she sighed before grinning impishly. 'But the men are simply outrageous, pinching one's bottom at every opportunity. I remember I ended up so bruised, I could barely sit down for a week.'

Peggy laughed. 'You're such a tonic, Dolly. I do wish you weren't living so far away.'

'Well, I'll be here for a while, so we must make the most of it while we can.' Dolly engaged the gears and shot off down Camden Road to screech around the corner into the High Street, scattering a gossiping group of women who were ambling across the road.

'Dolly, you're going to kill someone in a minute,' warned Peggy, holding onto her seat for dear life as Dolly swerved to avoid a drunk who'd staggered out of the Crown and into the road. 'Please slow down. I'd like to get there in one piece.'

Dolly slowed for about three seconds, and having driven over the humpback bridge, put her foot on the accelerator again. 'Ron told me about the girl you're visiting. It's terrible what damage can be done during a bombing raid. It sounds to me as if she was very lucky to escape with her life.'

'It'll take a long time for her to recover,' Peggy replied, still holding onto her seat as they went roaring up the steep hill towards the hospital. 'But she'll have a home with me when she does.'

'Poor child,' murmured Dolly around the cigarette she was lighting with one hand while she steered with the other. 'I understand she has no one left of her family back in Poland.'

'They were killed before she came over here looking for her brother.'

'Well, she's lucky to have you, Peggy. You're a wonderful woman and a brilliant mother – far better than I ever could be.'

Peggy didn't know how to answer, so said nothing. Dolly adored Carol and Pauline, but she'd left them with her parents while they were still very young, realising she'd be hopeless at providing the best and most stable upbringing. Dolly was an enigma, for she was bright, intelligent and probably the best, most discreet friend Peggy had. But no one knew anything about her life, and somehow, Peggy couldn't imagine her settling into quiet retirement down in Bournemouth.

'How's life in Bournemouth?' Peggy asked.

'Boring,' said Dolly, flicking cigarette ash out of the quarter-light. 'But I do have some fun tweaking the noses of those dreadfully snobbish women at the WI.'

'I can imagine,' said Peggy dryly. 'Whatever made you want to join them in the first place?'

Dolly shrugged. 'I thought I should do my bit – and I have learnt how to make jam and sponge cake.'

Peggy laughed. 'Good grief,' she spluttered. 'I never thought I'd hear the like.'

Dolly chuckled. 'I didn't say I was any good at it – but I gave it a go just to show willing.' She drove at speed through the hospital entrance and screeched to a halt on the gravel drive, sending a splatter of small stones across a nearby flower bed.

'I'll wait here for you – perhaps have a wander about to see what the place is like. Take your time, Peggy, I'm in no rush to get back to my sour-faced daughter and poor bewildered Frank.'

'You could come in and meet Danuta if you'd like,' offered Peggy.

Dolly shook her head. 'Perhaps when she's feeling better. There's nothing worse than having to be polite to strangers when one doesn't feel like being any such thing.'

Peggy hurried off and was soon entering Danuta's quiet room. The girl was sleeping, and Nurse Hopkins was sitting by the bed making notes in a folder.

'Hello, Susan,' Peggy whispered. 'How's our girl doing today?'

'She had a restless night, Peggy, so the doctor ordered some stronger medication. I doubt she'll wake for some hours, but I'm sure that if you sit and talk to her, she'll know you're there.'

Peggy thanked her and sat down as Susan Hopkins quietly left the room. Danuta was breathing evenly, and her skin felt cool, so she didn't have a temperature, and it seemed that any infection was being fought by the strong medication that was slowly being fed into her by tubes.

'I expect you've already heard from Ron, but there's been some wonderful news today,' Peggy began softly. 'Rome has fallen to the Allies. Everyone is expecting the invasion to come any day now, and then we will take Paris and drive on into the heart of Berlin.'

Peggy felt very emotional as she touched the girl's bandaged hand. 'And it's all because of the wonderfully brave things you and people like you have been doing over there, my darling. I'm so very proud of you.'

Danuta's fingers twitched beneath Peggy's gentle hand, and that was when she knew the girl could hear and understand her despite the heavy medication. Encouraged, she carried on talking for almost an hour before kissing her goodnight and returning to Dolly.

15

Ron dodged out of the way and softly but firmly booted Adolf up his tail feathers as he tried to attack him for the second time. Closing the gate on the enclosure, he exchanged glares with the vicious old tyrant.

'To be sure you were named well,' Ron muttered. 'And once we've got your namesake defeated, I shall take great pleasure in wringing your ruddy neck.'

Adolf's coxcomb bristled and he strutted off before flying onto the roof of the coop and emitting a series of loud, defiant crows as his hens pecked greedily at the food Ron had scattered on the ground.

Ron clasped the bowl of eggs – there were only three today – and looked up at the massed flight of Flying Fortresses, Lancaster bombers, Tornadoes, Spitfires and Hurricanes. They'd been thundering overhead since before dawn with a definite air of purpose and in greater numbers than usual, their fuselages unusually painted with broad stripes; wing and tail lights blazing even though it was daylight.

Something was definitely up. Ron could feel it in his bones, and with a growing sense of excitement he went indoors, switched on the wireless and then hurried out to the front of the house and along the cul-de-sac until he had a clear view down the hill to the Channel.

The sight took his breath away and made his heart thud with pride. Bombers, heavy transporters, fighters and even gliders were amassing from all directions and heading towards the French coast, their vast numbers stretching across the sky as far as the eye could see, lights flashing as they blocked out the sun and cast deep shadows over the calm Channel waters.

Thousands of battleships, corvettes, motor gun boats, motor torpedo boats, minesweepers, cruisers, tank and troop carriers were dark smudges out on the horizon, and the echoes of heavy bombardment carried across the Channel as bright flashes of gunfire were followed by oily plumes of black smoke rising above the distant shore.

'It's started, Harvey,' he breathed, stroking the dog's head. 'It really has begun.'

Harvey barked and wagged his tail, clearly confused by Ron's odd behaviour at this time of the morning, but he seemed to catch his excitement, and his barking became more enthusiastic as he chased after Ron, who'd raced up the steps and back into the house.

'It's started,' Ron yelled, banging on Peggy's door before racing up the stairs to tell the others. 'It's started! The invasion's on!'

As the girls came onto the landing and hurried downstairs to join Peggy and Daisy, who were now standing on the front step, Ron banged on Cordelia's door. 'I hope you're decent, old girl, because I'm coming in.'

Cordelia was in her dressing gown and slippers, and after her initial shock, looked at Ron askance. 'What do you think you're doing in here? Get out at once.'

Ron snatched up her hearing aid from the bedside chest and thrust it at her. 'It's the invasion,' he yelled. 'Hurry up, or you'll miss it.'

'I can't hear a word you're saying,' she retorted, fiddling with the hearing aid and almost dropping it.

'God love you, woman, you'll be the death of me,' Ron groaned, sweeping her up into his arms and hurrying down the stairs.

'Put me down this instant, you great bully,' Cordelia protested, wriggling furiously in his arms. 'This is most indecent, and I will not stand for it, do you hear?'

'To be sure 'tis not me that's deaf,' he grumbled good-naturedly, carrying her across the hall and out to join the others on the front step.

Cordelia stopped struggling. 'What is it? What's happened?' she asked, her voice rising in excitement.

Ron carried her down the steps and along the cul-de-sac before gently setting her on her feet. 'Look,' he said, pointing to the skies and the plumes of smoke rising beyond the mass of warships.

'Oh,' she breathed through her fingers. 'Oh, my goodness. So it's happening at last.' She turned to

Ron, still trying to get the volume on her hearing aid at a comfortable level. 'Why didn't you tell me instead of grabbing hold of me in that rough fashion?'

Ron wiggled his eyebrows and grinned. 'You know you enjoyed it, so stop complaining and watch the show.'

Cordelia huffed and drew the collar of her dressing gown tightly to her chin, but she soon forgot to be cross as she stood with the others to watch in awe as the invasion unfolded before them.

'I hope Fran isn't trapped in theatre and missing all this,' shouted a radiant Peggy above the noise. 'It's a terrific show.'

'I expect everyone's watching who can,' replied Ron, noting the swarms of people who'd gathered on the long hill that went down to the promenade, and those who were leaning out of their windows to wave flags and shout encouragement to the airmen. 'This is history in the making, Peggy, and an opportunity not to be missed.'

Peggy eased Daisy off her hip and the little girl clapped her hands and danced about in delight, laughing and waving to the planes while Harvey, not to be outdone, dashed back and forth barking excitedly.

They stood there in their nightclothes watching for almost half an hour, and then Peggy glanced at her watch. 'The news will be on soon,' she said. 'Let's go in to hear what's happening over there.'

Ron helped Cordelia up the steps and they trooped indoors. The wireless had warmed up, but music was playing, so Peggy put the kettle on while Sarah and Ivy rushed off to get dressed for work, and Rita put bread on the hotplate for toast.

The planes were still going overhead and making the most fearful racket, so Peggy turned up the volume on the wireless, poured out the tea and quickly made sure that Cordelia hadn't got cold from being outside in her nightclothes. Tension was high, the anticipation and excitement showing in all of them as they gathered around the table, their focus on the wireless.

The music stopped, and everyone edged forward in their chairs as the announcer's voice broke the tense silence in the kitchen.

'Here is the eight o'clock news for today, Tuesday the sixth of June, read by Frederick Allen,' he began.

'Supreme Allied Headquarters have issued an urgent warning to inhabitants of the enemy-occupied countries living near the coast,' he stated solemnly. 'The warning said that a new phase in the Allied air offensive had begun. Shortly before this warning, the Germans reported that Havre, Calais and Dunkirk were being heavily bombarded and that German naval units were engaged with Allied landing craft.

'This new phase will particularly affect people living roughly within twenty-five miles of any part of the coast. The Supreme Commander of the Allied Expeditionary Force has directed that wherever possible an advance warning shall be given to the towns in which certain targets will be intensively bombed. This warning will be perhaps less than one hour in advance of the attack. The warning will be conveyed in leaflets dropped by Allied planes.'

A breathless hush filled the kitchen as the planes carried on thundering overhead and the announcer continued.

'The German news agency reported that Allied airborne troops have landed in the area of the mouth of the Seine. That Havre has been heavily bombed, and German naval forces were engaged with Allied landing craft. Calais and Dunkirk were being attacked by strong Allied bomber formations. The agency added that so far, no Allied airborne troops have been landed at these two points.'

The man paused and Peggy stilled Daisy, who was getting restless and banging a spoon on the table.

'Here is the rest of this morning's news,' said Frederick Allen.

'The latest news from Italy is that the Allied advance continues beyond the Tiber from Rome. The Italian General Bencivenga has assumed military and civil governorship on Allied authority. King Victor Emmanuel signed a decree yesterday, transferring his powers to the Crown Prince. The King now retires from public life, and his son becomes Lieutenant General of the kingdom, until the Italian people have an opportunity of deciding by free vote the country's future form of government.

'A Te Deum, in thanksgiving for the deliverance of Rome, will be sung in all Catholic churches in England and Wales next Sunday.'

Peggy made a mental note to go to the special mass, and rather hoped Ron might accompany her – but it was a forlorn wish, for he hadn't been inside a church for years unless it was for a wedding or christening.

Frederick Allen's voice broke into her thoughts. 'President Roosevelt has congratulated General Sir Henry Maitland Wilson on the splendid success in Italy, but warned that ultimate victory still lay some distance ahead. The distance would be covered in due time but the going would be tough and costly.

'In further news, last night's Russian communiqué reported another twenty-four hours of successful defence against continued German heavy attacks north and north-west of Jassy, on the Romanian Front. Red Air Force bombers carried out a concentrated attack on the railway junction and other military objectives, and dozens of fires were burning before the raid was over. The Germans have lost forty-one tanks and thirty-nine aircraft during the past twenty-four hours.'

As Frederick Allen went through the headlines again and gave further, more detailed instructions on what the citizens of enemy-held areas should do when ordered to evacuate, everyone started talking at once.

Peggy was as excited as a schoolgirl, for it seemed her prediction was right, and that before long the

Allies would be marching through the streets of Paris. She quickly finished her cooling tea, mopped Daisy's face clean of blackberry jam and carted her off to the bedroom to get them both dressed for this most auspicious of days.

Sarah and Ivy helped Cordelia upstairs shortly afterwards, all three chattering like sparrows as they discussed the news and what it might mean – while a rather more subdued and thoughtful Rita followed slowly behind them.

Ron waited until the kitchen was clear of women and then leant back in his chair and smoked his pipe. There was no doubt about it, he thought; peace was on its way, but as Roosevelt had warned, the struggle would be long and hard, and the brave young men out there in ships, tanks and planes would be called upon yet again to make terrible sacrifices.

He placed his hand on Harvey's head as the dog sat at his knee and rested his nose on his thigh. Ron understood the excitement the news had engendered – he'd felt it himself – but for the women's sake, he hoped their delight in the invasion would not bring tears. Untold numbers would be killed or maimed before peace was finally won, and with Brendon and Jack Smith caught right in the middle of this invasion, and his Jim fighting in Burma, none of them could rest easily until victory was assured.

His thoughts turned to Seamus and Joseph, the two grandsons he'd already lost. Frank and Pauline must be terrified for Brendon, for although Pauline had refused to believe it, their only surviving son was out there somewhere in the Channel taking part in the invasion. He could only hope that Dolly's presence would fortify Frank and help to keep Pauline from going over the edge – but by the sound of things, Pauline saw her mother's arrival as an unwanted intrusion, and would no doubt vent her spleen accordingly.

'As long as she doesn't come round here causing trouble,' he muttered around the stem of his pipe. 'She's the last thing Peggy needs right now.'

And then there was Anne's husband Martin, Kitty's Roger and brother Freddy along with Cissy's young pilot, Randolph Stevens. At least they were safely in the POW camp Stalag III, and not up there supporting the invading troops in their fighter planes. They'd been on the point of exhaustion when they'd been shot down and captured, but he knew that if they caught wind of today's news, each and every one would be champing at the bit in frustration that they could play no part in it.

But what of his younger son, Jim, caught up in the fierce fighting in the Far East? The Japs were on the run from India and pouring into Burma and Siam, but despite the few victories by the Americans in the Pacific, there was no hint that the arrogant emperor was about to surrender. Ron didn't know much about the Japanese, but he'd learnt enough to realise that surrender would mean loss of face – a heinous shame that could only be atoned by ritual suicide.

Ron grunted and tapped the dottle from his pipe into the ashtray on the table. When you were up against people like that, it would take a miracle to defeat them.

He said none of this to Peggy as she came bustling into the kitchen, closely followed by Sarah and Ivy. 'I'll be off to see Frank and Pauline before I go to the hospital,' he announced, fetching his coat and cap. 'Dolly will pick you up again tonight, and Lil will bring Daisy back after her tea.'

Peggy kissed his cheek. 'Thanks, Ron,' she said, still breathless with excitement. 'Give Pauline my love, and try to be nice to her. She can't help the way she is.'

Ron grimaced, dragging on his coat and ramming his cap on his head. 'I'll be back late tonight. The Anchor will be busy after all the excitement of the invasion, and without Rosie to lighten my life, it'll be hard going.'

Ron had reached the top of the track leading down into Tamarisk Bay with Harvey when he saw Dolly striding towards him in tailored slacks, light sweater and jacket, clearly out of sorts. 'Are you off to see Danuta?' she asked.

'Aye, but I was going to see Frank and Pauline first.' He regarded her quizzically. 'What's up with you on this very fine day, Dolly? I've never seen your feathers so ruffled.'

'I'd advise you to steer clear of Pauline for now,' she said darkly. 'If I stay with her much longer, I shall commit murder.'

Ron chuckled as he took in the flush on her cheeks and the brittle brightness in her lovely eyes. 'Perhaps I'll give Tamarisk Bay a miss today, then, and walk with you.'

Dolly hooked her hand into the crook of his arm and they set off across the rough grassland as the planes took off and landed at Cliffe in a never-ending stream. 'You could always stay with us, you know,' Ron told her.

She hugged his arm to her side. 'Bless you, darling Ron, that would be lovely, but I have to soldier on with Pauline for Frank's sake. He's such a lovely great bear of a man and so bewildered by her ever-changing moods. I really do worry that one day he'll have had enough of it all, and simply walk out.'

The same thing had occurred to Ron over the years, but Frank wasn't the kind of man to walk away from his responsibilities. 'He loves her despite everything,' he said, 'and I think he believes that if he sticks by her, she'll eventually come right.'

He took a deep breath and expelled it on a sigh. 'Losing those boys was her undoing, Dolly, and now Brendon's mixed up in this invasion, it's no wonder she's falling apart.'

'That's just it,' Dolly said flatly. 'She's not getting hysterical or bursting into tears every five minutes. She's showing absolutely no emotion and has stopped talking altogether. Refuses to acknowledge me or Frank and has taken to cleaning that little house to within an inch of its life. It's more worrying, actually, because I've never seen her like this before, and neither Frank nor I know how to deal with it.'

'We all have our way of coping with things that worry or frighten us,' said Ron as they reached the country lane and headed for the stone bridge.

'I know, and I suppose I should be more patient,' said Dolly ruefully. 'But there are times when I wish I could shake some sense into her.' She stopped on the bridge to look down at the crystal-clear water that raced beneath it.

'Pauline is so very different to Carol, who's coped admirably with losing her husband and baby – and the fact she was evicted from her home so the Americans could practise for today. Carol's even had the courage to accept my failings as a mother, and to forgive me for keeping Felix a secret all these years – but Pauline has seen the whole thing as a personal assault, and refuses to believe a word I say.'

Dolly lit a cigarette and watched the planes landing, refuelling and rearming before taking off again. 'There's a steely calmness in Carol that I wish Pauline shared, but I fear she's too like her father – caring only for herself and blind to the needs of those who love her.'

'Things will be better once this war is over and Brendon comes home,' soothed Ron.

'I sincerely hope so, but if Pauline thinks he'll move back in and stay with her, she's in for a shock. Brendon has really fallen for little Betty, and I suspect he might very well settle down with her in Devon.'

'I don't think he'd be that cruel, especially if you and Carol go off to stay with Felix in America,' muttered Ron. 'He'll stay a while to appease his mother, but he has a life to live, and plans for his own future with Betty – and who knows, Betty might want to leave Devon for pastures new, and a ready-made family to look out for her.'

Dolly nodded and they began to walk up the track. Despite the turmoil in the skies and out in the Channel, bees and butterflies were buzzing and flitting in the hedgerows, skylarks were singing above the meadows and the air was filled with the scent of warm earth, dry grass and wild herbs.

'You're right as always,' she conceded. 'Betty was raised in an orphanage, and so has never known what it's like to be part of a family; having you and Peggy close by will help enormously should Pauline prove to be a bit of a tricky mother-in-law.'

Ron said nothing as he watched Harvey galloping along ahead of them in pursuit of a red admiral butterfly. He rather pitied any poor girl who had Pauline as a mother-in-law – for like Doris, she'd probably resent her arrival into her son's life, seeing it as losing her boy, rather than gaining a daughter, and, ultimately, grandchildren.

However, from what he'd heard about Betty from Brendon and Peggy, the girl had fought her own battles with being abandoned at an orphanage after contracting infantile polio, and the misguided opinions of the school board which thought cripples had no part to play in the education of children. She'd won all of those fights, and would know how to deal with Pauline – he'd bet his life on it.

They finally reached the five-bar gate and headed down the manicured lawns to the broad terrace. It seemed most of the patients were taking advantage of the fine morning, for wheelchairs were clustered together as the occupants discussed the news of the landings with the nurses and orderlies who were assisting the amputees and the blinded.

'It's when you see things like this that you want this war over and done with as quickly as possible,' murmured Dolly as they approached. 'So many young lives already ruined, and who's to say how many more there'll be before we have peace?'

'How come you managed to get down here with all that's going on?' asked Ron.

'I promised Hugh I'd be back by the end of the week.' She shot Ron a wry smile. 'He's very under-standing when it really matters, and I suspect he's as relieved as I am that Danuta's home and on the mend.'

'I'm sure he is,' said Ron, weaving through the wheelchairs on his way to the double doors that led into the building. 'But there is the rather vital matter of finding out who betrayed her – which I suspect is the main purpose of his largesse.'

Dolly stopped in the doorway, her expression solemn. 'That's always been the priority, Ron, but the debriefing can only begin when she's clear of mind and well enough to answer all the questions we have.'

'Is the suspect one of yours, do you think?'

Dolly's expression was giving nothing away as she regarded him silently and then headed for Danuta's room.

Ron let her go on ahead, promising to catch up in a few minutes. He had a question of his own to ask – one that had been bothering him ever since his first visit to see Danuta. Now it was time to ask the only person who might give him a straight answer.

Before leaving for work, Peggy had made sure Cordelia was dressed and back downstairs, and that Rita was coping with the knowledge that her father, Jack, was more than likely embroiled in the landings. The girl was clearly making a stoic effort to put on a brave face, and was planning to spend the morning at the fire station.

Peggy headed for the factory, her loyalties torn between her duty to Solly and the needs of Rita and those who relied on her for comfort and mothering in this new and rather frightening turn in the war. The planes were still going back and forth in endless succession, but the thunder and roar of their engines was like a heartbeat, drumming away, each throb bringing this war nearer to an end.

She held Daisy's hand as they walked along the pavement, waving and smiling to friends and acquaintances along the way, not daring to stop and chat as it was getting very close to the start of her shift.

Having deposited a happy Daisy at the nursery, she exchanged a few words with Nanny Pringle, who was positively beaming as she told Peggy there would be jelly and ice cream for the children at lunchtime thanks to Solly's wife Rachel.

The atmosphere in the factory was a little less light-hearted than it had been the day before because so many of the women had husbands, brothers, sons and lovers in the forces that were taking part in the invasion – and suddenly the war, and the very real danger they were in, was too close for comfort. There was an underlying sense of excitement that this could be the end of the war, but on the whole, the women were careful not to get too carried away, and set to work, always on the alert for the next news bulletin.

It came at midday and utter silence fell throughout the factory as John Snagge's mellow voice announced a special bulletin.

'D-Day has come,' he said. 'Early this morning the Allies began the assault on the north-western face of Hitler's European fortress. The first official news came just after half-past nine when Supreme Headquarters of the Allied Expeditionary Force – usually called SHAEF from its initials – issued communiqué number one. This said, "Under the command of General Eisenhower, Allied naval forces supported by strong air forces began landing

Allied armies this morning on the northern coast of France."

'It was announced a little later that General Montgomery is in command of the army group carrying out the assault. This army group includes British, Canadian and United States forces.

'The Allied Commander in Chief General Eisenhower has issued an order of the day addressed to each individual of the Allied Expeditionary Force. In it he said, "Your task will not be an easy one. Your enemy is well trained, well equipped and battle-hardened. He will fight savagely. But this is the year 1944. The tide has turned. The free men of the world are marching together to victory. I have full confidence in your courage, devotion to duty and skill in battle. We will accept nothing less than full victory. Good luck, and let us all beseech the blessing of Almighty God upon this great and noble undertaking."

'This order was distributed to assault elements after their embarkation. It was read by the appropriate commanders to all other troops in the Allied Expeditionary Force.

'His Majesty the King will broadcast to his people at home and overseas at nine o'clock tonight.

'No details have yet come in from the Allied side of the progress of the operations. The Germans, who have been broadcasting news of the attack on all their services except their own home service, say that the points assailed extend from Cherbourg to Havre, with the main weight of the attack in the area of Caen, which is some thirty miles west of Havre, and some sixty miles east of Cherbourg. They speak also of landings by paratroops, especially in the Havre area, and of stiff fighting. The important airfield at Caen has been one of the main targets for recent Allied air attacks.

'There have been no reports of enemy air activity on this side of the Channel during the night or so far this morning.

'The oppressed nations received the first news that big events were about to happen when a SHAEF representative broadcast to them that a new phase of Allied air offensive had opened. People in enemy occupied territory who live near the coast were warned to leave their homes as soon as they received warning of the coming attack. It would come about an hour before the attack and then they ought at once to make with all speed for the open country.

'After communiqué one had been issued, General Eisenhower broadcast to the people of Eastern Europe, announcing the landing as part of the concerted United Nations' plan for the liberation of Europe. He asked them to wait for the signal to rise and strike the enemy.

'"The day will come," he said, "when I shall need your united strength. Until that day I call on you for the hard task of discipline and restraint."

'Addressing the French people especially, General Eisenhower expressed his pride at having under his command the gallant forces of France.

'As the initial landing was being made in France, he emphasised the importance of his warning message. "A premature rising of all Frenchmen may prevent you from being of maximum help to your country in the critical hour. Be patient. Prepare. Great battles lie ahead."

'General Eisenhower concluded, "I call upon all who love freedom to stand with us. Keep your faith staunch. Our armies are resolute. Together we shall achieve victory."

'Later, SHAEF announced that General de Gaulle had arrived in this country and would speak to France sometime today.

'Communiqué one and General Eisenhower's message was broadcast to the peoples of Norway, Denmark, the Netherlands, Belgium and France in their own languages. Later, King Haakon of Norway, Dr Gerbrandy the Prime Minister of the Netherlands, and the Prime Ministers of Poland and Belgium themselves spoke to their fellow citizens.

'This is the end of the special bulletin.'

There was a general scraping of chairs as the women moved away from their machines and gathered in groups to discuss what they'd heard. But Peggy wanted to quietly absorb everything, so she went outside into the yard and lit a cigarette. She'd noted she hadn't been the only one to be moved by Eisenhower's speech to the men under his command, and as the others stood around, the mood was thoughtful rather than celebratory.

'It's quite frightening, isn't it?' she said to Gracie, who'd come to sit on the wall beside her.

Gracie looked up as the planes continued to roar back and forth and the dull thuds of the distant battle were carried to them across the water on the light wind. 'Clive's up there somewhere,' she murmured, 'and the only comfort I can take from it is that he's probably safer there than on those beaches.'

Peggy had a sudden terrifying image of Jack Smith wading ashore to be met by a barrage of gunfire. She shivered. 'I was so excited about it all this morning, relieved that finally something was happening, but at what cost, Gracie? I have a nephew out there on a ship, and little Rita's dad is more than likely on one of those beaches. It's all suddenly too real – and far too close.'

Gracie put her arm about her waist. 'We have to stay strong, Peggy, for their sake and for our children.'

Peggy pulled herself together as she finished the last of her cigarette and stubbed it out. 'It's either sink or swim, isn't it? At least we've got a choice, unlike those poor men over there who have to obey orders and put their lives at risk every moment of the day.'

She shot Gracie a rueful smile. 'I've often wished I was a man, able to fight the enemy, give Hitler a bloody nose and do all the things I simply don't have the strength or knowledge to do. Now I'm glad I'm a woman – for although we aren't in such danger and have a choice unlike those men – there are times when it seems to be the much tougher option.'

'You don't need to convince me,' laughed Gracie. She pulled Peggy to her feet. 'Come on, time for work before we have to start all over again when we get home.'

Peggy followed her inside and quickly used the washroom. Emerging from the stall to wash her hands, she came face to face with the odious Olive Grayson who was wearing an intense expression that warned Peggy she had hurtful and probably malicious gossip to impart.

'I've been trying to get to talk to you all day,' she said, barring Peggy's path to the basins. 'You'll never guess what I 'eard from a mutual acquaintance.'

'I haven't got time to listen to your gossip, Olive,' replied Peggy firmly.

'Oh, I think you'll find time for this,' said Olive, her eyes glinting with malice. 'It concerns that floozy what runs the Anchor.'

Peggy started to wash her hands, determined not to rise to the bait.

But Olive was not to be denied. 'I see Ron's taken charge while she's gorn off. His devotion's quite something, ain't it? But I wonder if 'e'd be that keen if 'e knew who she'd gorn off with.'

Peggy turned off the tap and dried her hands on the scrap of towelling while she forced herself to remain calm. She finally turned to Olive, her expression deliberately cool. 'What goes on between Ron and

Rosie is their concern,' she said flatly. 'You need to mind that flapping tongue of yours, Olive, because sooner or later it will get you into trouble.'

Olive smirked. 'I only pass on what I sees and 'ears, and this latest 'as come from the 'orse's mouth, so to speak.'

Peggy pushed past her, heading for the door, but Olive's dirty hand clamped on her shoulder, forcing her to a standstill.

'I 'eard tell Rosie were seen in a posh car with that there Major Radwell,' Olive rattled off in Peggy's ear. 'Early morning it were when they drove off up to the main road from the station – too early for most decent people to be out and about, dressed to the nines,' she added spitefully.

Peggy tamped down on the spike of alarm this statement engendered, and forced herself to face the woman. 'You're making it up,' she retorted.

'Ask yer snooty sister. She were there,' replied Olive triumphantly.

'Where?'

Olive rolled her eyes. 'At the station; where else? Blimey, Peg, I never took you for a thicko.' With that she slammed out of the washroom, leaving the door to clatter back and forth behind her.

Peggy stood there for a long moment before she could gather her senses and return to her machine. But Olive's words resounded in her head for the rest of the day.

*

Ron had returned to the Anchor, suddenly weary from the long walk and the distressing sight of Danuta, who was still heavily sedated and not making much sense. His low spirits were compounded by the lack of any messages or letters from Rosie, and the information he'd gleaned from Nurse Hopkins. It appeared that Major Radwell had been discharged from the Memorial the day Rosie had left Cliffehaven, and hospital gossip had it that he'd left in a chauffeur-driven car, with a large picnic hamper stowed beside the driver.

Ron's heart was heavy as he switched on the old wireless he'd brought downstairs so everyone could keep up with the invasion news. He reasoned that he could be putting two and two together and making five, but the coincidence was just too great – and he didn't believe in coincidences. Rosie had taken Monty with her, and what better transport was there than a chauffeur-driven car – what better company than a man who had enough influence to get travel permits? The thought made him feel quite ill, but he was determined not to show it.

He and Brenda worked well together behind the bar, and as the girls from the factories poured in after their early shifts, and the men from the Home Guard took up their usual places by the back window, he forced a smile, pulled pints and kept up his usual banter to disguise his broken heart.

He was glad of a bit of a rest when the one o'clock news came on, so he perched on a stool at the end of the bar by the till, and filled his pipe as Frederick Allen began to broadcast.

'D-Day has come,' said Frederick. 'Allied troops were landed under strong naval and air cover on the coast of Northern France early this morning. The Prime Minister rose in the House of Commons just after midday to give the latest news of the situation.'

The distinctive gravelled voice of Churchill filled the bar. 'During the night and early hours of this morning, the first of a series of landings in force on the European Continent has taken place. The assault fell upon the coast of France.

'An immense armada of upwards of four thousand ships, together with several thousand smaller craft crossed the Channel. Massed airborne landings have been successfully effected behind the enemy's lines, and landings are proceeding at various points at the present time.

'The fire of the shore batteries has been largely quelled. The obstacles which were constructed in the sea have not proved so difficult as was apprehended. The Anglo-American Allies are sustained by about eleven thousand first-line aircraft which can be drawn upon as may be needed for the purposes of the battle.

'There are already hopes that actual tactical surprise has been obtained. Of course, I cannot commit myself to any particular details as reports are coming in in rapid succession. So far, the commanders engaged report that everything is proceeding according to plan – and what a plan. This vast operation is undoubtedly the most complicated and difficult that has ever occurred. It involves tides, winds, waves and visibility both from the air and sea standpoints, and the combined employment of land, air and sea forces in the highest degree of intimacy and in conditions which could not and cannot be fully known.

'We hope to furnish the enemy with a succession of surprises during the course of the fighting. The battle will grow constantly in scale and intensity for many weeks to come. I shall not attempt to speculate upon its course, but this I may say, that complete unity prevails throughout the Allied armies. There is brotherhood in arms between us and our friends of the United States. There is complete confidence in the Supreme Commander, General Eisenhower, and General Montgomery. The ardour and spirit of the troops, as I saw for myself as they were embarking in the last few days, was splendid to witness.'

This rousing speech was greeted with a roar of cheering by the members of Parliament in the House of Commons, and echoed resoundingly by those who raised their glasses in the Anchor.

Frederick Allen was going through the main points again, and finished the broadcast with a reminder that the King would be speaking to his people scattered across the world this evening.

Ron turned the volume down as the chatter broke out and demands for more beer sent him down to the cellar to change another barrel and bring up the crates of bottles. No matter what was happening outside these four walls, business at the Anchor was brisk, and before the day was over, he'd have to put in an order at the brewery.

16

Peggy was emotionally drained by the end of the day, and besieged with worry about how to find out the truth of Olive's gossip before Ron got to hear of it. There was little doubt that Ethel had stoked Olive's thirst for tittle-tattle, for they were two of a kind – but the thought that Doris had somehow become involved just made things worse.

To put the tin lid on what had turned out to be a stressful day, Daisy proved to be overtired and not in the best of moods when she picked her up from the nursery.

'Too much jelly and ice cream,' said Nanny Pringle sagely. 'I did warn Mrs Goldman that such things are inclined to overexcite small children, but of course it has been a very special day, and Mrs Goldman is such a generous benefactor that one can't really complain.'

Peggy rested her hand lightly on Daisy's tousled dark curls as the child grizzled and whined and clung to her legs. 'Oh dear,' she sighed, glancing across to the van waiting outside the gates. 'Poor Lil has enough to cope with, and Daisy's clearly out of sorts.'

'I'm sure Lil will manage as magnificently as always,' said Nanny Pringle comfortably. 'She would have made an excellent nanny, and those four orphaned boys they've taken on are proof of that.'

Peggy untangled Daisy's arms from her legs and hoisted her onto her hip to murmur soothing words against her damp cheek. She felt awful about dumping her on Lil after not seeing her all day, and the fact that Daisy was overwrought and needing her tea and bed didn't make her feel any better.

'I'm so sorry, Lil,' she said, reaching the van. 'Daisy's not in the best of moods, and I think I ought to just take her home and forget about visiting the hospital this evening.'

'Aw,' said Lil, stroking Daisy's back and trying to coax her out of her grizzling. 'She won't be no bother.'

Daisy's arms tightened around Peggy's neck, her chubby legs clamping round her waist. 'Thanks, Lil, but it's best I just get her home before there's a full-blown tantrum.' Peggy peered into the cab. 'Sorry to waste your time and petrol ration, Fred. I do appreciate your kindness.'

Fred waved away her apology. 'I'll be here tomorrow same time if you need me.'

As Fred drove away Dolly opened the passenger door on her car. 'Climb in and I'll give you a lift home,' she said quietly. 'I can see Daisy needs you more than your girl tonight.'

'I feel horribly guilty,' Peggy admitted as she settled into the car with Daisy on her lap and still clinging to her like a limpet. 'Poor Danuta will think I've abandoned her.'

'I'm sure she won't,' soothed Dolly. 'But if it will make you feel easier, I could always pop in to see her and pass on a message for you.'

'That's a lovely offer, Dolly, but I can't expect you to do my visiting for me. After all, you and Danuta have never met and—'

'Stuff and nonsense,' said Dolly. 'Ron has told me all I need to know about the girl. She obviously means as much to you both as a daughter – and if it was one of mine lying there, I'm sure you'd be the first to offer help.'

'Oh, Dolly, you are kind.'

Dolly squeezed her hand and smiled. 'It's what friends are for,' she said softly. 'You run yourself ragged for everyone, now it's time for someone to take care of you.' She silenced Peggy's protest by raising a finger. 'I want you to promise that once you've got this little one in bed, you'll follow suit and get a good night's sleep.'

Peggy slumped in the seat with Daisy heavy against her chest, her cares weighing on her heart and in her mind. 'I'll try,' she replied, 'but sleep is hard to come by when there are so many things to worry about.'

Dolly eyed her sharply. 'Have you heard from Jim lately?'

'A few scrawled notes on bits of paper torn from a notebook. He can't tell me much because of the censorship, but at least I know he was still alive and uninjured on the day he wrote them.'

She felt the prick of tears and hastily blinked them back. 'As for Anne and the boys, the letters are few and far between, but I suppose they're busy on the farm now it's calving time and the school holidays are yet to begin.'

Peggy sat up straight and eased Daisy to a more comfortable position on her lap. 'How are you getting on with Pauline?'

'About as well as you get on with your sister Doris,' Dolly replied dryly. 'Coming down here was a mistake, Peggy. I simply can't get through to her, and now she's refusing to talk to me or Frank.'

'Oh, lawks,' sighed Peggy. 'Still, that has to be better than tears and tantrums, surely?'

'Not really. It just makes for a nasty atmosphere,' said Dolly briskly. 'I'm beginning to wonder if I should just leave her to it. Poor Frank will have to deal with her on his own, but with me out of the picture she might buck up and behave.'

'Please stay a while longer,' pleaded Peggy. 'It's selfish, I know, but we hardly get to see one another, and having you here does ease the burden.'

'It strikes me you have too many burdens on those narrow shoulders at the moment, Peg. I'm sorry I can't be here often, or for very long, but while I am, I want you to tell me what's bothering you. And don't deny it – I can see it in your eyes and in your demeanour.'

Peggy looked down at Daisy's head resting on her shoulder. The child had fallen asleep, her thumb in her mouth. 'Let's drive down to the seafront,' she murmured.

Dolly turned the key in the ignition and quickly drove away from the factory and turned left into the High Street which ended in a T-junction, and left again onto the seafront road that ran parallel to the promenade.

She parked and they both stared out of the window to the gun emplacements and ugly rolls of barbed wire that had been strung along the promenade to cut off the mined beach. The pier was an isolated lump of twisted, rusting metal marooned offshore, the remnants of an enemy fighter plane still visible through the shattered roof of what had once been the grand ballroom and theatre.

'It's not exactly an imposing sight,' Dolly remarked. 'But it looks as if things are still happening over there.'

Peggy watched the planes making their ceaseless journeys back and forth, and could see and hear the barrages of gunfire coming from the warships in the Channel as smoke rose from the distant shores to darken the horizon and throw a veil over the setting sun.

'Brendon's out there,' she said, 'and so is Rita's father along with countless thousands of others. My troubles seem very small compared to what they must be going through.'

'Tell me anyway,' coaxed Dolly, offering her a cigarette and opening the windows to let the smoke out and the fresh air in. 'A trouble shared is a trouble halved, as they say.'

So Peggy told her about her worries over Danuta, Jim, Rita and Sarah; the estrangement from her sister Doris after an all too brief armistice; and her concerns for Ron's future with Rosie. She admitted that she felt besieged by everything, from the constant onslaught of hardship to the enforced separation from her family – and that the effect of this war had slowly worn her down. She'd tried so very hard to stay strong, to keep her fears and her tears private, but now it was as if a dam had broken and it all came pouring out of her.

Dolly listened without comment, and when Peggy fell silent, exhausted but strangely unburdened at last, she threw the butt of her cigarette out of the window and took Peggy's hands. 'Ron's old enough and ugly enough to handle whatever is thrown at him,' she said firmly. 'From what I've heard over the years, Rosie isn't the sort of woman to throw everything away on a whim – or because he made a fool of himself after drinking too much.'

Her gaze was steady as she looked into Peggy's eyes. 'Gossip is dangerous, Peg. The only way to discover the truth is to go to Doris and find out exactly what she saw that morning.'

'I'd certainly get the truth out of her, which is more than I can say for Ethel,' said Peggy. 'She wouldn't know the truth if it bit her – and if she did see Rosie with the Major that morning, why is she keeping it to herself? She must know Ron would be fretting – and yet she's said nothing, not even to Stan.'

'Perhaps she has something to hide,' said Dolly.

'If that's the case, why tell Olive when she knows that woman can't keep anything to herself?'

Dolly took a deep breath and then expelled it. 'I have no idea,' she admitted. 'But if Ron does get to hear about this, both she and Olive will find they're on dangerous ground.' She regarded the sea which had become choppier as the day had progressed, and was now splashing with greater vigour against the tank traps and the shingle beach.

'This has to be cleared up quickly before the gossip spreads and things turn nasty,' she said decisively. 'And the only way to do that is to talk to Doris.'

Peggy looked once again at her sleeping child and knew she had neither the energy nor the will to go toe to toe with her domineering sister tonight. 'I'll make time tomorrow morning when I can be sure she's in,' she said reluctantly.

Dolly nodded and switched the engine back on. 'If you don't get any joy from her, I'll have a word with Stan. I've never met this new wife of his, but by the sound of it, she's trouble. Perhaps he can persuade her to tell the truth and shed some light on what's really going on here – because I don't believe Rosie has left Ron in the lurch for another man.'

Peggy had to smile at Dolly's fierce defence. It was clear her friend had a huge affection for Ron and Rosie, and was determined to get to the bottom of things. 'I'm so glad Ron's got you on his side,' she said fondly. 'Was there ever a time when you might have been tempted to …?'

Dolly laughed. 'He might have the same twinkling eyes and the soft Irish brogue that drew you to your scallywag Jim, but there was never anything like that between us. I've loved him like a big brother since I was a girl, admired his skills, his mind and his courage – but he would never have fitted into my world, nor I into his.'

Peggy thought she heard a note of wistfulness in her voice, but made no comment on it as Dolly drove up the hill towards Beach View.

After kissing and hugging Peggy goodbye, Dolly drove back to the seafront and headed towards Havelock Road. She stopped by the little park which had now been turned into an allotment and switched off the engine before lighting another cigarette and letting her thoughts wander.

Havelock Road was considered to be one of the smarter areas of Cliffehaven, and Doris had moved into the large detached house with Ted on their wedding day over thirty years before. It still looked quite grand, she noted, but the signs of war were here too, in the massive guns positioned on the hill above the end of the cul-de-sac, the two empty plots filled with the rubble of what had once been fine houses, and the overgrown gardens and cracked pavements.

Dolly had met Doris and Ted on several occasions, and had never quite come to terms with the fact that Doris and Peggy were sisters, for they were chalk and cheese, and clearly rubbed each other up the wrong way.

Ted Williams had always struck her as a diffident man, cowed by his bossy wife who seemed to think his skills on the stock market gave her the right to demand whatever she needed in her quest to climb the social ladder – so it had come as a tremendous surprise to hear that he'd been having an affair for several years, and somehow found the courage to leave Doris and demand a divorce.

Dolly smiled, remembering how she'd cheered when she'd received Peggy's letter telling her about it. She hadn't felt the least bit sorry for Doris, who, to her mind, deserved being taken down a peg or three. Doris was rude, overbearing and utterly scathing of Peggy's home and family, talking to Ron as if he was a servant and deriding all the good Peggy had done for those poor girls she'd taken in as the war had progressed.

It was little wonder that Peggy was reluctant to approach her sister about what she'd seen that morning, and Dolly had known instinctively that if this tangle of gossip was to be unravelled, she was best placed to do it. Although the thought of having to be polite to Doris made her grit her teeth.

She looked at her watch and decided she'd wasted enough time sitting here. Danuta would wonder where she'd got to, and Pauline would, no doubt, accuse her of neglect if she didn't show her face soon.

She checked her make-up in the rear-view mirror, repaired her lipstick and climbed out of the car. Knowing how much store Doris set by appearances, she was glad she was wearing her beautiful new Norman Hartnell two-piece. She draped the mink stole loosely about her shoulders to ward off the evening chill, gathered up her Chanel handbag and walked towards Doris's house.

Her high heels tapped on the uneven pavement, and then crunched over the freshly raked gravelled driveway. She noted there was fresh paint on the windows and doors, and spring flowers added a blaze of colour in the weed-free beds which had been sharply cut from the manicured lawn. Doris clearly wasn't about to permit a little thing like a world war to disrupt her from keeping up appearances.

Having rapped the knocker twice, Dolly stood back and waited. She could hear voices coming from the open windows upstairs and guessed it was the factory girls Doris had been forced to take in as evacuees, and who, according to Peggy and Ivy, she treated no better than poor skivvies. There were so many things about Doris that riled Dolly, that she began to wonder why she'd come. A telephone call would have sufficed – but then seeing the whites of her eyes was far more informative.

She was about to knock again when the door opened to reveal an immaculately turned-out Doris in twinset and pearls and a tailored tweed skirt. Glossy leather shoes and nylon stockings completed the look, and Dolly wondered how she'd managed to get hold of the nylons without chatting up some American.

'My dear Dolly,' Doris said warmly. 'What a lovely surprise. Do come in. I was just about to have my evening sherry.'

Dolly was very tempted to just ask her questions and then go, but she realised she'd get more from Doris by being friendly. 'That sounds like a marvellous idea,' she said, stepping into the hallway.

Doris led the way into her magnificent drawing room, and then closed the door on the lively chatter coming from upstairs. 'You'll have to excuse the noise,' she said. 'Those ghastly girls have yet to learn to keep their voices at a respectable level – and today's excitement seems to have made them worse than usual.'

She waved grandly to the expensively upholstered couch. 'Do sit down, Dolly, and I'll pour the drinks.'

While Doris was busy with decanters and glasses, Dolly took her time to admire the panoramic view of the Channel through the large bay window that dominated one wall. She eased the fur from her shoulders and perched elegantly on the overstuffed couch, understanding now why Peggy was always so terrified of creasing it or denting the military row of cushions lined up along the back. She glanced around the room and decided it looked like the furniture department in Harrods – all style and very little comfort.

Doris handed her an exquisite crystal glass full of sherry and sat down at the other end of the couch. 'I think a toast is in order, don't you?'

'Certainly.' Dolly raised her glass. 'Here's to peace.' The sherry was very good, which probably meant it was black market – as were the cigarettes Doris was offering her from a gold case. Sobranies were as rare as hens' teeth these days, and couldn't even be found in Mayfair. It seemed Doris had useful contacts – or was that Ted? She set the thought aside. Delving into Doris's shady dealings wasn't the reason for her visit.

'Well, this is all very pleasant,' said Doris once the cigarettes were lit and Dolly's outfit and mink had been zealously given the once-over. 'You're looking very well, Dolly. Is that a Norman Hartnell suit?

'From his latest collection.'

Doris nodded her approval but couldn't quite hide her envy. 'I heard you were in Cliffehaven and wondered if you might find time to call.' She sipped her sherry delicately. 'I suppose you're staying with Margaret as usual?'

Doris's fake plummy voice was already getting on Dolly's nerves – as was the woman's refusal to call her sister Peggy – but she managed to smile pleasantly. 'Actually, I'm with Pauline and Frank,' she said. 'Peggy has enough to do without me cluttering up the place, and with Brendon away at sea, I wanted to be on hand for Pauline, should she need me.'

'I'm sure you're a great comfort to her,' said Doris, her vowels almost strangled in her effort to maintain what she considered to be an upper-class accent. 'My Anthony is married now and living some distance away, but I know it's a tremendous comfort to him when I make my very rare visits to him and his little family.' Her gaze went to the silver-framed photograph on a side table. 'That's my little grandson, Teddy,' she said proudly.

'He looks a bonny little chap,' Dolly said, dutifully admiring the laughing baby. 'I'm so glad you manage to get to see them all when travel is so very difficult these days.'

'One has ways and means when one knows the right people to approach,' said Doris smugly. 'You also must have influential friends to be able to come down here at such a time.'

Dolly nodded in silent acknowledgement, delighted that the conversation was going in the right direction. 'It certainly helps,' she agreed, 'but I was rather surprised to learn that Mrs Braithwaite obtained a travel permit. I didn't think she moved in such elevated circles.'

Doris lifted her chin and sniffed in disdain. 'She's no better than she should be, and women like that always find a way to get round authority,' she said snootily.

Dolly thought that was a bit rich coming from a woman who clearly flouted the law by purchasing things off the black market and probably used bribes to circumnavigate the extremely strict travel bans. But she showed none of her thoughts, and kept her smile.

'I always thought Mrs Braithwaite was rather respectable – for a landlady of a pub,' she added for Doris's benefit.

'Hmph. Respectable is as respectable does,' said Doris scathingly. 'No *lady* would own a public house, let alone be seen with the likes of Ronan Reilly – a most disreputable and unsavoury character.' She gave a delicate shudder. 'But then you must know that, having been friends with Margaret for so many years. I don't know how you can bear to be under the same roof as him when you stay at Beach View.' Doris soothed her ruffled feelings with another sip of black market sherry.

Dolly held her temper and puffed on her cigarette. 'I did hear that Mrs Braithwaite has had her head turned by a certain rather dashing major,' she said, with all the eagerness of a genteel gossip. 'Do tell me how that came about.'

Doris stubbed out her cigarette. 'Well,' she began eagerly, 'I understand the Major started going into the Anchor once he'd recovered enough from his surgery to be out and about.' She leant closer. 'The poor brave man lost half his left arm, you know,' she said conspiratorially, 'and I suspect he was feeling rather lonely and out of kilter once he realised his army career was over. Mrs Braithwaite was no doubt on hand to soothe his troubled soul,' she added spitefully before sitting back with a holier-than-thou expression that Dolly wanted to swipe off her face.

Doris continued, unaware of how close she was to getting a bloody nose, 'Mrs Braithwaite was, shall we say, very friendly towards him; giving him free drinks and keeping him company after hours; having lunch with him at the Officers' Club and coffee in the Lilac Tearooms. You mark my words, Dolly, that woman was quite brazen about it. It's clear she saw an officer and a gentleman as well as a good army pension and a much easier life – it's no wonder she went off with him.'

Dolly feigned shock. 'Went off with him?' she gasped. 'But Mrs Braithwaite is still married. There can be no future with the Major – or with anyone until her husband dies.' She edged a little closer to Doris, inviting more intimacy. 'Are you sure she went off with the Major, Doris, or does this come from some gossip you've overheard?'

Doris drew herself up and looked down her nose at Dolly. 'My dear Dolly, I *never* listen to gossip. I'm sure you would agree that the only truth is what can be witnessed by our own eyes – and I assure you, I saw them together at the station that morning. In fact I even spoke to her very briefly.'

'Goodness,' breathed Dolly, suitably wide-eyed and agog for more. 'What did she say? How did she explain what she was doing with the Major?'

Doris's gaze slid away and she seemed to play for time before answering by lighting another cigarette. 'We hardly had a proper conversation,' she said finally. 'I'm not in the habit of passing the time of day with women like that.'

Dolly wanted to shake it out of her but knew she had to keep her patience and let Doris tell the story in her own way. 'But I heard the Major had hired a car and driver when he'd left the Memorial, so what were they doing at the station?'

'She asked – no, demanded – that I take a letter to Reilly. As if I had the time or the inclination to run errands for her. The bare-faced cheek of the woman quite took my breath away.'

'How ghastly for you,' Dolly murmured without a shade of sympathy. 'So what did you do?'

'She forced me to take the wretched thing, and before I could protest, she'd climbed back into that ridiculous car and was being driven off.' Doris puffed furiously on her cigarette, clearly still ruffled by what she saw as impertinence by someone from the lower orders.

'In the circumstances, I couldn't blame you if you didn't deliver it,' said Dolly carefully.

'Well, of course I didn't,' retorted Doris. 'My time is far too taken up with all my important charity work to be delivering barmaids' letters to Beach View. I gave it to Ethel, who most kindly offered to take it over there after she finished work.'

'That was kind of her,' said Dolly, who was wondering what Ethel had to gain by not delivering it.

'Where was Stan? I'm surprised he didn't offer to take it off your hands.'

Doris shrugged. 'I am not in the least familiar with the comings and goings of a lowly stationmaster, but I did note he wasn't there that morning, which was probably why that ghastly woman, Ethel, was in charge of the signal box.'

'I've yet to meet this Ethel,' said Dolly, 'so I'm rather curious to know what she's like.'

'She's as common as muck,' said Doris flatly. 'Goes about in dungarees and a headscarf, and always has a roll-up stuck in the corner of her mouth.' Her own mouth twisted in disgust. 'Definitely not our sort of woman at all.'

She brightened, fingering her strings of pearls. 'You really must stay and have supper with me, Dolly. The girls must have almost finished cooking it by now, and I so enjoy your company.'

Dolly looked at her dainty gold watch and gave a little gasp. 'I'm so sorry, Doris. I would have loved to, but I have an appointment elsewhere this evening, and I'm already in danger of being horribly late.'

She got to her feet and gathered up her handbag and fur, certain that Doris must be able to hear the furious beat of her heart and see the dislike in her eyes. The thought of staying a minute longer was too much to bear after what she'd heard.

'I suppose you're off to some lovely supper party at the Officers' Club – or is it dinner at one of the big houses close to the golf course?' Doris didn't wait for an answer, but clasped Dolly's hand. 'We are so alike,' she said, 'our social life is a whirl of parties and dinners with the best kind of people. Why, we even have a similar taste in pearls and furs. I so love mink, don't you?'

'Indeed.' Dolly eased her hand from her clasp and headed for the door. She couldn't get out of here soon enough. 'Thank you for the sherry, Doris,' she said, reaching for the latch. 'If ever you're in Bournemouth, do drop in so I can return your hospitality.'

Dolly was aware that Doris was watching her as she hurried across the gravel, to the freedom of the deserted pavement and then the sanctuary of the car. Her hands were shaking as she turned the key and crunched the gears.

'One of these days, Doris Williams,' she growled, 'you'll feel the back of my hand right across that snooty face.'

Taking the little car into a screeching turn at the end of the cul-de-sac, she roared back towards the town, catching a glimpse of Doris standing at her gateway, her hand limply raised in mid-wave.

Dolly had quickly realised that it would do no good at all to go storming up to the station to confront Ethel. It would cause trouble for poor Stan, and probably make things very difficult between him and his sly wife. Yet she still didn't see what Ethel would have to gain by keeping that letter. Was it out of curiosity to see where Rosie was going and why – or was it spite?

She drew the little car to a halt outside the Nissen hut which had replaced the booking hall and left-luggage store after it had been flattened in a bombing raid which had also destroyed an entire estate of houses. Climbing out of the car, she poked her head through the makeshift counter that had been cut out of the corrugated iron, and caught Stan eating a biscuit.

She grinned. 'Hello, Stan. I hope that biscuit's part of your diet.'

He started and placed a meaty hand over his heart. 'You gave me a fright, and no mistake, Dolly. I thought you were Ethel come to check up on me.'

Dolly laughed and submitted willingly to his bear hug. She'd known Stan almost as long as she'd been friends with Ron, and could still see the boyish delight in life in his smile that she remembered so well. She stepped back from the embrace and patted his chest. 'There's a lot less of you to hold onto,' she teased. 'But you're looking very well, Stan.'

'I'm half-starved,' he said mournfully. 'Ethel keeps a tight rein on what I'm allowed to eat.' He glanced worriedly over her shoulder. 'You won't tell her about the biscuit, will you?'

'Your secret's safe with me,' she promised. 'I'm so glad you've recovered, Stan. Everyone was so terribly worried about you.'

'My Ethel has seen me through,' he said, reaching for a small framed photograph he kept on the counter.

'She's a wonderful woman, and I don't know how I would have managed without her.'

Dolly dutifully admired the sharp-featured woman in the photograph, glad to have the opportunity to see what she looked like so she would be able to recognise her again. Then she gazed round the cramped space of this makeshift ticket office and left-luggage store. 'I'm surprised she's not keeping you company,' she said lightly. 'It must get very boring sitting here on your own for hours.'

'Ethel's on night shift up at the armaments factory all this week,' he replied, setting the photograph almost reverently back on the counter. 'But you don't have to worry about me getting bored, Dolly. There's always something to do.' He pointed to a collection of freshly planted seed trays and small garden tools that needed mending or sharpening. 'They keep me out of mischief, right enough.'

Dolly smiled at him fondly. 'I seem to remember you, Ron, Fred, Alf and Chalky were always getting up to some mischief or other when you were boys – and I bet that hasn't changed.'

He shot her a conspiratorial wink. 'Well, we do have a couple of enterprises in hand at the moment. Will you stay for a cuppa?'

'I'm sorry, Stan, but I can't. I'll pop in tomorrow, and perhaps get to meet Ethel at last. I've heard a lot about her from Peggy.'

'She gets back at seven, has a sleep until about two, and starts her shift at six. I'll tell her you called in.'

Dolly hugged him again, wishing she had time to reminisce and catch up with what the others in the gang had been up to, for Ron and Stan had been an intrinsic part of her formative years – the brothers she'd never had, her conspirators in mischief and adventure, and confidants in times of trouble.

She returned to the car and drove quickly up to the Memorial to check on Danuta and explain Peggy's absence before she returned to Tamarisk Bay and her daughter's cold company. She'd already decided how to deal with Ethel in a way that would avoid Stan finding out how devious his wife was – but it would mean an early start tomorrow.

17

Peggy felt drained after letting her pent-up emotions out with Dolly and could easily have followed her friend's advice and gone to bed once Daisy was settled, but there had been a marvellous delivery of letters waiting for her, and they'd perked her up no end.

Once tea was over and Daisy asleep in her bed, Ivy, Rita and Sarah decided it was time for Cordelia to dye her legs with gravy browning to make it look as if she was wearing nylons. There was a huge amount of laughter and chatter as Cordelia willingly succumbed to their gentle ministrations, and everyone fell about when she tried to draw a pencil line up the back of her leg and ended up with a wriggly line that started at the ankle and finished up going across her knee.

'I've started a new fashion,' she said defiantly, lifting her skirt and admiring her handiwork. 'A straight line is very boring. This is far more fun.'

Peggy was delighted to see them so happy, but the siren call of those letters couldn't be ignored any longer, so she took them into the bedroom so she could absorb them properly in peace and the soft glow of Daisy's night-light.

Anne was very busy down in Somerset with end-of-term tests and the arranging of a sports day at the village school. Her little girls, Rose Margaret and Emily Jane, had recovered from a bout of measles which had spread through the school like wildfire, and even infected one of the German POWs who was working on the farm. Calving was in full swing and the harvest would begin once the weather became more clement. Life was quite hectic, and she apologised for being so slack in not writing as often as she should.

Peggy was delighted to learn that Anne had received a card from Martin, who said they were being treated quite well, and that they'd just received Red Cross parcels for the first time. These had proved to be a huge treat and helped no end to boost morale amongst the men, who had no news of how the war was going or what was happening to their loved ones. Like Anne, Peggy could only conclude that the Germans in charge of the camp were heavily censoring the prisoners' mail, or just not delivering it.

Peggy read her very young granddaughters' almost illegible scrawl at the bottom of the letter, smiled at the row of rather wobbly kisses, and the two drawings of what were supposed to be new-born calves, but more resembled purple and yellow beetles.

The letters from Bob and Charlie were rather more sobering, and Peggy experienced a deep ache of dread as she read them. Bob had left school and was now working full-time on the farm, which he loved. He'd joined the local Civil Defence and was also a part-time junior plane spotter, learning the craft of identifying enemy and Allied planes as they flew over the sprawling Somerset hills and reporting back to HQ. Bob wrote that he was hoping to remain on the farm and not be called up when he turned eighteen next year, but if the call came, he was prepared to do his duty for his country and make both his father and his grandfather proud.

'Oh, Bob,' she sighed tremulously. 'They're already proud of you. Please God stick to being a farmer and serve your country that way.' She finished the letter, the words blurred by her unshed tears, and carefully tucked it back in its envelope.

Charlie's writing, as usual, was appalling and it took a while to decipher the single page. The scrawl was typical of her youngest son, for it was written in haste and great enthusiasm, without much care for spelling or punctuation. He clearly had far more interesting things to do than write letters home, and she suspected Anne had had to sit him down and make him do it before he disappeared off again for the day.

Peggy pushed away the memories of the eight-year-old boy she'd been forced to send away once the nearby school had been bombed. He'd always had scabby knees and a dirty, impish face beneath a shock of dark, unruly hair – but his eyes always shone with mischief and a simple delight in life, which clearly hadn't changed even though he was now thirteen.

Charlie's excitement at having managed to fix an old farm truck that everyone had abandoned as unrepairable leapt from the page. He was about to embark on a new project, which entailed restoring an ancient car he'd found in one of the barns, for if he could get it to go, he'd be able to drive it round the farm.

Peggy raised an eyebrow at this, for Charlie was harum-scarum, and the thought of the damage he could do behind the wheel of any motor made her shiver.

She returned to the letter to discover that he was looking forward to going up to the senior school in the autumn, but only because he'd been assured a place on the rugby and football teams, and would at last be allowed to wear long trousers like Bob.

Peggy's smile faded as she read the final paragraph. Charlie hoped the war would last long enough so he could enlist into the Royal Electrical and Mechanical Engineers and join his father out in Burma, which sounded far more thrilling than being stuck in a classroom.

Peggy's heart missed a beat, and she prayed fervently that the invasion meant neither of her sons would ever have to fight – let alone be sent to a jungle. Her hands trembled as she held the letters to her heart. Where had the time gone? How was it that Bob was now on the brink of manhood, and Charlie was racing towards it when all the memories she had of them were of impish little boys?

The knowledge that they'd grown and matured far from home and without her guidance lay heavily on her heart, for they had dreams and ambitions she'd known nothing about, and if they'd had worries or fears, they'd have turned to Anne or Aunty Violet for comfort and counsel instead of being able to come to her.

The tears rolled unheeded down her cheeks at the realisation that her little boys would virtually be strangers when they came home. *If* they came home. What if Charlie decided he preferred tinkering with farm machinery to having to start again at a new school where he'd know no one and couldn't play rugby? What if Bob stayed in Somerset to help Violet run the farm? Reaching for Jim's photograph, she held it close and curled onto the bed to sob quietly into her pillow as Daisy slept on, unaware of her mother's anguish.

Peggy had little idea of how long she'd lain there, but as the tears dried, she kissed Jim's photograph and fought to find an inner calm to sustain her before she read through his all too brief note.

The lined and rather grubby paper had been torn from a notebook as before; the pencil he'd used was faint, making the words he'd scrawled difficult to read. He missed her, fretted when there was no mail and was overjoyed when a great bundle of letters arrived all at once. He hoped his father was well and behaving himself, that Daisy was thriving and Cissy not too badly affected by what she must be experiencing at the airfield – for although they were isolated, the forces broadcasts were keeping everyone up to date on what was happening back home.

He sent his love to Cordelia and the girls, promising to write to everyone when he had time, but every day was busy and at night he was too tired to concentrate on anything but sleep.

Jim wrote briefly about the skilful and daring exploits of the glider pilots and the heroic Americans who could throw their planes about as if they were toys, using them to cut telegraph wires, pick up gliders, and land on the most makeshift of runways to deliver mail and supplies and airlift out the wounded.

Peggy noted that he made no mention of any fighting, or the hardships he must surely be suffering, and had to accept that she didn't really want to know. The bulletins on the wireless were enough to give her bad dreams; she didn't need any more details for her vivid imagination to work on and worry about.

Jim finished his letter, as always, with a kiss.

Peggy gathered up the letters and added them to one of the shoeboxes she'd stored in the bottom of her wardrobe. There were three boxes now, every one of them full. They were visible proof of how long she'd been parted from her scattered family, and only served to reinforce her yearning to have them all safely home. Feeling restless, Peggy changed into her nightclothes, wrapped Jim's dressing gown around her and went to wash her face and tidy her hair before she had to face the others.

She went into the kitchen and, despite her low spirits, had to chuckle. Cordelia and the girls had finished mucking about with gravy browning, and were now sitting round the table, their faces plastered in some sort of gooey paste. 'What on earth is that?'

'It's the latest beauty treatment,' said Cordelia, the paste cracking on her face as she spoke. 'Rita assures me I'll look years younger once it's washed off.'

Peggy eyed it with some scepticism. 'What's it made of?'

'Flour and water,' said Rita, trying not to move her mouth too much. 'It's supposed to tighten everything up and get rid of wrinkles.'

Peggy giggled. 'If you believe that, Rita, you'll believe anything. And at your age you don't have wrinkles.'

'Why don't you give it a go, Aunt Peg?' said Ivy.

'I'd rather have a cuppa, dear,' she replied, reaching for the teapot and still chuckling. 'Honestly, you're all as daft as brushes,' she managed, looking at the four white faces covered in cracked paste. 'Have you seen yourselves?'

'It's just a bit of fun, Aunty Peg,' said Rita, 'and it's not as if anyone can see us.'

'It's a good thing Ron's not here,' said Peggy dryly. 'I dread to think what he'd have to say about it.'

'It wouldn't do him any harm to give it a go,' said Cordelia, the paste slowly cracking enough to drop off her face and into her lap. 'He's got more wrinkles than a bloodhound.'

Everyone laughed, the paste crumbled to dust and there was a rush to the sink to wash it off before clustering around Cordelia's compact mirror to see the results. It was agreed that none of them looked any different, but it didn't really matter.

Peggy's spirits had been lifted by the warmth and affection of those around her. There was no place like home. The people in this little gathering had become family – and once Danuta was well and the war was over, these old walls would once again welcome back those who'd been away for too long.

She sipped her tea and lit a cigarette as the others settled down to wait for the nine o'clock news and the message from their king. Sarah turned up the volume on the wireless to combat the noise of the planes which were still going back and forth, and they were treated to a rousing performance from a French choir of their national anthem, the 'Marseillaise', which was then followed by a military band playing 'Land of Hope and Glory'.

Everyone sat very upright on the edge of their seats, enthralled by the stirring music of the two nations. Peggy's heart swelled with pride for the bravery and fortitude of the men who'd gone to free the French from beneath the boot heels of the Nazis, and looking round she noted she wasn't the only one to be so moved.

The music faded into silence and everyone edged forward in eager anticipation.

'Here is the news read by Joseph Macleod. This bulletin will include a message from His Highness, King George, and end with the latest war report, including the voices of Generals Eisenhower, Montgomery and De Gaulle. It also has messages and recordings from correspondents in the field.'

There was a short pause in which could be heard a buzz and whine of atmospherics, and then the King's now familiar, halting voice filled the kitchen. He was speaking not only to the people of the vast British Empire which spread across the world, from New Zealand and Australia to India and Great Britain, but also to those people in Canada and North America whose sons were now in combat to overthrow Hitler – and to the armed forces of the Allied nations.

'Once more,' he began hesitantly, 'a supreme test has to be faced. This time the challenge is not to fight to survive, but to fight to win the final victory for the good cause. Once again, what is demanded from us all is something more than courage and endurance; we need a revival of spirit, a new unconquerable resolve.'

Peggy closed her eyes and tried to block out the roar of the planes overhead as the King urged people of every faith to pray for strength and guidance to endure the days and weeks ahead as the fight for victory gathered momentum – and to never lose hope or faith in the great cause.

It was a short speech, but a moving one, and Peggy hoped that somehow Jim might get to hear it even though he was probably miles from civilisation, for surely it would hearten him and the men who fought alongside him to know that the entire free world was praying for them.

Her thoughts were broken by Joseph Macleod continuing with the news.

'All still goes well on the coast of Normandy. Mr Churchill, in a second statement to the Commons this evening, reported that in some places we've driven several miles into France.

'Fighting is going on in the town of Caen, and six hundred and forty guns of the Allied navies bombarded the German coast defences in support of our troops. Our great airborne landings – the biggest in history – have been carried out with very little loss. On the beaches, opposition was less than expected but heavy fighting still lies ahead.

'All through the night and today, air support has been on a vast scale. Thirty-one thousand Allied airmen have been over France today alone. Every one of the big fleet of American transport planes which carried the first troops and equipment to the Continent was painted with broad blue and white stripes so that friendly forces would know them. They carried coloured lights to help the pilots keep in formation. This brightly lit armada, stretching more than two hundred miles across the sky and travelling only a few hundred feet up took more than an hour to pass. Yet on the other side no flak came up. There was only small arms fire.

'Then, there were all our own airborne forces going out. The gliders and parachute troops in great numbers, with their own umbrella of night fighters. The Germans say we also dropped many life-sized dummies by parachute. They looked like men but exploded when they hit the ground.'

Peggy was still aware of the planes thundering back and forth as the newscaster continued to reiterate the details of the Allied landings which they'd heard in previous bulletins that day. She found her attention was wandering as her eyelids drooped, and although it would have been interesting to hear Eisenhower and the other generals speaking, she needed sleep more.

She kissed everyone goodnight and wearily trudged up the stairs to the bathroom before creeping into her bedroom and falling onto the bed, still in Jim's dressing gown. She didn't bother to draw the blackout curtains, for she was absolutely certain the Luftwaffe were far too occupied over northern France tonight to have the time to come and be a nuisance over here.

As Ron had predicted, the Anchor was busy. The regiment of Reserve and Civil Defence soldiers who manned the guns on the seafront and along the hills had come in as soon as their duty period was over to take up the benches by the fire and get stuck into pints of beer. The members of the Home Guard had gathered in their usual corner with their backs to the soldiers, drinking the place dry and reminiscing about how they'd won the First War in an attempt to impress the young boys in the group with their exploits.

Ron stood behind the bar drying glasses, keeping an ear open on the news and his gaze fixed on the gathering by the fire. He was always amused by the way the two factions studiously ignored one another, for they were very similar – although to mention the fact could cause heated debate and even a bout of fisticuffs amongst the older ones. None of them could fight their way out of a paper bag, and it usually ended up with lots of shoving and shouting, fists raised like aged prize-fighters, but judiciously too far from their opponent to land or receive a blow.

The soldiers might preen and make fun of what they called 'Dad's Army', yet they themselves weren't hardened, battle-weary veterans, but men rapidly approaching their half-century, serving out their call-up until they were discharged and transferred to the Home Guard.

Ron wondered if all the jeering, backbiting and jostling for position around the fire was because the soldiers saw their future in those old men, and the Home Guard were reminded of their youthful past, and none of them liked what they saw.

He finished drying the glasses and mopped up the spills from the counter as the factory girls clustered close to the wireless to listen to the first of the war reports that would now be broadcast every day to keep the people at home informed of progress. The bulletin tonight was a long one, he noted, glancing up at the clock above the bar. It was a quarter to ten, and Joseph Macleod was still introducing recorded messages from correspondents who were with the Allied armies in France.

Ron had just finished serving a round of drinks to his old friends in the Home Guard when he saw Dolly coming through the door. He grinned at her in surprise and delight. 'Well, to be sure, 'tis honoured I am that you've come to visit. What can I get you?'

'A very large gin if you've got any,' she said, settling on the high stool by the till where she had a good view of everyone in the bar. 'And have one yourself, Ron. I expect you've earned it tonight.'

Ron regarded her keenly as he poured the gin into glasses and opened a bottle of tonic water. 'You look upset,' he murmured. 'It's not Danuta, is it? She hasn't taken a turn for the worse?'

'No, nothing like that,' Dolly said quickly. 'When I left she was sleeping peacefully, happy in the knowledge that Rome has been liberated and our armies are slowly advancing into France. I'm just tired after a rather fraught exchange of views with my daughter.'

She poured some of the tonic water over the gin, raised her glass in a silent toast and drank half of it down. 'That's better,' she sighed, her gaze once more trawling the knot of women who were by the wireless.

'Are you looking for someone?' Ron asked.

She smiled and shook her head. 'I just enjoy watching people,' she replied smoothly. 'How are you doing, Ron? Still no word from Rosie?'

'Not a peep,' he replied with a frown. 'I simply can't understand it, Dolly. She's never ignored me like this before.' He heaved a sigh. 'Perhaps she's teaching me a lesson on what it feels like to be taken for granted, and to be sure, 'tis to my sorrow that I fully deserve it. I've made meself a promise that I'll change me ways once and for all, Dolly. Rosie deserves better than what I've given her over the years.'

'Try to keep that promise, Ron, but don't be too harsh on yourself,' Dolly soothed. 'I'm sure she'll be back soon, and you can sort things out between you then.'

'Aye, I hope so,' he said mournfully.

Dolly made a concerted effort to cheer him up. 'By the way, I popped in to see Stan earlier. He's looking very well now he's lost all that weight, but it seems that this new wife of his is a bit of a hard taskmaster.' She giggled. 'You should have seen his face when I caught him eating a forbidden biscuit. He thought I was Ethel spying on him.'

'Aye, he likes to have a treat now and then, but it does him no harm, Dolly. He's sensible enough to know he can't risk getting so out of shape again.'

He went to help Brenda with a large round of drinks for the factory girls, and while he was serving, he watched Dolly chatting to one of the girls and wondered what her real reason was for coming in tonight. She did look tired, but there was an alertness in her, as if she was waiting for something – or someone.

'Would you be after another of those?' he asked her, noting her glass was empty.

'I'd love one, but I have to drive back to Tamarisk Bay. It's bad enough during the day, but with hooded headlights it's positively hair-raising.'

'Then why don't you come back and spend the night at Beach View? There's an empty room, and I don't like the thought of you driving over there in the dark.'

'Bless you, Ron,' she said, affectionately patting his cheek. 'I've driven in far worse conditions, and I have things to do very early tomorrow.' She must have read the question in his eyes, for she grinned. 'Curiosity killed the cat, Ron.'

'Satisfaction brought it back,' he replied, wriggling his eyebrows.

Dolly laughed. 'I'm sure it does, but patience is a virtue, Ron. Goodnight.' She blew him a kiss, slid from the stool and was gone before he could think of a suitable answer.

'Women,' he muttered. 'Why do they always have to talk in riddles?'

Brenda broke into his thoughts. 'Have you put that order in to the brewery, Ron? Only we're very low on everything, and the bitter's almost run out.'

Ron gasped in horror. He'd sensed all day that he'd forgotten something important. 'I'll phone the order through first thing tomorrow.'

'I've made a list so you don't forget anything,' Brenda said, sliding the slip of paper towards him. 'Make sure you do it before nine o'clock, Ron, because without beer, we can't open the pub.'

Ron swore under his breath and took the slip of paper into the back hallway and pinned it firmly on the board above the telephone. As if he didn't have enough on his mind, he'd now have to face that smarmy drayman, Leg-Over, who thought he was God's gift to women and constantly tried to make a play for Rosie. No doubt he'd heard about Rosie's defection and would make a point of remarking upon it – thereby tempting Ron to violence.

But no matter how much he loathed the man, he knew he'd have to show some restraint. Keeping in with Leg-Over, who was the brewery owner's nephew, meant keeping the brewery sweet. Falling out with either of them could see Rosie losing the business she'd spent so many years building up – and that would definitely see the end of any hopes he harboured for reconciliation.

*

Dolly pushed the note to Peggy through the letter box and then headed back to Tamarisk Bay. It was pitch black, and the noise of the aircraft was a constant presence as she steered the car out of Cliffehaven and along the narrow country lane which led past the Cliffe estate and eventually circumnavigated the airfield before heading east to the next big town.

She sat forward to peer out of the windscreen, gripping the steering wheel as she slowly followed the meandering track up the hill, the pale, hooded headlights barely picking out the lumps of chalk and flint scattered across it. Feeling tired and tense, she breathed a sigh of relief when she finally saw the two large white-painted boulders Frank had placed on either side of the steep slope which led down to the isolated bay.

Dolly decided to leave the car at the top of the track, and once she'd switched off the engine, she climbed out, took a deep breath of the cold air and eased the tension in her shoulders. The sound of a latch clicking home made her instantly alert, and she spun round, expecting to see Pauline, armed with grievance and ready for another argument.

'Oh, Frank,' she breathed in relief as the giant figure approached. 'What are you doing out here at this time of night?'

'I couldn't sleep,' he replied. 'So when I heard the car, I thought I'd come out to make sure you got down the track safely in those daft shoes.'

'Bless you, Frank. How kind you are,' she said, wishing her daughter could see how very lucky she was to have him. 'I never seem to have the right footwear when I come down here,' she said, glancing ruefully at the high-heeled pumps.

Frank grinned despite the weariness and worry that was etched into his face. 'You wouldn't be Dolly without your high heels and furs.' He offered her his arm and they slowly made their way down the treacherous slope of earth and shale.

When they reached the bottom, Dolly stilled him. 'I'm doing no good here, Frank,' she said. 'So I think it's best if I leave tomorrow and let you and Pauline work things out in private.'

She saw he was about to protest and forestalled him. 'My presence here is making things worse. We both know it. And although I'm sorry to run out on you, I really do think things will improve once I'm gone.'

'She's finding it hard to take everything in,' said Frank, staring out to sea where flashes of gunfire and the flames of burning buildings could be seen on the horizon. 'And with Brendon out there somewhere ...'

'I do understand,' she consoled. 'My revelations about Felix and Carol couldn't have come at a worse time, and I feel horribly guilty.'

He put his great arm about her shoulders to hold her to his side. 'There's nothing to feel guilty about, Dolly. I've learnt since losing Seamus and Joseph that life is too precious to waste in regrets – that we must live it to the full and grab those moments of happiness while we can. I'm glad you and Felix have found one another again. You deserve to be cherished, Dolly, because you are one very special lady.'

'Oh, Frank,' she breathed, close to tears. 'I never realised how eloquent you could be.' She looked up at him and smiled affectionately. 'You're very much your father's son, which is probably why I regard you so highly. But if we stand out here for much longer, I'll freeze to death,' she added, to take the solemnity out of the moment.

Frank grinned and led the way to the front door. 'Perhaps if you wore that mink instead of carrying it over your arm, you'd get the benefit of it,' he teased. 'Come away in and warm up with a tot of the brandy I've been keeping for a special occasion. It's a fitting drink to wish you well, and raise a toast to the boys out there.'

18

Ron had left the house early because he wanted to get up to the Memorial to see Danuta before he had to return to the Anchor to telephone in the order to the brewery before nine.

He knew he would be pushed for time, so was setting a fast pace when he suddenly heard a plaintive mewling and realised that Queenie had chosen today of all days to follow him up here. Stifling his irritation, he stopped and looked back.

The cat was several hundred yards away, yowling pathetically as Harvey nudged her encouragingly with his nose, to no avail.

Ron grunted as Harvey ran up to him and then raced back to Queenie. 'Lord preserve me from blasted animals,' he grumbled, stomping back down the hill. 'They eat you out of house and home, the cat thinks she's a dog, the dog thinks he's human – and neither of them listen to a ruddy word I say.'

Queenie had put on a fair bit of weight since the previous summer, and it was becoming a strain on her three working legs to walk very far, so when she struggled heroically to get to Ron, his irritation with her fled.

'Ach, ye daft wee thing,' he crooned, scooping her up and letting her snuggle against him for a while so she could get her breath back. Her little heart was pounding, her ears lay flat against her head as she panted, and her claws dug into his neck as yet another squadron of planes hammered overhead.

He tried to soothe her by stroking her fur, but she was as tense as steel, and he was worried that if one more thing spooked her, she'd be off and he'd never find her. 'To be sure me pocket is the best place for you,' he murmured, gently unhooking her claws and tucking her away into the deepest recess of his poaching coat.

He felt her squirming against his thigh before she finally settled down, and once he was sure she felt safe, he resumed the long walk to the hospital at a rapid pace.

Leaving Harvey outside to partake of cooked breakfast and anything else the patients wanted to give him, he quickly made his way to Danuta's room. Opening the door, he was confronted by the unwelcome sight of Matron Billings.

'Morning,' he said cheerfully, praying that Queenie didn't stir or start mewling again.

'Good morning, Mr Reilly,' she replied, with little pleasure or warmth. She closed the folder of medical notes she'd been reading. 'The patient is responding nicely to her new medication, but her temperature is a little high, so I don't want you cluttering up the place for too long.'

She glared at him over her spectacles. 'There has been far too much coming and going of late. My patient needs rest and quiet – and I doubt you are the person to provide either.'

'To be sure, Matron, I'll not be stopping for long,' he assured her with a twinkling smile in the hope it might thaw her out a bit.

'I shall make sure of it, Mr Reilly,' she replied icily before sweeping out of the room.

'Poor Ron,' murmured Danuta. 'I think that woman does not like you.'

'Believe me, darlin', the feeling's quite mutual,' he replied, perching on the chair by the bed. 'Don't worry your wee head about that old trout.' He took her small bandaged hand and held it gently. 'How are you this fine morning?'

'A bit hot and uncomfortable,' she admitted, 'but I am always better when I see you.'

''Tis with regret that I'll not be able to stay long this morning,' he replied, taking note of the rather worrying high colour in her cheeks, and the brightness of fever in her eyes. 'I have things to do at the Anchor.'

'It is lovely that you come,' she replied softly. 'I do know how difficult it is for you and Mama Peggy to make the journey each day when you are both so busy.' She shot him a sad, sweet smile. 'I am looking forward to meeting Daisy, although it will remind me of my sweet Katarzyna. Do you still tend her grave for me, Ron?'

'Of course. I go every week or two to tidy up. I planted spring bulbs for her, and the sexton – the man who looks after the church and the graveyard – has planted a pure white rose by her headstone.' He saw the tears gathering in her eyes and enfolded both her hands in his. 'I'll take you there so you can see for yourself when you're well again.'

Danuta closed her eyes and a teardrop glistened on her lashes. 'You are so kind,' she whispered.

Ron wanted desperately to change the subject and bring a smile back to her wan little face. 'I hear Fran popped in yesterday, and that Cordelia will be coming in this afternoon.'

'Fran told me all about her Robert,' Danuta replied, a smile tweaking at her lips. 'I think there will soon be a wedding.' She winced and clutched her side as she moved against the pillows. 'It's just the stitches,' she explained. 'They are pulling when I move.'

'Then keep still, wee girl, or ask me to help shift the pillows so you can be comfortable.'

Danuta grinned, reminding Ron suddenly of the young girl who'd taken such delight in driving the ambulances during her stay at Beach View, and using her knowledge as a theatre nurse back in Poland to boss the first-aiders about when she saw they were making a mess of things.

'It is good to know *Babunia* has a friend to take her out,' she said. 'I am to meet Bertie this afternoon. She sounded very well on the telephone – just the same as I remember.'

Ron grinned. 'She doesn't change much, although she can get very grumpy in the mornings, and her hearing's getting worse.'

'I will remember to tell her to switch on her hearing aid – like before when I live with you.' Danuta gave a deep sigh and momentarily closed her eyes. 'I have missed you all so much. I hope Beach View has not changed.'

'It's a wee bit older and shabbier, but the walls are still standing and it's much the same. The heart of the home is still Peggy's kitchen, and before long you'll be sitting there with Harvey at your knee while you chatter away with Fran and Cordelia and the girls. It'll feel as if you've never been away.'

There were shadows in her green eyes as she looked at him, and her smile was wan. 'I have lived many lifetimes since I last sat in Peggy's kitchen,' she said wistfully. 'I wish that I was there now.'

'Well, you'd better hurry up and get better,' he said gruffly. 'The sooner you're out of this bed, the sooner you can come home.'

'Is Harvey still outside?'

Ron nodded. 'Aye, and it's more than my life's worth to let him in here. Matron would have me head from me shoulders, so she would.'

Danuta giggled and it warmed Ron's soft old heart. 'I tell you what, though,' he said, reaching into his coat pocket. 'I do have someone you've yet to meet.' He drew a sleepy and subdued Queenie from his pocket.

'Oh, she is beautiful,' gasped Danuta as he gently placed the cat beside her. 'Poor little one has a bad leg – like me. What is her name?'

'We call her Queenie, because she rules the house and even has Harvey do her bidding.' Ron watched the cat stretch and begin to purr beneath Danuta's gentle hand, and before either of them could stop her, she'd wriggled beneath the blankets and was curling up to sleep in the crook of Danuta's arm.

They both heard Matron's voice outside in the corridor and Ron quickly retrieved the cat from the bed and stuffed her unceremoniously back into his coat pocket.

Queenie was having none of it, and she hissed and howled and fought to claw her way out.

Ron pulled the coat as tightly as he could over his chest to keep her in, and turned his back on Matron as she crashed unceremoniously into the room.

'What's going on in here?' she demanded.

'Nothing,' said Ron, hastily backing away while he fought to contain a hissing, spitting, clawing Queenie in his pocket.

'What's that? What have you got in your pocket?' the woman snapped.

'To be sure 'tis nothing,' he stammered, backing away as Matron advanced.

In two strides she had him cornered and whipped back his coat.

A ball of black fur and fury shot out, used Matron's large bosom as a springboard, and flew round the room like a whirling dervish.

'Get that cat out of here at once!' stormed Matron, slamming the door shut and barring Ron's escape.

Queenie shot up the curtains and hung there for a moment before performing a circle of death around the walls and then leaping across the bed to use the few pieces of furniture to get about the room without touching the floor.

Danuta was in tears of laughter and pain as she clasped her stomach. 'My stitches,' she gasped. 'Oh, it hurts, but it's so funny.'

Herding cats was not Ron's idea of fun and he was having a déjà vu moment as he chased Queenie round the room. This was all too reminiscent of what had happened with the ferrets in the Crown – and no laughing matter.

Danuta collapsed against her pillows in a fit of giggles interspersed with little yelps of discomfort as her stitches pulled.

Queenie had no intention of being caught. She skidded past Matron, shot round the walls and then leapt onto the bed to hiss and growl at Matron, her tail fluffed to three times its normal size, her back arched before she buried herself beneath Danuta's bedclothes.

Ron approached carefully. If he frightened Queenie she could do untold damage to Danuta with her sharp claws. 'Keep still, wee girl,' he warned her.

Danuta clamped her lips together to stifle her giggles, and Ron glared at Matron Billings. 'Not a word,' he rumbled. 'And no loud noises, neither.'

Matron was about to answer when Ron held a grubby finger up to silence her. 'You want the cat gone? Then do as I say.'

Much affronted, Matron pursed her lips and glared at him, but mercifully said nothing.

Ron approached the bed and sat at the end by Danuta's feet. 'Come on, Queenie,' he coaxed softly, reaching tentatively beneath the blanket. He felt her whiskers tickle the back of his hand as she sniffed his fingers, and could hear the way she was panting – a sure sign that she was frightened.

'It's all right, girl. You're safe now,' he continued, daring to let his fingers slowly move over her head and down her back to stroke away the fear. He continued stroking her as he lifted the blanket and swiftly cradled her in his arms.

Queenie stiffened immediately she saw Matron, but Ron continued to stroke and talk softly to her as he edged past the woman and reached for the door handle. 'Come on, Queenie, that's enough excitement for the day. Let's go home.'

He slipped through the door and into the silent, deserted sluice room. Queenie was calm and purring again, so he very gently tucked her away in his pocket and breathed an enormous sigh of relief.

Stepping back into the corridor, he could hear Matron Billings reading the riot act to Danuta, but knowing the girl was perfectly capable of withstanding anything that woman had to throw at her, he hurried away with an easy conscience.

'Come on, ye heathen beast,' he said to Harvey, who was gobbling down bacon, toast and eggs, much to the delight of a group of injured airmen. 'Let's get out of here before we're both shot.'

Peggy was woken by the sunlight streaming through the window, and because it had been so long since she'd experienced such a thing, she lay there for a moment, delighting in the sense of freedom it gave her simply because the blackout curtains had not been drawn, and she could see the sky and the screeching gulls that were sitting on the roofs of the houses in the row behind Beach View. She felt lighter, too, the burden of her cares eased somewhat after sharing them with Dolly – and although those worries still lurked, they didn't seem quite so daunting.

She eventually slipped out of the bedroom to go and make a pot of tea in celebration and to listen to the progress report of the invasion on the wireless. It was with surprise that she spotted some letters in the wire basket that hung beneath the letter box, for the postman wasn't usually this early.

Retrieving them eagerly, she noted that Sarah had another air letter from Australia, and what looked like a letter from Delaney. Cordelia had several from her distant family members in Canada; there were two for Rita, two for Ivy, one from Jim to Ron, and four for Fran – which was hardly surprising, as she had a very large family over in Ireland, and they were all great letter writers.

Peggy sifted through them and, with a frown, plucked out the pale blue envelope which had clearly been hand-delivered. She recognised the writing as well as the expensive stationery, and wondered why Dolly had popped the letter in the box without calling in – but came to the conclusion that perhaps it was just a note to report on her visit to Danuta the previous evening, and it had been too late to disturb everyone.

She carried the pile of letters into the kitchen and placed them on the table. Setting the kettle on the hob, she tore open Dolly's letter.

Dearest Peggy,

I know you really didn't want to face Doris, so I've already been to see her. There is a faint hope that Rosie's mysterious departure can be fully explained, but please don't say anything to Ron until I've dealt with it. You'll know if I've been successful.

Regretfully, I shall be on my way home by the time you read this. Pauline and Frank are better off alone to work things out between them, and although I'm sorry we couldn't spend more time together, I have other commitments which I've ignored for too long.

I hope your girl Danuta recovers very soon. It was lovely to meet her this evening, and please don't feel

*guilty about not visiting. She fully understands how
very busy you are, and how difficult it must be for you
to see her every day. She seems to be quite bright and on
the mend, and tells me she was delighted to get a
morning visit from Fran, and a telephone call in the
afternoon from her 'Babunia' Cordelia – which I
understand means grandmother in Polish.*

*The knowledge that Danuta has a warm and loving
family to return to on her recovery fills me with great
pleasure, for she seems in need of wonderful people like
you and Ron to cherish and care for her.*

*I will write or ring whenever I can, and the next time
I manage to get down to Cliffehaven, I'm taking you out
on the razzle – a visit to a beauty parlour followed by
drinks, dinner and maybe even a bit of dancing thrown
in. Stay safe, my dearest friend,*

Dolly

Peggy gave a sigh of disappointment that was
tinged with relief that she wouldn't have to see Doris
today. Dolly had once again proved to be a steadfast
and thoughtful friend, and although Peggy had hoped
she would stay longer, she fully understood why it
was probably best that she left Pauline and Frank to
sort things out between themselves. Having heard
Pauline's hurtful and unforgiving diatribe against
Dolly, Peggy could only imagine how uncomfortable
things must have been for everyone at Tamarisk Bay.

She read through the two pages again, the decisive,
fluent writing somehow epitomising the energetic

woman who'd penned it. Peggy would have loved to have been a fly on the wall when Dolly confronted Doris, for although Doris thought Dolly was the bee's knees, Dolly could barely stand to be in the same room with her. However, Peggy was intrigued to know what she'd learnt, and how the mystery of Rosie's silent absence could be explained in such a way that wouldn't bring untold hurt to Ron.

Realising it would do no good to waste time speculating on it, she made a pot of tea and sat down at the table someone had already set for breakfast. She eyed the stack of mail, her finger slowly shifting it back and forth until Jim's letter to Ron sat before her.

She was sorely tempted to open it, for she'd suspected for quite a while that he told his father much more than he'd ever revealed to her – and although she really didn't want to know *too* much, it was frustrating to think they didn't trust her to cope with the unvarnished truth of Jim's situation.

Peggy knew they only wanted to protect her, and she blessed them for it, but it really was irritating that they thought her incapable of dealing with the realities of the campaign in Burma when the BBC Home Service trumpeted the latest news into her kitchen with increasing regularity.

She shoved the letter back into the pile and her gaze fell on the one with the American Services' franking which she suspected was from Delaney. It irked her that the man clearly had no compunction about writing to Sarah when he had a wife and children back in America and absolutely no right to be playing fast and loose with her girl's feelings. The man had no morals, and if she'd dared, Peggy would have ripped up the letter and thrown it in the fire – along with any more that landed in her letter box. But that wasn't Peggy's way, and with a little grunt of disgust, she reluctantly pushed it to the bottom of the pile.

She sipped the tea and waited for the house to come to life. Fran would be home soon from her night shift at the hospital, and Ivy from hers at the factory. Rita was probably planning to spend another day at the fire station helping with the administration, and Cordelia would be up soon because Bertie Double-Barrelled was taking her out to lunch and then up to the Memorial to visit Danuta.

Sarah would be coming down, dressed and ready for her day up at Cliffe. Peggy found it a bit worrying that the WTC was about to move away from the area, for Sarah enjoyed her work and had made lots of lovely friends amongst the other girls. However, she was a competent secretary, and Peggy had few fears that she wouldn't find another job in the town. In fact, she remembered, she had a friend who worked at the Council offices in the High Street, and they were always looking for typists. Perhaps she could put in a word for her?

She glanced up at the clock, surprised that Ron had yet to put in an appearance. He was definitely up and about, for there was a bowl of lovely eggs on the drainer, so she could only conclude that he'd gone with Harvey up into the hills.

The absence of Queenie was not unusual, for she liked to roam at night, and quite often followed Ron and Harvey on their early morning walks, even though Ron usually had to carry her home in his pocket, for although she was a game little thing, going all that way wasn't easy on three legs.

Peggy decided that real scrambled eggs for break-fast would go down a treat, and so she wrapped Jim's dressing gown more tightly about her, and went down the concrete steps into the garden to col-lect some tomatoes which she planned to slice and serve on the side with toast.

The planes were still noisy, and it seemed Adolf was trying to outdo them with his crowing. As she passed the coop he took off from the roof of the hen house and came at her with talons and spurs poised to attack.

She dodged away from the wire-netting fence, never quite sure if it was strong enough to contain him, and headed for Ron's early fruiting tomato plants, glad she didn't have to go into the coop every morning to collect the eggs.

'Vicious brute,' she muttered, selecting three of the largest and reddest fruit. 'It's no wonder Ron's always threatening to put you in the pot.'

'I wondered how soon you'd go off again,' said Pauline sourly. 'But you've really excelled yourself this time. You managed to stay for more than one day.'

Noting the sarcasm, Dolly finished loading her suitcase into the boot of her borrowed car. 'I stayed because I thought you might need me,' she said calmly. 'But it's clear you don't, so it's best if I go before things get more difficult.'

Pauline folded her arms tightly round her waist, her back to the churning sea that was hissing over the shingle, the wind blowing her hair over her face and flapping at the hem of her dressing gown. 'That's just typical. The minute things get awkward you're off, leaving your usual mess behind for others to clear up.'

Dolly had had very little sleep and was in no mood for another set-to. 'I have tried to put my house in order, Pauline,' she said wearily, 'now it's time to see to yours. I've apologised until I'm blue in the face, but it seems you're determined to be unforgiving, so there's no point in me staying.'

'You don't care about me, or Carol,' Pauline retorted. 'Everything is always about you. Carol might see things differently, but I'm not willing to just accept all the lies you've told and pretend to be happy for you as you sail off to America for your new life without a thought for me.'

Dolly would not be drawn into another endless circle of unresolved argument. She glanced across at Frank who was leaning against the boat winch, looking as if he had all the cares of the world on his shoulders and hadn't slept for a week.

'Take care, Pauline,' she warned quietly. 'Frank is a good man – but even good men grow tired when there's no light at the end of the tunnel and each day is a battle that never seems to have a hope of being won.'

'What do you mean by that?' snapped Pauline.

'You'd know very well if you bothered to pay attention to your husband and consider his feelings in all this,' Dolly said. 'Have a care, Pauline, or you really will find yourself alone.'

She saw the fear flash in her daughter's eyes, and wondered if perhaps she'd gone too far – and then decided she'd pussy-footed around her daughter long enough, and that Pauline needed to hear a few home truths.

'Frank loves you, Pauline,' she said, not attempting to reach for her hand, knowing any sign of affection would only be rejected. 'As do I. But love wears thin when it's constantly rejected and ignored, and if you keep up this sort of carry-on, you'll only have yourself to blame if everything crumbles about you and you are truly left alone.'

Pauline's jaw was working, her eyes sparking fury as she glared back. 'Just go,' she rasped. 'Go and good riddance. You're not welcome here – ever again.'

Dolly understood that Pauline's attack was her way of defending herself, but she felt the stab of her words like a knife to the heart. She climbed into the car and drove away, but once out of sight of the row of cottages, she brought the car to a standstill in the lee of a sprawl of high gorse. In a great flood of tears she released the pent-up heartache and regrets she'd held behind the dam of resolve she'd built so carefully over the past few days.

She'd been harsh to her girl – some might say cruel – but Pauline had made it her mission to push and push and push from the moment she'd arrived. And the shaming thing was, her daughter's accusations had struck home and she had every right to be angry.

Dolly fully accepted that she hadn't been a good mother, and that she was now paying the price for that, and for keeping Carol's relationship to Felix a secret by weaving a web of lies in the mistaken belief that she was protecting Carol.

She gave a tremulous sigh. Her whole life was a lie – necessarily so during the years of both wars, but a burden which was growing harder to bear as time had gone on. She hated lying to Carol, Pauline and Frank – who all thought she was living out a care-free retirement in Bournemouth – and loathed keeping secrets from sweet, trusting Peggy.

However, the fateful events in Devon had proved to her that all lies – no matter how well meant or nationally important they might be – could eventually be uncovered, usually with disastrous consequences. She'd been incredibly lucky that Felix was an honourable man and would never reveal her link with the SOE – but how much longer would that luck hold should fate intervene again?

Eventually managing to pull herself together, she dried her tears and repaired her make-up before lighting a cigarette and examining her options. Her work at Bletchley was important and so secret that she'd signed a lifetime pledge never to reveal what part she'd played in helping to prepare the agents before they were dropped into enemy territory. It was work she loved and which gave her great satisfaction – although sometimes there was the most awful heartache when things went wrong, as they had done with Danuta.

But even to think of giving it up was impossible – especially now the tide of war was turning. The agents and saboteurs trained at Bletchley would be in high demand as the battles grew in strength and the Allies pushed deeper into Europe, and she was an intrinsic part of the team who saw to it that they were fully prepared.

Then there was Danuta. The previous evening, the girl had told her the names of those who'd betrayed her. To walk away without seeing justice done would betray Danuta and all the men and women who risked their lives working secretly within enemy territory, and such a betrayal would haunt her for the rest of her life. And what would her resignation achieve?

'Absolutely nothing,' she muttered, turning the key in the ignition and setting off for Cliffehaven.

She parked the car at the end of Mafeking Terrace so she had a clear view of the factory gates. Checking her watch, she realised she'd only have a few minutes to wait until the shift was over.

The girls she'd spoken to last night in the Anchor had been only too eager to describe Olive, for it seemed most of them had suffered from her vicious gossip. But Olive wasn't her target today, just as she hadn't been the only reason for Dolly's visit to the Anchor the previous night. She'd gone to see Ron, and to find out if Olive had spread her vitriol far enough for him to hear it – or was actually in the pub awaiting her chance. In which case, Dolly would have headed her off somehow. But it seemed Ron was none the wiser, and as there was no sign of the woman, Dolly had left satisfied that she could clear up this mess before it went any further.

She watched the women start to stream through the gates, giving cheeky lip to the guard, giggling and gossiping, glad to be free of work for a few hours before they had to start again tonight. She had a clear image of Ethel in her head from Stan's photograph, but soon realised it wouldn't be easy to spot her, for dressed in dungarees or trousers, their hair tucked away beneath knotted scarves, it was almost impossible to distinguish one woman from another.

She scanned the endless, noisy stream, quickly dismissing the young and the overweight, but homing in on the ones who clearly worked in the armament factory until she saw the sharp, foxy features she'd been searching for.

Dolly climbed out of the car and moved through the swirl towards the woman in the red headscarf. Small and skinny, with the yellow complexion of a 'canary girl' who handled explosives all day, Ethel had a face like a smacked haddock and a voice like a foghorn as she complained about her supervisor to another woman who clearly didn't want to hang about listening.

Dolly kept watching her as she approached, aware that she too was being regarded with some curiosity by the other women as they hurried past.

'Ethel Dawkins?

Ethel turned and eyed her up and down suspiciously, the fag drooping from the corner of her mouth as she swiftly tucked her large metal lunch box under her arm. 'Yeah? Who wants ter know?'

'I'm an old friend of your husband, Stan,' Dolly replied pleasantly, moving in so Ethel had no choice but to step away from the other women who were swirling round them. 'I popped in to see him yesterday and he said you'd be coming off shift, so I thought I'd come and introduce myself.' Dolly stuck out her hand. 'Dolly Cardew.'

Ethel eyed the outstretched hand and reluctantly shook it briefly. 'Pleased ter meet yer, I'm sure,' she said, her eyes still bright with suspicion as they took in the expensive clothes and shoes, her arm firmly anchoring the tin to her side. 'I gotta get 'ome,' she muttered. 'Stan will be wanting 'is breakfast.'

'There's something I'd like to discuss with you first,' said Dolly, continuing to advance so slowly that Ethel was almost backed up against the wall of the dairy before she realised it. She noted the way

Ethel was gripping the lunch box, and wondered what was hidden inside it.

'Oh yeah? And what would that be, then?'

'I believe you have something that doesn't belong to you,' said Dolly.

The arm tightened further on the box as her companion made her escape. 'I ain't got nothing that ain't mine,' she retorted, her eyes narrowing. 'Who are you? What right you got coming 'ere with yer nasty accusations?'

Dolly had now manoeuvred Ethel into the corner between the wall and the fence. 'If you have nothing to hide, Ethel, why are you being so defensive?'

'I don't like yer snotty tone,' snapped Ethel, the long ash dropping from her fag down her front. 'You ain't the police, so I don't 'ave to answer your questions.'

'What's in the tin, Ethel?'

'Nothing. Just me lunch.' Her gaze darted from side to side, looking for help or escape, but the other women had gone and the guard had shut the gate on the stragglers and was heading for the canteen. 'What's it to you anyway?'

'It matters to me if there's a letter in there,' said Dolly, her calm tone belying her readiness to ward off any attack the woman might be planning. 'A letter to Ron from Rosie, which you seem to have forgotten to deliver.'

'I don't know what yer talking about,' Ethel barked. 'Now sling yer 'ook before I lump yer one.'

Dolly saw the bunched fists and the light of battle in Ethel's eyes. She grabbed her skinny wrist and swiftly twisted her arm up her back, forcing the woman's face to be pressed against the wall, the tin to clatter to the pavement.

Dolly held her fast, keeping her legs splayed to avoid being kicked by Ethel's heavy boots. 'That's an interesting lunch, Ethel,' she said, regarding the two tins of butter, the packet of tea and tin of condensed milk which had spilled onto the pavement and were rolling into the gutter.

'Let go of my arm,' Ethel shouted, kicking and struggling.

Dolly gave an added twist to the wrist, forcing the arm higher until Ethel yelped in pain. 'Tell me where the letter is and I'll let go,' she said quietly.

'I ain't bloody telling you nothing, you cow,' yelled Ethel.

'How about I call the guard?' Dolly murmured close to her ear. 'He's only over there, and I'm sure he'd be very interested to see what you had in your tin. Nicked it from the canteen, did you? That's theft, Ethel, and I'll make sure you do time for it if you don't tell me what I want to know.'

Ethel groaned and sagged against the wall. 'It's in me pocket. But you'll pay fer this, you toffee-nosed slag.'

Dolly kept her grip on the skinny wrist with one hand and delved into the grubby pockets with the other to find yet more tins – as well as the letter, which had been opened.

'I were going to deliver it,' whined Ethel. 'I just forgot, that's all.'

'Of course you were,' said Dolly, shoving the letter into her jacket pocket before letting go of the wrist and taking a quick step back and to one side, to avoid the haymaker punch the woman was winding up to aim at her head.

Unbalanced, Ethel staggered, tripped over one of the tins and went sprawling into the gutter.

Dolly looked down at her in disgust. 'That's the best place for a liar and a thief,' she said coldly. 'I hope Stan never finds out what sort of low-life he's married.'

Ethel rubbed her wrist and scowled as she scrambled to her feet. 'I'll tell my Stan what you done to me – you *bitch*,' she spat.

'No, you won't,' said Dolly. 'Because then you'd have to explain why I'm a bitch – and I don't think he'd be too happy to hear how you steal food and other people's letters.'

She was about to return to her car when she stopped and looked back at Ethel, who was now on her hands and knees scrabbling about for her ill-gotten booty. 'What did you stand to gain by not delivering it?'

'That ain't none of your flaming business,' yelled a red-faced Ethel.

'I could make it my business,' Dolly said softly, her high heel stabbing down on the packet of tea and missing Ethel's fingers by a whisker.

Ethel cowered. 'That bitch what owns the Anchor was due for a payback,' she gabbled, hastily getting to her feet. 'Thinks she's so bleeding clever with her fancy clothes and 'er hold over poor old Ron all the time she's playing fast and loose with that posh major.'

Her face was ugly with jealousy and spite. 'Well, I soon put a spike in 'er balloon, and that's a fact,' she said with a nasty sneer.

Dolly turned away and headed back to the car, unable to bear being in her presence a moment longer. 'Poor Stan,' she murmured, settling behind the wheel. 'How on earth did you get so taken in by that hard-faced, jealous harridan?'

She glanced across at Ethel, who'd collected her booty and was now striding with righteous indignation down the hill. Dolly gave a shudder and switched on the engine. She had a fair idea of how Ethel had snared him. He'd been lonely, flattered by the attentions of a much younger woman, and so smitten he'd turned a blind eye to all the faults others must have seen in her. She knew from her letters that Peggy had had her doubts about the match – as had Ron. Dolly could only hope that her old friend would never have cause to lose those rose-tinted spectacles, for if he did, he would end up being very badly hurt.

It was with a heavy heart that she drove down the hill, over the bridge past a few stragglers from the factory and along the High Street before turning into

Camden Road. She pulled up outside the Anchor, relieved to find that it was still too early for the shutters to be drawn back, which probably meant that Ron was on his morning walk to the Memorial with Harvey.

Dolly drew the envelope from her pocket. It was grubby from frequent handling, and torn carelessly open, which suggested that Ethel had never had any intention of delivering it.

Dolly was caught on the horns of a dilemma. She didn't really want to read the letter, for it was none of her business and there had been prying enough, but what if it was Rosie's final farewell to Ron? He was already hurting at the thought she might have left him, and Dolly couldn't bear the thought of him going through the agony of having his suspicions confirmed in Rosie's own hand.

And yet she couldn't believe that of Rosie; sweet, vivacious Rosie who didn't possess a cruel bone in her body. If she'd wanted to end things between them, she'd have respected Ron's feelings and done it face to face, not by letter – especially not one carelessly left to another to deliver.

There was, of course, the possibility that the letter contained a reasonable explanation for her sudden departure, which would give Ron hope and clear up any lingering suspicions.

Dolly sat there for a long moment, turning the envelope over and over in her hand before coming to a decision. Climbing out of the car, she thrust it through the Anchor's letter box, her curiosity unsatisfied but her conscience clear.

Driving back out of Cliffehaven, she stopped for a moment on top of the hill to open the window and bid a fond farewell to the town she'd loved since childhood.

It sprawled back from the horseshoe bay into the surrounding hills, the terraces and quiet streets looking peaceful in the early sun as the barrage balloons glinted above the factories and the calm sea lapped at the shore – but the smoke and flames were clearly visible on the other side of the Channel, and the combined Allied air forces were continuing their ceaseless flights.

Dolly gave a regretful sigh. How different it was from those far-off summer days when she'd spent hours on the beach and in the rock pools while a band played on the pier and there was the heavenly scent of toffee apples and candy floss in the air. But there was hope those days would return once peace was restored, the barbed wire removed and the holidaymakers coming once more, and that was what she would cling to.

She drank in the scene, relieved that although she and Pauline had parted on bad terms, her visit had not been a complete disaster. She had the names of the double agents; Danuta was on the road to a slow recovery with a loving home to go to when she was discharged from the hospital; and Dolly had high hopes that Ron and Rosie would find their way through this recent upset and be happy together again.

She blew a kiss towards the town, engaged the gears and roared away, the tyres screeching as they fought for purchase on the tarmac. Her mission completed, she could now return to London and the office building in Baker Street where some of the most closely guarded national secrets were kept, and focus entirely on what she had to do to help bring this war to an end.

19

Peggy was dressed and Daisy was eating her breakfast by the time Sarah came downstairs. 'There are a couple of letters for you,' she said. 'It's been a bumper delivery today.'

Sarah blushed scarlet as she noted the one with the American franking and hastily put them both in her trouser pocket.

'Aren't you going to read them?' Peggy put the scrambled egg, toast and tomato before her. 'It's not often the post arrives before you have to go to work.'

'I'll read them during my lunch break,' Sarah replied, not quite meeting Peggy's steady gaze.

Peggy sat down beside her. 'Look, dear, I might not approve of you and Delaney, but it's really not my business. Don't feel you can't read his letters because of me. And judging by the postage date, he must have written that just before the invasion began.'

'I'll read it later,' Sarah replied firmly, and swiftly changed the subject. 'How lovely it is to have real scrambled eggs for a change. The hens must be laying really well, even though the planes are making such a terrible racket.'

'It's still all go over there,' said Peggy, wiping Daisy's mouth clean and helping her get down from her chair. 'I listened to the war report earlier, and it seems everything is going to plan, so I suppose we'll all just have to put up with it for a while yet.'

'You'll never guess what I just seen,' said Ivy, rushing into the kitchen and dropping her coat and gas mask onto a nearby chair.

'A pink elephant walking down the High Street?' teased Peggy.

Ivy giggled. 'Nah, better than that. I saw your posh mate, Dolly, having a right set-to with Ethel.'

Peggy looked at her in astonishment. 'Really? Are you sure?'

'As sure as I'm breathing,' said Ivy, plumping down at the table and eyeing Sarah's breakfast greedily. 'Can I 'ave some of that? I'm starving.'

Peggy smiled indulgently and fetched her plate from the warming oven. 'I really can't imagine Dolly getting involved in fisticuffs – especially with Ethel,' she murmured, putting the plate in front of the girl.

'Well, she was,' said Ivy, digging into her breakfast. 'Cor, this is blindin', Aunty Peg,' she said dreamily through an enormous mouthful of egg, toast and tomato. 'There ain't nothing like proper egg for breakfast, is there?'

Peggy held on to her patience as Ivy continued to shovel the food into her mouth. 'What did you see exactly?' she asked once the girl was mopping up the last of it with a heel of bread.

'Your mate had Ethel pinned up against the dairy wall, 'er arm halfway up 'er back, 'er ugly mug pressed into the brick.' Ivy grinned. 'Ethel was kicking and struggling and yelling blue murder, but Dolly 'ad a firm grip on 'er, and she weren't going nowhere.'

'But what …?' Suddenly Peggy had an inkling as to why. 'Did you hear anything of what was being said, Ivy?'

'Nah. I were too far away, more's the pity. But I could see everything well enough. When Dolly grabbed her, Ethel's famous lunch tin fell on the ground and there was tins of butter and milk and packets of tea strewn all over the pavement.' She gave a sniff. 'I always thought she were a thief, but to rob the Red Cross is low, even for 'er.'

'So what happened next, Ivy?' prompted an impatient Sarah. 'Do get on with it. I have to leave for work.'

'All right, all right. Keep yer 'air on. It won't matter if you're a few minutes late.' She wriggled in her chair, clearly enjoying her moment. 'Dolly were saying things close to Ethel's ear, and must have got fed up with 'er not takin' no notice, 'cos she forced her arm a bit further up and Ethel sort of sagged – all the fight going out of 'er.'

'And?' Sarah was reaching for her coat.

'Dolly searched the pockets of her overalls, found what she were looking for after chucking out a couple more tins of butter, and let 'er go.'

'What was it she found?' asked Peggy.

'I dunno, but it were small enough to put in her own pocket.' Ivy's eyes gleamed. 'That Dolly's quite something for a posh old gel,' she breathed in admiration. 'Ethel was winding up to punch 'er lights out, and she just stepped to one side cool as yer like, and let Ethel's weight behind the punch send 'er staggering. She landed on her arse in the gutter,' she finished, exploding into laughter. 'I ain't seen anything that funny in years.'

'And that was the end of it, was it?' asked Peggy, trying to control her own giggles.

'Sort of. Your mate Dolly put one of them pointy heels right through a packet of tea and only missed Ethel's fingers by a gnat's whisker. There was a bit of shouting again from Ethel who called her a bitch and so on, and then Dolly walked away and drove off in 'er car.'

Ivy drank down her tea, clearly thirsty after all that talking. 'I weren't the only one to see it neither,' she said, just as Sarah was heading for the door. 'The factory estate supervisor come out just in time to see Ethel picking up her stuff. I shoved off quick, not wanting to get involved, but I reckon from the look on 'is face that Ethel's in for a right earwigging – and probably the sack.'

'Oh, lawks, I hope not. Poor Stan,' sighed an anguished Peggy. 'It'll be all over town before you know it, and he'll never live down the shame if she gets sacked for theft.'

Ivy shrugged and poured a second cup of tea. 'I know it ain't fair on 'im, but thieves are the lowest of the low,' she said. 'They steal from people what can't afford to lose anything, and Ethel's got away with it for too long. She deserves everything she gets.'

'Don't forget the jam you brought home,' Peggy reminded her.

Ivy bristled. 'I 'ad that off Fred's Lil, fair and square,' she protested. 'She saw me coming home from work and offered it to me knowing 'ow much you and Daisy like yer jam.'

'I'm so sorry, Ivy, said Peggy, feeling wretched. 'I jumped to an unfair conclusion when you came back with it.'

'I should've said straight off,' conceded Ivy. 'Sorry for jumpin' at you like that, Aunty Peg.'

'You had every right to,' said Peggy, still fretting over poor Stan and the consequences of Ethel's thieving.

Her thoughts turned to Ron and she wondered if he was back from his walk to the hospital yet, and if she'd have time to pop into the Anchor to see if Dolly's surprising exploits had indeed retrieved a letter – and if they had, to find out what it contained.

But a glance at the clock told her she had less than ten minutes to get to the factory, and Daisy still needed to be dressed in her coat and shoes, and the slow walk would take at least eight of those minutes. Her curiosity would not be satisfied until this evening, she realised in frustration.

*

There was no time to get back to Beach View and drop off Queenie, so Ron let himself in through the Anchor's side door, Harvey barging past him to get upstairs to his favourite place on Rosie's couch as he trudged wearily after him.

Ron still couldn't come to terms with the fact that Rosie wasn't there to greet him with her lovely smile and sparkling blue eyes, her gorgeous figure wrapped in a silk dressing gown that whispered against her body as she walked – and although the scent of her perfume was still discernible, the place felt empty and soulless without her.

Her absence made him feel like an intruder, and as the days had gone on without any word from her, he was beginning to lose heart. He had no idea where she was or how to get in touch with her, and if she was with the Major, then he could only surmise that she'd made her choice and forgotten all about him. His heart ached at the thought, the spark of hope he'd kept alive in danger of flickering out as each silent hour passed.

He took a deep, restorative breath, filled Monty's bowl with water and left it in the kitchen for Harvey to drink, and then went into the spare bedroom. Easing off his coat, he laid it carefully on the bed so Queenie wouldn't be disturbed, and then closed the door firmly behind him. Queenie might panic when she woke to find herself in strange surroundings, and Rosie certainly wouldn't appreciate her doing the wall of death on her new wallpaper – besides, he'd had enough shenanigans for one day.

Ron looked at the clock and went back down the stairs to place the order with the brewery, going over the list twice to check that he'd remembered everything.

The clerk assured him the delivery would be made before opening time, and feeling much relieved, Ron went down into the cellar, which he'd helped Rosie turn into a makeshift air-raid shelter.

There were overstuffed chairs and couches, a couple of low tables and rugs to make it homely, and a kettle and primus stove to make tea. Ron had fixed up a sort of bar in one corner, so all tastes could be catered for – although drinking and smoking in air-raid shelters was frowned upon by the authorities.

He weaved his way through the furniture, hoisted the wide wooden ramp away from the far wall and set it in place beneath the hatch that opened in the pavement above. It was firmly locked at the moment, but he'd open it when he heard Leg-Over's dray horse plodding down the road, for it was a danger to life and limb if left open, and he didn't want some unsuspecting pedestrian ending up in a broken heap on Rosie's cellar floor.

Returning upstairs, he regarded Harvey fondly as he lay sprawled and snoring on the couch, his belly full of things he had no business eating. The old rogue was still as slim as a greyhound and as energetic as his pup, Monty, but he was tiring more easily, and slept for longer these days. He was getting to be an old boy, a bit like himself, Ron thought mournfully. The mind was deluded into thinking they were still young and sprightly, but the body was starting to let them down.

Thoughts of Monty brought him back to Rosie's absence, so to dismiss the ever-present anxiety, he went into the kitchen and placed the kettle on the hob. While he waited for it to boil, he filled his pipe and watched Camden Road slowly come to life.

Queues of housewives were quickly forming outside the shops where awnings had been drawn out over the pavement to give the place a bit of colour in the welcome sunshine. No one seemed to be taking any notice of the planes which continued to roar back and forth on their mission to bomb the hell out of enemy installations on the other side of the Channel, and Ron sensed an air of stoicism in the women who were patiently waiting to collect their rations and girding themselves for many more months of hardship before their men could come home and things return to normal.

He opened the window and puffed on his pipe, deep in thought. He very much doubted things would ever be the same again, for this war had brought so many changes to everyday life it would be a long time before the country settled down and accepted that the old ways were a thing of the past, and that new challenges lay ahead.

Victory back in 1918 had brought challenges none of them had expected, for food had been scarce and poverty rife; the returning men finding not a home for heroes, but a tired, dispirited country where there were few jobs and the injured amongst them were reduced to begging in the street.

And then the flu epidemic had swept the world, killing more than had died in the trenches, and the little spirit there was had withered to nothing.

He stared unseeing out of the window, the memories of that time sharply imprinted on his mind. It had been nothing less than a miracle that he and his sons had survived the horrors of the trenches, but on their return home it had been a fearsome struggle to blank out all they'd witnessed and try to survive the homecoming. He and the boys had gone out day after day and sometimes throughout the nights, into deeper and more dangerous waters to bring in the catch, but they counted themselves fortunate to still have the fishing boats Ron's father had willed to him, for they'd kept them alive during those long, tough years.

The kettle began to whistle and broke into his dark thoughts, and as he made a pot of tea and brought it back to the sitting room, he berated himself for letting his profound sadness over Rosie make him so gloomy. Things would be different this time, for twenty-five years had passed, and although they were once again at war with Germany, the world had moved on.

People were better educated and far healthier; huge advances had been made in engineering, medicine, communications and technology, so there would be jobs aplenty. New houses and schools would have to be built, whole towns and cities raised from the rubble which would offer a promising future for the next generation of bright young things like his grandsons.

Sinking into one of the armchairs, he stretched out his legs and relaxed for the first time since waking. It was barely nine thirty, but it felt much, much later after all he'd been through today, and as his eyelids drooped, he settled his head back into the soft cushions and let sleep claim him.

Startled awake by the sound of the horse's hooves on the street below, Ron spilled cold tea all down his front and cursed. Brushing it off his sweater and jacket with irritation, he hurried downstairs, grabbed the trapdoor key and slammed through the side door.

'Morning, Ron,' said a smirking Leg-Over. 'Cutting it a bit fine, weren't you, phoning in your order so late?'

'I've been busy,' Ron muttered, patting the patient old dray horse before slotting the key into the brass fitting and heaving up the weighty hatch until it was tethered firmly to a hook on the Anchor's wall.

'On your lonesome, I hear,' continued Leg-Over, making no effort to unload the barrels and crates from the dray. 'Still, you can't expect a looker like Rosie to ignore the attentions of a much younger man with better prospects than a scruffy pensioner like you.'

Ron gritted his teeth, refusing to rise to the goading as he hoisted eight crates off the dray and carefully placed them on the pavement before reaching for one of the barrels. He worked quickly and efficiently, determined not to let Leg-Over rile him, but it was getting harder by the minute as he stood there needling him while he watched him work.

Once all the barrels were lined up on the pavement, Ron wiped the sweat from his brow on his jacket sleeve. 'I'll go down and give you a shout when I'm ready to catch them,' he said. Not waiting for a reply, he hurried back through the side door and into the cellar.

Peering up at Leg-Over's ugly mug, he yelled, 'Right you are! Let's be having them.'

Leg-Over slid the crates down with unnecessary speed and Ron just managed to catch them and move them out of the way before the first barrel began rolling ponderously down the ramp. 'Slow down,' he shouted. 'You'll crack the barrel.'

'Then you'd better work faster, old man,' Leg-Over retorted, sending the second barrel down.

Ron swore under his breath, determined not to let Leg-Over get the better of him, but he promised himself that one of these days, he'd land such a punch on the man's nose he'd be out cold for a week.

'Right you are,' shouted Leg-Over once everything was in the cellar and the empty barrels in the dray. 'That's it. Give my love to Rosie when you see her. If you see her again,' he added with a snigger.

The wooden hatch slammed back into the hole, leaving Ron in the pitch black of the cellar.

Muttering dire threats to get his own back on Leg-Over, he switched on the single light bulb and removed the ramp. He manoeuvred the heavy barrels across the concrete floor towards the pumps, and then stacked the crates by the bottom of the steps so they'd be easy to grab when the bar got busy.

Once he was satisfied that all was in order for opening time, he returned to the pavement, locked the hatch and hung the key back on its hook by the telephone. Sweating profusely and covered in muck from handling the barrels and crates in the dusty, cobwebbed cellar, he went upstairs to have a quick bath so he'd look reasonably respectable by the time Brenda appeared and he had to open the doors.

Ron was feeling refreshed after his bath, and in a better frame of mind. He combed his thick, unruly hair, winked at his reflection in the steamed-up bathroom mirror and went to check on the animals.

Finding them both still sleeping, he put some food down, closed the door behind him and went down the stairs and into the bar. He switched on the lights, checked there were clean glasses under the counter, and enough crates to see them through the next couple of hours.

He fetched a pint glass and pumped some of the new beer into it, giving it a good inspection before he threw it away and pumped some more until it ran clear. The first pouring from a new barrel was always cloudy – especially if it hadn't had time to settle – but this looked the business, and as he was feeling quite thirsty, he refilled the glass and drank deeply.

He savoured the pint as he regarded the room, noting how neat and clean it looked, with the chairs and tables tidied away, the cobwebs dusted from the inglenook, and the floor swept. Brenda was worth her weight in gold, he decided, for she did the things he hadn't thought to do, and remembered things he should have.

He finished the beer and rinsed out the glass, then took the tea towels off the pumps and gave the counter a quick wipe over – not that it needed it, for the wood gleamed richly from many years of Rosie's loving polishing.

Satisfied that she would be pleased at how well they were managing, he headed for the door. There were a few minutes still before opening time, but there were letters on the mat and hope sprang eternal that at last there might be something from Rosie.

He gathered everything up and sifted through the bills and private letters until he came to the envelope with his name on it in Rosie's handwriting. Frowning at the fact it bore no stamp, and had clearly been opened and much handled, he tossed the rest of the post on top of the dilapidated piano and sat on the stool, eager to see what she had to say.

Ron,

I'm writing this in haste, for I don't have much time before I have to leave. I hope Sergeant Williams returned Flora and Dora safely, and I'm sorry I couldn't deliver them myself, but it was very late when I found them and I didn't want to disturb the household.

I received some sad news by telegram this mid-morning, and having spent the rest of the day trying desperately to find a way of sorting things out, I was unable to get hold of you or anyone at Beach View – which is why I must leave so swiftly and without warning.

My poor James died yesterday after a particularly bad episode, and of course I must go and see to all the arrangements before his family take over and go against his wishes. Thankfully, he was sound enough in mind for a little while to write a will before he was committed to the asylum, and although his family want him to be buried in their village churchyard, he'd always had an abhorrence of the idea and so expressed the wish to be cremated, and his ashes scattered across the Channel.

You will no doubt have heard about the lunch I had at the Officers' Club with Major Radwell. Henry's a good companion, and has turned out to be a most helpful friend. When I found it impossible to obtain a travel warrant to get to the asylum, he called in a lot of favours and secured warrants for both of us as he was being discharged that day from the Memorial. He even hired a chauffeur-driven car to take us all the way up there,

*so I could travel in comfort and take Monty, who would
have been an added burden to you when you have so
many other commitments. I'm sure Henry will prove to
be an enormous help when it comes to all the paperwork
that's bound to be involved, and I feel rather blessed to
have him at my side during this difficult time, since
I couldn't have you.*

*I will give this letter to Stan, whom I trust will pass
it on with little delay, for once again I will need your
help in keeping the Anchor going while I'm away. You
will have Brenda to help you, and can rely on her to
remind you of all the things you'll probably forget.*

*I'm so sorry I didn't get the chance to speak to you
and smooth things over between us before I had to flit.
But I should be home within a fortnight, and we can talk
then. Thank you for all the years of love, support and
laughter you've given me. I will hold onto those
memories as I sadly turn the final page on my marriage
to James and try to come to terms with what his
passing will mean.*

*I will write no more of my thoughts now, for I am
tired and will probably not make much sense. As you
will note, there is no address on the letter, for I have
no idea of where we'll be staying.*

With love,

Rosie

Ron scanned through the pages again, desperately
trying not to read into them things that weren't there,
but failing miserably. They might just be friends,

Rosie and the Major, but they were clearly on first-name terms, and what did she mean about where *they* were staying? Did they plan to be in the same hotel or boarding house? And it seemed the Major's eagerness to help was over and above what should be expected from a mere friend.

Ron tried to stop his jealousy from ruining what should have been a moment of joy. Rosie had written to him, after all, and there was a very real reason why she'd had to leave Cliffehaven. Of course it was sad that James had died, but it meant that Rosie was free at long last to marry him, so why was he being so sour?

He re-read the last but one paragraph, trying to figure out what she meant by having to come to terms with what James's death would mean for her. They'd talked about it often enough – planned their future together for when the time came. Now it had, it seemed she was having second thoughts, and that could only mean one thing. Major Henry Radwell.

Ron's emotions were mixed, his thoughts confused as he sat there in the shaft of sunlight that streamed through the coloured glass of the small window in the door. He couldn't honestly say he felt much about James's passing, for he'd never met the man, but he understood that it would affect Rosie after all these years of sorrow. He wasn't sure what to make of any of it, for parts of her letter held promise, and other parts felt as if she was holding back.

'What's the matter with you?' Brenda said cheerfully as she opened the door and stepped inside. 'You look as if you lost a bob and found a farthing.'

'Nothing a pint won't fix,' he muttered.

'So the order's arrived then, that's good,' she replied, her gaze falling on the grubby envelope in his hand.

He shoved it in his pocket just as the telephone began to ring in the hall. There seemed to be an added urgency to its tone, so he hurried out to answer it.

'Ron, it's me, Stan. I need your help, old friend.'

Ron gripped the receiver. 'What's happened? Where are you?'

'I'm at the police station. Ethel's been brought in for stealing ...' His voice broke and he couldn't continue.

'I'll be right over,' said Ron, slamming down the receiver. 'Would you be after minding things for a wee while, Brenda? Only I've got something important to do.'

She regarded him with undisguised curiosity, realised he wasn't going to enlighten her and gave a sigh. 'Only if you promise to be back in time for closing,' she said. 'I've got my daughter coming over with the grandchildren this afternoon, and it's a rare treat, so I don't want to miss a minute of it.'

'I can't promise how long this will take. I'm sorry, you'll have to lock up on your own.'

He was halfway out of the door before he remembered Harvey and Queenie were still upstairs. He dithered, and then decided the animals would be all right shut in up there for a couple of hours.

Hurrying down Camden Road and up the High Street, his thoughts were in a whirl. He couldn't care less what happened to Ethel, but his old friend Stan must be going through all kinds of agonies.

The police station stood tall and imposing half-way up the High Street, and Ron hurried up the steps and pushed through the swing doors into the reception area where two policemen were trying to deal with a belligerent drunk, while the duty officer attempted to take down the man's details.

Ron could hear Ethel and another woman yelling blue murder from somewhere in the building; but his whole attention was on Stan, who sat slumped on a nearby chair, his head in his hands, a forgotten cup of tea cooling beside him.

He hurried to him and squeezed his shoulder. 'It's all right, Stan. I'm here now.'

Stan looked up, his face ashen, eyes haunted with despair. 'Oh, Ron,' he rasped, gripping Ron's hand as if it was a lifeline. 'My Ethel's in awful trouble and I just don't know what to do about it.'

Ron was about to question him further when Bert Williams emerged from a nearby room and acknow-ledged him with a nod. 'I'm sorry we've kept you waiting so long, Stan,' he said. 'But there are procedures to go through, and they always take time.' He cast a glance at the other officers and the raucous drunk. 'Let's talk in here where it's quieter and more private.'

Ron steadied Stan by holding his arm as they traipsed into the small office where in happier times they'd shared a glass or three of whisky and put the world to rights during the long reaches of the night.

The man standing by the window was a stranger to both of them, so Bert made the introductions. 'This is Colonel John White,' he said. 'He's actually retired from the army, and is now the supervisor of the factory estate, and responsible for bringing Ethel and her crony in.'

He sagged into the well-worn chair which creaked under his weight as the three men guardedly shook hands. 'I think it's best if he explains the circumstances,' he added.

John White might have long retired from the army, but he'd retained the bearing and polish of his years as a soldier. He remained standing by the window, his thick silver hair glinting in the sunlight that struggled through the unwashed glass, his highly polished shoes and neatly pressed suit at variance with Bert's rather scruffy uniform.

'I have been shocked by the amount of pilfering that has been going on in the estate,' he began, 'and because my son is a POW in Germany, I'm particularly disgusted that some choose to steal from the Red Cross.'

He looked at Stan without a trace of pity. 'Mr Dawkins, your wife has been under suspicion for some time. Earlier this morning, I called for a constable, and he and I caught her red-handed as she tried to pass some stolen goods on to her friend and co-conspirator, Olive Grayson. The Grayson woman has admitted to selling such goods on the black market, and both of them have now been charged.'

He glanced towards the door. 'As you can hear, they are now being detained in the cells, awaiting the duty solicitor.'

'It's got to be a mistake,' muttered Stan. 'My Ethel wouldn't—'

'This is the proof, Mr Dawkins,' he interrupted, placing a box of tins and packets on Bert's desk. 'They were found upon her person at seven thirty this morning, and as they are clearly marked with the Red Cross stamp, there can be no doubt they were stolen.'

His gaze hardened as he regarded Stan. 'As her husband, I find it hard to believe you knew nothing of this.'

'But I didn't,' Stan managed, shaking his head in bewilderment. 'Absolutely nothing. I swear it.'

'Stan's not a liar, neither is he a thief,' said Ron evenly. 'I'd stake my life on it that he's telling the truth.'

A heavy silence fell in the room, and the men winced at the language Ethel was using as she proclaimed her innocence and accused Olive of stitching her up. Olive's reply to this was equally laced with expletives, and Bert finally lost his patience, opened the door and barked an order to one of the constables to go and shut them up.

'I'm sorry, Stan,' Bert said as he returned to his chair. 'Ethel's been caught good and proper, and I had to charge her.' He leant forward, his elbows on the desk. 'And I'm going to have to search the cottage, Stan. There's a real possibility she's been hiding stuff there until she can pass it on. My constable found a stash of stolen goods hidden at Olive's place.'

Stan buried his face in his hands, the tears seeping through his fingers. 'I can't believe it,' he sobbed. 'I simply can't believe my Ethel would do such a terrible thing.'

Ron watched his old friend disintegrate before his eyes, and he put a brotherly arm about his shoulders to try and comfort him.

'Stan has lived in this town all his life,' he said to John White. 'He returned from the First War where we fought together in the trenches, and took over the post of stationmaster from his father. His military record is exemplary, and he was awarded a Military Cross for bravery under fire. His reputation in Cliffehaven is of the highest standing, for he's an upright, honest man with a strong sense of duty. He suffered a heart attack last year, and something like this could easily bring on another.'

Ron paused to let all this information sink in. 'Stan is an innocent man and doesn't deserve to be punished, but if this gets out, he will lose not only his home and the job he loves, but his reputation. I'm asking you – no – begging you to find a way to shield him from it.'

John White looked at Stan with something approaching pity before he turned to Bert Williams.

'You know Mr Dawkins better than I do,' he said. 'What is your advice?'

Bert chewed his lip, clearly distressed by the whole distasteful business. 'Everything Ron said is the truth,' he said eventually. 'And I wholeheartedly agree that Stan should not be punished for his wife's actions. To that end, I will conduct a discreet search of the cottage without the presence of other officers, and make arrangements for both women to be transferred to another district to stand trial.'

He looked up at John White. 'What happens to Stan will depend on how many people saw you and the constable bringing the pair of them in. This town thrives on gossip, and something like this will be common knowledge by lunchtime.'

'As far as I'm aware there were no witnesses. It was between shifts and too early for most people to be out and about. The Grayson woman lives alone in a caravan parked off Briar Lane, and because of the hour I asked the constable to refrain from ringing the bell on the police van in case it disturbed the residents – of whom there was no sight.'

John White took a deep breath. 'I can see what a shock this all is to Mr Dawkins, and I'm sorry to have caused him such distress. But it's my duty to stamp out theft on the estate, and I had no option but to carry out that duty when it became blatantly obvious what was going on.'

'I hope your constables will keep this to themselves, Bert,' said Ron.

'You can be sure of it, Ron,' he replied firmly. He pushed back from his desk to signal the distressing meeting was over. 'I'll need you and Stan to witness my search of the cottage,' he said dolefully. 'These things have to be done by the book, I'm afraid – and I shall also need a statement from Stan once he's feeling more up to it.'

'What will happen to Ethel?' rasped Stan, his breathing ragged.

'She and Olive will stay here until the duty solicitor arrives and then be quickly transported out to another station.' He placed a meaty hand on Stan's shoulder. 'Do you wish to see her, Stan?'

He shook his head. 'I couldn't bear facing her now I know what she's really like.'

'I'm sorry, old chum,' Bert murmured. 'It's all a bit much to take in, isn't it? Best you let Ron get you home. I'll follow on with Colonel White in a few minutes so we're not all seen together.'

A very concerned Ron guided Stan out of the back door of the police station and along a warren of narrow streets until they reached the cottage. His old friend seemed to have aged, his once sturdy figure suddenly becoming frail and unsteady as they entered the dark little cottage and Stan almost collapsed into the fireside chair.

'How do I tell Ruby what's happened to her mother?' he asked, staring into the empty hearth.

'I should let Bert tell her,' said Ron, filling the kettle and putting it on the gas ring. 'He's more experienced at such things.' He found the quarter-bottle of whisky he'd brought over a few nights before and emptied it into two mugs as he waited for the kettle to come to the boil. 'Drink this, old pal. It'll steady your nerves.'

Stan swallowed it down in one and rested his head back in the chair, his eyes closed. 'Thank goodness April's working at the telephone exchange today and Vera Gardener's looking after little Paula. I couldn't have borne it if she'd been here to see Bert doing his search. It's all so shameful, and I have no idea how to tell her what Ethel's done.'

Ron sank the whisky and made the tea. 'She's your niece and won't judge you, Stan. You're not responsible for what Ethel's been up to.' He glanced up at the clock. Brenda would be locking up in ten minutes, and if she hadn't found the animals by now, they'd need letting out.

'I'll have to leave you for a bit, Stan,' he said, handing him the mug of tea. 'But I'll be back as soon as I can.'

Stan seemed to suddenly come out of his stupor, for he glanced at the clock, checked his pocket watch and got to his feet. 'I've been neglecting my duties,' he breathed. 'Lord knows what's been happening this morning. I've missed two trains already, and there are bound to have been complaints to Head Office. At this rate, I'll lose my job without Ethel's help.'

Ron followed him outside, slamming the door behind him and still carrying his mug of tea as they headed down the path to the gate which led straight to the platform. He was very worried that Stan would keel over with all the stress of the morning, but when he saw the little figure working in the signal box, he knew his old friend had love and support enough for him to be able to go and fetch the animals.

Ruby came flying down the steps of the signal box and flung her arms around Stan. 'I'm so sorry, Uncle Stan. What Mum done was unforgivable.'

'But what ...? How ...?'

Ruby eased him down onto the bench. 'Bert Williams phoned through to the factory office to tell me what were going on,' she explained. 'I told 'im straight she could stay there and stew for what she done to you, and come straight up 'ere to see to the early trains 'cos I knew you'd be down there trying to 'elp her.'

'But she's your mother,' breathed Stan. 'Surely you should be looking after her, not me.'

Ruby gripped his hands. 'I'll see 'er later. It's you what matters now. I told Mum to stop 'er thieving, and now she's only got herself to blame for the mess she's in. Her and that Olive 'ave been at it for months, and I don't mind telling you, Uncle Stan, that sort of thing not only makes me sick to me stomach, but it rubs off on others what 'ave done no wrong. I can't remember the number of times I've 'ad me bag and pockets searched, just because she's my mother.'

As the train came chuffing and puffing into the station, Ron finished his tea and headed back to the

Anchor without asking Stan about the letter Ethel had hidden – the poor man had enough to contend with today.

Ruby had lived at Beach View for a while after she'd escaped her brutal husband back in the East End, and he and Peggy had come to admire her courage and fortitude – and her downright good sense. Stan would be all right now she was with him.

20

The letter from Delaney seemed to be burning a hole in Sarah's pocket all morning, but she was kept so busy with invoices, wage packets and the paperwork involved in getting the timber delivered, that it was well into her lunch break before she finally had a chance to escape the office to read it.

She locked the door and found a quiet, secluded spot in the formal gardens near the manor house and sat down on a stone bench beneath a rose arbour. It was peaceful amongst the high, sheltering rhododendrons, the sounds of the axes and saws in the forest as distant as the booms coming from across the Channel, and although the planes were still noisy, their racket had become so familiar of late she didn't really notice it any more.

The letter had been written, as Peggy had observed, the day before the invasion, and she fondly pictured him sitting in his officer's billet, his forehead creased as he concentrated on what he had to write. She slit the envelope open to find four closely written pages, and settled down to enjoy them.

My darling Sarah,

My precious, sweetest English rose, I cannot express how much it meant to me to see you the other day, and as I sit here waiting for my orders, my thoughts are full of you, fearing that I may never see you again, but praying that fate will bring us together at some time in the future.

The mission I am being sent upon will probably prove to be the most dangerous and daring of this war, but of course I cannot reveal what it is — yet I'm sure that by the time you receive this you will know, and understand why it was so important to me to write to you.

This war has brought us together, and because I have no idea whether I will survive the days and weeks ahead, I want you to know that although my love for you is true and steadfast, I am guilty of having lied to you — and for that I am profoundly sorry and ashamed.

When I came to England, I decided, probably foolishly, to invent a wife and children, for I didn't want to be distracted as so many of my fellow officers were, and lose focus on my military commitments and the part I would have to play in this war. I have never married, Sarah. There are no children. But my family do own a ranch and that is where I shall return, God willing, once the war is over and I've been discharged of my military duties.

I beg you to forgive me for lying to you. I have wanted to tell you so many times, but it never seemed to be the right moment, and then I'd fallen so deeply in love with you, I'm ashamed to say I didn't have the courage to speak out. I was terrified you would end things between us, and I didn't want to lose you.

But now there is a very real chance that I may not come back, and I didn't want to die with such a deception on my conscience – or to have you discover after I'm gone that I was untruthful to you.

I love and admire you so much that there are no words to express it. I know you were reluctant to show your feelings for me because of Philip and the promises you made to him before you left Singapore, and I'm sorry that in my pursuit of you, I must have caused you some distress as well as a good deal of heart-searching. It was never my aim to make you choose between us, but I lived in hope that you would turn to me – and after our last meeting, I dared to believe that my love is reciprocated, and that we are meant to be together.

I so wish things were different, my sweet Sarah. Your loyalty to Philip is admirable, and I deeply regret making things difficult for you – but I will never regret loving you.

I won't write again until you reply to this, for you'll need time to absorb what I have done, which I hope most sincerely you find it in your heart to forgive. And should you decide not to, then despite my broken heart, I will understand.

I send a kiss and a prayer that we will meet again – if not in this life, then perhaps the next.

Ever yours,
Delaney

Sarah's hands were trembling as she read through it again. It was a beautiful letter, written with such feeling that she could almost hear his quiet, drawling voice in every word. She could just about understand why he'd lied – even though it did seem a very silly thing to do – but it was difficult to accept that he'd kept silent for so long. Why hadn't he said something during those precious few hours they'd spent together recently? Surely it must have been clear that she'd given him her heart?

'Oh, Delaney, how I wish you were here,' she murmured. 'Of course I forgive you. How can I not when I love you so?'

She heard the distant booms and bangs from the northern shores of France, and felt an icy prickle of dread run down her spine as she looked up to watch the unceasing flow of Allied planes taking off and landing at the nearby aerodrome. Delaney was right when he'd said he would be in the middle of the fiercest, most dangerous and daring battle of the war, and her heart clenched at the thought of him leading his men from the landing craft onto those beaches and into the hell-fire of enemy guns.

The war reports being broadcast every day on the special radio frequency said there were few casualties, but she suspected that was government propaganda – a ruse to keep morale high amongst the civilians – for surely, with so many thousands of men involved, there would be untold numbers of dead and wounded?

She tenderly folded the letter back into the envelope. She would write back as soon as she returned to the office, and send the letter off with all the other post. She didn't want him distracted and becoming careless when so much was at stake, and she couldn't bear the thought that if she delayed in replying, he might be killed and would never know how very much she loved him.

Sarah trembled inside, her emotions a mixture of joy and dread, for surely such happiness wasn't possible in these uncertain, deadly times. To dream of a future together was almost tempting fate – and yet there had to be hope, for without it there was nothing.

She took a deep breath and let it out on a tremulous sigh as she realised Philip and her father, if they were still alive, might be thinking exactly the same; living on hope, surviving with only one thought on their minds – to return home to the women who loved them.

What Delaney was asking of her, and what her heart yearned for, would break the promise she'd made to Philip. Could she ever be truly happy with Delaney while living with the knowledge that Philip might have defied the odds simply because he believed she was waiting for him still?

She closed her eyes, battling the demons that had been her constant companions since the moment she'd met Delaney. She'd tried so hard not to be drawn to him, holding fiercely to the promises she'd made to Philip in the belief that he'd come through – and yet as time had gone on with no word of what might have happened to the man she'd last seen at the Singapore docks, that belief had dwindled and Delaney had crept into her heart.

Her thoughts turned to those carefree days on the rubber plantation in Malaya when the future had seemed so certain, and she was a young girl in the throes of first love. The memories of that time were as ephemeral as a half-forgotten dream, difficult to capture, and as elusive as smoke, for they seemed to belong to someone else – a very different Sarah to the one sitting here in the manor house gardens.

Sarah and her younger sister Jane had led a comfortable, privileged life amongst the ex-pats until the Japanese had invaded, and they'd both had to grow up very quickly as they were torn from home and family and forced to flee to England.

How very different they were now compared to those girls who'd arrived, bewildered and uncertain they'd ever see their parents or Sarah's fiancé again. Jane had been dependent and childlike following a riding accident, but she'd left Beach View a confident, bright young woman to take up a secret posting with the MOD, and Sarah, who'd merely played at working for her father when she found time in the heady whirl of her social life, was now happily fully employed by the Women's Timber Corps, and feeling very much at home with her

Great-Aunt Cordelia and the wonderfully motherly Peggy.

Sarah smiled. At least Peggy and Aunt Cordelia would approve of Delaney now that it turned out he wasn't married, but how would they feel when she told them she was planning to marry him and set up home with him in America?

She hugged that joyful thought, warmed by the hope it brought her, until the images of that long ago tropical night when Philip had proposed came to haunt her. They'd been on the veranda at the back of the house which stood on stilts and overlooked the vast rubber plantation, the darkness of the encroaching jungle behind them. Her father Jock and her heavily pregnant mother were in the airy sitting room behind the long, delicate muslin curtains which undulated gently in the warm breeze that smelt of frangipani and mimosa.

Sarah closed her eyes again, trying to capture the scene, and the emotions of that moment, but the images were faint, as if she was watching it through the muslin, the participants a blur as they stood there against the backdrop of verdant green.

She gave a little sob of anguish as she realised she could barely remember what Philip had said to her that night, for the events which had swiftly followed had been so terrifying they'd erased nearly everything that had come before. That quiet moment in which she'd accepted his ring was the last they'd shared, for within a matter of days, they were running for their lives.

Her thoughts inevitably turned to her mother, who'd gone into labour – a difficult and life-threatening labour which had kept her in Singapore as the Japanese advanced. And to her father – big, robust, capable Jock, who'd refused to leave her, but who'd been determined to see his daughters safely away on one of the evacuation ships. Unlike the night of Philip's proposal, she could remember that last farewell all too clearly.

She and Jane had clung to one another on the deck, the enemy aircraft roaring overhead and strafing the dockside as Jock and Philip waved goodbye and ran for cover. And then had come the deadly game of hide and seek as the Japanese torpedoed some of the rescue ships, and their captain had taken the brave decision to hide between a group of small islands and then return for the women and children still stranded on the docks.

Sarah opened her eyes, surprised to find she was still in the manor house garden, for the sights and sounds of her escape from Singapore had been so vivid. There had been so much fear as she and Jane had clung to one another in the hold of that ship, not only for their lives, but for their parents and Philip, who they'd left behind.

It had been a miracle that Jock had managed to get their mother and baby brother on board the very last ship to leave Singapore, and although she was now living on the other side of the world, at least they knew she was safe. But there had been no word since of Jock or Philip, and the rumours coming out of that part of the world made it hard to believe that either of them could have survived.

Now all she had were fading photographs which had been taken in happier times and in a very different world – so remote from her present reality that it was difficult to comprehend.

Sarah's stomach rumbled, reminding her that she hadn't had her lunch. She checked her watch, noted she had another ten minutes before the canteen closed and drew her mother's letter from her trouser pocket. It was quite a thick letter considering she'd received several over the past few days, but perhaps it contained more photographs.

She tore it open eagerly and began to read. But by the time she'd got halfway down the first page, she could barely make out the words through her tears.

21

Burma

Jim, Ernie and Big Bert had calculated that this was their forty-fifth day behind enemy lines, but at least they were on the move and not under siege like the men who were pinned down in India, trying to drive the Japs from the Kohima to Imphal Road which they'd blocked following their withdrawal from the Kohima Ridge – a siege that had lasted weeks.

Their commanding officer had explained that the fighting was continuing fiercely in the area, for it was vital that the enormous supply dumps and rail-heads at Dimapur were defended. Should it fall to the Japanese, it would be disastrous for the Allies, and a huge bonus to the Japs who, it was reported, were desperate for supplies now the Allies had bombed their stores of rice and made it almost impossible for anything to be flown in. Consequently, General Slim had called for reinforcements to form a rearguard, clear the road and mop up any Japanese who were retreating back into Burma.

Jim tried to ignore the swarms of flies and mosquitoes as he eased the straps of his backpack to a more comfortable position on his shoulders and cursed the monsoon rains which had turned the earth to a quagmire and soaked him to the skin. He wouldn't have minded if the rain was cold – in fact, he would have welcomed it – but it was warm, and doing very little to alleviate the dreadful heat and humidity that rose sharply along with the number of noisome insects the minute the sun came out.

Jim and the rest of the column had encountered the enemy many times during the past few days, but they'd managed to get rid of them and carry on with very little delay, and, thankfully, few casualties. Like his fellow soldiers, Jim felt a certain pride in the fact they could come across the enemy unexpectedly during the night, kill them and continue their march without losing cohesion or discipline – it made them feel they could achieve anything.

The terrain they were travelling over now was nothing short of hellish. They'd crossed gorges and mountains, climbed cliffs and fought their way through dense jungle and forests of lethal bamboo which bore steel-strong barbs of up to ten inches long that could rip through flesh and have your eyes out in a split second of carelessness. At the same time they'd been involved in skirmishes with the enemy who would appear as if from nowhere, and had to be dealt with before they could move on.

The quiet order to halt came down the line, and everyone drew breath and eased their aching backs while they waited to be told what to do next. The

Gurkhas, Jim noticed, were hardly sweating, and looked as fresh as they always did as, in pairs, they carried the enormous Bren guns between them on their shoulders, their sturdy bodies wreathed in ammunition belts.

Jim mopped his brow with his filthy handkerchief and eased the straps once again, wondering if he had time to roll a smoke. But within minutes, the long column began to move, and as he reached the edge of the jungle, he finally saw what the holdup had been.

The cluster of Burmese villages was small, but surrounded by large paddy fields and cut off from the jungle by a road. Armed and ready for the surprise enemy attack which they expected to come from the village, the men were crossing the road into the paddy fields. About a third of the column had reached the paddy and another third were still crossing the road. Jim and his platoon waited for the order to go, but as they were about to step out of the camouflage of the jungle they heard the unmistakable drone of enemy Zeros.

There were ten of them and they were coming from the north, flying quite low, and clearly patrolling the road.

Every man, mule and horse froze where they were and not one head was lifted to see what the enemy planes were doing, knowing that a white face or movement of any sort could be spotted and they'd be wiped out in a single run by those Zeros.

There was muttering behind him as the sound of the engines died and they began to move forward. It was late afternoon and the rain had started again, pounding down on them as they crossed the road and began to follow their commanding officer through the paddy fields towards where they would split up and form smaller ambush platoons.

They reached the point where they would stay for the night, and almost before they'd had time to draw breath, snatch a mouthful of K-rations or a drink of water, the sappers were ordered to dig in. 'Here we go again,' moaned Ernie.

'The faster we dig, the quicker we can eat,' encouraged Jim, the rain battering down on his hat. 'Come on, mate, we're all dog-tired, so don't waste your breath, because you'll be getting no sympathy from anyone.'

They caught a small Japanese convoy that night, their anti-tank guns setting the leading truck on fire, the machine guns and grenades finishing the job at close range, and marking up over forty of the enemy killed.

On the second night when they'd been ordered to withdraw and move a few miles north, they had rather more to do. They mopped up a weak enemy battalion and a platoon of Japanese who'd been coming down the road before they were the target of a surprise and frankly insane attack by a Japanese company.

Jim and his men had watched in disbelief as the Japs had come at them across open paddy fields, bayonets fixed but without supporting fire. The machine guns made short work of them, but it was a shock to discover that they had no ammunition in their rifles. It seemed that rather than suffer the ignominy of surrendering, they preferred to die with their so-called 'honour' intact.

With the Zeros constantly buzzing overhead on patrol and to protect the Jap convoys using the road, the USAAF were called in to get rid of them. Which they did swiftly and efficiently before destroying a huge store of rice which intelligence had spotted several miles away hidden in a deserted Burmese village.

Jim and his platoon had dug in on the rugged slopes of a hill where kanyin trees overshadowed the teaks. They cleared the lesser growth to form clean lines which gave them a good view of the road beneath them, then took it in turns to sleep and eat. Jim had been dreaming about Peggy and Beach View when he woke for no apparent reason and automatically reached for the carbine resting between his knees.

He was instantly alert, listening for any sound that might have been the cause of his waking so abruptly, but there was no bird call, enemy rustle or animal snuffling – not even the snores and breathing of the men around him. He could see the bulk of Big Bert on watch at his machine gun, and the huddled figures of the Gurkhas lying in wait with their Brens while the other men slept in a rough circle behind them. Looking down the hill he could see the deeper shadows of massed men, mules and horses at rest within the hollows and defiles of the terrain and the long, empty road running through the valley.

Jim realised it was the silence that had woken him – a silence which was like nothing he'd experienced before coming to Burma, and seemed to hold a special quality. He relaxed and looked up through the kanyin trees which stood two hundred feet high, their vast upper branches forming broad, leafy canopies that were smothered in red and white flowers.

It was like being in nature's cathedral, he thought, with the long, straight trunks forming the walls and aisles, the canopies the roof, above which sailed a full, orange moon. He lay there watching the way the leaves and blossoms of the kanyin trees formed beautiful patterns against the moon, and how a pale mist was rising from the valley to drift up the slope and silently fill the aisles between the trees and entwine its way along the trunks. It was at moments like this he could forget his reason for being here, and just revel in the wonder of nature's mysterious beauty.

Dawn came and cast a pearly light over everything, chasing away the mist and bringing with it the distinctive tenor bell call of the Sambhur stag, one of the red deer which roamed wild through Burma and India.

When Jim and the others had first heard it, they'd taken it to be the Japs conducting their usual ploy of using bird calls to signal to one another, but one of the officers had put them straight, even going so far as to quote a poem by Kipling about the deer.

Neither Jim nor Ernie had heard of Kipling, and thought poetry was something that only officers and women would appreciate, but they'd been quite impressed by this one, and Jim had written to Peggy to tell her to look it up in the library.

He nudged the others awake and took his turn at the machine gun while a small cooking fire was lit and the billy boiled for tea. Having eaten their breakfast, they moved on to find out what lay on the other side of the hill, which intelligence had told them was more heavily timbered, and covered in jungle undergrowth.

The Japs came from nowhere, almost catching them off guard. Machine guns rattled off bullets and Bren guns roared as grenades exploded and the earth shook. Jim hit the ground and squirmed for cover behind a tree to fire back at the shifting shadows through the thick undergrowth.

He was distracted by movement beside him, and saw Big Bert climbing a nearby tree, a Bren gun on his back as if it weighed nothing. Perched up there he must have had an excellent view of the enemy position, for he began to shout directions to the men beneath him as to where to fire.

Jim followed his directions, admiring his courage, but thinking he must be insane to do such a thing. Catching sight of several Japanese moving to flank the tree, he shouted, 'Look out, Bert, they're coming left and right!'

'Yeah, I seen 'em,' he shouted back, opening fire and dispatching them all before killing off a couple more he'd spotted in the trees to his right. He clambered down, cursing the fact he'd run out of ammo, then grabbed a fresh magazine from a startled Gurkha and shinned back up the tree like a monkey, shooting the gun as he went.

Jim was occupied in exchanging fire with a couple of Japs when he caught a glimpse of two young Gurkhas running out to flank so they could see the enemy more clearly and follow Bert's orders. One was in charge of the Bren, the other the loaded magazine, which he'd slap into the gun the minute the other shouted change.

Jim had seen them practising this manoeuvre many times, but he didn't have the chance to watch, for a Japanese machine gun had opened up, the bullets thudding all around him as he repeatedly fired back and lobbed off a few grenades – but it was difficult to see his target in the shifting shadows of the jungle, and despite all his efforts, the machine gun was still in action. There was only one option open to him. Get nearer and finish the bastard off.

Jim edged away from the tree and began to crawl towards the enemy machine gun, the bullets of which were zipping all round him. He felt the sting of the bullet as it scored a burning path across his cheek and through his earlobe. It hurt like hell, but he shook his head, ignored the warm trickle of blood he could feel running down his neck and continued to crawl closer to the machine-gunner, his thumb firmly pressed down on the pin of the primed grenade.

Bert and the Gurkhas were still keeping the Japs busy, and Jim had to flatten himself to the ground as someone from his platoon lobbed a grenade, missed the true target by a country mile and nearly blew him to smithereens.

He lay there cursing, his face buried in mud and muck as everything exploded around him. He felt clods of earth and bits of tree land on him, and when he judged it safe enough, he rolled to one side, burrowed beneath the undergrowth surrounding a tree and saw he was within feet of the enemy gunner.

He took his thumb off the grenade and lobbed it, hit the deck and covered his head with his hands as once again bits of Jap and jungle splattered down on him.

With a grunt of disgust, he knocked away the severed foot that was still wearing a boot, and aimed his carbine at a Jap he'd spotted a few feet away, and who was lining him up in his sights. He pulled the trigger.

Nothing happened, so he quickly rolled away and sank deeper into the undergrowth, the enemy fire following him too closely for comfort. 'Tree two o'clock,' he yelled above the rattle of gunfire and the boom of the Brens.

Jim wrestled with the carbine, but it was jammed solid, the barrel too hot to handle. He heard the strangled cry and thud of the Jap's body as it hit the ground following a barrage of fire, but he was too busy fighting to free his gun to take much notice.

He cursed the gun, cursed his luck and the blasted Japs, who were still firing at him. Just how many of the bastards were there?

He glanced up and saw the Ghurkha on the Bren take a burst of enemy fire in his face and neck. The youth rolled away from his gun, his hand coming up in death to signal the other man to take over. Which he did immediately.

He continued to fight the blasted gun, and had just got it clear when something heavy fell on him and sent him sprawling. He found himself on his back staring into a very dead and chewed-up enemy face. He shoved him off, smeared the blood and gore from his own face, spat to clear his mouth and crawled away to join in the fire-fight.

When it was over, Jim was astonished to discover it had lasted a mere fifteen minutes, for it had felt much longer than that. Big Bert had miraculously survived his heroics, and would probably be awarded a medal of some sort, while Ernie was complaining he'd sprained his wrist when he'd tripped over a tree branch and fallen into a shallow defile. The medic put a sling on the wrist and saw to the damage on Jim's check and ear by slapping antiseptic on it which stung like hell for several minutes after.

Jim was aware that he'd been extremely lucky, but was a bit put out that his good looks had been marred by the loss of an earlobe – but then consoled himself by the thought that a battle scar might actually enhance his reputation amongst the ladies.

They counted the dead – thirty enemy, three of their own and five injured, but not seriously – and then hoisted their weapons and as one moved back into the jungle to face the next skirmish. They felt invincible – the knowledge they could encounter death at any moment making them even more determined to survive.

22

Peggy thanked Frank profusely for his and Lil's kindness, giving him a kiss and a hug before she went indoors. They were such good people, and lovely friends to help her out like this, and she wondered what she could do by way of showing her appreciation.

She went into the house and up the steps to the kitchen. It felt like many hours since her sandwich lunch, and she was very ready for her tea – but first she would check on Daisy and make sure she was settled for the night.

'Hello, Cordelia,' she said, surprised to find her alone in the kitchen. 'Has everyone deserted you this evening?'

'I've had my dessert, thank you, dear. Ron's rhubarb was delicious, but it could have really done with more sugar. Lil dropped some fish off, so I made a pie. And I don't mind telling you, it's one of my best.'

'I'm sure the rhubarb was delicious and the pie wonderful as usual, but that wasn't what I asked,' said Peggy loudly, making winding signs for her to turn up her hearing aid. 'Where is everyone?' she asked once Cordelia had stopped fiddling with it.

'I presume Ron's at the Anchor – I've yet to see him today. Lil put Daisy to bed and I checked on her a few minutes ago and she's asleep. Fran and Ivy are on their night shifts, and Rita's gone off some-where – probably to the fire station.'

Peggy frowned as she took off her scarf and coat. 'But I thought she was expecting to see Peter Ryan this evening?'

Cordelia looked at Peggy over her glasses. 'Rita got a letter from that rather cheeky Australian this morning. It appears he's refused to stay grounded while all this hoo-ha is going on, and has joined the local squadron.'

Cordelia gave a little sigh. 'She also got a letter from her father – a sort of farewell in case he doesn't come back, which obviously upset her tremen-dously. I do wish he hadn't done that, but I can understand why he felt the need.'

'Poor little love,' murmured Peggy. 'She's been through too much already, what with losing Matt. If anything happens to Jack, she'll be inconsolable, for he's all she's got.'

'She's got you, Peggy,' said Cordelia firmly. 'You've filled the gap left by her mother and taken her under your wing since she was a little girl. All the while you're by her side, she'll never be alone.'

'That's sweet of you to say so, Cordelia,' said Peggy, kissing her cheek. 'But it doesn't stop me worrying.'

She hurried off to check on Daisy, who was indeed fast asleep, clutching a knitted rabbit that Lil must have made for her. Peggy softly ran her fingers through the dark curls and kissed her lightly on the forehead, regretful that she'd spent so little time with her today and vowing she would devote the majority of the weekend to her.

Returning to the kitchen, she fetched her plate of food from the warming oven and sat down at the table. 'Where's Sarah?' she asked before tucking into the delicious fish pie.

'She came in briefly, pushed her supper around the plate without eating much of it, and went out again. There's something on that girl's mind, you mark my words. I tried to ask what was wrong, but she said it was nothing and not to worry about it. She was just tired.' Cordelia sniffed. 'I don't believe that for a minute, but if she won't share her troubles, what can I do?'

'It's probably Delaney,' said Peggy through a mouthful of gorgeously rich pie. 'There was a letter from him this morning, and I expect, like Rita, she's worried about what might be happening to him on those beaches.'

'Hmm. You could be right, but it's her father and Philip she should be thinking about – not some American fly-by-night who's leading her astray.' Cordelia stuffed her knitting into the bag at her feet and stroked Queenie, who was sitting on her lap.

'It was lovely to see Danuta again after so long, but she did look tired and very frail,' Cordelia went on. 'It strikes me she was incredibly lucky to survive that enemy raid, but it's strange we heard nothing about it on the wireless as they've been so few and far between of late.'

'I shouldn't set too much store in that, Cordy, they can't report everything,' said Peggy smoothly. 'She was feeling a little perkier this evening. Her temperature was down, and she was full of Ron's exploits this morning.'

Cordelia chuckled. 'She told us too, and it did make us laugh. But I have to say, Ron really is his own worst enemy. I mean, what on earth was he thinking about, taking Queenie all the way up there, let alone letting her loose?'

Peggy scraped the last of the fish pie from her plate and savoured it. 'Who knows what goes on in that man's brain? I've given up trying to fathom it out.'

'I doubt there is much of a brain to fathom,' said Cordelia tartly.

'That's a little unfair,' Peggy said mildly. 'He's bright enough – but he just doesn't think of the consequences before he acts.' She decided to change the subject. 'How's Bertie? We haven't seen him in ages. Is he well?'

'As fit as a fiddle and far too energetic for a man of his age,' said Cordelia with a hint of pride. 'We had a lovely lunch at the golf club after he'd played eighteen holes this morning, and he was planning to fit in another nine once he'd dropped me off here from the hospital.'

'I saw you had lots of letters from Canada today,' said Peggy. 'How are things over there?'

'They had a tough winter and were snowed in for a couple of months, but life is going on as usual, it seems, and they've told me to expect another food parcel.' Cordelia gave a little chuckle. 'It's very thoughtful of them, and I know it will be a treat, but receiving food parcels makes me feel as if I'm a charity case. I shall be glad when this war's over and the rationing stops.'

She picked up her handbag and cardigan, grabbed her walking stick and got out of the chair, tipping Queenie unceremoniously onto the floor. 'Sorry, Queenie,' she muttered. 'I forgot you were there.'

Queenie was most put out and stalked off with her tail in the air.

'Are you going up already?' asked Peggy in surprise.

'I've heard the news twice today, and have no real interest in hearing it again. It's been a busy day and I'm tired. Besides, I have a new library book to start, and I prefer reading in bed.'

She put her hand on Peggy's shoulder to stop her getting up. 'I can manage the stairs perfectly well,' she said. 'You stay there.'

'But—'

'It's much easier going up than down,' Cordelia said firmly before she kissed Peggy's cheek and headed for the hall. 'Goodnight,' she called over her shoulder.

'Sleep well.' Peggy tiptoed to the door, listening intently as Cordelia slowly climbed the stairs, poised to dash out and catch her should she fall.

She found she'd been holding her breath, and as Cordelia reached the landing, she let it out on a long sigh. She would have to do something to make Cordelia's life easier – although the elderly lady would refuse to accept she needed help and would be most put out at what she'd see as interference. Yet it was clear she was finding the stairs a hindrance these days, and every time she went up and down them, Peggy dreaded it.

Returning to the table, she sat down and mulled over the problem. It would be easy to swap rooms with her, but then she wouldn't be close to the bathroom or lavatory, and she quite often had to get up in the night now. Cordelia hated using the commode, and getting to the outside lav meant going down those concrete steps and out into all weathers – which was definitely not on.

Peggy fretted over the problem until the nine o'clock news began.

'Here is the news read by Stuart Hibberd.

'All the landing beaches in Normandy are now cleared of the enemy. Reinforcements and supplies are getting across safely. More airborne landings were made during the night when five waves of glider troops seized fresh positions on the Cherbourg Peninsula.

'Heavy armoured fighting has started inland. A German tank attack near Caen has been beaten off. Allied aircraft flew more than thirteen thousand sorties yesterday. The RAF had more than a thousand planes out during the night on roads and railways behind the beachheads.

'German attacks to the north of Jassy in Romania have got weaker and easily pushed back. In Italy the Fifth Army, pushing ten miles on from Rome, are now spreading out along the highways to the north.

'The general picture from the coast of Normandy this evening is that the perils of D-Day have been successfully met, though the main battles at sea, in the air and on the land are still to come.

'Letters to men taking part in the assault have already been sent across the Channel. This is announced today by the Post Office, which says that the postal service between the United Kingdom and our forces on the Continent have been planned as an integral part of the military organisation.'

Peggy's mind began to wander. Never mind the invasion; there seemed to be more and more problems to be faced here at home, and she felt rather beleaguered by them. Cordelia couldn't go on as she was; Rita needed extra attention at this difficult time; something was troubling Sarah; and there was still the question over whether Dolly had sorted out the problem between Ron and Rosie.

Her head was spinning with it all, and as the newscaster began to talk about the huge Japanese losses in Burma and going through the long list of the different regiments that were fighting alongside the Chindits, she switched the wireless off. Jim and the Burma campaign was the straw that would break her resolve, and she needed to stay strong to continue her own battle here.

Brenda had taken the night off, so Ron was only half-listening to the wireless as he served the clamouring customers, mulled over Rosie's letter, and kept an eye on Sarah. It was unusual for the girl to come in here alone, and as she sat deep in thought on a stool at the end of the bar, he could tell that something was worrying her.

He waited for a lull then took his pint of beer with him and leant on the bar to talk to her quietly beneath the surrounding chatter. 'This isn't really the place for confidences,' he said, 'but I'm here to listen if you'd like to tell me what's troubling you.'

She looked at him, her blue eyes bright with unshed tears. 'I know you mean well, Ron, and usually I would have come to you for advice. But this time it's too difficult – too personal – and I must deal with it on my own.'

Ron had a sudden and rather alarming thought, but wasn't sure how to express it without causing offence. 'Is this to do with your man, Delaney?' he asked.

'He's part of it,' she admitted. 'But things have happened and ...' She tailed off, her expression forlorn.

'To be sure, I'm sorry to be asking, wee girl, but would you be in a similar situation as young April found herself in?'

She looked at him like a startled fawn and then reddened before shaking her head. 'I rather wish it was as easy as that,' she replied. Then she took a breath, finished the drink she'd made last for the past hour, and lit a cigarette.

Ron frowned as he watched her. She was clearly on edge, but thankfully not pregnant, so whatever it was plaguing her couldn't be that serious. 'I've always found that a problem shared is easier to deal with. If you won't confide in me, then go to Peggy. She doesn't judge or tell you what to do, but talking it over with her will help you decide how to fix whatever's on your mind.'

Sarah nodded. 'I know, but I don't like to bother her. She already has enough on her plate without taking on my problems.' She squared her shoulders and did her best to appear in charge of the situation. 'Don't worry, Ron. I'll sort everything out myself in time, you'll see.'

He reached for her hand and gave it a squeeze. 'Go home to Peggy, wee girl. You'll not be solving anything by sitting here. You won't regret it, I promise.'

Ron watched as the girl shot him an uncertain smile, slid from the stool and made her way through the throng and out of the door. He'd been meaning to tell Peggy what had happened this morning with Stan and Ethel, but if Rita and Sarah were in need of her then he wouldn't say anything for now. He'd see how things were in the morning, sit her down quietly and tell her then.

He turned back to serve the customers, his heart heavy at the thought of what a burden they all were to Peggy – motherly, sweet Peggy who was never too tired to listen, console or advise. What would they all do without her?

'Pray God we never have to,' he muttered.

Peggy had washed up her dishes and set the table for breakfast. It was a chilly, blustery night, so she was glad of the fire in the range as she settled down to write letters to her scattered family.

On hearing the slam of the gate a little while later, and feeling the cold snap of wind coming under the kitchen door from outside, she rose from her chair to put the kettle on, suspecting it was either Rita or Sarah in need of home comforts and a cuddle.

As Sarah stepped into the kitchen, Peggy could tell immediately that she was deeply troubled and bravely trying not to show it. She reached for her hands and drew her towards the fire. 'Come and warm yourself,' she said quietly.

Sarah sat down and Peggy perched on the arm of the chair and drew her into her side. 'Why don't you tell me what's worrying you so we can put whatever it is right?'

Sarah made no reply, but Peggy could feel her trembling from all the emotions she'd clearly been holding in for too long, and wasn't at all surprised when the girl burst into tears. She held her close. 'That's it, Sarah. Let it all out. I'm here now.'

'I don't know what to do,' Sarah sobbed against Peggy's shoulder. 'It's awful. I feel so awful.'

'I'm sure it's not half as bad as you think,' Peggy soothed. 'You've just been bottling things up, making them seem far worse than they really are.'

Sarah fumbled in her pocket and thrust a letter at her. 'It's worse than awful – it's … it's impossible,' she finished on a fresh bout of tears.

Peggy held her close and fumbled the letter from Delaney out of the envelope. She read through it carefully and silently cursed the stupidity of the man for making things far more complicated than he'd needed to by lying. And yet she couldn't understand why Sarah was so distraught.

She kissed the top of Sarah's head before stroking back her hair. 'He was very silly to lie to you, but it seems he's genuinely sorry – and it's a beautiful letter, Sarah,' she murmured. 'So why are you so upset?'

Sarah fumbled in her pocket again and wordlessly handed her the air letter from Australia.

Peggy opened it and began to read.

My darling Sarah,

I have received some wonderful news today, and as I sit here in the glow of evening at my writing desk penning letters to you and your sister, it is as if the world is suddenly a much brighter place, full of light and colour rather than the silver of the eucalyptus trees and the dull red of the earth, for at last there is word from Malaya.

402

*The letter from your father was dated January 1942,
and has been passed on from Borneo, through Indonesia
to East Timor and then to Darwin before finally reaching
me here in Cairns. I know it would be foolish to get my
hopes up too high, for the news coming out of the Far
East is horrifying, and after more than two long years in
Japanese hands, anything could have happened to them.
But the fact your father managed to write to me at all,
and that the letter arrived in the post this morning, is no
less than a miracle – and now I'm clinging to the hope
that another miracle will be performed and both of them
will survive and come home to us.*

Peggy held the sobbing girl closer, understanding now why she was so distraught, and continued to read.

*Do you remember Amah who looked after me as a child
and cared for you and your sister so beautifully and with
such devotion? It was such a terribly sad day that we
had to say goodbye not knowing what might happen to
her and the other Malay servants. She risked her life to
discover where Jock had been taken after he was arrested
by the Japs, and managed to get into Changi prison
where he was being held. She was so brave, so loyal, and
once this war is over, I will go back to Singapore to find
her and repay her for her courage.*

*I have transcribed here the letter Jock wrote, for the
original is barely legible and far too precious to send on
another long journey around the world.*

My Dearest Sylvia,

Amah has come to Changi in the guise of a kitchen helper for our captors, and at great risk to her own life has offered her assistance in getting news to you and our girls. I don't have much time to write, so I will be brief.

I was taken prisoner shortly after you set sail for Australia, and I can only pray that you and our son arrived safely, and that our girls are secure in England with their great-aunts. The conditions here in the prison are appalling, with little food or fresh water and no medical care for the many wounded.

I'm sad to say that Philip was brought in this morning, and we now share a cell with ten others, most of them members of the civilian militia he'd joined. We are alive and unharmed, which is more than I can say for many others, and have learnt very quickly that this new regime views any protest as an excuse for brutal reprisals, and that they have a blatant disregard for the rules of the Geneva Convention governing prisoners.

There are rumours that we'll be taken to an internment camp later today, so we live in hope that the conditions will be better there and that the Red Cross will be able to help the wounded amongst us. Amah tells me that most of the Chinese fled when the Japs invaded, but my old friend Lee Shing is still here until tonight, and will take this letter with him.

I've addressed it to your parents in Australia in the hope it will find you, and pray it doesn't fall into the wrong hands, or cause the death of either of these two brave, loyal friends.

I also pray that before too long we shall all be reunited. God go with you all.

Jock.

Peggy turned the page to find that Sylvia continued with her letter, but she was finding it hard to read on.

There is a line from Philip at the bottom of Jock's letter. He says, 'My darling Sarah, my thoughts of you and the future we planned will give me the strength to survive whatever lies ahead until we can be together again. Wear my ring in remembrance of me and the promises we made, and know that I will always love you, Philip.'

Peggy dropped the letter in her lap. 'Oh, Sarah, darling,' she breathed, holding her close. 'Oh, my poor, poor little girl. It's no wonder you're in such a state.'

Sarah huddled against her, burying her head in her shoulder. 'How can I write to Delaney now and tell him how I feel? It's unthinkable to plan a future with him after getting that wonderful, heart-breaking letter from Pops, who was clearly trying to be so brave and strong for us.'

Peggy continued to hold her, unable to find the words of consolation the girl needed, for the situation she found herself in was so impossibly hard, it would have challenged even the great wisdom of King Solomon.

Sarah's sobs eventually quietened, and she drew back from the embrace, mangling the damp handkerchief in her restless fingers. 'Philip asked that I wear his ring in remembrance of him and the promise we made to each other – but it's been sitting in a box in a drawer for over a year,' she said bitterly. 'What sort of girl does that make me, Peggy?'

She got to her feet and lit a cigarette, then began to pace the floor. 'I've betrayed him by falling in love with Delaney, and if he doesn't survive whatever horrors the Japanese are inflicting on him and Pops, then I'll never forgive myself.'

'Sarah, it's not your fault,' Peggy protested.

'Of course it is,' Sarah rasped. 'My fault entirely. I made promises I didn't keep, let my head and heart get turned when I should have known better, and lived in a stupid dreamworld of romantic nonsense, all while Philip could be going through the worst kind of hell.' She plumped down on a kitchen chair and burst into tears again.

Peggy went to her and held her, rocking her like a baby in her arms. 'Sarah,' she began quietly, still holding her. 'Sarah, that letter was written almost two and a half years ago and anything could have happened since. I'm sorry to have to say it, but they might not even have survived Changi prison, let alone the camp they were sent on to.'

Sarah kept her head buried against her.

'You can't torture yourself like this and sacrifice your chance of happiness with Delaney if that is what you really want – and I think you do.'

Sarah shook her head and pulled back from Peggy's arms. 'It no longer matters what I want,' she said, suddenly calm and coldly determined. 'I'll write to Delaney, explain the situation and wait for Philip. If he survives, then I will be the best wife I can be for him. It's the very least I can do.'

Peggy's heart ached at the thought of her throwing her life away on the very tenuous hope that Philip would survive. 'Don't you think Philip deserves a wife who stays with him out of love, not a sense of duty?' she asked carefully.

'I'll learn to love him again,' Sarah said stubbornly.

'And what if he doesn't come back?' Peggy asked softly. 'You will have made an enormous sacrifice, but to what end?'

'That'll be my punishment for not staying faithful,' Sarah retorted.

'Please, Sarah,' Peggy sighed. 'Don't make any hasty decisions now. You're overwrought and not thinking clearly. We've both heard the reports coming out of Malaya, Burma and Siam, and it would be a miracle if anyone comes out of those camps alive.'

'As Mother said in her letter, miracles happen. She's not about to lose faith in them surviving, and neither will I.' Sarah lit another cigarette. 'Pops is strong and fit for a man his age. He's used to the heat and humidity and the rigours of managing a rubber plantation. Philip's young and sturdy, a gifted polo player and sportsman. They'll come through.'

Peggy realised the girl was determined to believe her brave words, but the fittest of men could be poleaxed by malaria, typhoid or an infected wound, and as the Japs had refused to allow the Red Cross to send parcels or enter their POW camps, there was no way of knowing what else the prisoners were being subjected to.

There had been rumours of servicemen being used as slave labour – of mass graves in the jungles outside the camps, and even of women and children forced to endure the most awful hardships in places unfit for swine.

Peggy voiced none of these thoughts. Sarah knew as much as she did, but was choosing to ignore it as she clung to hope. 'Will you show your mother's letter to Cordelia?' she asked hesitantly.

Sarah shook her head. 'Best not to. She'd only fret.'

'Just promise me you'll take time to think things over before you write to Delaney,' Peggy urged.

Sarah stubbed out the cigarette, got to her feet and shook her head. 'He deserves a quick reply,' she said. 'It wouldn't be fair to let him go on hoping, and a clean cut is best. He'll understand that.'

Peggy very much doubted it, and suspected that Delaney would be hurt and confused by her sudden change of heart, and probably blame it on himself for having lied to her. It couldn't be a worse situation for either of them.

'Just be careful, Sarah,' she warned softly. 'Delaney needs to have a clear head over there in France, and a letter like that—'

'Don't, Peggy,' Sarah interrupted, her voice breaking. 'It will be a hard enough letter to write, and I can't ... I can't allow myself to think about that.' She grabbed her handbag and gas-mask box, gave Peggy a swift hug and ran out of the room.

Peggy sank into the fireside chair and covered her face with her hands in sorrow – not only for Sarah, but for her mother and the men they waited for. The cruelties of war came in many guises, affecting each and every one of them in a different way. For Sarah and Sylvia it was the gnawing fear of not knowing what had happened to Jock and Philip amid the horrifying rumours coming out of the Far East. For her, it had struck at the very core of her family, scattering her loved ones to the four winds, leaving her bereft and in dread of seeing the post boy walking to her front door with a telegram in his hand.

Ron was escorting Rita back from the Anchor, where she'd cheered up somewhat after an hour with her fire service colleagues. They talked as they slowly went along Camden Road, Rita swinging along on her crutches while Harvey watered every lamp post, downpipe and wall he came across.

'I know it's easy for me to say,' he said, 'but try not to worry about your dad. Jack's never been gung-ho about things – so I doubt he'll do anything reckless.'

'Yeah, I know,' she replied. 'I just wish he hadn't written me that letter. It choked me up no end, and sort of brought the war too close for comfort. I couldn't bear to lose him, Grandpa Ron.'

'Of course you couldn't,' he replied, pausing to put his hand on her shoulder. 'Just remember you aren't alone, Rita, and that Peggy or I will always be here if you should need us.'

She leant towards him and nudged his arm before grinning up at him. 'Yeah, and I count myself very lucky to have you. But it works both ways, Grandpa Ron. What's been bothering you lately?'

'Women trouble, as usual,' he muttered. 'But it's nothing I can't deal with.'

Rita giggled. 'Well, you're experienced enough in such things, so you should know how to charm your way out of whatever you've got yourself into.'

They crossed the road and Ron came to a halt at the end of the cul-de-sac. 'Sarah has things to talk over with Peggy, so it's best you go in through the front tonight,' he explained.

Rita nodded her understanding, blew him a kiss and swung away towards the front steps.

Ron watched until she'd slipped indoors, and then strode up the hill and along to the back gate.

Queenie came out of nowhere like a black streak and almost tripped him up as she shot between his feet and up the steps to the kitchen.

Harvey was about to follow her when Ron heard the unmistakable sound of Peggy's sobbing coming through the open door and grabbed his collar. 'Go to your bed,' he ordered softly, pointing to his basement room.

Harvey had heard the sobs too and with a whine of distress looked up at Ron in appeal.

Ron gently took his head in his hands and looked into his eyes. 'I'll sort it, Harvey,' he said. 'Go to your bed and stay there.'

Harvey's tail was between his legs as he reluctantly obeyed. Ron shut the bedroom door and quietly went up the steps into the kitchen.

The sight of his little Peggy huddled in the chair and sobbing her heart out was too much to bear, and he crossed the room in three strides to scoop her up into his arms.

'I've got you now, wee girl,' he soothed, settling into the chair with Peggy on his lap, her head nestled into his neck. 'There we are, there we are. It's all right. I'm here to look after you.'

It broke his heart to hear her crying, for although he suspected she'd spent many a night sobbing into her pillow, she'd never been so openly distressed. He experienced a momentary stab of fear at the thought she might have received bad news of Jim or one of the family, but it soon became clear that she was simply beaten down by the worry and fear this war had brought, and that Sarah's plight had proved to be the breaking of her.

Ron held her in his arms as she told him about the letters Sarah had received that day, and the choice the girl had made. He listened to her worries for the girl and her young American, and held her close as she listed all the numerous worries and fears that had beset her since the children were sent away and Jim was called up.

'Now, Peggy, girl, you're letting all of this get on top of you,' he said once the flow of words and tears came to an end. He stroked her hair and could feel the tension in her slight body, and the tremor of her distress running through her.

'You've spent your life loving and caring for us all, and once this war began you took on those girls and treated them as daughters. You've listened to our woes, consoled, advised and stood by us in times of trouble – and now it's our turn to look after you.'

'I don't need looking after,' she muttered.

'Yes. You do,' he said firmly, lifting her from his lap and settling her into the other armchair. He took her hands in his. 'We've all been selfish,' he said. 'Too taken up with our own lives and worries to see that you're wilting beneath the weight of all the responsibility we heap upon your slender wee shoulders. And it's going to stop.'

'But Sarah and Rita—'

'Sarah has to make her own decisions, right or wrong. It's what adults have to do. Rita knows she can come to me, but she's a tough little thing and is quite capable of getting through what ails her at the moment. I can't do much about Anne, Cissy, the boys and the grandchildren, but you have no need to worry about them, Peggy. They're healthy and safe down in Somerset, and will come back the minute the war's over.'

'But Bob's ... And Charlie's ...'

'Stop it, Peg,' he said gently. 'Those boys will come home, you'll see. All this talk of enlisting and fighting alongside their father is just a result of all the propaganda they're being fed day after day on the wireless and in the papers.'

Peggy withdrew her hands from his grip and cupped his face. 'Dear Ron. What would I ever do without you?' she sighed.

'You'd probably have less work and fewer shenanigans to put up with,' he said lightly, glad she seemed more like herself.

'I heard about your latest set-to with Matron,' she said with a ghost of a smile. 'Whatever possessed you to take Queenie up there?'

'Ach, the daft wee thing followed me and I had no choice.' He chuckled and shook his head. 'You should have seen Matron's face. I thought she'd explode.'

Peggy lit a cigarette and regarded him through the smoke. 'And what about you, Ron? Have things been resolved between you and Rosie?'

He frowned. 'Sort of,' he mumbled. 'I got a letter this morning, hand-delivered and already opened.' He quickly explained Rosie's reason for leaving so suddenly, and went on to tell her about his suspicions that Ethel had been the one to keep the letter.

413

Peggy's expression cleared and she smiled before telling him about the unpleasant scene with Olive in the washroom, which had led Dolly to Doris, and then into a full-frontal attack on Ethel outside the factory to retrieve Rosie's letter. 'There's no doubt at all that she had it,' Peggy finished.

'Phew,' breathed Ron. 'That's quite some bit of detection work.' He grinned. 'I wish I'd seen Dolly rough-handling Ethel.' He cleared his throat. 'It clearly wasn't Ethel's morning, because she ran into even more trouble later.'

Peggy eyed him sharply. 'Ivy told us about her thieving, and how the supervisor saw her stuff fall out of her lunch tin and pockets. Has she been sacked?'

Ron took her hand and carefully went over the morning's events. 'She and Olive Grayson have been sent down to Hastings to await their trial,' he said finally. 'We won't see either of them again in a hurry.'

'And Stan? How's he coping with the shame of it all?'

'I doubt he'll ever really get over that aspect of it, but once he recovered from the shock, he managed somehow to pull himself together and return to his old routine. Ruby and April are looking after him wonderfully well, and so I have every hope he'll soon be our old Stan again.'

'Oh, that poor, poor man,' sighed Peggy. 'We all tried to warn him she was no good. I so wish we'd been proved wrong.'

'Love is blind, Peg. It makes fools of all of us.'

'It's bound to get out,' Peggy fretted. 'You know what this town's like for gossip. Stan will have a hard time keeping his head up after this.'

Ron explained what Bert Williams had arranged to keep Stan's good reputation intact. 'Stan, Ruby, April and I decided that if questioned over Ethel's whereabouts, they'd say she'd walked out on Stan and returned to London where she felt more at home. Once the flurry of gossip over that has died down, she'll be forgotten and life will go on.'

'It's been quite a day, hasn't it?' Peggy threw the cigarette butt into the fire, kissed his cheek and then got to her feet. 'As long as Stan's all right, and you're all right, nothing much else matters,' she murmured. 'Goodnight, Ron. Thanks for being so loving and sweet to me. I shall sleep well tonight, and I hope you do too now you know where Rosie is.'

Ron saw to dampening down the fire for the night and filled the kettle for the morning, then checked the air-raid box was fully stocked before turning out the kitchen light.

He went down the steps, and although he was bone-weary after the long and traumatic day, he didn't go to his room, but went outside and looked up at the stars he could just see twinkling amongst the scudding clouds.

It would be dawn in Burma now, but did his son look up at that same moon and think of his home and family? He suspected he did, but it couldn't ease the constant ache of worry that weighed heavily on his heart. Peggy was not alone in her fears, but he would never admit it to her. It was his responsibility to look after her properly from now on – to see when she was feeling low and be there to lean on when she needed support – for his silly old tender heart couldn't withstand seeing her so vulnerable to all her fears and cares again.

23

Ron had slept like the dead and woken refreshed to start a new day with renewed energy and a determination to stay positive regarding Rosie. He had to believe she'd come back to him when she returned to Cliffehaven, or he didn't know how he'd cope. And he vowed to himself that if he was lucky enough to be given a second chance with Rosie, he wouldn't take her for granted ever again.

He went outside and watched as Adolf bullied the hens, attacking them with his beak and claws, making them squawk as they tried in panic to escape him.

Ron had seen enough. He grabbed a towel from the overhead drying rack, opened the pen and gave Adolf a boot up the bum. As the vicious old beast tried to flutter up to the roof of the coop, he threw the towel over him and made a grab for his neck.

'Right, you bastard,' he growled. 'It's goodnight Vienna for you.' One strong twist and Adolf's reign of terror was over.

Ron carried him into the shed, chopped off his head and strung him up from a ceiling hook. The meat wouldn't be tender enough for a roast dinner, but he'd make good tasty stock once he was plucked and gutted.

Wishing he could deal with Adolf Hitler the same way, but boosted by the accomplishment of a long-overdue job, he went back indoors, turned on the wireless and made himself a cup of tea.

Sarah joined him at the breakfast table a few minutes later, her face wan and her eyes bruised and reddened from tears and lack of sleep. Ron wanted to comfort her, but as her talk with Peggy had been in confidence and he wasn't supposed to know anything about it, he made no comment on her appearance, and filled the awkward silence between them with idle chit-chat until she left for work.

In Ron's opinion, she was making a terrible mistake by holding onto the hope that Philip was still alive. He wondered if she'd written that letter to the American, and dreaded to think how it would affect him. Ron knew from bitter experience how terrifying it was to have to face the enemy guns on landing beaches, but the poor wee man would have to do it after receiving what the Yanks called a 'Dear John' letter and that would make the going even tougher.

He drank more tea and came to the conclusion that he couldn't do much about Sarah and her tangled love life, for things would pan out one way or another, and only time would tell if she'd made the right decision. He fed the animals and then ate some of the porridge from the pot, sneaking a bit more sugar from where Peggy had hidden it in the cake tin on the top shelf of the larder. Happy with his lot, he filled his pipe and settled back to listen to the early news.

According to the reporter, the Allies were making satisfactory progress in Normandy. The American 5th Army was now forty-two miles beyond Rome, and the troops which had been held up for five months on the Adriatic were finally advancing. There was no change on the Russian Front, and only sporadic fighting near Jassy. All air-force activity was, for the moment, fully focused on Normandy.

Ron glanced out of the window as yet another flight of heavy bombers thundered overhead with their usual escort of fighter planes. At least the weather seemed to be improving, for the sky was blue and almost cloudless.

'Good morning,' said Peggy, coming into the kitchen still in her nightclothes, her face showing signs that she'd had a reasonable night's sleep. 'I'm sorry about last night,' she said, pouring a cup of tea. 'I don't know what came over me.'

'You'll not be apologising to me for letting go once in your life,' he said sternly. 'I want you to promise that the next time things get on top of you, you'll come to me and talk it over.'

'I doubt I'll let things go that far again,' she murmured, 'but thank you, Ron. I know I can count on you.'

He reached across, patted her hand and grinned. 'I've something to tell you which might cheer you up. I've sorted out Adolf.'

She stared at him in disbelief. 'How on earth did you do that?'

He chuckled. 'Not Hitler, but our Adolf, the tyrant of the chicken coop. He's as dead as a doornail and I'll be plucking him later for you to boil him up into some lovely stock.'

Peggy giggled. 'I almost feel sorry for him. What an ignominious end for such a dictator. Shame someone doesn't do the same to the human Adolf.'

Ron put a bowl of porridge in front of her. 'The news is all good according to the war report earlier. Hitler will get his comeuppance soon enough, I'm thinking.'

'I sincerely hope so,' Peggy muttered, digging into the porridge.

He sat back down and regarded her sternly. 'You do too much, and it's time everyone pulled their weight in this house, so I'll be having a word with all the girls later.'

'Don't you dare,' she said. 'Those girls do enough. They work long hours, do their own laundry and clean their rooms as well as babysit Daisy, help with the shopping and cooking, and keep Cordelia amused.'

She cocked her head and regarded him with a twinkle in her eyes. 'Before you start throwing your weight about, think on your own behaviour. Have

420

you tidied your room, Ron? Is your dirty washing in the basket, or strewn about on the floor in there – and when was the last time you stood in a queue to do the shopping?'

He desperately tried to remember. 'Last week,' he said triumphantly. 'To be sure I fetched the bread.' Her expression didn't bode well and he knew his charm wouldn't get him out of this situation. 'I'll be seeing to me room today,' he muttered. 'With all the goings on of late, I've not had a minute to meself, and me shrapnel's playing up something dreadful.'

Peggy flicked a tea towel at him and burst out laughing. 'Get away with you, you old scallywag. There's nothing wrong with you a good woman couldn't cure. Sort out your room before you go up to the Memorial. You've got plenty of time.'

He smiled sheepishly and went down to his basement room. Standing in the doorway, he suddenly saw it through Peggy's eyes and was quite shocked at how much he'd let things slide.

The bed was a jumble of blankets, sheets and pillows, all liberally covered in cat and dog hair and dirty paw marks. The floor was littered with underwear, discarded boots and socks; and his fishing gear was stacked by the chest of drawers, which spewed out his collection of vests and sweaters. The curtains were still drawn over the window that overlooked the basement corridor, and as he pulled them back, he realised the frame was dark with mould and the glass was filthy. He caught a whiff of ferrets, farts and dog-breath, and attempted to throw the window open, but it was stuck fast with grime and grease.

He fetched a bucket of hot water, a cloth and a scrubbing brush and set to work with a will. He managed to get the window open at last, and began to gather up the dirty washing. Once that was done, he started on the rest of the room, his shame at letting it get into such a state growing by the minute. It was all very well lecturing others about helping wee Peggy, but it seemed he was the worst offender.

'To be sure I can turn over a new leaf as well as anyone,' he muttered, gathering up the discarded newspapers and tying them into a neat bundle to use for toilet paper or rekindling the fire.

'Leopards rarely change their spots,' said Peggy, who'd quietly come to the doorway to watch him. 'But you're doing a good job so far. Keep it up, Ron.'

Ron gritted his teeth as she chuckled and walked away. As much as he loved Peggy, he did wish she wouldn't creep up on him like that. Rosie was the same. Was it something all women did to catch their man out – or just a habit of the women he loved? Either way, he knew he'd have to turn over a new leaf, for Peggy was at the end of her tether, and Rosie would stand no nonsense on her return and he had to be on his best behaviour. If she'd have him.

An hour later he emerged from the basement in triumph to find that Peggy was helping Daisy with her breakfast, Rita was preparing to go to the fire station, and Cordelia was immersed in her newspaper crossword.

'I would like you all to come and see my room,' he declared. 'To be sure it is now the finest room in the house, with not a speck of dust to be found, and a window so clean you wouldn't know it was there.'

They encouraged Cordelia to leave her crossword and turn on her hearing aid, and then dutifully trooped downstairs.

Ron stood back admiring his room as the women crowded round him. All his clothes were folded away, his boots hidden in the bottom of the wardrobe, his fishing tackle neatly stored on top of it. The bed was freshly made, the furniture polished, and there was a pot of hyacinths on the chest of drawers which now had all its knobs firmly back in place. He'd shaken the rug, scrubbed the floor, put fresh bedding in for Flora and Dora, and even swept away the cobwebs which had hung like cargo nets from the ceiling.

'It was about time you did something useful,' grumbled Cordelia. 'But I doubt it'll stay like this for more than half a day.'

'It looks lovely, Grandpa Ron,' said Rita, giving him a hug. 'And smells nice too, for a change.'

'Very nice,' said Peggy, holding tightly to Daisy as she watched the ferrets sleeping in their cage tucked beneath the high bed. 'But you've still got a long way to go to convince me you'll do this every day.'

Ron crammed his hat onto his head. 'To be sure you women are never satisfied,' he grumbled. 'I work me fingers to the bone all the while me shrapnel's moving and giving me hell, and all I get is sarcasm. Come on, Harvey. Let's be up to the Memorial for some added insults from Matron just to brighten our day.'

He stomped off into the garden as the others broke into laughter. He'd show them he was a reformed character, and then they'd be laughing on the other side of their faces, so they would.

Ron followed Harvey down the path and through the gate, and as he began the long climb to the top of the hill he felt his spirits soar as the skylarks trilled high above him. It was a beautiful day, his old pal Stan would eventually get over Ethel with help from all who really loved him, and Rosie would soon be home where she belonged.

He took a deep lungful of the cool, clean air and watched the sun spark diamonds on the water. Anything was possible on a day like this, and although Rosie might be having second thoughts, he knew in his heart that they were meant to be together, so all was right with his world.

Peggy's world was still a bit rocky, for her worries were legion and mostly unresolved. And yet she had to admit that her crying session last night with Ron and her heart-to-heart with Dolly had made her feel a little better. She had been trying to ignore how much the anxiety of living in wartime had affected her recently, and it felt such a relief to let it out. As the sun was promising a lovely day, she decided to leave the house early and take Daisy to the park for an hour before she had to be at work.

The large recreation ground lay to the west of the town, and looked very different to how it had once been. The bowling greens had been turned into communal vegetable plots; the cricket pavilion was now the meeting place and storage facility for the Civil Defence and Home Guard, and where there had once been carefully maintained football and cricket pitches there were more vegetables, with only a solitary bit of rough ground set aside for rugby and football.

Cliffehaven's main public shelter lay beneath it all – a dark, rather frightening place that stank of lavatory buckets and too many people confined into a single space, which everyone avoided like the plague unless it was absolutely necessary.

Peggy was about to turn off the High Street and head for the children's playground when she heard her name being called. She stopped and turned to see Pauline coming towards her with a determined expression that didn't bode well.

Not wanting Daisy to witness any unpleasantness, she let go of her little hand. 'You run on ahead, darling,' she said. 'I'll be with you in a minute.'

As the toddler eagerly trotted off towards the other small children playing in the sand pit and on the swings, Peggy turned to face a clearly furious

Pauline. 'Good morning, Pauline,' she said pleasantly. 'It's a bit early for you to be out, isn't it?'

'I have an early shift at the Red Cross,' Pauline said, slightly out of breath after her fast walk. 'But that's neither here nor there. Do you know what trouble you've caused by interfering in my business?'

'I haven't interfered in anything,' Peggy protested, determined not to be cowed by her hectoring tone.

Pauline folded her arms and glared. 'You told Mother what I said to you in confidence. And within days, she's on my doorstep. I'd call that interfering.'

'I'd call it coincidence,' Peggy replied evenly. 'Your mother comes and goes as she pleases, and I certainly played no part in her latest visit.'

'I don't believe in coincidences,' Pauline retorted. 'You must have talked to her, otherwise why would she turn up when I'd made it plain she wouldn't be welcome?'

'The only time I talked to her was when she was already here,' said Peggy. 'Dolly came because you hadn't answered her letter, and she'd hoped that she could persuade you to see things her way.'

'Carol and I have always had to see things from her point of view,' Pauline said bitterly. 'My sister might be soft enough to fall for her old flannel, but I'm not – and I made that very clear to her.'

'Which is why she left before she'd planned to,' said Peggy. 'She was in despair at the way you behaved towards her, and could see she wasn't helping the situation by staying, and that you and Frank needed to sort things out on your own.'

'What goes on between me and my Frank is none of your damned business,' snapped Pauline. 'And as for being in cahoots with Mother when you knew how I felt about her – well, that just goes to prove you're no real friend, Peggy Reilly.'

'I'm sorry you feel that way,' said Peggy calmly. 'But my friendship with Dolly has very little to do with you, and quite honestly—' Peggy bit off the words, realising how close she'd come to causing a real rift between them by telling Pauline that if she wasn't her sister-in-law then she'd probably have nothing to do with her. 'We're family, Pauline, and family has to stick together at all costs – especially during the hard times.'

'There wouldn't be so many hard times if people like you didn't poke their nose into other people's business – and just because we're related doesn't mean I have to like you, Peggy. I thought I could trust you with my thoughts and feelings, but it turns out I was wrong.'

Peggy glanced across at Daisy, who seemed to be playing with the other children. She looked back at Pauline, who still had the light of battle in her eyes, and decided she'd had enough.

'You've clearly decided that me, your mother and the entire world is against you,' she said briskly, 'and I spend little enough time with my daughter to want to waste it arguing with you. Once you've stopped to think what your selfish attitude is doing to Frank and those who love you, perhaps you'll have the decency to come and apologise.'

She didn't wait for her reply, but turned away and hurried towards Daisy, who'd tripped over something and was yelling fit to burst as she sprawled on the grass.

It took some minutes to pacify Daisy, and once she was happily playing again, Peggy shot a furtive look over her shoulder. There was no sign of Pauline, and with a sigh of relief, she returned to pushing Daisy back and forth on the swing.

The hour was over all too soon and Daisy complained bitterly as Peggy lifted her from the swing and carried her back towards the High Street. She tried coaxing her into a better mood by talking about her best friend Chloe, who would be waiting for her at the nursery, and peace was restored by the time they reached the entrance.

However, Peggy seemed fated that morning, for as she waited at the kerb to cross into Camden Road a shiny black car pulled up beside her and Doris climbed out.

'Hello, Margaret,' she said with a smile. 'This is a surprise.'

Relieved that Doris wasn't on her usual high horse, Peggy smiled back. 'Hello, Doris.' She took in her sister's lightweight suit and smart hat. 'You're looking very well. Are you off somewhere nice?'

'A fund-raising coffee morning at the Officers' Club,' Doris informed her, bending down to tickle Daisy under the chin. 'My goodness, hasn't she grown since I last saw her?'

As Doris was clearly trying to be nice for once, Peggy didn't remind her that it had been several months since her last visit to Beach View and it was therefore hardly surprising that Daisy had grown.

'Yes, she's getting bigger and more independent by the day,' she said instead. 'But Doreen's been terribly kind and has sent on the lovely dresses and shoes that her girls have grown out of, so I'm never short of things for her.'

'And how is our sister?' asked Doris. 'She rarely writes, but then I suppose she's too busy now she's saddled with that fatherless baby as well as the two girls, while holding down a job.'

'Yes, very busy,' Peggy murmured, glancing at her watch. 'Look, I'm sorry, Doris, it's been lovely bumping into you, but I have to be at work in ten minutes.'

'Ah, yes. That ghastly factory,' Doris sighed. 'I do wish you'd find something more suitable, Margaret. Couldn't Mr Goldman have given you an office post instead of sending you down on the factory floor with all those common women?'

'I can't type,' said Peggy, refusing to rise to the bait.

Doris grimaced as she looked down at Daisy. 'Do wipe that child's nose, Margaret. It's quite disgusting.'

Peggy quickly mopped Daisy up, but her daughter was getting restless and they were in danger of being late. 'I really must get on, Doris. But there is one thing I'd like to ask before I do. Why did you give Rosie's letter to Ethel?'

Doris raised one finely shaped eyebrow. 'I was extremely busy that day and she kindly offered to deliver it. Why do you ask?'

'Ethel not only didn't deliver it, but she opened it and read it. It finally got to Ron yesterday.'

'Well, that's all right then,' said Doris, digging into her expensive handbag.

'Actually it was far from all right,' said Peggy. 'Rosie needed him to run the pub while she went north to arrange her husband's funeral. Luckily for her he'd taken it on anyway, but because that letter wasn't delivered, he was in absolute pieces thinking she'd left him for that Major Radwell.'

'Well, I wouldn't blame her if she had,' said Doris with a sniff. 'You know my thoughts on Ron, and although I don't approve of the Braithwaite woman, I'm sorry her letter wasn't delivered as promised.'

'Thank you, Doris, I appreciate your apology.'

Doris dipped her chin in gracious acceptance and slipped a threepenny bit into Daisy's rather grubby hand. 'What do you say, Daisy?'

'Tank you, Dor, Dor,' the child replied, suitably awed by such largesse.

'Thanks, Doris. I'll get her some sweets for a treat later if I can find any.'

Peggy decided that as Doris was being so nice, she should do something in return. 'It would be lovely if you could come over for a cuppa or lunch one day. I'm busy this weekend, but what about Saturday the seventeenth?'

'I'm afraid that isn't possible,' said Doris. 'I'm hosting a luncheon that day in aid of a children's charity Lady Chumley and I have set up to help local children who've lost a parent or been made homeless by the war. It's just a small gathering of twenty or so of Cliffehaven's elite.' She regarded Peggy thoughtfully. 'I suppose you could come if you wanted, but I'm afraid it isn't a suitable event for small children.'

Peggy had to bite the inside of her lip to prevent herself from smiling at the insincerity of the invitation and the idea of hosting a children's charity event at which children weren't welcome. The thought of attending such a function, where she would have to smile and be polite to the snobbiest women in Cliffehaven, made her shudder. She'd done it once before and sworn she'd never do it again.

'That's a kind offer, Doris, but I make a point of spending most of the weekend with Daisy now I'm working.'

Doris looked faintly relieved and dug into her handbag again to pull out a small leather-bound diary with a tiny gold pencil attached to it. 'I could come for afternoon tea on the Sunday,' she said, the pencil poised above the page. 'Would four o'clock suit you?'

'That would be lovely. Now I really must go. See you on the eighteenth.'

Peggy scooped Daisy onto her hip and ran across the road towards the sprawling factory, rather pleased that her snooty sister had been nice to her for a change.

24

Over a week had passed since Ethel and Olive's arrest, and as Ron made his way back from the Memorial on that Saturday morning, he was looking forward to dropping in on his old pal Stan for a cuppa and a chat before he had to open the pub.

Ron's spirits were high, for the truth behind Ethel and Olive's disappearance had not been revealed, thanks to Bert and John White keeping a tight lid on it. Stan was coping very well now the rose-tinted spectacles had finally been removed and he could see what sort of woman Ethel was. He was mortified that he'd been such a fool to marry her when nearly everyone had advised him against the match, and was almost pathetically grateful that Ruby and April were standing by him.

Stan's reputation and kindness over the years had earned him much sympathy, and he'd been astounded by the number of people who'd made a point of visiting him to offer help when the story got round that Ethel had left him after a most interesting tussle with some smartly dressed woman outside the factory. Ruby had been to visit her mother very briefly, but she'd said little about it, and Ron suspected it hadn't been an easy meeting.

He tramped down the lane, Harvey galloping ahead of him in pursuit of a bird that had rattled out of the hedgerow to fly past his nose and flutter annoyingly just out of reach. Ron's mood had been lifted not only by the fact that Danuta was recovering quite rapidly and would soon be able to come home to Beach View, but because he'd had a short note from Rosie in the post the previous afternoon, telling him she would be returning to the Anchor on Monday evening. There was no indication of how she felt, and in what capacity she'd be coming back, or for how long. Two days of not knowing felt like for ever, but if he kept busy they'd hopefully pass quickly.

Ron reached the country road and climbed the steep hill until he reached the top, where he could see Frank already waiting for him in what was left of the old farmhouse the army had requisitioned at the beginning of the war.

Harvey greeted Frank, who made an enormous fuss of him, so taking advantage of this, Harvey flopped on his back to encourage him to rub his stomach, and squirmed in ecstasy at Frank's rough handling.

'Daft beast,' Ron muttered before taking his son into a strong embrace. 'How are you, my wee boy?'

Frank slapped his father on the back and grinned. 'I'm all right, as it happens, Da. Pauline's in a better mood now she's had a couple of letters from Brendon, and she's feeling quite pleased with herself for being promoted at the Red Cross as a co-ordinator. She actually gets a small wage now, and I've told her to treat herself, so she's off to the hairdresser's this morning for a shampoo and set, whatever that is.'

The two of them sat down on one of the fallen rafters, and while Ron lit his pipe, Frank smoked a cigarette and idly stroked Harvey's ears.

'It's a bit worrying that Gerry's got this new pilot-less rocket thing, isn't it?' Frank said. 'I've yet to see one close up, just a few lights in the sky and the whirr of a motor, but the report of what happened in London the other day made it sound as if they can cause a lot of damage.'

Ron grimaced. 'Aye. Poor old London always gets the worst of anything Gerry throws at us. Just be thankful we're living down here and out of harm's way.' He puffed on his pipe and watched as the Air Artillerymen struggled to manoeuvre yet another huge anti-aircraft gun in place.

'It looks like they're expecting more to come over. That's the eighth new gun I've seen up here, and there's talk of having hundreds of barrage balloons erected along the seafront and over the factory estate.'

'I reckon Hitler's trying to get his own back because of our successful invasion,' said Frank. 'This new weapon feels to me like a last-ditch attempt to stop us getting any further into Europe.'

'That won't happen, whatever he throws at us,' said Ron. 'We've got Gerry on the run all along the

435

Italian Front; we've taken Pescara and San Stefano, and are in command of over fifty miles of the Normandy coast.'

'It's good news for us all round, isn't it?' said Frank. 'The Russians have finally launched an offensive on Leningrad, and the Japs are still retreating from Kohima. If this keeps up, we'll soon see the back of Hitler and have our Brendon and Jim home.'

Ron grunted, unwilling to point out that there would be many more battles and lives lost before anyone could expect real peace, and although the Superfortresses had begun to bomb industrial targets in Japan, the war in the Far East was far from over.

'Da?' Frank's voice broke into his thoughts. 'Da, do you think it would be all right if I asked you and Peggy over for a cup of tea tomorrow? Only Pauline's regretting what she said to Peggy last week and wants to make things up with her – and although she'd kill me for saying this, she's too embarrassed to make the first move.'

'I'm glad she wants to smooth things over, but tomorrow isn't a good day. We have the delightful Doris coming for afternoon tea.'

Frank grimaced. 'That wouldn't do at all. Pauline and Doris fell out, and Pauline can't stand the sight of her.'

'She's not the only one,' said Ron, tapping the dottle from his pipe and getting to his feet. 'I plan to make myself scarce while she's there, and spend the afternoon getting the Anchor all shipshape for when Rosie gets back.'

He shoved the pipe in his pocket. 'But I've got a better idea. Peggy's planning a picnic in the recreation ground this afternoon as long as this weather holds, so you could meet us there after Pauline's been to the hairdresser.'

'That sounds a splendid idea,' said Frank, looking much relieved. 'I'll get some bottles of beer and have a rummage through the cupboards to see what else I can bring.'

Ron embraced his son, revelling in the size and strength of him, and wishing wholeheartedly that he could hold his Jim like this. 'To be sure I'm sorry I can't stay longer. But I promised to drop in to see Stan before I open up the pub.'

'I'll see you later then.' Frank almost squeezed the life out of his father in a bear hug and gave Harvey a hefty pat then went off with a cheery whistle down the track to Tamarisk Bay.

Peggy didn't know how to feel when Ron told her Pauline and Frank were coming to the picnic, but as long as Pauline behaved herself, she supposed it was better to patch things up rather than leave them as they were.

She'd done an hour at the Red Cross earlier this morning and was feeling quite excited by the idea of a picnic, but kept looking out at the sky, praying the weather wouldn't change as she and Cordelia spread margarine on bread and sliced corned beef and Spam as thinly as possible to put in sandwiches.

'The forecast said it would be fine today,' said Cordelia, 'so there's no need to keep looking out there.' She was now slicing tomatoes, the sharp knife getting dangerously close to her fingers.

'Let me do that,' said Peggy, quickly easing the knife from her. 'I need you to organise the picnic basket and help Sarah make sure we have enough blankets and chairs to sit on.'

Cordelia raised an eyebrow at this, but said nothing as Ivy dashed into the kitchen holding up a paper bag in triumph. 'Look what Alf the butcher sneaked me from under the counter. Sausages! Proper bangers!'

Peggy gasped with pleasure as she viewed the string of eight fat, glistening sausages. 'Fry them slowly on a low heat so they don't burn on the outside and stay raw in the middle – and remember to prick them first. We don't want them bursting,' she warned Ivy, who was a bit inclined to fry everything on a very high heat and as quickly as possible. 'We can eat them cold with the salad I picked from the garden.'

Peggy started to worry they wouldn't have enough food, for not only did she have the residents of Beach View to feed, but Ivy's Andy, Fran's Robert, Kitty and Charlotte as well – and now Frank and Pauline. And how on earth was she going to get everything and everyone down to the recreation ground? There was the picnic basket and table, the blankets, deckchairs, bottles of beer and lemonade, the primus stove and kettle so she could make tea, and that was without taking extra coats and umbrellas in case it rained. Cordelia would find it a trial to walk all that way, but as there was no other solution they'd just have to take it slowly.

'John Hicks said Andy could borrow the fire station van,' said Rita, somehow reading Peggy's mind. 'He's also donating two packets of custard creams a grateful lady gave him after we'd put out her chimney fire.' She grinned impishly. 'And if Pete can wangle an hour off from his flying duties, he's promised to bring cake and ginger beer.'

'I didn't realise he'd been in touch again,' said Peggy carefully.

'He popped into the fire station yesterday, just for a chat,' Rita replied, rather too nonchalantly. 'And to show me the motorbike he's bought. It needs a bit of work, but it's going well enough for getting about on short trips.'

Peggy saw the brightness in her eyes and the colour in her elfin face and gave her a hug. 'That's nice, dear,' she said, glad the girl was more cheerful and relieved that young Peter was proving to be a stalwart friend. 'Let's hope he can get away so he can show it off to the rest of us. But please promise me you won't give me another heart attack by going for a ride on it.'

Rita grinned. 'I've already had one,' she admitted. 'But I promise to behave this afternoon.'

Peggy's heart was full as she revelled in the bustle going on around her, and the knowledge that in a few short days, Danuta could very well be a part of it again. She couldn't wait to collect her girl from the Memorial, wrap her in her arms and bring her back to Beach View to convalesce.

Andy brought the van promptly at one and they spent some time loading it up. Peggy decided at the last minute that it might be a good idea to bring Daisy's pushchair, so if she got tired, she'd have something to take a doze in.

Andy helped Cordelia up into the cab while Peggy squashed in beside her with Daisy on her lap. Ivy, Rita, Sarah and Fran piled into the back with all the things that Peggy considered would cover any and every eventuality.

Andy slammed the back door and climbed in behind the wheel. 'Are we all ready for a picnic?'

'Yes,' they yelled back.

'Hold tight then and give us a song to help us along the way.'

There was some chattering in the back and then the girls began to sing 'Little Brown Jug'. Cordelia and Peggy joined in with great enthusiasm and Daisy clapped her hands as she sang her own version.

They arrived at the recreation ground to find Charlotte, Kitty and Robert waiting for them with their own picnic basket. The back doors were opened, everyone was helped out, and within minutes there was a long, happy line of people heading across the abandoned football pitch, each carrying something.

Blankets and chairs were placed near the trees, far enough from the children's playground that they wouldn't be pestered by sand flying from the sand pit, but near enough for Daisy to enjoy herself. Picnic baskets were opened and Kitty's revealed cheese sandwiches, a collection of savoury biscuits, a bottle of milk, some very thin slices of ham and jars of homemade piccalilli and pickled beetroot.

'As Charlotte and I get extra rations of cheese and milk, we thought we'd share it. We also saved up some coupons for the ham, and Doris's Ted gave us a couple of slices more as a treat.'

Everyone applauded, and then gasped as Robert produced a bottle of gin, some tonic water and a large packet of chocolate biscuits. 'My mother sent the biscuits,' he said shyly.

'Oh, but that was lovely of her,' said Peggy, her mouth watering at the thought of real chocolate.

Andy hefted over a crate of beer. 'A gift from Aunt Gloria,' he explained, digging in his pocket for the bottle opener. 'She said that if the Crown was quiet, she might pop over later with some scones she baked this morning.'

Peggy liked Gloria, for although she was bold and brassy, she had a heart of gold, but as Ron was joining them later, it could be a bit awkward. His current predicament with Rosie had spiralled from his last visit to the Crown, and while no one could have foreseen the seismic consequences of that day, they were now unavoidable. Rosie's reason for leaving Cliffehaven might now have been explained, but her feelings towards Ron and Major Radwell were still a mystery.

Beers, gin and tonics and sandwiches were handed out. Daisy sat contentedly gnawing on half a sausage and Cordelia was fussing over Charlotte and Kitty, who looked as if they were about to have those babies any minute.

Peggy sipped the lovely gin and lifted her face to the sun as the talk went on around her. It had been too long since they'd been able to do this, and she hoped that the weather would continue to be nice throughout the summer, for it did the heart good to be outside, surrounded by the people she loved.

The burble and pop of a badly tuned motorbike broke the peace and they all turned to watch Peter Ryan ride across the field towards them. 'G'day,' he said cheerfully, unwinding his length from the heavy motorbike.

Rita introduced Robert, Charlotte and Kitty, and having grinned in delight at them all, he dug into the panier on the back of the bike and lifted out a large tin. 'With the compliments of the AAF,' he said, taking off the lid and placing the tin in the middle of the rug.

There were oohs and aahs and little squeaks of pleasure as they saw the plump Victoria sponge that was filled with cream and jam and dusted with icing sugar.

Pete winked at Peggy. 'Florrie in the canteen at Cliffe is a bit partial to an Aussie accent,' he explained. 'Besides that, she's a ripper cook. That's a bonzer cake, isn't it?'

'There's only one way to find out,' said Rita, digging him in the ribs. 'Stop talking and get cutting.'

Peggy noted the easy interaction between them and her misgivings fled. Peter Ryan was a lovely young man who'd clearly brought a new light into Rita's life, and Peggy couldn't deny that her romantic heart was warmed by the thought. What would be, would be, she thought dreamily.

The cake proved to be delicious, but as tempting as it was, they thoughtfully left enough for Frank, Pauline and Ron, who turned up an hour later with Harvey.

'Come and sit by me, Pauline,' said Peggy, noting that the other woman was looking rather hesitant at joining the party. 'Your hair looks nice. Have you just had it done?'

The ice slowly melted between them and eventually Pauline surprised Peggy by actually apologising for her outburst the other day. As the chatter once more rose in volume, Harvey patiently sat begging at each of them in turn for more food, and Daisy fell asleep in her pushchair, Peggy knew that harmony was restored and everything would be all right.

She lay back on the blanket, shielded her eyes against the sun and gazed up at the clear blue sky thinking how wonderful it was that in this moment it didn't feel as if they were at war. It was like the old days, although the picnic would have been on the beach back then, and music would have been coming from the bandstand as they ate ice cream and hot chips smothered in salt and vinegar.

She let her eyelids droop, drowsy from gin and the sun and good rich food, delighting in the song of the skylarks and only vaguely aware of the buzz of a distant engine that must be a plane flying very high, and therefore not from Cliffe.

'Strewth!' shouted Peter, leaping to his feet. 'Everybody take cover. Now!'

Startled out of their stupor, they all looked at him in confusion. 'It's just a plane,' said Rita.

'That's no flaming plane,' Peter shouted. 'It's a V-1. And it's heading this way.' He hauled Rita to her feet, grabbed Daisy's pushchair and shoved it under the trees, startling the toddler awake and making her cry.

The other men were galvanised into action. Cordelia and the two pregnant girls were unceremoniously plucked from their chairs and carried into the bushes under the trees, where they ended up knee-deep in a weed-choked, hidden ditch.

Peggy snatched Daisy out of the pushchair and joined them, while Sarah and Ivy raced to help the mothers of the small children playing nearby get them out of the open.

They all huddled there, eyes turned skyward as children cried and Harvey whined in confusion.

They could hear the buzzing of the engine more clearly now, and see the large, pilotless plane coming nearer and nearer – untouched by the barrage of gunfire that was coming from the top of the cliffs and the nearby hill at the end of Havelock Road.

'It'll be all right as long as that engine keeps going,' said Peter, one arm around Rita, the other round Cordelia. 'It's when it stops we could be in trouble.'

Peggy watched, her heart beating so painfully she could scarcely breathe as she held Daisy and prayed for this awful thing to fly over them and land somewhere it would do no harm.

And then the engine cut out.

Frozen in fear, they watched the thing tip towards the earth, gaining speed as it silently dropped like a stone behind the trees in Havelock Gardens.

'Down! Get down,' shouted Ron, grabbing Harvey to his chest and throwing them both to the ground.

The explosion rocked the ground and sent shock waves through them all. The wind of it blasted through the trees, shedding them of leaves and breaking branches, the sound reverberating endlessly in their heads as more explosions followed and lethal debris was flung into the air to rain down all around them.

Peggy shielded Daisy with her body and tried to burrow deeper into the hedge as the child screamed in terror and those around her scrambled to find better shelter.

The terrible explosions finally stopped. The deadly rain of rubble and uprooted trees petered out. And in the terrible silence that followed, Peggy dared to look out from her hiding place.

A great pall of black smoke was rising beyond Havelock Gardens and spreading like a giant mushroom into the clear blue sky. 'Oh, dear God,' Peggy breathed. 'That's Havelock Road.'

She grabbed Ron's jacket sleeve. 'It exploded in Havelock Road,' she yelled, her head still ringing and her ears numbed from the explosion. 'I've got to find Doris.'

'You'll be doing no such thing,' he said, releasing her grip on him and helping her out of the ditch as Andy and Peter raced across the field on the motorbike to get the services out. 'The fire brigade will be here in a minute. Harvey and I will go to see if Doris is all right.'

Peggy tried to soothe Daisy, but she was too distraught herself, so Pauline took charge of the child with great calm and soon had her tears dried and her fears allayed by a chocolate biscuit.

Cordelia was trembling with fear and cold, the muddy water from the ditch dripping from her lightweight coat as Frank gently sat her in one of the deckchairs and wrapped her in a picnic blanket. Charlotte and Kitty were soaked to their thighs, and clearly shaken, but their experiences of flying with the ATA stood them in good stead, and they calmly went to help the mothers of the little ones who'd so recently been playing happily on the swings.

Peggy took it all in as if she was watching it happen from a great distance. 'I must go and see what's happened,' she said fretfully. 'I can't just stand about here when my sister could be . . .' Unable to complete the sentence, she broke free from Frank's staying hand and began to run.

The urgent clanging of the fire engines' bells got louder as they approached from Camden Road. A convoy of Civil Defence trucks followed with an ambulance not far behind it. People were pouring out of the houses and shops to stand and stare, while nurses ran from the hospital and members of the Home Guard collected nearby.

Peggy took it all in as she chased after Ron and Robert, who were now running towards that awful cloud of black smoke.

She'd lost her shoes in the ditch, but she barely noticed as she ran headlong out of the recreation ground and swerved to go down the hill and into Havelock Road as the three fire engines hammered ahead of her, their bells ringing, the firemen clinging onto their sides.

She could see the smoke more clearly now. It was rising from the end of the cul-de-sac where the hill swept down to the beach, and there were flames rising with it – terrible flames that burnt bright red and orange. But something was wrong with what she was seeing, and as she chased after the fire engines and trucks, she realised with horror what it was. The huge gun was no longer there.

Peggy collided with Ron and would have fallen if he hadn't caught her. But she had eyes only for the inferno before her – the swirling black smoke and the great swords of flame that pierced through it, devouring what was left of the two end houses.

The shattered remains of the anti-aircraft gun could be seen lying at the core of the house next to Doris's, the corpses of the men who'd manned it flung like stringless marionettes into the vegetable patch that had once been the quiet little park.

Trees had been uprooted and lay leafless in the road as the hungry flames ran in rivers to feast on them. Garden walls had been obliterated, drain-pipes torn from their tethers and twisted out of shape – and everywhere was the glitter and twinkle of broken glass.

'Doris is in there,' she yelled to John Hicks, the fire chief. 'She's got twenty guests for lunch, and there are two evacuees as well. You've got to get them out!'

He gently put her aside and calmly organised his men to cover the bodies of the soldiers and aim their jets into the heart of the raging fire. 'I'm not sending anyone into that,' he said. 'I'm sorry, Peggy, but it's highly unlikely there's anyone still alive in either house.'

Peggy felt numb as she tried to comprehend what he'd said. Doris couldn't be dead. It was impossible to even think of such a thing. She was larger than life, bossy and overbearing and definitely not the sort of person to be hit by a bomb.

'Move back, Mrs Reilly. Come along. Let the firemen do their work.'

Peggy stared at the man in the tin hat and Civil Defence uniform and stood firm. 'I'm not going anywhere.'

She ignored him and stared dumbly as the roof at the back of Doris's house collapsed and brought down the side wall, which flattened the garage. The flames were gathering energy and greedily feeding on this new bounty, probably drawn by the fumes of the petrol Doris had hidden in there.

'She's got petrol in that garage, and there's a car too,' she yelled, tugging urgently at John Hicks's jacket.

He swore under his breath, ordered the Civil Defence to get everyone well away, and his men to aim their hoses at the garage. He swore again as Andy raced towards the garage and began to heave away the fallen masonry to get to the petrol cans inside.

Before John could stop them, Ron, Frank, Robert and Peter were by Andy's side, tugging, heaving, chucking things to one side in their desperate bid to prevent another explosion.

Peggy saw the new blossom of flames at the same time as John. 'Get out of there!' he yelled. 'The whole lot's going to blow any minute.'

The jets of water soaked them as they reluctantly retreated. John ordered the fire engines and other vehicles to be quickly backed up the road, and then turned to Peggy and the others and yelled at them to run as far and as fast as they could.

Peggy dithered, but Ron grabbed one arm, Frank the other, and she was lifted off her feet and carried right out of Havelock Road and down to the promenade, where they pressed her down to the ground behind the tea kiosk and shielded her with their bodies.

Half crazed with fear, she fought them. 'Where's Daisy? Where's my Daisy?' she screamed.

They had no chance to reply, for the explosions came one after the other in a great booming salvo that shot flames, masonry and burning petrol cans high into the air.

Peggy stopped struggling and burst into tears. No one could have survived that. Her sister was gone. But where was Daisy? Was she safe?

She felt herself being lifted and held in strong arms, and in her sorrow, fear and bewilderment, thought for a minute that Jim had come home. But it was Frank. Dear, dependable, kind Frank. Closing her eyes she leant against him, thankful he was there, but longing for it to be Jim.

The tears flowed and she buried her face in his shoulder as he carried her away from the shouts of the firemen, the thick, choking smoke and the demonic crackle of those flames that were devouring her sister's beloved house. She couldn't bear to think of how it must have been inside when that V-1 hit, and could only pray that death was instantaneous, and they'd known nothing of it.

'Mama. Don't cry, Mama.'

Peggy opened her eyes and as Frank gently put her on her feet, she fell to her knees and clasped Daisy to her, kissing her little face and thanking God she'd come to no harm. 'Is everyone else all right?' she asked Pauline once she felt calmer.

Pauline nodded. 'Kitty and Charlotte have gone home and Peter has taken Rita off on his motorbike because John Hicks ordered her in no uncertain terms to leave. Robert and Fran have cleared up what they can of the picnic, and Sarah has gone back with them to Beach View to try and calm Cordelia down. She was in a bit of a state, and soaked through from being in that ditch. I wouldn't be surprised if she goes down with a nasty cold after this. Ivy's gone to the Lilac Tearooms to get refreshment for the firemen and rescue teams, and Da's standing by with Harvey to go in once the flames are extinguished in the very remote hope that someone might still be alive in there. Now come on, Peg. I'm so sorry, but there's no point in us standing about getting in the way. Let's get you and Daisy home.'

Peggy let Frank take Daisy and then steadied herself by clinging to his arm as they turned their backs on the inferno that was still gushing flames and smoke into the air. They eased through the gathering crowd, and had to wait for another fire engine to pass before they could cross into Camden Road.

'It looks like John's had to call for outside reinforcements,' muttered Frank.

Peggy could barely see through her tears and her heart was aching with loss. She and Doris had fought all their lives and yet she'd always felt a bond with her – a special bond that only sisters could share. And now she'd never have the chance to tell her she loved her, to give her a hug and …

Peggy stared in disbelief as the ghost of her sister came running towards her. She blinked and looked again, certain she was having some sort of hallucination. But when Doris flung herself into her arms, she knew it was for real.

She wrapped her in a close embrace. 'Thank God,' she breathed. 'Oh, thank God you're alive.' They clung to one another, their tears mingling as Doris gabbled incoherently and Peggy tried to soothe her.

Peggy finally drew back and lovingly smoothed Doris's hair from her tear-streaked face. 'I love you, Doris,' she said, 'and I'm sorry I don't tell you that often enough.'

'I love you too,' she sobbed. 'And I'm sorry I've been so mean about you working at the factory. I knew you needed the money and I should have helped you out.'

Peggy shook her head. 'None of that matters now,' she said softly. 'As long as you're alive, that's all I care about.'

Doris was trembling as she glanced towards the smoke that was still rising above the houses and drifting along the cul-de-sac. 'What happened? Was it a gas explosion? Did everyone get out in time?' she asked brokenly.

Peggy shook her head. 'I'm sorry, Doris. It was a V-1 rocket and it all happened too quickly for anyone to get out.'

'No, oh, no,' she groaned, sinking onto a low garden wall. 'And it's all my fault,' she sobbed. 'If I hadn't asked them to lunch they'd still be alive.' She buried her face in her hands and cried in anguish.

Peggy sat next to her and put her arm round her shoulder. 'Don't torture yourself, Doris,' she begged. 'It's not your fault. It was a million to one chance that the rocket came down where it did.'

'I can't believe it,' spluttered Doris, mopping her face with a handkerchief, unaware she'd become the centre of attention from the bystanders and gawkers now the flames were dying down. 'I simply can't believe they're all gone.'

Peggy held her and waited until she was calmer. 'I thought you'd gone with them,' she said, her voice ragged with emotion. 'I really thought I'd lost you, Doris, and it was the worst moment of my life.' She took her hands and held them tightly. 'I can't tell you how relieved I am you weren't in there. But where were you?'

Doris sniffed miserably and dabbed her eyes. 'I'd forgotten to pick up the smoked salmon I'd ordered for lunch. It's Lady Chumley favourite.' She took a quavering breath. 'But the specialist place I'd ordered it from is in the next village. And then when

I finally picked up the salmon the blasted car broke down, and I had to walk all the way back in my new shoes.'

'So the car wasn't in the garage?' asked Peggy sharply.

Doris shook her head. 'No, it's parked on the side of the road about three miles away.'

'How many people were in the house?' asked Frank. 'The firemen will need to know when it comes to a search.'

'There were twenty for lunch, including me. The two evacuees were supposed to stay and help serve, but as usual they skipped off without a word and left me in the lurch.'

Doris fell silent and then took a shallow, ragged breath. 'Their disobedience saved their lives, just as my forgetfulness saved mine. But when I think of Lady Chumley and Mrs Anstruther-Fox and Camilla …' She broke down in tears again.

Peggy looked up at Frank and he helped them both to their feet. 'Let's get you both home,' he said gently.

'But I don't have a home any more,' wailed Doris. 'I've lost everything.'

'You have your family, Doris,' said Peggy. 'And from now on Beach View will be your home. Come on. Let's get back there and help you settle.'

Epilogue

Ron had lit the fire in the hearth and pulled the curtains on the dreary night. Rosie's sitting room was warm and cosy, the freshly washed chintz covers on the couches and chairs glowing with faded colour, the cushions plump and inviting. There was a glorious bunch of Stan's roses in a vase on the mantelpiece, and he'd made a plate of sandwiches for her in case she was hungry after the long journey. There was a fresh bottle of gin on the sideboard, all the glasses had been washed and polished, and even Harvey had had a bath and brush so his brindled coat gleamed in the firelight as he stretched out on the hearthrug.

Ron looked at his watch. The Anchor had been closed for almost an hour and all was quiet, for most people were in bed at this late hour, but Rosie would be here soon, he was sure of it. He eased a finger round the starched collar of his shirt and adjusted his tie. Peggy had sponged down his best suit, Fran had cut his hair and trimmed his eyebrows, and he'd polished his shoes to a shine this morning, so he knew he looked respectable – even though this get-up was horribly uncomfortable.

He relaxed back into the couch, mulling over the events of the past two days. The fire in the houses had eventually been extinguished, and a subsequent search through the dank, stinking, blackened shells had revealed that the house next to Doris had thankfully been empty, the occupants working at the Red Cross warehouse.

The tragic remains of the women attending Doris's lunch had been found. The majority of the bodies had been located in the drawing room as expected, but there seemed to be evidence that a few of Doris's guests had been in what turned out to be the charred remains of Doris's bedroom at the moment the V-1 hit. What they'd been doing there was a mystery, but to shield Doris from any further upset it was decided not to say anything to her – although it would all come out at the inquest.

There had been nothing to salvage from what had been a beautiful and expensively furnished house. Doris had cried over her loss, but been thankful that at least everything had been insured and she'd been wearing her diamond ring that day, her mink coat lying on the back seat of the car, which was now parked outside Beach View.

Ron looked at his watch again and then tried to relax into the comfort of the couch and in the tranquillity of this little room. Beach View was always noisy, which he didn't mind at all, but since Doris had moved in the atmosphere was already different, even though she'd only been there two days. She'd had Peggy running about after her and had insisted upon having the large bedroom at the front, which meant Rita and Ivy had to move to the top of the house.

Doris seemed to be genuinely mourning the loss of her snooty friends, but when it dawned on her that their loss meant she was now the leading light in the town she'd perked up no end and begun to plot and plan how she'd run things her own way from now on. She'd also taken full advantage of Peggy's sweetness and relief that she was still alive, and seemed to delight in telling everyone what to do – especially him.

Ron gave a deep sigh. It was a very great shame that her estranged husband had decided to be away this particular weekend. Where Ted was, or who he was with, no one seemed to know, but as far as Ron was concerned, the quicker he got back and took Doris off their hands, the better. He could only pray the man was willing to do such a thing, for if Doris stayed much longer, Adolf the rooster would not be the only victim of manual strangulation.

Ron began to get worried as the little clock on the mantel chimed one and then two. There was still no sign of Rosie and he was beginning to fret that something might have happened to her – or that she'd changed her mind and wasn't coming after all.

He began to pace the floor, going repeatedly to the window to see if he could spot a car coming down Camden Road. But the silence was profound, the foggy night closing in as the minutes ticked away and the clock chimed three.

Ron slumped into the chair again, positive now that she wasn't coming. Lost in his misery he was startled by the slam of the back door, and scrambled to his feet. And there she was, his lovely, smiling Rosie, home again and walking straight into his arms, where she belonged.

Dear Reader,

Here we are again back in Cliffehaven with Peggy Reilly and all the lovely people who live at Beach View. The five long years of war is still dragging on, but there is now a glimmer of hope that the tide is turning, and very soon the men will be coming home.

It has been six years since the first Cliffehaven book was published, and to my great joy, I've been able to live, love and cry with the Reillys and their evacuees right through those war years – and it's not over yet! I never imagined how dearly you would take Peggy, Ron, Cordelia and Rosie to your hearts and I'm fully aware that if anything happens to Harvey, I shall suffer the dire consequences!

I've had such pleasure in introducing them all to you, for they are now an intrinsic part of my own family, and like my family, I'm never quite sure what they'll get up to next, but it's great fun finding out, even when they make me cry.

I hope you enjoyed *With a Kiss and a Prayer* and I look forward to your comments on Facebook.

Until the next book, *As the Sun Breaks Through*, I wish you good health and contentment throughout 2018.

Ellie x

Did you love *With a Kiss and a Prayer*?

Look out for the next Cliffehaven novel

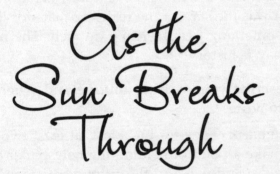

ELLIE DEAN

Pre-order now in paperback and e-book

Out 23 August 2018

Interview with Ellie

1. What made you want to become a writer?

I've always loved reading and making up stories. I am an only child, raised by my grandmother and her sisters, who opened up the world of books to me. Yet it was the family story which always intrigued me and I knew that one day I would have to sit down and write it. I eventually achieved this, and it was the start of me realising that storytelling was something I could really do well. The rest, as they say, is history!

2. Describe your writing routine and where you like to write.

I have black coffee for breakfast, at least two cups, and make a point of reading the newspaper before doing the Sudoku, and the cryptic crossword. This gets me into a working frame of mind and wakes up my brain. I have an office in my house that overlooks paddocks and the South Downs, and I sit down there before ten every morning. I check my emails and Facebook, and then read through what I've written the day before. Editing this gets me into the next scene that I want to write. I work through from ten until around six, five days a week. If a deadline is looming however, then I might work over the weekend and at night. I find that sometimes I do my best work after midnight!

3. What themes are you interested in when you're writing?

The theme of family, and of the intricate threads that bind people together or tear them apart. People react differently to situations, and I find it fascinating to watch my characters evolve throughout the book.

4. Where do you get your inspiration from?

Inspiration comes from everything and anything. A conversation overheard – a newspaper article, a line in a book or a song.

5. How do you manage to get inside the heads of your characters in order to portray them truthfully?

Once I have the plot and the title, then I must have the actors playing their parts. I wait for them to come to me, to show themselves and tell me about their lives. It might sound weird, but that's how I work. It's like meeting new friends. You don't know everything about them immediately, but as they talk, you can discover who they are, where they come from, their social background, their aspirations, their failures, etc. As an author I become this person, with their viewpoint, their likes and dislikes and the reactions they will have to any given situation. An author must evolve into these characters to make them fully rounded, and it doesn't matter what gender they are – people are very similar underneath the skin.

6. Do you base your characters on real people? And if not, where does the inspiration come from?

I don't actually base my characters on anyone, but there are certainly shades of people I've known and loved or disliked intensely. People like to think I've based a character on them, but that isn't so – and yet I might have picked up a habit of theirs, or the way they say things, which leads them to think that it is them.

7. What's the most extreme thing you've ever done to research your book?

I flew a Spitfire. It was a simulator, unfortunately, but it certainly gave me the feeling of flying – and I got a certificate to prove it!

8. What aspect of writing do you enjoy most?

I love doing most of it. Working out a story, plotting it, finding my characters and taking them through the trials and tribulations of the book to a satisfying end. I enjoy the research too, for I've learned a huge amount about World War II, and I'm constantly surprised by what I uncover. The writing is harder and it seems to get harder the more I do it. Probably because I'm aware of the pitfalls, and because, at times, it feels as if I'm trying to knit fog – but once I have written THE END, the joy is in the editing. With the story complete, it's great to go through it again and turf out all the things that shouldn't be there, and to make it as good and as polished as possible.

9. What's the best thing about being an author?

Not having to get dressed in the morning to go to work or to go outside when the weather is foul or to battle with commuter traffic.

10. What advice would you give aspiring writers?

Learn your craft. Do your apprenticeship by writing, writing and writing – and reading. Persevere, take advice and don't get precious about your work. The publishing world is tough, so be prepared to develop a very thick skin.

11. What is your favourite book of all time and why?

There are so many favourites, it's hard to choose. *Exodus* by Leon Uris was the first adult book I read when I was about eleven, and it inspired me to one day write a brilliant story. *Delicious* by Nicky Pellegrino because I adore Italy and the Italians, and this book is redolent with the scents of olive oil, garlic and herbs!

12. If you could be a character in a book, or live in the world of a book, who or where would you be?

I'd be the female captain of a pirate ship, sailing the Caribbean and being romanced by someone dashing and handsome – like Ross Poldark!

Lose yourself in the

Find Love. Find Hope.
Find Cliffehaven.

world of Cliffehaven ...

Ellie DEAN
Can love survive in a time of war?
Where the Heart Lies

United by love, separated by war...
Ellie Dean
Always in my Heart

It was a time of friendship, family, love and loss...
Ellie Dean
All My Tomorrows

The *Sunday Times* Top Ten Bestselling Author
Only love can get you through the heartache of war
Ellie Dean
Sweet Memories of You

The *Sunday Times* Top Ten Bestselling Author
Wartime can bring friendship and love as well as heartache
Ellie Dean
Shelter from the Storm

The *Sunday Times* Top Ten Bestselling Author
Does absence make the heart grow fonder?
Ellie Dean
Until You Come Home

The *Sunday Times* Top Ten Bestselling Author
ELLIE DEAN
The Waiting Hours
Can the tide of war heal her broken heart?

Hear more from

ELLIE DEAN

SIGN UP TO OUR NEW SAGA NEWSLETTER

Penny Street

Stories You'll Love to Share

Penny Street is a newsletter bringing you the latest book deals, competitions and alerts of new saga series releases.

Read about the research behind your favourite books, try our monthly wordsearch and download your very own Penny Street reading map.

Join today by visiting
www.penguin.co.uk/pennystreet